RACHEL GRANT

# BODY OF EVIDENCE

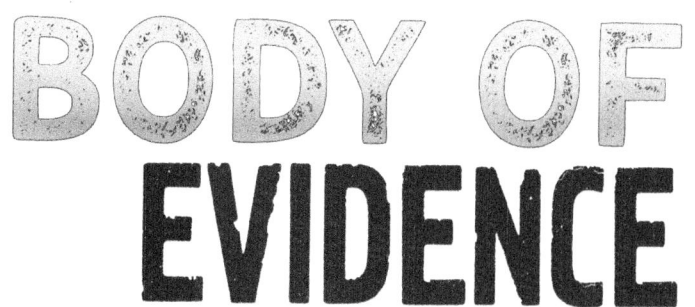

Janus Publishing, LLC

ISBN-13: 978-1490974187
ISBN-10: 1490974180

Cover art and design by Naomi Ruth Raine

Copyediting by Linda Ingmanson

This one is for Mike
October 2, 1951 – August 28, 2010

Friend, brother-in-law, next-door neighbor, aspiring writer, poet, and microbiologist.
I have never known a finer human being.

"No Matter"

Three books perch like falcons
beside my chair,
awaiting my imperial pleasure.
In the fireplace,
maple and cedar are galloping off
in stallions of flame.
January has taken care of the yard work.
The phone has been assassinated.
The dog has even stopped slobbering.
However you define paradise,
this is part of it.

- Michael Grant

# Chapter One

*Democratic People's Republic of Korea (DPRK)*
*October*

"Rise, Mara Garrett."

Mara understood only a handful of Korean words, but she'd learned that phrase early in this farce of a trial and was on her feet before the interpreter finished speaking. Tremors radiated from her belly. *This is just a formality. I'm one step closer to getting home.* Her token lawyer had warned her she would probably be sentenced to ten years' hard labor; then the real negotiation for her release would begin. With her conviction and harsh sentence, North Korea would be in a stronger bargaining position.

Of course, North Korea, the most secretive and unpredictable regime on earth, wasn't known for negotiating. They would make demands, and the US would either meet them or not.

She'd traveled the world for her job with the Joint POW-MIA Accounting Command, conducting excavations to retrieve the remains of American servicemen who'd died in wars fought by the United States in the last century. Her work for JPAC was hazardous. She'd faced down poisonous insects, dug up unexploded ordnance, and suffered third-world diseases. But never, not even in her wildest imagination, did she think her work could lead to being arrested in North Korea.

But that was what happened when she ended up alone on the edge of the Demilitarized Zone.

She looked to her lawyer for some sort of reassurance and caught the glint of a camera lens. Cameras hadn't been permitted in the courtroom during the trial; the presence of one now filled Mara with a foreboding chill. It seemed the North Koreans expected a dramatic, newsworthy reaction.

She stood straight with her head high so the camera wouldn't see her clenched hands behind the table. She refused to give them the spectacle they wanted.

The judge spoke. She forgot to breathe while waiting for the translator. Finally, the man said, "Mara Garrett, you have been convicted of spying. The penalty is death by firing squad. The sentence will be carried out in twenty-four hours."

The room tilted. A shriek built in her throat, while her bones turned to jelly. Sheer will kept her face blank while she battled dizziness. She'd been alone when she was arrested but had spent the last two months worrying her coworkers had been detained as well. For their sake, she needed to take the blame. If they were being tried in another courtroom, her admission of guilt could prevent them from receiving the same sentence. She pressed her nails into her skin and fixed her gaze on the lens. "This is my fault. My JPAC team is blameless."

The judge spoke again, yelling now, and the translator matched his tone. "You are guilty and have been sentenced!"

"It was a mistake," she said, desperation building in her voice. "I was separated from my team by accident." But that wasn't true, and she feared they saw through the lie.

Panic threatened as a guard grabbed her arm and tugged her toward the door. He wasn't taking her to the firing squad. He couldn't be. Hadn't they given her twenty-four hours?

They'd almost reached the exit when the door swung open and slammed against the wall. The guard jerked to a stop. Framed in the opening was a portly, highly decorated military man.

A rapid-fire exchange between the judge and the newcomer ensued. Mara twisted in the guard's grip and watched in horror as the judge angrily ejected the cameraman from the room.

Panic morphed into bone-melting fear. What the hell was happening?

The military official waved a magazine in the air. In a haze, she recognized the Asian edition of *TIME* magazine from the bold font and familiar red border.

At last the man looked away from the judge and addressed her, causing the translator to jump to his feet and race to her side to voice his words. "Our leader, in his infinite wisdom, has decided to grant you amnesty on one condition."

Hope flared but was soon tempered with the fear that this interruption was a stress-induced fantasy, like the ones Mara had suffered years ago after her father's death. Each time the fantasy faded, hope went with it, and she was slapped with grief as fresh and intense as the day he'd died.

Hope would break her, making it her captors' ally. She knew

that better than anyone.

"Our beloved Dear Leader once got your President Clinton to come groveling."

No. *Not again.* This wasn't a pathetic fantasy. It was an all too real nightmare. Cold sweat dripped from her brow. The idea of a rescue mission headed by a former president terrified her. She wasn't a reporter dipping her toes in the Tumen River. She was the niece of a former vice president of the United States, and as such could be seen as a valuable bargaining chip.

The North Koreans knew exactly who she was. Because of her family connections, it was especially important she downplay her significance. A presidential envoy would open the door to other outrageous demands, and she was horrified by the thought that the unpredictable dictator could gain the upper hand with the US because of her.

Her situation wasn't helped by the fact that her uncle was facing trial on ridiculous corruption charges. She could only assume her arrest had added to the ongoing media frenzy in the United States, further convincing her captors of her importance. She'd repeatedly begged her interrogators to tap a low-level politician as envoy, but each time her pleas were met with disdain.

"Our leader wants to meet the man on the cover." The translator pointed to the magazine. "If he comes to P'yŏngyang before your execution, we will allow him to take you home."

The man stood too far away; she couldn't see the face on the cover. She had no idea who had been selected. But even more important, was twenty-four hours enough time for an envoy to fly to North Korea?

The official waved the magazine as if it offered hope, but there was no such thing as hope. She was going to die.

METAL CLANGED AGAINST metal as Mara's cell door crashed open. She pushed to her feet with shaking arms. Her twenty-four hours must be up. She looked from one guard's face to another. "Did the envoy arrive? Am I being released?"

The two men looked at her blankly and said nothing. None of her guards ever spoke English. Too bad she hadn't learned the Korean words for execution or firing squad. *On my next trip to North Korea, I'll be more prepared.*

*Or at least bring a better linguist.*

The guard held up a blindfold and handcuffs and gestured for her to step forward, answering her in the universal language of executions. Her vision dimmed in the already dark cell, and she rocked back on her heels. With a hand on the cold concrete wall to steady herself, she closed her eyes. She took a slow, shallow breath. In a matter of minutes, this nightmare would be over.

She should welcome the restraints. She didn't want to see the guns or look into the eyes of the men who had been ordered to kill her. She didn't want to instinctively raise her hands, as if she could ward off bullets. Handcuffed and blindfolded, at least she could die with dignity.

Ironic that after years of devoting her life to bringing lost US servicemen and women home, it was unlikely her body would return to American soil. As a convicted spy, she would receive no such gesture of respect.

The guard wrapped the cloth around her head. His vacant eyes and hollow cheekbones would be the last thing she'd ever see. She recalled the unseen face on the cover of *TIME*. But he represented hope, and hope was a treacherous bitch.

A guard pushed her toward the door, and she left her cell for the last time.

If footage of yesterday's sentencing had been aired in the US, her mother had to be out of her mind right now. Her mother had been through so much already, and the last year had been especially hard after a US attorney seeking to make a name for himself had filed charges against Uncle Andrew. Now her mother would lose her only child.

A thousand regrets hit her as she was guided down corridor after corridor. She'd allowed her work to consume her life. She had been too busy to visit her family on the mainland. Several times her uncle had flown out to JPAC deployments, just so he could see her. The last time she'd seen him, they'd been in Egypt, nearly a year and a half ago.

And she never should have agreed to the North Korean deployment, not with the trial drawing near. If she were a better niece, she'd have taken a leave of absence and gone to DC to stand by him.

Had her actions hurt the others as well? Were the members of her JPAC team also facing execution? She'd been alone when she was arrested, but the Korean People's Army was just as likely to have arrested everyone at the site, holding her team accountable because she'd fled. Panic caused her steps to falter. A guard pressed her shoulder and barked at her in Korean. *This is really happening.*

She crossed a threshold, and for the first time in weeks felt the cold bite of outside air on her skin. Taking a deep breath, she caught the acrid scent of burning leaves, a smell she hadn't experienced since childhood.

She realized fall had started while she was in captivity. Living in Hawai'i, she often longed for seasons—yet another sacrifice she'd made for a job that meant everything to her. But the work she'd loved had gone to hell when she'd trusted the team linguist, Roddy Brogan, at a critical moment.

Roddy had led her off the site and into the North Korean wilderness. Scared to death, she'd fled him, and because of that, she would die. But why had he done it, and what had happened to him?

Her boots met pavement with a soft thud. She knew she passed in front of a line of people. The firing squad. She heard their breathing and with eerie perception sensed soldiers aligned with the renowned North Korean military precision.

The wind carried a man's voice. His tone held the feeling, the inflections of English, but she was unable to make out his words. Could it be the envoy? No. She couldn't allow hope. The sounds were nothing but the feverish imaginings of a desperate mind.

*Don't think. Don't hope. Just walk.*

The guard jerked her to a halt. Hands on her shoulders positioned her. A cold brick wall pressed against her spine.

*Don't think. Just breathe.*

This was it. The hands fell away, and footsteps retreated. Tears burned her eyes.

*Don't cry. Just breathe.*

A shout echoed in the air. The clicks of rifles being raised met her ears. Her legs shook.

*Breathe.*

"Stop!" The distant voice rose over the sound of pounding, rapid footfalls. The accent was unmistakably American. "Tell them—you've been ordered to stop!"

More Korean shouts followed.

Her throat seized.

Voices exploded in Korean.

"Lower the guns, dammit!" The American now stood so close,

she felt the vibration of his words as much as heard them. In a rush, she realized he must be standing between her and the firing squad, shielding her.

Another Korean shouted. A tap followed. Had the guns been lowered?

Her whole body shook as hands worked the blindfold knot behind her head. The cloth fell away, but she was afraid to open her eyes.

"Mara, it's okay," the American said, his voice gentle this time. "I'm taking you home."

Slowly, afraid to believe his words, she opened her eyes. She squinted in the light until the man before her came into focus. The handsome face was vaguely familiar.

Seconds ticked by in silence as she searched her memory. Then recognition hit her.

Of all the people he could have asked for, the North Korean dictator had demanded Curt Dominick, the ambitious US attorney who was prosecuting her uncle.

Her knees gave out.

# Chapter Two

CURT DOMINICK LUNGED and caught the woman. She'd crossed the courtyard with such dignity and grace, she'd reminded him of the goddess Athena, but holding her, he noted she hardly weighed a thing. She was really more pixie than Olympian.

Why did her size surprise him? Between the dossier he read on the flight, the intense media coverage since her arrest, and his own research into her family, he knew everything there was to know about Mara Garrett. He shouldn't be thrown off by something as inconsequential as height, yet he was.

She was pale, with an understandably haunted look in her eyes, and she appeared to have lost weight in her two months of captivity. Her gaze locked with his, and he could see the fear she'd masked with sharp posture and firm footsteps, a display of inner strength he hadn't expected her to possess.

She was a reporter's wet dream: all-American girl, thirty years old, petite, blond hair, wide, luminous blue eyes, pert nose. Gorgeous even on her worst day—which this most certainly was. He couldn't help but see her easy beauty even now, when she couldn't muster the warm, dimpled smile featured in so many photographs. The fact that her work was physical, cerebral, and humanitarian had caught the media's attention, but it was her family ties that ensured her face had graced the cover of every major magazine and newspaper in the US since her arrest.

Every inch of her life had been dissected by the media, and according to the US State Department, P'yŏngyang hadn't appreciated their depiction in the drama—understandable, since it appeared the North Koreans were justified in arresting her—but that tidbit had been withheld from Mara Garrett's adoring press.

As a result, P'yŏngyang was out for blood. American blood. And, as the niece of a former vice president—even a disgraced one—Mara Garrett had blood that ran red, white, and blue.

Once she was steady on her feet, he let her go and turned to his North Korean handler. His heart still hammered from the execution he'd almost been too late to prevent. He'd traveled seven thousand miles and had to run the last five hundred yards. The jolt he'd felt at seeing her before the firing squad couldn't begin to compare to how she must have felt, but instead of comforting her, he had diplomatic duties to fulfill, playing nice with the same bastards who'd demanded his presence with an insanely short amount of time to fly from DC to P'yŏngyang. "I'll sit for the photos with your leadership, but she will not be photographed."

From the corner of his eye, he caught her rubbing her cheek against her shoulder and realized she was wiping away tears. He whirled to face her guard. "Handcuffs off. Now." His words came out as a harsh bark. He wanted to throttle all of them for putting her through this torture.

Cuffs removed, she rubbed her wrists. "Thank you. For"—her voice cracked, and she cleared her throat—"for coming for me."

He wiped away another tear with the pad of his thumb, and his heart began to slow. "North Korea in the fall?" He smiled. "I wouldn't miss it."

He caught a glimpse of her dimple and felt a tug in his gut. Damn, he was as base as the tabloid-reading public, all because she was pretty. Irritated with himself, he turned to his escort. "Let's get the photos over with."

"Follow me," the man said.

The firing-squad soldiers shouldered their weapons and marched in the opposite direction, while they were led into the ornate building. Inside, the woman was whisked away by another handler before Curt came face-to-face with the leader of North Korea. He sat for the photos with his face carefully blank. Like President Clinton, he tried to look like an empty suit.

Four long hours after landing in P'yŏngyang, he and Mara were reunited on the jet. He took a deep breath of relief and studied her across a small table in the main cabin. She appeared even smaller huddled under a plush blanket. She looked out the window; her whole body trembled as they raced down the runway.

The nose of the plane lifted. A second later, they were fully airborne. P'yŏngyang faded into the distance as they climbed to cruising altitude. Curt pulled out his cell phone and a minute later said, "Mr. President, we're in the air."

MARA COULDN'T STOP trembling. She burrowed under the blanket and tucked it around her knees, but the quaking wouldn't stop. She leaned her forehead against the window and forced herself to breathe slowly. Below, North Korea faded from view.

She took another deep breath and exhaled, fogging the glass and erasing the outside world. The knot of tension in her belly began to uncoil.

"Here, ginger ale should help."

She turned to see the man who'd saved her life standing in the aisle, frowning at her and holding out a drink. With ice.

The clink of the ice against the glass conjured the memory of the lukewarm water her captors had provided with her daily serving of kimchi. She'd eaten while sitting on the cold hard floor of her tiny cell, surrounded by thick concrete walls that blocked all sound and light. She'd endured many things while imprisoned, and lukewarm water didn't even rate a mention on the most detailed list of grievances, yet the sight of the clear cubes triggered a rush of emotions. Sadness, joy, guilt, and fear all tumbled over one another. Pathetic to face a firing squad only to be brought low by a handful of ice.

She rubbed her temples, trying to hide her struggle to stave off tears. She was lucky to be alive to have this nutty breaking point, and she had the man in front of her to thank for that.

The fact that he was the US attorney prosecuting her uncle only made his heroic actions more baffling. Marginally composed, she accepted the cold glass. "Thanks," she said and downed the soda in one long drink. She set the empty glass on the table, revived by the sugary jolt, and then faced him. His hazel eyes studied her, causing her belly to flutter and cheeks to heat.

Her emotions were seriously whacked if Curt Dominick—of all people—caused a fluttery reaction. But he'd flown halfway around the world at a moment's notice to save her. Didn't that warrant a major change in her opinion of him?

She shook off her reaction. She could freak out about it later; right now she had questions that needed answers. "This plane is empty," she said. "Where is everyone?"

"P'yŏngyang insisted I come alone. No envoy team. Just me and the pilots."

The information surprised her, but he'd misunderstood. "No, I meant where is my JPAC team? Where is Jeannie Fuller? Where is Evan Beck? Where are the others?"

He startled. "You don't know?"

She shook her head. "No one would tell me. And I had to be careful with what I said—I didn't know if they were being tried as well. If they were, then my words could be used against them." She paused and stared at the condensation gathering on the glass in front of her, seeing instead Roddy's easy confidence as he drove her away from the safety of the site and straight to the Demilitarized Zone. "But I'm here, and they aren't. Where are they?" She held her breath, grateful she'd finally know the truth. If her team was safe, then keeping her silence about what Roddy had done would be worth it.

"They arrived in the US two days after you were arrested."

Her pent-up breath left in a rush. "*All* of them?"

"Yes."

*Including Roddy.* Don't focus on that. Think about the team. Jeannie, her best friend and coworker, was safe. As were several men she'd worked with for years.

She turned again to her rescuer. His intent gaze met hers, those clear, hazel eyes probed, assessed. "The State Department needs to know what happened to you. You need to tell me everything."

The State Department or Curt Dominick? The man was gunning for her uncle. She had to be careful with what she said, because Roddy was only a contractor to JPAC. His true employer was Raptor, the private security firm her uncle had taken a job with after his term as vice president ended.

The man before her had charged her uncle with using his influence as vice president to get the US government to award numerous contracts to Raptor, only to receive a payoff when he took a job with the mercenary organization a few months after leaving office.

Uncle Andrew had warned her that Curt Dominick would one day come calling and ask about the work Raptor did for JPAC, and the US attorney would twist her words if she wasn't careful. But he had also said Curt Dominick had more ambition than human decency, yet the man had shielded her from the firing squad. That exceeded human decency and made him on the verge of godlike in her estimation.

Pressure built in her chest, and she rose from the plush seat. Curt didn't budge from his position in the aisle, trapping her between the table and chair. "Excuse me," she said.

He was tall, six feet at least, and intimidating with his probing gaze.

She squared her shoulders. "I need to walk. Even a plane aisle is better than my six-by-six cell."

He stepped back and swept an arm out.

The jet smelled of forced air and wealth. The deluxe interior struck her as ridiculous after two months inside a dark, concrete box. The oil painting on the bulkhead appeared to be a signed original—and she was fairly certain she'd seen the artist's work featured in a DC gallery a few years ago. "This isn't a government jet," she said.

"No. It was donated by a billionaire who was anxious to be associated with your rescue."

She cringed. She was certain the media attention had made her efforts to convince the North Koreans she wasn't important that much harder. They'd wanted no one less than the secretary of state or sitting vice president as envoy. She really shouldn't have been shocked Curt Dominick had been chosen. After all, in a moment of desperation, she'd tossed out his name. It would forever be her dirty little secret that she'd chuckled at the idea of him being distracted from prosecuting her uncle.

But never, not once, had it occurred to her the man would actually be selected. He wasn't a cabinet member or a heavily tattooed and pierced former basketball player, so what did he have to offer? She could only assume the fact that he was prosecuting her uncle had been a delicious irony to the dictator.

"Start talking, Mara. We need to know what happened the day you were arrested."

She needed a minute. She didn't want to think about that day, let alone talk about it. But the State Department *did* need answers.

She turned to face him, then wished she hadn't. His closed expression was an unwelcome change from the man who'd removed her blindfold in the courtyard. Her guard went up, and she looked away before answering. "On the last morning, I found unexploded ordnance not far from the remains of the pilot of an F-86 Sabre."

"A bomb. Is that unusual?"

She shrugged, aiming for nonchalant. "We dig in combat-plane wrecks. It happens." Anxious and wondering how much she should reveal, she turned and strode down the aisle to the galley, where she opened cabinets, making a show of looking for something to eat, even though nausea threatened with every bump of the aircraft. "Our ordnance-disposal expert—Evan Beck—ordered the site cleared so he could defuse it." She raised her voice to be heard over the omnipresent whine of the aircraft. "We argued, because his plan wasn't standard protocol."

She stretched on tiptoes and reached for a box of crackers she didn't want. Without warning, his hand appeared next to hers and snatched the box from the high shelf. She leaned into the sharp edge of the counter to widen the distance between them.

"What is standard protocol?" His voice was low, harmonic with the hum of the jet but audible because he stood uncomfortably close.

"In North Korea? The team stuck together. Always."

"That had to be awkward after you and Evan broke up."

She stiffened, rattled that he knew about her relationship with Evan. Yet she shouldn't be surprised. "We broke up almost a year ago. When it ended, we remained friends." Not really, but that was no one's business but her own. She faced him and crossed her arms over her chest. "We worked together in remote places. We had to get along."

"I'm not interested in either the start or end of your relationship, or your justification for or against said relationship. I merely wish to establish that you and Mr. Beck were not mere coworkers. Your interactions were clouded by emotion."

She plucked the box from his hand and tore off the lid. "Thanks—for the crackers and the douse of cold water. Nice to know where I stand."

"You are standing inside a private jet loaned to the US government for your extraction from North Korea. I have spent eighteen of the last twenty-two hours on this jet during a week in which I do not have an hour—let alone twenty-two—to spare, so I could save you from a situation I have every reason to believe you caused. *That* is where you stand."

She narrowed her gaze. "If you ever decide to run for public office, don't give interviews. Your appeal drops every time you open your mouth."

He laughed. "Thanks for the tip."

She crossed the aisle and set the box on the table, glad he couldn't see her answering smile.

"You argued with Beck," he prompted.

Her smile faded. "As forensic archaeologist, I was in charge of the excavation." She'd worked so damn hard for that title. Her job had given her purpose when circumstances conspired to make her nothing more than a trophy. Not many people knew she was former Vice President Andrew Stevens's niece, but after learning of her connection to power—and later her connection to infamy—they usually wanted to exploit it. JPAC wasn't just a job, it was her calling, but odds were she'd never work for them again. "But when it comes to bombs uncovered during excavation, the ordnance disposal technician has final say, so we had to evacuate."

Turbulence bounced the jet, pitching her toward Curt. He grabbed her shoulders and steadied her. He was a brick wall and just as warm. It was a sad testament to her mental state that she didn't care. He'd saved her life, and hero was now stamped on his forehead in indelible ink.

"We should sit down and buckle up. Turbulence can be rough."

She glanced at the seat, aware his hands remained on her shoulders. "I've been trapped for so long—"

He released her, but his touch lingered on her cold skin. "You said the site was evacuated."

"Yes. I was angry and hiked up the dirt track to the vehicles first. Roddy Brogan, our team linguist, was right behind me. He took the driver's seat and started the engine."

"You're saying Roddy Brogan drove?"

"Yes. I was surprised too. We never drove ourselves anywhere." She paused and bit her lip. "North Korea is…different. In other countries, our military escort surrounds us with guns either down or facing out—protecting us. In North Korea, the guns were trained *on* us. We weren't treated like guests invited by the government in a show of goodwill; we were treated like the enemy. Our KPA—Korean People's Army—escort didn't trust us. We followed protocol at all times, because failure to do so could mean getting shot." She glanced down at her boots. "Or arrested. So when Roddy took the driver's seat and said he'd been instructed to drive the third Nissan because the regular driver had to stay behind to guard Evan, it was not standard protocol."

"But you believed him."

"He speaks Korean. I don't. And he was in the driver's seat, and we were headed for the barracks, so I didn't have much choice. I thought we were fine, until Roddy passed the turn to the barracks." The moment returned with full clarity. The jolt of fear. The immediate instinct to leap from the fast-moving vehicle, quashed by the knowledge she wouldn't survive a tumble down the steep, rocky hillside.

"That's when Roddy told me he was taking me to the border—to the Joint Security Area within the Demilitarized Zone. He said"—she stopped and caught her breath—"he said he'd overheard our KPA escort talking. They knew I was a former US vice president's niece. He said they knew Uncle Andrew had been indicted on corruption charges, and the North Korean government wanted to use me in some sort of power play. Roddy said he'd decided to make a run for the Joint Security Area and hoped they'd let us cross." She shook her head. "He claimed he was trying to protect me. But he was crazy. The KPA would never let us cross the Demilitarized Zone. I begged him to take me back to the site."

"You didn't believe his story?"

"No. The KPA knew who I was before I even entered the country. JPAC didn't try to hide it. So Roddy's claims made no sense. And even if he was telling the truth, I knew I was in more danger because we'd left the site without an escort." She paused. "It was the scariest moment of my life—topped only by everything that happened after."

"What happened next?"

She frowned. "I was arrested, tried, and convicted of spying, and sentenced to death by firing squad."

"No. I meant what happened in the Nissan with Roddy."

She shook her head. Silly of her to have expected a bit of compassion. "We saw a vehicle coming our way. Roddy took a narrow offshoot into the woods to hide. He shut off the engine and told me to be quiet. I begged him to go back, but he wouldn't listen."

"What did you do?"

"I rammed the side of my hand into his Adam's apple and bolted."

Curt scanned her from head to toe. "You overpowered a Raptor operative who was a former Army Ranger."

Either he was impressed, or he didn't believe her. "I had surprise on my side. I could demonstrate if you want."

He smiled slightly. "I'll take your word for it."

"I had a good head start—and I'm a runner—so I managed to lose him in the woods. After about ten minutes, I stopped to get my bearings. My safest course was to return to the site. If I could get back to the site, then we—my team—could deal with Roddy. Everything would have been fine. I had to guess which direction and how far we'd come. The trees were so tall, it was dark and I couldn't navigate by the sun. My backpack—with my compass—was in the Nissan."

"Why did you flee Roddy? Wasn't it more dangerous to take off alone?"

"I had a moment to react. I knew the rules, and Roddy forced me to break them, so I fled the person who was endangering me the most. I was petrified. Of Roddy, of being found by a KPA soldier before I could get back to the site. An American alone in North Korea just doesn't happen. And with this"—she grabbed a handful of blond hair—"it's hard for me to go unnoticed in Asian countries." She took a deep breath. "I was stunned when I came out of the woods and found myself on the edge of the DMZ."

The horror of that moment was still with her. She'd relived it a thousand times in her cell. She relived it now. She'd screwed up in the biggest way. What if Roddy had been telling the truth? What if he could have gotten her over the border? Her eyes filled with tears.

Curt's voice remained emotionless. "Then you were arrested?"

She nodded, unwilling to describe what followed. He didn't need the details.

"Prior to that day, was Roddy someone you trusted?"

The truth had a bitter taste, but she knew the State Department would ask her the same questions. This was only the beginning. "I trusted him because of JPAC, but sometimes the fact that he was a subcontractor employed by Raptor and not JPAC led to friction. They aren't there to provide security. They work with us in the field as medics, or linguists like Roddy, or ordnance disposal technicians like Evan. But sometimes they think they should be in charge. When you spend months at a time with someone in foreign countries, tension can really build, and most of the time Roddy was like an annoying little brother."

That same annoying little brother had returned to the US with the rest of the team. How had he managed it? And given what she'd found in North Korea, she couldn't help but wonder what awaited her at home.

# Chapter Three

MARA PACED THE aisle, reminding Curt of a caged tiger—or in her case, kitten—all sleek movement and feral energy. "You aren't what I expected," he said.

She paused and frowned. "And you aren't *who* I expected."

"No doubt you counted on someone higher up, but for some reason, North Korea demanded me." He'd wanted to blame her for this ill-timed mission of mercy, but according to the State Department, he'd come to the North Korean leadership's attention thanks to the *TIME* article. If there was anyone to blame, it was the editor-in-chief.

She shook her head. "No. I wanted someone lower, much lower."

He grinned. "You got a lawyer as your envoy. Some would say you can't go much lower than that."

Her smile was faint. "You aren't just any lawyer; you're the overzealous US attorney who is trying to destroy my family."

"It's your uncle who did the damage. I'm just the one who refuses to let him get away with it. For the record, I warned the secretary of state I didn't think you'd be happy to see me and weren't likely to tell me a damn thing. But he insisted I question you anyway."

"You were wrong. When my blindfold came off and I saw your face I was…beyond happy to see you. You saved my life. I'm grateful."

During his early days as a prosecutor, he'd been given the nickname The Shark, and it had stuck. Much as he hated the name, sometimes he wished he really were as ruthless as it implied. A true shark would be unaffected by those vulnerable blue eyes. Nor would a shark be so gut-wrenchingly moved by how bravely she'd faced the firing squad.

He needed to keep her family ties front and center in his mind. He dropped onto the couch, thinking she might respond better if he didn't tower over her. "Tell me about Raptor."

Her mouth tightened. "My uncle says you're obsessed with his work for Raptor—which is nuts. He took the job as Raptor's chief of operations *after* his term as vice president was over. How could his work for Raptor have anything to do with your trumped-up charge of taking bribes while he was vice president?"

"A grand jury indicted him on the influence-peddling charge."

"Don't make it sound like you had no part in it. *You* convinced them. You took a wonderful, noble man and destroyed his reputation to make your own."

Her words were laughable. There was nothing noble about former Vice President Andrew Stevens, not by a long shot. "I convinced the grand jury with solid evidence. And if your uncle were as smart as he's reputed to be, he'd have turned state's evidence on Raptor's CEO instead of taking the fall himself."

"Has the CEO been indicted?"

"I don't have the evidence to indict Robert Beck as a co-conspirator."

"Why do lawyers say 'co-conspirator' when 'conspirator' means the same thing?"

That made him smile. "Because we like to make things sound complicated."

She resumed pacing. "Like charging my uncle with 'influence peddling' when the words 'taking bribes' would be clearer."

"Don't forget 'obstruction of justice' instead of 'cover up.'"

She stopped and frowned. "Has Uncle Andrew been charged with obstruction?"

"It was added to the charges against him weeks ago." He couldn't nail Andrew Stevens or the CEO for selling arms to a Sudanese war criminal, but he could damn well convict the corrupt former vice president for covering it up.

She dropped into a chair and pulled her knees to her chest. She looked small, delicate, and exhausted. Remembering the hell she'd been through today, he felt like a shit.

She met his gaze with a faint smile. "Why couldn't the North Koreans have demanded George Clooney as envoy?"

He laughed. "Maybe Clooney was too busy arranging a human rights march, whereas I had a lull in my schedule between kicking kittens and destroying the lives of honorable men for personal gain."

Her smile deepened, flashing that warm dimple, and he felt a jolt of heat that made him want to curse. "Get back to Raptor, Mara."

She cleared her throat. "My interrogators asked about my uncle's work for Raptor, repeatedly."

"What did the Democratic People's Republic of Korea want to know about your uncle's job as chief of operations for Raptor?"

"Like you, they were suspicious about Raptor's role with JPAC. They wanted to know if Uncle Andrew was paid to use his influence as vice president to get Raptor mercenaries placed on JPAC recovery teams."

He leaned forward. If his numbers were correct, that was the million-dollar question—and that figure didn't include the company shares Stevens had received, worth quite a bit more. "What did you tell them?"

She met his gaze with a defiant glare. "The truth. He didn't have anything to do with JPAC's decision to hire Raptor. JPAC contracted crew positions to Raptor before my uncle's term in office was even over. He had *nothing* to do with the private security company at the time."

As much as he wanted to pursue this line of questioning, they were supposed to be talking about her arrest in North Korea. Her version bore little resemblance to what he'd been told, yet it sounded strangely plausible. How else could she have gotten to the DMZ? She didn't speak Korean, and as she'd pointed out, her blond hair and blue eyes were tantamount to waving an American flag.

He took a sip of his drink. "According to JPAC, you left the site alone. None of your coworkers knew where to find you when the Korean People's Army showed up with weapons drawn and demanded JPAC leave the country."

Mara jolted to her feet. "No way! Call Roddy." Her voice shook with anger. "I want to talk to him."

"You can't. Not until you've been debriefed by the State Department."

She struggled to regain her composure. "Then let me call Jeannie."

"Jeannie?" he asked, even though he knew perfectly well who she meant. He wanted to hear her take on the JPAC assistant forensic archaeologist.

Mara shot him a skeptical look. "Jeannie Fuller—my coworker. She's my best friend, and she *saw* me leave with Roddy. She'll set things straight. I want to call her."

"You can't."

"Dammit! Why not?" She leaned over him, her face so close that her hair tickled his cheek. Her blue eyes locked on his while she patted his breast pocket. "You've got a phone right here." She touched his cell through his jacket, "And I want to use it."

Christ, he was jealous of his phone. He never reacted to women this way. The glimpse he'd had of Mara Garrett's inner strength had gotten to him, but that didn't change who she was...or who he was. Gripping her invasive hand, he stood, forcing her up and back. "No," he said.

He stopped, her hand caught beneath his. She touched his chest, not the cell phone, and his heart kicked up a notch. With only inches separating them, he'd have to be made of stone not to be affected by her. Her chest rose with each angry breath as her eyes pierced him with a sharp glare.

"You may not speak with your team. You may not speak with your uncle." The State Department had set the rules, but he had no problem enforcing them. "You will not get your story straight with anyone in JPAC or Raptor before the State Department debriefing."

*GET MY STORY straight?*

Her team—including her best friend—had said she'd left the site alone. They knew she'd left with Roddy, and they'd lied. And Curt Dominick thought she wanted to get her story straight? She just wanted to get the story, period.

Curt stood before her, his face no longer merely impassive or remote. He was downright glacial. She knew his nickname, The Shark, and now she understood he wasn't just ruthless in the courtroom.

When *People* magazine placed him in their Sexiest Men of the Year issue, NPR's Nina Totenberg had done a story on Curt Dominick, explaining that legal-news junkies had a new, swoon-worthy star. Nina really should have done a better job describing his chin or mentioned the dark mole on his right cheekbone, but more important, Nina had failed to prepare Mara for the man's megawatt looks, commanding presence, and utter lack of heart.

Now, face-to-face with The Shark, she stumbled backward until her knees hit the arm of one of the recliners. "Do you have to be such a prick?"

His eyes glinted with amusement. "Sweetheart, you think I'm a prick now, but you haven't seen anything yet."

The man before her wasn't a rescuing superhero. He was the powerful US attorney who prosecuted mobsters and politicians. He was formidable, harsh, exuding distrust, and she was stuck on a plane with him for at least fifteen hours. "Is there a shower on this flying yacht?" Her words lacked the punch she'd been aiming for and were clouded by weariness. "I haven't had a hot shower in months."

"There's a suitcase full of clothes for you in the bedroom." He waved toward the rear of the jet, but his voice was less harsh. "After you shower, try to get some sleep." He pulled out his cell phone. She'd been dismissed.

She walked toward the bedroom on legs that ached from constant tension. Pre-North Korea Mara would have seen Curt Dominick as an interesting challenge. Post-North Korea Mara didn't have the emotional wherewithal for challenges.

"Palea? It's Dominick. Bring Roddy Brogan in for questioning. Now."

She halted midstep and whirled to face him. He met her gaze and offered a slight, almost imperceptible nod. Heat started in her belly and spread outward.

He held her gaze even as he continued to speak into the phone. "I don't care that it's one in the morning in Honolulu. Roddy Brogan needs to answer some questions." His rich, deep voice, uttered words she'd never expected him to say, while his intense stare held her rooted to the spot. He *had* listened to her. He was following up on her allegations.

In one area, at least, her uncle had been wrong about Curt Dominick, making her wonder what else her uncle was wrong about.

CURT WATCHED HER escape into the cabin as he told his friend, Honolulu FBI agent Kaha'i Palea, what he needed. Conversation complete, he returned the phone to his breast pocket.

He had a job to do. He'd hoped she'd give him something on Raptor, but he had no idea what to make of her claim Roddy Brogan had essentially abducted her. But he wasn't operating at top capacity. Everyone had a breaking point, and after being awake for most of the last thirty hours, he'd passed his—probably right about the time he was a complete ass to a woman who'd just survived a firing squad.

He grabbed a blanket and stretched out on the wide sofa. The moment he closed his eyes, images of the petite archaeologist bombarded him: her proud posture as she marched blindfolded down the cobblestone path; the anger in her eyes as she called him on his dickish behavior.

More images followed, but these weren't based on memories. A carnal fantasy of slipping into the shower with her and washing the grime of imprisonment from her skin; her blue eyes darkening as he thrust into her for the first time.

He jolted awake.

*Shit.*

He sank back into the couch. It wasn't like him to have sexual dreams about women he'd just met, but he could cut his subconscious some slack. After all, he'd been researching the woman for months, and she was as impressive on paper as she was in person. Smart, savvy, and hardworking, she'd graduated with honors from Stanford University and held a masters degree in archaeology from the same institution.

Her uncle had visited her deployments several times when he was vice president, and an Associated Press reporter had interviewed her during one such photo op in Vietnam. She'd explained how her career choice stemmed from personal family history. Her maternal grandfather—the former vice president's father—had been shot down over North Korea in 1951 and never returned. Then she'd described the loss of her own father when she was in her teens, and how the only place she'd been able to grieve was at his graveside.

When asked what working for the Joint POW/MIA Accounting Command meant to her, her dimple had appeared and her face lit up as she responded, *"I'm providing closure for families like mine. I'm bringing them home."*

That clip had been played thousands of times in the last months. In the US, Mara Garrett was a hero. But inside this jet, she was a puzzle he needed to solve.

She idolized her uncle. Understandable, given the fact that he had taken over as father figure when her dad died. But a problem for Curt because her uncle was a corrupt son of a bitch who'd sold out the country he'd sworn an oath to defend and bear allegiance to.

Curt had hoped she'd prove to be a pretty twit who'd created an international incident, but she might be the victim after all. He rolled to his side and tried to get comfortable. He needed to sleep so he could hit the ground running when they reached DC. Once there, the State Department would take Mara Garrett off his hands, and he would lead the prosecution of her uncle.

Whether she was a pretty twit or an alluring victim didn't matter. She was somebody else's problem, and after tomorrow, he'd only see her in his dreams.

AFTER TWO MONTHS of cold sponge baths, hot spray sluiced down Mara's back. She rolled the lavender soap between her hands, building a thick lather. Like the ice cubes earlier, the luxury of scented soap and running water undid her, and tears slid down her cheeks.

She should be overjoyed. She was on her way to the mainland. But nothing felt right. Her best friend had lied. Roddy had flown home to Honolulu with the rest of the team. And US Attorney Curt Dominick had rescued her from a firing squad. There was no universe in which those three statements made sense.

Released after two months of isolation and interrogation, she should also be free from the gut-wrenching fear, but painful knots still twisted in her belly. What was she returning to? The mound of lather grew, hiding her hands beneath a thick layer of bubbles. She needed to talk to her uncle. Maybe he knew something.

The water turned cold, startling her out of her emotional spiral. She shut off the spray and washed while bracing for the cold rinse. Her first hot shower in months and she'd ruined it. Once again, she'd failed to think things through and see the pitfalls of her impulsive actions.

Rinsed and clean, she shut off the frigid water. She leaned against the fiberglass stall, powerless against a noisy sob that engulfed her. The battle she'd waged to control her emotions for two months was over. She was alone and safe. She could let down her guard and really cry.

She slid down the slick wall and hugged her knees to her chest. Where was the euphoria of rescue? Why did she feel like the trouble had only just begun?

Jesus. Curt Dominick, of all people. Another painful, embarrassingly loud sob escaped. Even his selection as envoy was her fault. If he ever learned the truth, he'd hate her. More than he did already.

For a moment, when they stood in the courtyard and he held her, she'd met his gaze and the strongest, most head-spinning, gut-clenching emotion had shot through her. Hate was the last emotion she felt for Curt Dominick.

A LOUD THUMP jolted Curt from his light doze. He bolted to his feet. Mara. Was she hurt? He hurried down the short aisle. He'd been dozing for only a few minutes. It took him a second to get his bearings. Was she in the private cabin to the left or the shower to the right?

He shook his head to dispel sleep and heard a noise coming from the shower. He reached for the knob when the sound registered. A sob. His hand froze an inch from the door.

Shit. He was not cut out for this.

The woman had just been through a nightmarish ordeal. Her two-month-long imprisonment had culminated in a firing squad and ended with her being rescued by a man who was not known for his ability to sympathize.

Should he knock? Enter? Talk to her through the door?

Another sob sounded, and his heart twisted. He leaned his forehead against the panel. A better man would open the door, take her into his arms, and comfort her.

But he wasn't that man. Where she was concerned, he had to be a prosecutor first, last, and always.

# Chapter Four

Roddy Brogan was dead. He'd been shot on Oahu sometime in the last four hours, and the death scene had been staged to look like a suicide.

Curt hung up his cell and ran his fingers through his hair, distantly registering he'd missed an appointment with his barber yesterday. Or was it today? They must have crossed the international dateline already. But he had far bigger problems than a missed haircut.

If his information was correct, Roddy Brogan—gifted linguist and cold-blooded mercenary—had provided translation for the Sudanese weapons deal. The man's death could be the key to finally indicting the CEO, and Curt had a hunch Raptor's sharp talons were all over the death scene.

The trial would start in twenty-one hours whether he was there or not. Without changes to their itinerary, they would reach DC in thirteen or fourteen hours.

But if he changed their refueling stop to Oahu…he was looking at two hours—three at most—added to their travel time. Cutting it close, but doable.

He pulled out his cell and dialed his co-counsel, Assistant US Attorney Aurora Ames. She was going to freak when he explained the delay, but when she heard why, she'd understand.

Mara emerged from the bedroom when the plane started to descend, surprised they'd reached the mainland already. All she could see from the portside window was the vast blue ocean, but one of California's coastal airports or military bases must be ahead. She hoped someone from the State Department would join them for the rest of the journey. Then the official debriefing could begin.

Once that was behind her, she could return to Oahu and find out if she still had a job, but deep down, she feared she already knew the answer to that question.

She hadn't been able to sleep during the long flight. The dark, tiny room transformed into her cold cell every time she closed her eyes. She'd battled the illusion by turning on the bedside light, but the dim glow made sleep impossible.

Curt sat on the sofa with his laptop open before him, looking handsome and refreshed, his shirt crisp and tie straight, like he expected to argue before a judge at any moment.

Mara felt rumpled, frazzled, and haggard. Her hair was too long and had darkened after months of being out of the sun, the clothes provided for her were too big, and she had bags under her eyes from yet another sleepless night. She resented the hell out of the fact that he looked so damn good while she resembled an escapee from rehab.

"I'm glad you're up," he said, lifting his gaze from his computer. "I have something for you." He picked up a file from the seat next to him and handed it to her.

"What's this?"

"We're getting ready to land on Oahu, and I want you to understand why you have to continue with me to DC."

She dropped the file and turned to a starboard window. Sure enough, Oahu was in the distance as they passed Kauai. "Oahu? I'm going home?" Her heart surged with joy.

"No. We're just refueling here, then continuing to DC."

She glanced over her shoulder. "But surely I can stay—"

He picked up the discarded file and pressed it into her hand again. "No. We're going to DC. That's a subpoena. I'm calling you to testify for the prosecution in the case of the United States of America vs. Andrew Stevens."

CURT FELT A slight stab of guilt but shoved it aside. He had a job to do.

"I—I—don't believe you. You're supposed to be my hero, the man who flew halfway around the world to rescue me… My blindfold dropped, and I see the most handsome face I've ever seen in my life, and it's *you*, with a subpoena."

He ignored the jolt of pleasure her compliment caused. "I'm no one's hero, Mara. I've never been accused of being anything but a shark."

"Really? Maybe you should hire a new publicist!"

He couldn't help it, he laughed. She had a gift for making him laugh while insulting him.

"Why the hell would I testify against my uncle?" The hostility in her voice revealed a fire she'd shown only fleetingly earlier, and he was relieved she'd turned angry. An angry Mara would be far easier to deal with than the wounded sprite. He could be his usual, ruthless self without qualm.

"You'll testify because you've been subpoenaed."

"That's not what I meant, and you know it. I want to know why you think I can help your case. I haven't even seen my uncle since he visited me in Egypt a year and a half ago. I don't know a damn thing about influence peddling."

"You work with Raptor operatives, and you dated one for five months." Five months, two weeks, and three days, according to his information, but it tended to creep people out when he spoke in such precise terms.

"So I dated Evan. That doesn't mean I know anything about my uncle's work for Raptor."

"You know far more than you think you do."

"Like what?"

Two beeps preceded an announcement by the captain. "We've begun our final descent and are cleared to land at Marine Corps Base Kaneohe, Mr. Dominick. We'll be on the ground in five minutes."

He hit the intercom button, more thankful than he could say for the interruption. "We're preparing for landing," he said, then gathered his papers into a neat stack. After stowing his laptop and papers, he moved to the seat-belt-equipped recliner and signaled for her to sit. "This is just a refueling stop. So don't get any ideas about staying."

"If we only needed fuel, we'd have gone to California as planned. Why are we really here?" she asked as she dropped into the facing seat.

She was smart. No doubt about that. "I have business here."

"How long are we going to be on Oahu?"

"A few hours."

They were both silent as the jet approached the runway. Finally, Mara spoke. "You're making a mistake, you know. My uncle is innocent."

He looked down at his cell and typed out a text message for Palea, informing him of their arrival. "No, he isn't. He took bribes and covered up other crimes."

"You're chasing phantoms. I know him, and he would *never* take a bribe. No crimes were committed. There couldn't be a cover-up, because he has nothing to hide."

He met her gaze. "No, Mara, I'm chasing Raptors—whether the person I need to take down is your uncle or a field operative, I don't give a damn as long as they bring me closer to indicting the slippery weasel of a CEO, Robert Beck. And this stop on Oahu might give me the evidence I need."

She flinched at his mention of her ex-boyfriend's father. Yes, Mara Garrett had far too many connections to Raptor to be as ignorant as she'd claimed. She'd paint an ugly picture for the jury.

MARA EXPECTED A light breeze when she emerged from the aircraft, but the trade winds had taken a vacation from paradise, and the heavy air was a stifling eighty degrees. Her internal clock didn't know what time of day or even month it was, and Hawai'i's perpetual lush weather didn't ease her disorientation.

This should have been a triumphant moment. Her homecoming. But suddenly, Oahu felt as foreign as the first time she'd landed in Papua New Guinea. The air was thick, unforgiving, the familiar scent of tropical flowers masked by the acrid stench of hot tarmac.

She paused on the top step of the gangway. A few meters from the plane, a line of marines stood at attention in eerie similarity to the firing squad she'd faced in North Korea.

Curt waited at the bottom of the stairs with his satchel in hand. He urged her forward with an impatient wave. She descended. The moment her feet hit the tarmac, the marines saluted in perfect unison.

The show of respect hit her with the force of a fist. A civilian receiving a salute was a rare and precious gesture, bringing forth an instant rush of tears and a sudden, sharp shame. Although technically a civilian navy employee, she worked with all branches of the military. She'd trained with the troops to show she was no pedigreed token employee and could keep up with the vigorous physical requirements. She worked long hours in the lab and even longer hours in the field when deployed. As a result, she knew more than military rank and insignia; she understood their culture. These men didn't salute the self-assured, smug, and commanding US attorney. Nor did they salute because she was a former vice president's niece. No. They saluted the JPAC archaeologist. Her work was dangerous, grueling, and respected by soldier, sailor, airman, and marine.

These marines didn't blame her for screwing up in North Korea. They thanked her for her service to an important cause.

She cleared her throat and said, "Thank you." But the words felt inadequate.

A colonel stepped forward. "At ease." He shook Mara's hand with a firm grip and introduced himself as Colonel McCormick. To Curt he said, "I was surprised to hear you were headed our way, Mr. Dominick."

"The change was necessary."

"I've received orders from the secretaries of state and defense to provide you with whatever you need."

Curt inclined his head to request privacy for himself and the colonel. The two walked away, leaving her to stand awkwardly in front of the marines.

A minute later, he returned. "You'll wait on the plane while I attend to some business."

"Where are you going?"

"I'll be gone an hour, maybe two."

"You're not even going to pretend to answer my question."

"No." The man was colder than Antarctica in July and a secretive son of a bitch. She still couldn't believe he'd served her with a subpoena.

The colonel gave orders to the marines, then nodded to Curt.

"I've got to go," he said.

The muted smell of the tropics and slight breeze on her skin combined to strike her with an intense longing for home. "I want to go to my house."

"We don't have time, Mara. We won't be on Oahu long."

"It's in Kaneohe, not far from here. It's been months."

His voice softened. "I wish I could take you there. But I can't."

"I don't need a babysitter."

"You'll wait here."

"Fine," she said and turned toward the gangway.

"Mara."

She faced him. His eyes held the compassion she'd briefly glimpsed when they met in North Korea. He could make her knees weak with one penetrating stare, because she was a fool who couldn't separate the notion of "hero" from "rescue" even when her rescuer was the enemy.

His warm palm caressed her cheek. "I'll be back as soon as I can."

Tenderness from The Shark? Was it an act? "I'll be here."

"Good."

Through a main cabin window, she watched Curt and the colonel drive away, while the marines marched in unison, and the pilots crossed the tarmac to a nearby building. She was alone.

It was ridiculous for her to wait here when she could be doing something. She wasn't a prisoner anymore, and no one, not even the man who'd saved her life, had the right to detain her. She wanted to track Roddy down, but confronting him would be stupid. Jeannie was her best hope. Jeannie would tell her what the hell had happened on that August day.

Her tiny house was about ten miles away—less than five miles across the bay as the Nēnē flies. Once there, she could pick up her car and head to Jeannie's. She would be back on the base before Curt even knew she'd left.

A friend tended bar at the Marine Corps Base golf course on weekdays and could probably give her a ride home. She paused to wonder what day of the week it was and realized she had no idea. They'd crossed the international dateline during the flight. It was yesterday here and tomorrow in North Korea, but she had no name for today.

The first problem was clothing. She'd die of heat stroke if she walked a mile, let alone ten, in the clothing provided by the State Department. She searched the galley and came up with a serrated knife. After slipping off the clothes, she sawed through each pant leg, then hacked off the sleeves and high neck from the sweater. Dressed again, she paused in the doorway and glanced down at her frayed and unraveling ensemble. Telling herself she set a new standard for awesomeness, she stepped outside.

The fuel truck arrived, and she headed down the stairs. The tech was too busy hooking up the line to even glance her way. In seconds, she crossed the tarmac and circled the building. With luck, she'd have two hours before anyone even realized she was gone.

# Chapter Five

Andrew Stevens gripped the phone in a tight fist and managed to maintain a calm, reasonable voice. "She's on Oahu?"

On the other end of the line, the secretary of state's voice remained smooth and even, a sure sign he hadn't picked up on Andrew's tension. "This is a courtesy call. I'm not at liberty to divulge more."

"You can tell that bastard Dominick I'm grateful to him for saving her."

"I'll do that. They'll be in the air again shortly. You can have breakfast with her tomorrow."

Andrew gritted his teeth. They both knew the trial started tomorrow. "I'm busy tomorrow morning."

The man cleared his throat. "Yes. I guess you are."

On autopilot, Andrew said the necessary words of thanks and hung up. Mara was stuck with Curt Dominick until the trial started. If he didn't know his darling niece was loyal to a fault, he'd be very, very afraid. As it was, all he could do was pray she didn't unwittingly set the prosecutor on the scent of a charge bigger than obstruction of justice.

The right question, deftly applied, could unlock knowledge Mara didn't know she had, and Curt Dominick was just the man to ask those questions. Hell, the prosecutor had been compiling a list since July.

He punched in Raptor CEO Robert Beck's number. He could hope Mara would refuse to answer, and her knowledge would remain harmless, dormant. But he couldn't rely on hope. There was far too much at stake. Robert Beck could help. His son, Evan, was Mara's ex-boyfriend, and the two had remained close, even after the breakup. Evan might be able to wrest her away from the prosecutor.

Roddy Brogan's body had been removed hours before Curt arrived at the scene. Understandable, considering the rapid rate of decomposition in the balmy climate, but even without the corpse, the smell of death remained.

The gun that had apparently killed him remained on the floor. An FBI crime scene technician photographed blood splatters that streaked across the walls and floor. Suicide couldn't be immediately ruled out.

Curt turned to FBI Agent Kaha'i Palea. Palea had been up since Curt's one a.m. call and looked tired. "How did you know to look for Brogan here?"

"Years of fine-tuning my investigative instincts."

Curt raised an eyebrow.

The crime scene tech laughed. "It was dumbass luck. He'd run out of places to look and decided to check this place out because he was in the area."

Palea grinned. "You call it luck. I call it instinct. Po-tay-to, pa-tot-oh."

A loud boom rocked the floor and rattled the windows. The tech glanced from Palea to Curt. "Sonic boom?"

Palea shrugged. "They're getting sloppy on the base. Heads are gonna roll for that." The phone on Palea's hip chimed. He glanced at the display. "I need to take this," he said and answered the call.

Curt studied the weapon, so close to where the corpse had lain. Five years ago, at the age of twenty-three, Roddy Brogan had completed US Army Ranger training but was injured in a training exercise. Permanent nerve damage to his right—and dominant—hand forced a medical discharge, but a Raptor headhunter had snatched him up while he was still recovering, recruiting Roddy for his linguistic talents. From what Curt had been able to learn, during the last five years Roddy had become nearly as proficient with his left hand as he'd been with his right.

The weapon on the floor lay only inches from where Roddy's left hand had been. If he'd been murdered, the killer had known about his disability.

Palea closed his phone. "The serial number on the gun is a match. It's Roddy Brogan's Raptor-issued weapon."

"It seems unlikely Roddy could be caught off guard and killed with his own weapon," Curt said. *But petite Mara claimed she took him down with a swift chop of her small hand.*

"I know," Palea said. "He must have known his killer. Someone he trusted."

"I agree." He turned away from the crime scene to look out

the window. Plants crowded upon each other, threatening to take over the backyard. The nearest neighbor wouldn't have seen a thing through the thick foliage.

His phone vibrated in his pocket. He checked the number. Hawai'i area code. Few people in Hawai'i had his cell number. He left the bloody kitchen for the adjacent living room and answered. "Dominick."

"This is Colonel McCormick," a clipped voice said. Sirens wailed in the background. "Shit, Dominick. I need you to sit down."

Icy fear spread through Curt. He knew with sudden certainty the noise that shook the house a few minutes ago hadn't been a sonic boom. He held the phone in a knuckle-burning grip. "What's going on, Colonel?"

"There's been an explosion. The jet… It's gone."

The room around him narrowed to a small, airless tunnel, and the bright noon sun dimmed. "Mara," he said before his voice cut out.

"She was inside."

The putrid scent of death that permeated the house became stronger. He stumbled across the room and into the screen door. The door gave way, and he tumbled onto the porch.

His job had been to save her.

His fault. Jesus. He'd left her behind.

He leaned against the porch railing and realized he still held the phone in a death grip. "I'll be there in fifteen minutes."

"I'll send a car—"

The rest of his words were lost as Curt saw a vision walking down the long driveway. He didn't believe in ghosts or spirits or even angels and had always believed he'd been born without a faith gene. He was a man who relied on facts and evidence, and walking toward him was an ethereal, beautiful sprite. The sun glinted off her blond hair, and damn if it didn't glow.

The phone dropped from his hand and clattered on the wooden planks. His throat seized. He couldn't speak, couldn't breathe, couldn't even think.

Her brow wrinkled in confusion as she approached. Finally, the vision spoke. "Before you yell at me for disregarding your orders, I want to know what the hell you're doing at my house."

# Chapter Six

THE EXPLOSION HAD drawn all pleasure craft for miles, making his boat one of many on the water. He was just another fisherman, curious, watching fire trucks and ambulances race down the runway toward the fiery wreck that had been a luxury private jet a few minutes before.

The blast had taken out the windows of the nearest building. The medics would have plenty of patients to care for, but he hoped no one inside the building had been seriously hurt. He hated killing military personnel.

He hadn't believed his luck when he'd been told Mara's jet had rerouted to Oahu, providing him with the perfect opportunity to take her out before she reached DC and said the wrong things to the right people.

Now she was dead. Despite what Mara believed of him, this wasn't the outcome he'd wanted. But he had no other choice. Rectifying Roddy's fuckup in allowing her to escape him in North Korea was more important.

With binoculars, he watched the colonel at the periphery of the scene. The man held a cell phone to his ear. With the touch of a button, he accessed the speaker on the colonel's phone and eavesdropped on the conversation.

He smiled, hearing Dominick say he'd return to the base. When Dominick arrived, a sniper shot would be the cleanest way to take care of the last loose end. He had the long-range rifle ready.

The boat rolled over a low wave. He rocked with the motion, steady on his feet at the helm as he waited for Dominick to say more, but the conversation had halted.

Then a third voice carried over the line, and his blood ran cold.

His gaze returned to the scene on the airfield. Firefighters pumped water on the smoldering ruins. People limped out of the wounded building, and the colonel paced.

All for nothing.

Mara was alive.

IF SHE DIDN'T think it was impossible, Mara might believe the unfazable Curt Dominick was, well, fazed. He gripped the porch railing and looked as if he'd fall without the support.

"What the hell is going on?" she asked.

He stooped and picked up his cell phone. In that one swift motion, she saw him transform from rattled to composed. His left hand adjusted the knot on his silk tie, while his deep voice was clear and steady. "Colonel, Mara's here. She just arrived."

Damn, he'd probably been looking for her.

"I don't know," he said into the phone. "I'll find out." He stared at her but surprisingly didn't appear angry. He looked…hungry. Her belly fluttered at the intensity of his hazel eyes. "Keep this under wraps. I'll call when I know more." He shoved the phone into his pocket, his gaze still locked on hers.

She found his silence and stare unnerving. "I wanted to pick up some stuff." *Crap*. He hadn't said a word, and she'd already gone on the defensive.

"Dominick! I want you to see this." The words carried through the screen door.

Shocked, she pinned Curt with a glare. It was one thing for him to be here, quite another for a stranger to be inside her house. "Who's inside?"

Curt's cell buzzed. He fished it out and glanced at the caller ID.

"Don't you dare take that call without answering me. I have the right to know who is in my house."

He tucked the phone away. "The FBI," he said.

The sense of violation took her breath away. Finally, she found her voice. "I was subpoenaed, but that doesn't give you the right to search my house."

"We have every right—"

"Show me the warrant."

"We don't need one—"

"The hell you don't!"

"It's a crime scene. Your buddy, Roddy Brogan, ate a bullet in your kitchen."

The words knocked her backward. "Roddy's dead?" Her voice dropped to a pathetic croak. "Here?"

"His body was removed before we landed, but yes, he's dead."

"Is that why we rerouted to Oahu?" Her brain spun, and her breathing turned shallow.

"Yes."

"Roddy can't be dead." Panic rose. "He's the one who—"

"I know. He's the reason you were arrested on the edge of the DMZ."

Questions crowded against each other in her addled mind. "Why was he here?"

He leaned against the side of her house and crossed his arms. "I was hoping you could answer that."

She stiffened. "I can't possibly be a suspect."

"Did Roddy have a key?"

"I was in North Korea. Then I was on a plane—with you."

"Did Roddy have a key?"

Exasperation won out. "No."

"Were you and Roddy ever involved?"

"No."

"Never?" His tone conveyed disbelief.

"I wasn't interested. He was your typical sexist pig."

"And Evan Beck wasn't?"

She flinched, as she always did when Evan's name came up, but quickly recovered. It was futile to hope the eagle-eyed prosecutor hadn't noticed. She shrugged and aimed for flippant. "Egypt was lonely, and Evan was hot."

"Did you ever give Evan a key?"

"No."

"You dated for a long time."

"What's with the obsession over my relationship with Evan? Are you jealous, Curt?"

His eyes narrowed, but still, he smiled and shook his head. "They must have loved your mouth in North Korea."

She'd tried to rein in her glib tongue during interrogation but had failed on a few memorable occasions. She looked away, unable to suppress a shudder at the memory.

He grabbed her hands and squeezed. "I'm sorry. That was thoughtless of me."

Since her arrest, she'd had very little human comfort, and the touch of his hands triggered a sharp need. She stepped closer, and his arms enfolded her. A hand stroked her hair and the other rubbed her back. "I'm sorry, Mara. I'll try to remember what you've been through and not be such a prick."

She pressed her cheek against his chest and murmured, "Thanks." He smelled pleasantly musky, and his broad shoulders and firm body made her feel protected. Safe. She didn't want to think; she just wanted to feel.

"Dominick," a man called from inside the house. "I need you in here."

She took a deep breath and stepped out of his arms.

He studied her with unreadable eyes, then ran his fingers through his hair and glanced away. "I need to confer with Palea, but before I do, back to my earlier question. There's no sign of breaking and entering. I was trying to establish if there is any way Roddy—or his murderer—could have gotten a key."

"A copy of my key is at JPAC headquarters—so other JPAC teams can watch over my place when I'm deployed. I do the same for them."

His intense gaze was probing, analyzing. Filing away information about her in his sharp mind. But now she saw compassion in his eyes as well. One of the numerous walls that separated them had fallen. She wondered if the change would be permanent or fleeting.

"Ordinarily, we'd never let you enter a crime scene, but I'll make an exception for two reasons. One, you might be able to tell us what's changed since you were here last."

"What's the other reason?"

"You've been through hell. You can pick up a few personal items before we head to DC. I was going to throw together a bag for you."

She regarded him for a moment. "Curt Dominick, you might actually be a nice man."

He winked at her. "Don't tell anyone. You'll ruin my reputation." He turned and reached for the door handle, then glanced over his shoulder. "Brace yourself."

Inside, a man was taking pictures on the other side of the low partition wall that separated the kitchen from the living room. Another man pawed through her neatly stacked mail with gloved hands.

The second man looked up, and his dark, native-Hawaiian eyes widened at the sight of her. "This is a crime scene. She can't be here."

She bristled. "This is my house. Who are you?"

"Assistant Special Agent in Charge Kaha'i Palea. I repeat, you shouldn't be here." The man glared at Curt. "Dammit, Dominick. You've gotten sloppy."

"We need her. She can tell us what's out of place."

She headed toward the kitchen to look over the low partition wall.

"Wait—" the agent said.

She ignored him and rose on her toes to peer over the divider, to see what the other man was photographing. The smell of death was bad enough, but the mess in her kitchen was worse. Blood pooled on the floor, spattered the walls, cabinets, and dripped in red streaks down her airy curtains.

"The blood is new since I was here last." She turned away from the gruesome scene and landed right in Curt's arms. Tremors started in her center and spread to her extremities.

"There's always more blood than people expect," he said.

Her forehead pressed against his heart. The steady beat became a calming cadence. "God, I'm having a crappy day," she whispered.

His arms tightened around her. "You're determined to milk the firing squad, aren't you?"

The trembling dissipated in the wake of her laugh. She met his gaze. What a time for him to reveal he had a heart, let alone a sense of humor. "I'd be a fool not to," she said.

His cell rang again. Thankfully, he ignored it, but she forced herself to step out of his arms. Turning to face the carnage in her kitchen, she hugged herself and said, "I'd say Roddy had a worse day than I did." She turned her back on the mess. "Are you sure it was Roddy? I mean, given what's left in my kitchen, identification must be difficult."

The FBI agent nodded. "The medical examiner has already matched Brogan's tattoos for a positive ID."

Of course. The JPAC skull symbol had been tattooed next to a raptor on his shoulder. Roddy was really and truly dead. Later she'd process grief, horror, and outrage, but right now she was concerned about the living. "Have you checked on my neighbors? The gunshot must have terrified them."

"Roddy was considerate in his suicide and used a gun with a silencer," Agent Palea said.

"Raptor has the best toys," Curt added.

"You don't really believe this was a suicide," she said.

"No," said the agent.

"The ME has placed the time of death around the time the president announced we'd safely left P'yŏngyang," Curt said. "Listen, we have some questions for you, but I need to speak with Agent Palea alone first." Curt's gaze raked her from head to toe. "Why don't you change while we talk?"

"What, you don't like my outfit?"

With thumb and forefinger he pulled a loose strand of yarn at her collar. The sweater unraveled. He flashed a wry smile. "It's entertaining, certainly."

Thoroughly confused by Curt Dominick's unexpected attitude shift, she escaped down the hallway to her bedroom.

CURT WATCHED MARA leave the room with quick strides. The explosion had rattled him or he never would have made the stupid, cruel remark about her flippant tongue. But what worried him was his willingness to hold her, which had been triggered by an overwhelming need to appease the crazy part of him that feared she was a haunting angel—or demon.

As he followed Palea outside where they could talk in private, questions inundated him in rapid-fire succession. Had the jet been rigged to explode from the beginning? If they'd flown to San Francisco as planned, would they have exploded in the air? The pilots had guarded the jet in North Korea, but what if they'd missed something? Was Mara the target? Or had someone finally followed through with one of the many death threats he'd received?

Palea swung around and said in a low voice, "What the hell was that?"

"What do you mean?"

"With the sweater. And the embrace."

He gave Palea a look that usually made opposing counsel back off. "There's nothing going on. She's part of a case."

"She's also beautiful, vulnerable, and looks at you like you're Superman."

"She's got a little hero worship going, which is understandable, considering I arrived only moments before her execution. It doesn't have anything to do with *me*." Great. He sounded defensive.

"You're prosecuting her uncle. She could be using the oldest trick in the book to sway you."

"I'm not some novice assistant district attorney, so you can cut the condescending lecture. I was relieved to see her because that wasn't a sonic boom we heard. It was our jet—exploding. I ordered her to wait for me on the jet. If she'd listened to me, she'd be dead."

Palea's suspicious gaze fixed on the house. "For someone who just escaped an explosion, she seemed pretty nonchalant."

His cell phone rang again. Caller ID indicated the president's chief of staff. He also had missed two calls from the secretary of state. "She doesn't know about the explosion."

"What are you going to do?"

"The trial starts in thirteen and a half hours, and I'm stuck on Oahu without a jet. I need to make some calls. I can probably arrange a military flight."

"Before you do that, I want to show you something." Palea led the way back inside the house and headed down the hall to Mara's den. "I found this behind the file cabinet." He held up a clear plastic evidence bag containing a small padded manila envelope. "It's empty. Whatever was inside the envelope was dirty—soil and organic residue coat the inside. The postmark indicates it was mailed from the Camp Casey—South Korea—APO the day after Mara was arrested."

"When JPAC was evicted, they left the country through the Joint Security Area and went straight to Camp Casey," Curt said. "A day later, they caught a military flight back to Honolulu." He paused, considering multiple scenarios. "Anyone on the crew could have sent the package to Mara's address. You think Roddy came here last night to retrieve it?"

"The package would have arrived weeks ago."

"Maybe the package didn't matter until Mara was released," Curt said. He studied the printed address label. It revealed nothing about the identity of the sender. "You think he grabbed the contents before the shooter arrived?"

"Maybe," Palea said. "Then he heard someone and dropped the envelope behind the cabinet before meeting his killer in the kitchen. The killer might have lifted whatever was in that envelope from the corpse."

"Call the ME and tell him to look for the same dirt residue on the body." Curt leaned into the hall. "Mara?" She didn't answer immediately. "Mara," he said again, more loudly this time.

She stepped into the hall, tugging down her shirt. "Keep your panties on." She'd changed into khaki shorts and a sleeveless top that highlighted both her full cleavage and flat belly. She'd swept her long blond hair into a ponytail and looked refreshed, comfortable, and disturbingly sexy.

"You'll freeze in DC," he said.

She made a face. "I'm not wearing this in DC. I'm wearing it in Hawai'i. I packed mainland clothes."

"Ms. Garrett," Palea said. "I have a question. Follow me, please." He left the den and led them into the living room. "Who collected your mail while you were away?"

"The post office held it."

He pointed to the secretary. "Your mail is here."

She stopped short and looked puzzled for a moment before understanding lit her face. "I always have the post office hold my mail when I'm away, and set up delivery to resume on the day I'm scheduled to return. I was supposed to be in DPRK for two months, not three."

Curt and Palea exchanged glances. "The mail was inside the house," Palea said. "Not on the porch nor in the box."

"My neighbors have a key. They probably saw the stack and moved it inside for me."

"You didn't mention that your neighbors had a key," Curt said.

"You asked how Roddy could have gotten in—and Roddy would have gotten my key through JPAC. He doesn't know my neighbors."

The manila envelope wouldn't have been accessible to Roddy until the mail was delivered a month ago. An FBI agent would contact the post office for the exact date and check with the neighbors to ascertain if they'd moved the mail inside the house and if they'd noticed the manila envelope. But he didn't need to tell Palea how to do his job. "You have questions to answer, and I have calls to make," he said and walked outside.

His first call was to Colonel McCormick. The man didn't even bother with hello. "What did you find out?"

"I haven't told her about the explosion. I needed her mind clear for questioning."

"Get on it, man! I've got a crater where a jet used to be, and I need answers."

"And I've got a gallon of blood where a man used to be. I need answers too. The woman's been through an ordeal. If we push her too hard, she might break, and neither of us will get the information we need."

"Listen. I've got news copters over the bay threatening my restricted airspace, my assistant tells me they're reporting that you and Garrett are alive, and all the networks are demanding a statement. To top it off, the secretary of state and the president's chief of staff are on my ass because you aren't answering your phone. I don't give a shit how fragile Mara Garrett is. You need to stop pussyfooting around and find out what she knows or bring her here so *I* can."

"They're reporting we're alive? And how do they even know the jet that exploded was ours?"

"How the hell would I know? Maybe Garrett called someone."

"That would only make sense if she knew about the explosion." He looked back toward the house. He'd assumed he had more time—an hour at least—before word they were alive made headlines, but the news had leaked within minutes of the blast.

The bomb could have been set before he even left DC. Or it was planted after they arrived on Oahu. Either way, someone wanted one—or both—of them dead. And here they were, sitting pretty in the first place any smart assassin would look.

# Chapter Seven

"MARA, GET YOUR bag. We're leaving." Curt stood in the front doorway, tension coiled in his gut.

Mara glanced away from Palea and frowned at him. "In a minute—"

"Now. I don't have time to explain." He heard his abrupt tone and winced, but this wasn't the time for soft, coaxing words.

"I'm not done questioning her," Palea said.

"We have to go. She can answer your questions on the phone."

"What's going on?" Mara asked.

"I'll tell you, but only if you're in the car in the next thirty seconds." He brushed past her and headed down the hall. "Is your bag in the bedroom?"

"I haven't finished packing." She hurried after him.

"I don't care." He found her duffle and nearly crashed into her in the hall as he headed back to the front door.

"Curt, what's wrong?"

"I'll tell you in the car." To Palea he said, "I'll call you as soon as I can."

Palea nodded. "Be careful."

Thankfully, Mara followed without further argument. In the carport, he said, "Give me your keys."

"You aren't driving my car."

"Yes. I am. Keys. Now." He held out a hand.

She glared at him. "They're in the bag. Side pocket."

He dug out her keychain, then looked at the battered Honda Accord. "Does this thing even run?"

She rolled her eyes. "It runs fine. Are we going back to the jet?"

"We're going to the base."

"That's not what I asked. Curt, what is going on?"

"Get in. Get buckled. Then I'll tell you."

The car smelled musty, but thankfully, the engine purred. Once they were on the highway, she said, "Tell me, Curt."

"Someone blew up the jet. We needed to get the hell away

from your house before they figured out where you were and tried to kill you again."

She met his words with silence. Several minutes passed. He'd known this would be too much for her. How many hours ago had she faced the firing squad? Fourteen? Fifteen? The hollows under her eyes told him she hadn't been able to sleep during the flight, and now she had a blood-soaked kitchen and someone had just tried to kill her.

Crappy didn't begin to describe this day.

He signaled a left turn at a Kaneohe cross street. He'd find a restaurant and get her some food while he made calls. "No," she suddenly said. "Go straight. Take a left on Likelike Highway."

"We can stop. Regroup."

"No. Let's get to the base. Maybe that colonel can get us another flight."

"I hope so." They reached the busy intersection and stopped at the light. He cast a glance sideways. Mara huddled in her seat, appearing small and fragile, but he'd witnessed her formidable inner strength before and hoped to hell she could draw on that now. "You okay?"

"Not by a long shot. But I'm alive."

He patted her shoulder. "Good girl."

"Don't do that."

"What?"

"Condescend to me."

"I thought I was being encouraging."

"You withheld something from me—you found out about the explosion before I arrived at the house, right?—and now you're patting me like I'm a dog. Don't. Don't hold things back from me, and don't talk down to me. It demeans us both."

"Fair enough." The light changed, and he turned onto the highway. He was more than happy to skip the kid-glove treatment. "Did you call your uncle today?"

"No."

"How about your mother, have you called her?"

"How the hell could I do that? I don't have a phone." She hit her thigh. "Crap, I plugged it in to charge, and we left so fast, it's still at my house."

Traffic moved slowly. They inched along the highway toward the next light as the air blowing through the vents got progressively hotter. "Someone told a reporter we're alive." Sweat dampened his shirt. He fiddled with the controls.

"The air-conditioning only works sometimes." She rolled down her window.

"Maybe the person who gave you a ride off base talked." He rolled down his window, but the relief was minimal. The vehicle wasn't moving fast enough to create a breeze.

"I got a ride from a friend. I don't think she'd tell anyone, and like me, she probably doesn't know about the explosion."

"Who is she?" He loosened his tie.

"I don't want to get her in trouble."

"By getting you off base, she saved your life. She'll need to talk to investigators." The light changed, and he stopped unknotting his tie in favor of operating the stick shift.

"She doesn't matter. She's just a friend who gave me a lift when I needed one."

The prosecutor in him had to ask. "Like Roddy in North Korea?"

"No. Roddy *abducted* me."

A welcome breeze wafted in as they picked up speed. "Conveniently, Roddy is dead. He cannot confirm or deny your story." The road narrowed to one lane in each direction. He merged into the remaining lane, then resumed working the knot on his tie.

"I thought you were going to stop being a prick."

"And I thought you wanted me to stop being condescending. Which do you want?"

She huffed out a sigh and grabbed his tie, unknotting it while he drove.

"Thanks," he said as he popped open the top two buttons. Sweat had plastered his shirt to his skin, but now he could feel the airflow.

"At least you're easy on the eyes," she said. "This would suck completely if your face matched your personality."

A sharp laugh escaped. He glanced sideways and caught her amused expression.

Mara gasped. "Look out!"

He swung his gaze back to the roadway and saw a huge pickup truck coming at them head-on. He swerved to the right, but there wasn't enough shoulder to evade it. The truck clipped the Accord, sending it into a spin. He gripped the wheel and tried to recover control. He turned into the spin, and they came to a stop.

He glanced at Mara. "You okay?"

"I think so. You?"

They faced the wrong way on the highway. A line of cars was stopped before them, some having narrowly avoided their own collisions.

The behemoth white pickup that had started the accident had ricocheted to the left after clipping them, and now rested with the front tires off the road, the fender against a palm tree. The engine roared as the vehicle revved, then lurched in reverse, dropping off the curb with a thunk. The truck paused, then surged forward, barreling down the narrow highway and disappearing from view.

He pulled out his cell to call the police. To Mara, he said, "I got the license plate."

"You don't need it. I know that truck—but I can guarantee the owner wasn't driving."

Startled, he turned to her. "How do you know?"

Her face had lost all trace of color. "His brains are splattered all over my kitchen."

# Chapter Eight

"YOU'RE CERTAIN?" CURT asked.

Mara nodded, unable to speak as the enormity of what had just happened sank in. One moment they were driving and bickering, and the next, Roddy's beast of a truck tried to take them out in a head-on collision.

Curt turned her Honda around and took a right onto a neighborhood side street, where he parked and made a phone call. "Palea, the link we needed to connect the jet explosion to Roddy's murder just happened, which means you can get your ass over to the Marine Corps Base and take over the investigation." He quickly explained the accident and the fact that Roddy Brogan owned the truck. "Call the Honolulu special agent in charge and have her call the secretary of defense. I'll call the attorney general and secretary of state. I want you in charge of the investigation on the base within the hour." He glanced at Mara. "We've got to get out of here. It's clear she's the target. She was supposed to be on the jet, and whoever is after her recognized her car."

Curt's words to the FBI agent penetrated the haze that had clouded Mara's mind.

*I know the driver of the truck.*

*The driver of the truck just tried to kill us.*

*And he probably killed Roddy.*

Curt continued making calls while the meaning sank in. Even though Roddy had died in her house, she hadn't wanted to believe she knew his killer. It was impossible. She didn't know killers. Soldiers, yes. Cold-blooded murderers? No.

She was still reeling when Curt nudged her, offering his cell phone. Startled, she met his gaze. "It's the secretary of state. He wants to talk to you."

She'd met the secretary of state a few times when he served in the senate with her uncle. He'd always been nice but stiff—the consummate statesman. He'd probably worked hard to secure her return. She took the phone. "Mr. Secretary, thank you for everything you've done for me. And please, let the president know how grateful I am."

"I will, Mara. And you're welcome, but it looks like you aren't out of trouble yet."

"Yeah, the stop on Oahu isn't going well."

"Mara, is there any chance what's happening could be related to North Korea? The president and I need to know if we could have a problem with a madman with nukes."

She glanced at Curt. She wanted to tell the secretary everything. But she couldn't—not in front of Curt, and certainly not on a cell phone. Besides, she'd made sure the North Korean government didn't know a thing—so she wasn't lying. "You'll be happy to know this appears to be personal."

The man breathed heavily into the phone. "I'm sorry for your sake, but admittedly relieved. Be careful, Mara. And if you think of anything, call me. Dominick has my private number."

"Yes, sir," she said and ended the conversation.

"What's the fastest route to Hickam Air Force Base?" Curt asked.

"Get on H-3. Why?"

"We're going to catch a flight from there."

"You arranged a flight?" Wow—she'd spaced out for a bit but didn't realize she'd been *that* checked out.

"Not yet. But with the Kaneohe runway gone, Hickam is our best bet to get off the island quickly."

"We're just going to show up and demand a plane?"

"Yes."

"The military doesn't work that way. Hell, arranging for transportation for JPAC—and we *work* on Joint Base Pearl Harbor–Hickam—is a frigging nightmare."

He flashed a cocky grin. "Sweetheart, you've never traveled with me before."

THEY WERE GOING to Hickam. Evan Beck threw Roddy's truck in gear and headed for Likelike. They were taking H-3; he'd take the other tunnel, ensuring his targets wouldn't spot Roddy's oversized truck.

He blessed the Raptor tech who'd designed the device that could pull Dominick's cell phone number from Colonel McCormick's phone. But even better was the gadget that turned Dominick's cell into a microphone. Once he had the right cell phone number, he'd locked onto Dominick's phone. Able to eavesdrop on conversations even when the man wasn't using the phone, he heard everything he needed to track them down. Mara's voice was clear as day. He shook off the flicker of hesitation. He had a job to do.

His window of opportunity at Hickam would be brief. There were so many high-level government officials involved; the base commander would give Dominick an aircraft carrier if he could.

At Hickam, he'd be able to take Mara out with the Barrett Light 50. He'd get only one shot—the fifty-caliber round would be heard for miles—but it was the only rifle in his arsenal with the range he'd need.

He parked in the neighborhood that overlooked the airfield, obscured by a cluster of mango trees with low branches, but with a clear sight line from the back. He climbed into the truck bed and set up the Barrett. He hadn't used this weapon much, but he had a computerized scope so advanced the military didn't even have them yet. The scope would make his lack of familiarity with the gun irrelevant. Soon Mara wouldn't be his problem anymore, and his dad would get off his back.

He'd just gotten the rifle set up and the scope mounted when Mara and Dominick stepped onto the tarmac.

From the flurry of movement on the airfield, it became clear which jet they where heading for. Evan would have a clear shot when Mara climbed the steps. Leading as she was, when she reached the second step their heads would be at the same height. He'd already programmed the scope with her height, and it zeroed in on the exact place her head would be when she stood on the second step. Now he waited.

She and Dominick stopped fifty yards away from the jet and spoke with an officer.

Evan was an ordnance tech. For JPAC, he disposed of bombs, and for Raptor, he created them. Sniping wasn't his style, and as he waited for Mara to reach the crosshairs, he was reminded why. Waiting sucked.

Sweat broke out on his brow.

*Move.*

Finally, Mara resumed walking, Dominick next to her. Mara climbed first. In the scope, her head came into view. The height setting was dead-on.

Evan squeezed the trigger.

# Chapter Nine

THE GANGWAY ROCKED under Curt's feet as the side of the jet suddenly sprouted a hole. An earsplitting bang followed an instant later. In front of him, Mara dropped down. He did the same, covering her body with his.

*Holy shit*, what was that thing? In a flash, it had created a foot-wide hole in the jet's fuselage. The sound had reached them after the bullet pierced the jet, meaning the damn weapon was supersonic.

Mara groaned beneath him. He shifted his weight to his hands, which were braced on either side of her head.

What if the bastard fired again? Hell, the sides of the stairs might conceal them, but obviously the round could pierce metal just fine. They were completely vulnerable. "We've got to get out of here."

She rolled over, and they were chest to chest. Blood covered her face. He reared back. "Mara! Did shrapnel hit you?" Over his shoulder he yelled, "Medic! She's hurt!"

The airman who'd accompanied them to the jet had dropped to the tarmac. Now he inched forward and rose on his knees at the base of the stairs.

"I hit my head on the edge of the stair. It's just a cut." More blood spilled from the wound, staining her hair, running in rivulets down her cheek and nose, along her neck, and pooling in the groove above her collarbone.

He cupped her face in his hands, smearing blood across her cheeks. "Promise me you're okay."

She grimaced. "I promise. The cut stings, but my head is fine."

"I'm going to get you the hell out of here; then we'll clean you up. Okay?" He pulled at his shirt, buttons went flying, but he didn't give a damn. Bare-chested, he pressed his shirt against the cut on her forehead. "Hold this to stop the bleeding."

*Oh Jesus.* If she'd been one step higher… He couldn't think about that. Right now he had to get her out of here. He needed to do his fucking job and actually *protect* her for a change.

He swung around to face the airman. "I think the bullet came from over there," he said, pointing to a line of trees across the road from the airfield.

"Yes, sir, there's already a team checking the area out. If the gunman was there, he'll have fled by now."

Curt glanced again at the hole in the jet. "This jet isn't going anywhere."

"No, sir."

"Ms. Garrett and I are leaving. I want you to call FBI Agent Kaha'i Palea. He's going to be in charge of this investigation as it relates to the others. Tell him what happened and tell him I'll call him as soon as I can."

In minutes, Curt was back behind the wheel of Mara's Honda.

"How did the shooter know where to find us?" She leaned against the passenger window, holding his shirt in a ball against her forehead. She looked exhausted and her eyes closed as she said, "No one knew where we were headed."

"I don't know. We were only there, what, thirty minutes? Hardly time to drive through Honolulu traffic and get in position for that shot."

"Do you think the shooter was on base already?"

"Possible. Or there's a tracking device on your car—or on one of us."

Curt's phone vibrated in his pocket.

*My cell phone.*

Cell phones were vulnerable to hacking and being turned into microphones, but it required sophisticated computer skills. The few cases he'd prosecuted had involved corporate espionage or domestic-violence-related stalking. But a few months ago, he'd read a Homeland Security briefing that stated devices to lock onto cell phones by the less-technically savvy were in development and might already be in use.

From the moment Palea told him Roddy was dead, Curt had suspected Raptor. It was why he'd made the decision to reroute to Oahu. Anything that implicated Raptor could possibly be used against Stevens, and even better, lead to an indictment of Robert Beck. The man had betrayed his country numerous times in Iraq, Afghanistan, and in Egypt. And with Roddy's abduction of Mara in North Korea, he couldn't help but wonder if the Democratic People's Republic of Korea could be added to the list.

Raptor had the skill and equipment to blow up a plane and had long-range sniper rifles with enough firepower to blow a hole in the side of a military jet. But more important, Raptor topped Homeland Security's list of companies who were suspected of developing phone-hacking devices.

The phone in his pocket was probably acting as a beacon and microphone right this second, telling a Raptor operative where they were, and anything he said aloud would tell him where they were headed. He looked for a place to pull over so he could yank the battery out of the phone.

"Curt, I think you should let me call—"

He slapped a hand over Mara's mouth before she could divulge something important. He glanced sideways to see hurt and confusion on her bloody face.

He was a complete ass. But all he could do was shake his head, slowly remove his hand, and press his index finger to his lips. When she remained silent, he gingerly took the cell phone out of his pocket and held it out to her. He waited for a safe break in traffic, then faced her long enough to mouth the words, *Remove the battery*.

She cocked her head to the side but nodded. She dropped the shirt she'd been holding against the cut and pried off the back of the phone. A moment later, the battery was out. Curt took a deep breath but remained silent. What if the culprit hadn't been the phone? Whoever killed Roddy could have easily bugged the car.

They had a host of other problems. Right now, he was shirtless and she was coated in blood. They had no phone, no jet, little cash, and the trial started in, *fuck*, twelve hours.

She tapped his shoulder and pointed to the upcoming exit. The parts of her face not coated in blood were pasty white.

He changed lanes to reach the exit and followed her hand signals, hoping against hope she was leading them to a doctor, a fueled jet, a phone, a clean car, or a safe place to hang out until they could procure any of those items.

Unfortunately, she led them to a park. A crowded, Waikiki beach park.

*What the hell?*

He glanced sideways at her, and realized the blood had been flowing from her wound unchecked since she pried out the battery. He'd been following driving directions from someone who could very well be light-headed.

With hand signals, she told him to park the car. Lacking a

better option, he complied, but the moment the vehicle stopped, she flung open her door and bolted for the water.

*Shit!*

Curt had no choice but to follow her.

She zigzagged across the park, weaving between tourists in an almost drunken manner. But still, for a woman who was probably woozy from a head wound, she was *fast*. She was swimming for the breakwater before he reached the waterline. Did she think she could swim to the mainland? Had she lost her *mind* along with all that blood?

Curt had no choice but to kick off his shoes and dive after her. With several swift strokes he caught up to her in deep water, grabbed her by the waist, and pulled her against him. "What the hell are you doing?"

They were being hunted—probably by mercenaries—and she'd had him pull over so she could take a *swim*?

She draped her arms around his neck and flashed a blissful smile. "Isn't the water wonderful? I didn't think I'd live to see Hawai'i again, let alone get to swim in the ocean." Her voice held a worrisome dreamy quality.

"Mara, I think you've lost too much blood." Hell. She was underweight, probably hadn't slept, and had barely eaten. Add blood loss to that and it was surprising she was even conscious.

She threaded her fingers in the wet hair at his nape. "But salt water is good for the cut, and the blood's been washed away. Plus, if either of us is bugged, the bug has been destroyed by the water, right?"

Relief spread through him. Okay, she might not be firing on all cylinders, but she wasn't completely irrational either. "Some bugs are waterproof, but your thinking was sound."

She glanced down at the neckline of her tight-fitting top. "Is it crazy to think my clothes might have been bugged when Roddy's killer was in my house?"

"Yes, but I suppose it doesn't hurt to be careful. I think it was my phone, but the only way to be certain is if no one tries to kill you in the next hour."

She frowned. "I don't like your method of testing hypotheses."

He laughed. "I don't either, sweetheart."

They bobbed on the surface of the turquoise sea. The water was calm, almost flat due to the lack of trade winds, and the sun beat down on his bare shoulders as he treaded water with her in his arms.

Her wound, her predicament, this entire situation was his fault. If they'd just refueled in San Francisco, they'd be crossing the mainland by now. But he was determined to get something solid on Raptor, and now she was in danger. "I'm sorry, Mara. I seriously screwed up."

Her expression turned dreamy, and one hand stopped playing with his hair in favor of tracing his pecs. "You're really ripped. But you probably know that. I didn't think lawyers could be ripped. My uncle's lawyers were always slimy weasels…"

"Okay. Time to stop the blood flow. You probably need to eat or drink something too."

"I feel fine." Her hand slipped below the water and continued exploring his chest and belly. "Jesus. Where did you get this six-pack? It's unfair, really, that you're brilliant, successful, *and* hot…"

He caught her hand and pulled her snug against his body before she could take her exploration too far. "Mara. You need to stop. This isn't appropriate."

"Today I've been before a firing squad and survived *three* attempts on my life. Screw appropriate."

He was too transfixed by the sight of water sluicing over the deep V of her top and disappearing into the valley of her cleavage to respond. She flashed a dimpled smile. Her lips looked far too tempting. But even if her dizzy logic appealed, he had to be the voice of sanity.

Jesus. This couldn't be happening.

The feel of her nipples against his chest was enough to drive him insane, and unfortunately, given their current embrace, even in her light-headed state she had to be aware of his arousal. How the hell had he gotten into this situation? He, Curt Dominick, couldn't possibly be swimming in the Pacific Ocean twelve hours before the trial with his defendant's punch-drunk and far-too-attractive niece plastered against him.

That's it. He would indict the editor-in-chief of *TIME* the first chance he got.

MARA FOLLOWED CURT up the beach and back to the car, where he grabbed his bloody shirt and thrust it into her hands with firm instructions to apply it to the cut on her forehead. She didn't know what his problem was. She felt fine. Maybe a little dizzy, but otherwise better than she had in months.

So she'd lost a little blood and told him he was hot. What was the big deal? She noticed *ample* proof he was attracted to her. "A lifeguard could give us a bandage," she said.

"Yeah. And check you out for signs of a concussion. But I think you need something to drink first." He sounded so serious. So boring. Her head didn't even hurt. She was fine. Right now, all she wanted was to taste the salt water that rolled down his incredible chest.

Who would have thought her own private savior would be built like a superhero? She'd bet he screwed like one too.

"Mara, you need to stop. Jesus. *Please.*"

She must have spoken aloud again. She needed to stop that. It seemed to upset him.

He took her arm and dragged her up the beach to a burger stand. She ordered a Spam musubi—Hawaiian cuisine at its worst, but a snack she'd missed while in North Korea.

Curt made her drink a bottle of Gatorade first. She couldn't stand the stuff. Then the lifeguard who bandaged her forehead said she had to drink another one before attempting to eat. At last, Curt fed her small bites of musubi, insisting she eat slowly.

Exhausted, she leaned against the man by her side. He argued and cajoled and coaxed her to drink more. Gradually, with each swallow, the world came into sharper focus.

Sometime later, after drinking what had to be gallons of Gatorade, she felt less drunk but no less tired and wondered why Curt was shirtless. In bits and pieces, the last hours crystallized. The shot that had zinged so close to her head she felt the air flow against her scalp. Curt's body covering her—protecting her again—on the staircase. Most of the drive to the beach made sense. It wasn't until she was in the water that her memory became really fuzzy.

Oh hell. If her memory was even close to accurate, she'd hit on Curt like a cheap drunk. She felt her face flush and closed her eyes. "Did I say aloud everything I think I did?"

Still leaning on him, she felt his chuckle. "And then some."

"Keep in mind, I'm having a really, really shitty day."

"Noted and forgiven."

She met his gaze. His hazel eyes held concern and camaraderie. Somewhere during this crazy day, they'd become allies. "I feel better. Clearer."

"Good, because I don't know my way around here. I need your input."

"Do you really think your phone was bugged?"

"I think it had been turned into a microphone. We have to assume whoever is after you knows everything I've said today, up until the moment you pulled out the battery. Right now we're stuck. We need a phone so I can arrange a flight for us."

"We can go back to a base—"

"I'm done trusting the military. Whoever is after you got on and off the Marine Corps Base undetected and got on Hickam without a problem."

"Maybe he's been caught."

"As soon as we get a phone, I'll call Palea and find out." He paused. "Which brings us to another problem. Palea's phone is probably a microphone too. In fact, we have to assume everyone in my phone's address book is compromised. Somehow I need to get in touch with Palea and tell him that."

"You can't call anyone in your cell phone address book?"

"No one."

"And we can't go to a military base?"

"Definitely not."

The enormity of their situation hit her. She'd liked it better when she was light-headed. "Christ, Curt. How are we going to get off this island?"

# Chapter Ten

Robert Beck paced his office, waiting for his son to check in. The day had gone from promising to hell with each attempt Evan made to repair Roddy Brogan's screwup in allowing Mara Garrett to escape him in North Korea.

Even though Evan had used a Korean explosive to take out the jet, with repeated failed attempts on Garrett's life, no one would believe the North Korean angle for long, meaning Evan had compounded Roddy's error to such a degree that it was hard to see a way in which Raptor wouldn't be implicated.

If Evan couldn't silence Mara before she left Oahu, his son would have to take the fall for the company. The outcome was the last thing Robert wanted, but Evan had known the risks of failure. And now he couldn't help but wonder if his son's feelings for the woman had contributed to the fiasco.

His secure line rang, and Robert snatched the phone without hesitation. "My shot went high," Evan said without preamble.

"Didn't you use the scope? That fucker cost ten grand and should have delivered."

"We're in Kona conditions. I forgot to adjust the humidity setting."

Now he was certain. Evan still had feelings for Mara and couldn't be trusted to get the job done. "You know what this means?"

"I'll get her, Dad. I know her better than anyone. I can find her even though Dominick's phone went dead."

"His phone isn't sending signals? Did he realize you were listening?"

"I was too busy hauling ass off the base to listen. But I know Mara. I know exactly where she'll go next."

*Yes, but will you follow through?* "Where will she go?"

"Jeannie Fuller's house. She's Mara's best friend. I bet Mara is wondering why the hell Jeannie lied about what happened that last morning."

BACK AT THE car, Mara dug through her duffle bag and pulled out a shirt for Curt. The shirt, a men's size medium tee decorated with the unofficial JPAC symbol—a skull on one side with the words, "Search, Recover, Identify" above a globe and trowel on the other—conformed to Curt's insanely amazing abs like a second skin. "God, you look hot in that."

Concern returned to his handsome features. "I thought you were better. We can rest longer or get you more Gatorade."

She shuddered. "No. More. Gatorade." She touched the butterfly bandage on her forehead. The bleeding had stopped, and her mind was clear. "I'm fine. Wits present and accounted for."

He frowned. "Then no flirting, Mara."

The utter lack of warmth in his voice irritated her. He'd been so sweet—so not *him*. She hated the return of the cold prosecutor. "Why? Afraid you'll respond? Oh, wait, I forgot. You can't respond, because you aren't human; you're a shark."

He narrowed his eyes and leaned into her, backing her against her dusty car. "I'm human all right, Mara. And the same adrenaline that's flowing through you is also coursing through me, making me want very human things." He reached up and cupped her chin, his mouth only inches from hers. His thumb brushed across her bottom lip, and she needed to catch her breath as heat flooded her system. "But there's one thing you need to remember. I *will* send your beloved uncle to prison. No matter how much adrenaline urges us to be stupid, we can't forget who we are."

He was right, damn him. Who he was made the attraction she felt for him indecent. In her uncle's world, loyalty was everything.

And yet, her uncle was wrong about him. Curt embodied integrity and human decency. The simple fact that he'd flown to North Korea to save her should have been proof enough, but in the last few hours, he'd demonstrated compassion and caring that belied his reputation.

She'd battled hero worship from the start and used the fact that he was prosecuting her uncle as a shield, but for her, the fight was lost. "I know who you are," she said. "You're the man who saved me from a firing squad."

His pupils dilated, telling her he harbored similar foolish desires. "Don't, Mara. Don't make me out to be anything other than an envoy."

Apparently, he was more skilled at resisting desire. Well, he did have a reputation for control. She pressed her palms flat against his chest and pushed him back. "You were nicer when I was light-headed."

"Me? No. You were hallucinating. I was my same asshole self."

She smiled as she locked the car. She knew the truth. "So, what do we do now?"

"We need a place to hole up for the night. There is no way we're getting off this rock today."

"My landlord has a small fishing boat. I keep an eye on it for him when he's on the mainland and have a key. We can sleep there."

"Good." He nodded toward the shopping center across the busy divided roadway. "I'm guessing we won't have any trouble buying a prepaid cell phone at that mall." He pulled out his wallet, and she noted with chagrin the leather was damp. He counted his cash; the wet bills stuck together, slowing the process. "I've got nearly three hundred dollars, enough for a phone and minutes—and we're going to need a lot of minutes—but that's all. We'll have to get cash from an ATM after we buy the phone."

Together they crossed the street. "Is it too much to hope we won't be recognized?"

"Probably. You've been tabloid fodder for months. Hell, a week ago, you achieved the publicist's trifecta and made the covers of *People*, *TIME*, and *Vanity Fair*."

She dropped her jaw. "I was on *TIME*?"

"Believe me, it's not all it's cracked up to be," he said, deadpan.

Mara laughed—a true belly laugh, and her first in months. Finally, humor subsided, she pulled him toward the garage-level cell phone kiosks located on the sidewalk outside Sears. They purchased a prepaid, no-ID-required phone and cleaned out Curt's soggy wallet.

Intent on finding a cash machine, they entered the department store and headed for the mall entrance at the opposite end of the store. Passing through the electronics department, Mara caught sight of the news and came to a dead stop. Every oversized flat-screen TV along the shelves showed the charred remains of the jet, smoldering on the Kaneohe airfield in crisp high-definition color.

The fuselage of the Bombardier BD-700 was…*gone*. The largest remaining piece was the tail, canted at an odd angle on the tarmac, with only bits of the tail wings attached. Trained and accustomed to excavating crashed jets, she'd never come across one of that size that was so…pulverized.

And she was supposed to have been inside.

Curt's hand gripped hers and squeezed.

Footage of the wreckage was replaced by an AP photo of her uncle with her when he'd visited her JPAC team in Egypt. The Egyptian photo op had taken place during that happy window of time after his term as VP was over, but before Curt had convinced a grand jury to indict him.

Mara hit the volume button on the set. A reporter described her work for JPAC as more photos of Uncle Andrew and her flashed across the screen—all taken when he visited various deployments.

"Your uncle sure did like those JPAC photo ops. Did he get you the job at JPAC just for that purpose?"

Irritation surged at the often repeated question. "Uncle Andrew had never even heard of JPAC until I started working for them. I *earned* my position there."

Pictures of Curt with the North Korean leadership came next. He looked handsome but vacant, and a glance at Curt showed a wry smile on his face. "I do look like an empty suit," he said, sounding pleased.

"You look stern next to the beaming dictator."

"Diplomatically, that was the goal. Remember the photos of Clinton with Kim Jong-il? He practiced that blank face with Chelsea and Hillary for days before the trip."

"How do you know that?"

"I spoke to him when I was en route. He helped prep me for the meeting."

She faltered. She'd met Clinton once, at her uncle's inauguration, but didn't expect he remembered her. She was a lesser relative of the second family and not part of the limelight elite, which had suited her fine. Knowing former and current presidents had taken an active role in obtaining her release was humbling.

The reporter continued. "…as to why Ms. Garrett and Mr. Dominick are on the island of Oahu and not en route to Washington, DC, as originally reported, we have yet to receive an explanation. Back to you, Rachel."

Rachel Maddow smiled at the camera. "Rumors are running

rampant in DC tonight as US Attorney Curt Dominick takes a vacation on Oahu with former VP Stevens's niece right before jury selection begins in the Stevens's trial. Is this a sign the power prosecutor's case has fallen apart? Or is it a sign the *prosecutor* has fallen apart?"

Curt let out a low growl.

She tugged him toward the mall entrance. "C'mon. We need to get cash."

They quickly found a cash machine on the second floor of the mall. Curt looked at his watch. "Timing is critical from this moment forward. We need to be out of the mall in five minutes." He slid his card into the slot and withdrew three hundred dollars. "Your turn."

She slid her card. "I need to check my balance. I haven't used this account in months."

"Just hurry."

She typed in her PIN and navigated the menus. Seconds later, glowing white letters appeared on the small screen: *Current Balance $505,912.56.*

# Chapter Eleven

Mara leaned against the ATM as though standing without support were impossible. Curt read over her shoulder. "Holy fuck, Mara."

"That money isn't mine. I swear." Her voice shook. "I should have five, maybe six thousand here, plus ten grand in savings."

How many times had he heard a defendant swear the drugs/money/weapon wasn't theirs? "Withdraw three hundred, and let's get out of here."

As they hurried through Sears, his mind raced. They couldn't talk once they were in the car—what if it were bugged? They had to plan now. "We need a new car. And I need to talk to Palea."

"I need to talk to Jeannie—"

"Absolutely not. That's exactly who they'll expect you to turn to."

"They who?"

Curt jogged down the escalator inside Sears. "I think it should be obvious by now. Raptor."

Curt was five stairs below her before he realized Mara had halted. "Why would Raptor be after me? They work for my uncle—"

"Precisely."

"Dammit, Curt. Uncle Andrew would never—"

He raced back up the escalator before they drew attention. "Mara, we don't have time for this now! We need a plan. I need to call Palea and set up a meeting place with him. I can't use the new phone to call him. Palea's phone is probably compromised, just like mine was."

"From the ATM transactions, whoever is after me already knows we're at Ala Moana. Make the call from here."

She was right. Their location was already compromised. He sprinted down the last few steps, and this time, she followed.

They quickly located a pay phone. Palea answered on the first ring and let loose with what Curt assumed were foul Pidgin curses before adding, "Shit, Dominick, took you long enough to call!"

"I need your help, Palea. But both your phone and mine are out."

"You know this?"

"Yes. I'll tell you more in person. Pull the battery from your cell, then call me at this pay phone from a landline. Can you do that in the next fifteen seconds?"

"I'm on the Hickam airfield. No landline nearby. The shooter got away."

Curt swore, even though he'd expected both answers. "We need to meet someplace private. And I've got about thirty seconds before I need to get the hell away from here."

"Let me think."

He waited, tension coiling in his gut.

Finally, Palea said, "I have an idea. Remember that time we were having drinks and I told you about my favorite movie scene?"

Years ago, they'd met when he took classes at Quantico while Palea was training to be an agent. The laid-back Islander and the stiff Harvard Law student had struck an odd friendship. On one memorable evening over beers, Palea had vented about an FBI case that had gone sour in the courts. He'd then needled Curt with what he declared was his favorite movie scene of all time. "Yeah."

"One hour. Got it?"

Curt wasn't sure he did but hoped to hell Mara would. He hung up, then turned to her. "You know the scene in *Jurassic Park* when the lawyer gets eaten while sitting on the toilet? Where was that filmed?"

KUALOA RANCH, THE meeting place Palea had cryptically selected, was located just off the coastal highway on the windward side of the island. Curt noted the deep lines of exhaustion around Palea's eyes as they greeted each other in a secluded area far from the arched entrance to the valley.

Palea's day had been as long and eventful as Curt's. His investigation into Roddy Brogan's murder now included the exploded jet and the shooting. The military had resisted Palea's assumption of authority on both bases, but with Curt's backing, the secretary of defense and the attorney general had agreed.

"*Brah*, I seriously hope you've gone *lolo*," Palea said after they exchanged new cell phone numbers.

"Me too," Mara said. "But how else could they have known we'd gone to Hickam?"

Palea's answer was to fix Mara with a suspicious stare, but since she had been the one nearly shot in the head, the FBI agent's suspicions of her had no traction with Curt.

"Do you want me to arrange a flight?" Palea asked.

"No. Anything through government channels will be traceable. I have a plan. I just need to make some calls." He nodded to the Honda. "But we do need a new car. The flight I arrange probably won't be ready until tomorrow, and her car is known to the shooter."

"Take my Bureau car."

"That's risky. It's got a tracking device?"

Palea nodded. "All government vehicles do. Lay low until you're out of here, and if anyone asks, I'll say the Bureau car broke down. If they don't know you have my car, they won't have a reason to activate the device."

It was the best they could hope for under the circumstances. "Mara wants to talk to Jeannie Fuller, and I've got a few questions for her myself. Can you arrange that?"

Mara let out a surprised gasp. Curt had thought about this at length on the long, silent drive from Waikiki and had decided to hell with the State Department's rules. They needed answers, and Jeannie Fuller was more likely to open up to Mara than to Palea or him.

"She left the island early this morning," Palea said.

"Is she a suspect in Roddy Brogan's murder?"

Mara stiffened. "No way—"

"Now isn't the time, Mara." Turning to Palea, Curt repeated, "Is she a suspect?"

"Yes."

"Jeannie wouldn't—"

"Save it for later." Curt turned again to Palea. "Where did she go?"

"Her flight landed in LA several hours ago. We don't know where she went from there."

"What about Evan Beck?" he asked. "Have you found him?"

"No. He could have caught a Raptor flight off the island. We have no way of tracking him." Palea fixed Curt with a stare. "I know you think Raptor is involved, but this could be nothing more than an ex-boyfriend with too much technology at his disposal and a grudge against the woman who dumped him."

Curt had expected this, but still, it rankled. "That's not what's happening here."

"Beck may be Brogan's killer, but that doesn't mean this is part of a bigger Raptor conspiracy."

"Dammit, you're on this case because I trust that you won't cave if powers-that-be try to shut down an investigation into Raptor. Don't let me down."

"I'm not caving. I'm just saying this may not be the break you're hoping for. Even if Evan Beck was the gunman, you won't have shit against his father."

"Your job is to gather evidence against the operatives—starting with Evan Beck. It's *my* job to connect it to the CEO."

"You better know what you're doing, *brah*. If you fuck up, my career tanks with yours."

Silence stretched between them. Curt knew Palea had legitimate reason for concern. If Curt failed to gather the evidence he needed, Robert Beck could use his influence to destroy them both. But he refused to back down in the name of self-preservation. And he had no respect for the prosecutors before him who had.

MARA LISTENED TO the exchange with interest. The notion Jeannie was a suspect sickened her. Impossible. Jeannie wouldn't hurt anyone. On the flip side, she wished the notion Evan had killed Roddy didn't ring true.

Evan. Son of Raptor's CEO, coworker, ex-lover, and mercenary in every sense of the word. They'd spent five months together, and she'd ended the relationship when she learned he was capable of anything, so long as he was following orders. Murder was just another item on the mercenary-fieldwork continuum.

Curt believed Raptor was after her, and given the—*oh holy shit*—half-million dollars in her account, she had to admit he had a point. And Curt didn't even know about the bomb.

She climbed into the passenger seat of Palea's Ford sedan with the gruesome scene from her kitchen in the forefront of her mind. Had Evan done that? Nausea threatened. "Find your happy place, find your happy place," she muttered.

"Does that work for you?" Curt asked.

"No, but I figured it was worth a try."

"Maybe your problem is the place. Where is your happy place?"

"When I was in North Korea, it was Hawai'i. Today? It's anywhere *but* Hawai'i."

He chuckled. "You and me both."

Talking proved effective and nausea receded. "What about you? Where is your happy place?" she asked.

He was silent. He rubbed his hand across his chin, now sporting a day's worth of sexy stubble. Finally, he spoke. "The courtroom."

"Seriously?" His answer startled her, yet it shouldn't have. Hell, it was clear his work was his life. Good for him if he enjoyed it. She'd been the same way until two months ago.

"Nothing is like matching wits in a courtroom. Nothing challenges or invigorates me like proving a case. It's a chess game."

"I can't stand chess. I'm terrible at it."

"That's because you're impulsive. You don't think before you act. Like fleeing Roddy in North Korea."

"But being impulsive has merits. If I hadn't left the jet on the Marine Corps Base, I'd be dead."

He flashed a wry smile. "Well played."

She leaned back in the seat. She'd be more satisfied with her victory if their lives weren't at stake.

AT LAST THEY were heading south to the marina where Curt could make the necessary calls to get them a flight away from here. As he drove, the sun dropped below the mountain ridgeline and dusk descended with tropical speed.

Holy hell, night was falling and he was still on Oahu. Part of him still hadn't come to grips with the situation. It was inconceivable that he was five thousand miles away from the federal courthouse in DC the night before the trial was to start.

He was anxious to get to the boat, but they both needed food. Given that Mara had lost a lot of blood and had barely slept or eaten, he didn't know how she remained upright but had to respect her grit.

He pulled off at a roadside shrimp shack to pick up dinner. As they waited for their food, she leaned against him, clearly at the limit of her strength. He draped an arm around her in the sultry darkness, struck by a need to protect her that was almost primal. A seventh-degree black belt, he knew how to send out serious she's-mine-don't-fuck-with-her vibes. Wearing the skintight T-shirt, a day's worth of stubble, and standing in his most intimidating stance, there was no way in hell even his closest colleagues would recognize him right now.

"What day is it?" Mara suddenly asked.

"Here?" Leaning against him as she was, the top of her head rested against his chest, and he enjoyed the way she fit against his side.

"No, in Iceland."

He chuckled. "It's a reasonable question. It's Tuesday in North Korea." He glanced at his watch. "And Tuesday in DC, but here, it's still Monday."

"Meaning it was Monday when I woke up in North Korea, and it's *still* Monday. I'm starting to wonder if this day will ever end, or if I'm trapped forever on the day of my execution."

He pressed her closer to his side. "You get maudlin when you're tired."

She huffed and looked up at him. "I get maudlin when things start blowing up, I get shot at, and my only ally is the man who wants to send my uncle to prison."

"What, you're not milking the firing squad anymore?" He couldn't stop himself from tracing her lips with his finger. Damn, he must be tired. His control was slipping.

Those soft, tempting lips widened in a weary smile. "I'm saving it for the next time you revert to your unpleasant jerky self. Why play my best card when you're being civil?"

"I'm sure you won't have to wait long."

"So am I," she said dryly. "When *does* the trial start?"

He startled at the question. He hadn't realized she didn't know. But then, she hadn't even known what day it was. "In eight hours."

"I'm sorry, Curt. I had no idea."

He shrugged. "I'll miss the first day of jury selection. That's all."

"This is the biggest trial of your career, isn't it?"

He nodded. Truth was, it would be the biggest trial of any lawyer's career. But what surprised him the most was that she mentioned the trial without trying to convince him he was going after an innocent man or accusing him of destroying her uncle for personal gain. They had reached a truce.

Alarm trickled down his spine. Given the coming sleeping arrangements, he'd be better off if they were still at war.

The mouthwatering aroma of butter, garlic, and spices filled the car as they headed south again, and hunger eclipsed other worries. Adrenaline had dissipated, and suddenly he was starving. Mara fed him a garlicky bite as he drove, and the taste only made him ache for more.

But his other worries returned when she licked the buttery sauce from her fingers in a manner that made a different form of hunger roar to life.

From the age of sixteen, he'd played by a very stringent set of self-imposed rules. He had goals that required discipline and had learned the hard way that emotional involvement was dangerous to his control.

He'd vowed then to never again be led by his dick. Deeper emotions weren't allowed to enter into his liaisons. Ever. Making him the damned king of restraint.

He realized now that in the twenty-plus years since he'd chosen his path, he'd never been truly tested. Any relationship that threatened to break his emotional embargo was ended without regret. And now his lofty goals were finally within reach. If—*when*—Stevens was convicted, Curt was all but assured to be named the next attorney general of the United States.

But there was something about Mara Garrett that made him want to forgo control, to forget hazard.

And he couldn't place her on the next flight off the island and be done with her.

Stevens's niece was the last person he could get involved with. He'd be compromising his case, his role as prosecutor, and his career. Plus he'd known from the start there was the possibility she'd asked the North Koreans to make him the envoy. She could be the reason he was stuck on Oahu and would miss the start of the trial.

And right now, with the hum of desire running through his veins, he couldn't muster the outrage to give a damn.

# Chapter Twelve

THE SMALL FISHING boat was moored at the end of the long pier and was a welcome sight to Mara at the end of what was quite literally the longest day of her life. The small vessel rocked as she climbed aboard, the swaying motion nearly knocking her off her tired feet.

The corners of Curt's eyes crinkled with warmth as he boarded. "This is perfect, Mara."

She quickly opened the padlock securing the cabin hatch. "It's small," she warned.

He followed her inside. The cabin was so tiny she had to climb onto the V-shaped bunk just to make room for him.

Five feet across at the widest point, the cabin quickly narrowed to the apex of the bow. From bow to hatch it was maybe nine feet—three feet of cramped kitchen on one side of a narrow center aisle, the door to the tiny head on the other. The aisle was a short rectangle of space that ended at the foot of the six-foot-long, V-shaped bed, which filled the bow from starboard to port. She and Curt would have to share the small bed. There was no other option.

They ate sitting across from each other on the bed. "Ohmygod," she said through a mouthful of food. "This is the best meal I've ever had in my life."

"You know, earlier you said the same thing about Spam."

She laughed, and her cheeks warmed at the reminder of her behavior.

He cocked his head to the side. "Did they bring you a last meal in North Korea?"

"Yes, but for some strange reason, I couldn't eat it."

"I wouldn't mind strangling the person who decided not to tell you I was en route."

"They didn't tell me anything. Ever." She'd wondered why, of all the names she'd floated as potential envoys, the dictator had chosen him. "Did the *TIME* article mention you wanted me to testify in the trial?"

He nodded. "According to the State Department, the ultimatum included the phrase, 'He wants her? He can come get her.'" Curt paused. "I spent an hour with Kim. The whole time, he grinned and was jovial and very curious about my job. I'm a government employee, tasked with prosecuting politicians and mobsters. He's the leader of a dictatorship. There is no one equivalent to me in his world, and he was clearly trying to understand how the US can operate when a man beneath the president has the power to destroy him. In North Korea, the only threat to power is their own military. He asked about the headline on the cover."

"What did it say?"

He grimaced. "'US Attorney Curt Dominick: Bringing down American Government one Politician at a Time.'"

She couldn't help it. She laughed. No wonder Kim had bit. Given what she'd seen of the anti-American sentiment in North Korea, those words probably made Curt a superstar there.

"We'll never know his real reason for demanding me, but at the heart of it all, I got the sense his interest was genuine."

"What did you think of him?"

"I was scared shitless I'd say the wrong thing and end up in the cell next to yours."

"But the whole world knew you were there; he'd never get away with that."

"Mara, it's North Korea. They can do whatever the hell they want."

"But you were a diplomatic envoy. That would be an act of war."

"Some would say arresting a former VP's niece who'd been invited to the country was an act of war, but they weren't too concerned about that."

"They justified it. I was found on the edge of the DMZ—"

"And they could have found a way to justify arresting me. The State Department made it clear that by going in alone, there were no guarantees for my safety. The pilots had to stay on the plane to guard it. I was solo."

Curt was *scared*? He'd risked his life and freedom to rescue her? Oh shit. She'd had it bad when he was Superman, but now he was mortal, and ten times sexier.

"Don't look at me like that, Mara. I'm no hero. If there's a hero in this, it's you. You survived two months inside the DPRK, and your first words after sentencing weren't in defense of yourself. You took the blame and defended JPAC. Your words will go a long way toward keeping JPAC operational."

The garlicky shrimp hit her stomach with the density of a meteorite and twice as hot at his mention of JPAC, the organization she'd loved and the career that was now gone. "Congress tried to shut JPAC down after I was arrested, didn't they?" And if word got out about the bomb, JPAC's problems would be exponential.

He nodded. "They're funded for the next fiscal year, but hanging on by a thread."

She flopped back on the mattress and stared up at the ceiling. Every muscle in her body ached with exhaustion. Or maybe it was heartache. Or fear. "I'm a disaster."

"There is something you can do."

"Besides hide out on this boat forever? Do tell."

"JPAC will survive if you show Raptor was to blame. Help me bring down Raptor, Mara."

*Join me on the Dark Side, Luke.* Damn lawyer. He wanted her to commit to working against her uncle. She propped herself on her elbows. "I thought it was just Roddy. I didn't think it was the organization as a whole." That was the truth.

"And now?"

Her tiredness was so much more than jet lag. It was firing-squad lag, attempted-murder lag, losing-all-sense-of-safety-and-belonging lag. "You've made your point." She met his gaze. "Raptor might be trying to kill us."

"*Might?*"

He wanted her to admit her uncle could be behind it all. She couldn't. Not to herself, and certainly not to him. She didn't flinch from his gaze. Thankfully, his eyes didn't hold pity. In fact, what she saw could be desire, but the guarded prosecutor was hard to read.

She didn't understand him. Or herself. Maybe all the forms of lag that plagued her had caused this overwhelming attraction to manifest. Or maybe it was the simple fact that lusting after Curt was an excellent distraction from the horrors of the day.

Of course, lust didn't begin to describe what she felt. She *wanted* him. Now. Here. In sixteen different ways, some of which were illegal in more conservative states. She'd survived on little more than adrenaline and fear for months, and her body was craving life-affirming release. Curt was gorgeous, ripped, and proximate.

She was a starving woman presented with steak prepared just the way she liked it.

But he was the last man on earth she should get involved with. "Can you make your calls and get us off this damn island?" she asked.

RAPTOR'S SURVEILLANCE EQUIPMENT probably outclassed that of the CIA, and Curt had carefully considered which of his friends and colleagues would be off Raptor's grid. Lee Scott was the perfect choice. They'd met at a karate dojo when Curt was the elder teaching assistant and Lee a student, and had been friends for two decades. Curt trusted him completely. A private-sector computer and cell phone security expert, Lee worked outside political circles but knew the important players, he held government contracts that required him to pass high-level security clearance, and his expertise in phone systems ensured their conversation would remain private. Best of all, Lee's stepbrother had his own corporate jet.

Lee's perfection, however, did not extend to his attitude when called at one fifteen in the morning to field a request for a jet that didn't even belong to him. He groused in a sleep-laden voice, "You want me to call JT and ask him to send his jet to Oahu to pick you up?"

"Yes, please."

"Didn't the last jet you borrowed blow up?"

Curt grimaced. "Um, yeah." He paused and launched into his pitch. "You know I wouldn't ask if—"

"Forget it. It's yours."

Lee's quick capitulation startled him. "That easy?"

"If you're asking, I know it's important, and I know JT will agree."

Curt was humbled for a moment by Lee's simple faith in him, and emotion flooded him. Damn, apparently Mara's finagling past his guard had left him vulnerable to other feelings. He cleared his throat. "Thanks, Lee. I owe you."

In political circles, favors were currency and sometimes poison. He wasn't a politician, but US attorneys were appointed by the president and had to go through Senate confirmation. The easiest way to sail through was to owe no one, and up until this moment, Curt had been debt-free.

"No, Curt. It's impossible to owe a true friend anything more than a beer."

He laughed. "Fine. I owe you a beer."

"Well, maybe more than *one*. And not that crappy stuff you drink either."

Curt smiled, his gaze on Mara as she stretched out on the bed. "I owe you a keg of the good stuff, because I have another favor to ask." Her shirt rode up to reveal creamy smooth skin, flat belly, and perfect navel. Since when were belly buttons such a turn on?

He imagined tracing the indentation with his tongue and then trailing downward…

"You need advice on how to handle the archaeologist you picked up in DPRK. Now, I know a thing or two about archaeologists"—Lee's voice softened at the reference to his fiancée—"and all I can say is good luck, buddy."

He knew Lee was teasing, but still, the idea he'd somehow picked up on Curt's carnal thoughts was alarming. *What the hell is happening to me?* "I can handle her." He tried to put humor into his voice, to show amusement and prevent Lee from guessing he was losing his fucking mind.

Mara's eyes warmed in challenge at his words. With a wicked smile, she touched her flat belly, casually pushing her top higher, revealing more tempting, smooth skin.

He narrowed his gaze. The trial. The trial was starting, and he needed to focus, *dammit*, on what was important. Convicting Stevens and staying alive. In that order. "I need you to buy a prepaid cell phone and deliver it to my co-counsel, Aurora Ames. Tonight. Now. And tell her to pull the battery from her cell."

"You think her landline and cell are under surveillance?"

"She's the first person I'd monitor if *I* were looking for me. I want you to deliver it to her house."

"She's going to freak when a total stranger shows up at her door at three in the morning."

"She's going solo in the courtroom in a few hours. She must be wondering why I haven't called. If anything, she'll be expecting you." He gave Lee Aurora's address. "Don't call her and warn her you're coming over. The last thing I want is Raptor getting your phone number and connecting you to me."

Lee let out a low whistle. "Raptor? Shit, Curt. You're talking black ops."

Guilt stabbed at him for asking for help without warning of the risks. "If you don't want to get involved, I understand."

"I'll be fine. I'm worried about *you*. If Raptor's black ops missions were authorized, then you're going after the highest politicians in office."

"I'm already prosecuting a former VP." On the bed next to him, Mara flinched. She tugged her shirt down and sat up, all playfulness gone.

"There'll be enormous pressure to bury your allegations," Lee said. "You could be the one to go down."

"Raptor's not acting on legitimate—if there is such a thing—black ops orders right now. Their greedy CEO is making his own rules."

"Be careful, buddy."

Curt glanced around the tiny cabin. This was a nice, safe, hidey-hole, but he shared it with his defendant's enticing niece. This fishing boat might just be the most dangerous place on earth.

# Chapter Thirteen

MARA GOT UP from the bunk and searched the cabinets in an attempt to distract herself while Curt arranged a flight and cast aspersions on her uncle. She found a stash of men's clothing—fishing attire, which was perfect for Curt—and blankets for the bed. The bedding was a poor distraction, a reminder of the small bed and the enticing man who would share it with her.

Drawn to him like a mosquito to a bug zapper, she knew the coming hours would be a special kind of hell.

She slipped into the head to get ready for bed just as he said good-bye to whomever he'd called. Something about Curt brought out her provocative streak, the part of her that couldn't resist a challenge. She wanted to push him to turn reckless. Wild. She wanted to shake his methodical, lawyerly, suspicious heart, and make him see her not as a suspect, not as a victim, not as a defendant's niece, but as a woman.

She studied the gash on her forehead, a thin line of red visible under three butterfly bandages. She remembered Curt's gentle treatment of her, the way he'd held her, fed her, teased her. And she remembered the way he'd looked at her, desire in his usually shuttered eyes.

In spite of her fuzzy brain, she knew her memories were accurate. She also knew the man who'd been charming, funny, warm, kind, and ridiculously sexy was the real Curt.

She took a deep breath and opened the door.

He lay shirtless, stretched out on the bed, asleep.

This infuriated her. Which frustrated her. Did she have to be such a freaking basket case?

She dropped her heavy duffle bag on the foot of the bed, causing it to shake. He obliged by opening a sleepy eye. "Oh good," he said drowsily. "You're done."

He got up to take his turn in the head, but she didn't budge, forcing him to brush against her in the tiny space, her bust to his abs.

Big mistake. In the confined space, her ample chest crushed

against his skin with only her low-cut top between them. Need pounded through her with dizzying intensity. His eyes widened.

She cleared her throat. "I found more clothes for you." She pointed to the items.

"Thanks. I'll sleep in the JPAC one then." He grabbed the T-shirt he'd removed and reached for the door.

She wanted to run her hands over his chest and shoulders—and vaguely remembered doing so in the water. No fair. The memory was fleeting—she deserved a do-over. She wanted to run her tongue along his pecs and then trace his beautifully defined abs with her lips.

Reckless. Absolutely, horrifyingly reckless.

"No, Mara," he said into the heated silence, then escaped into the lavatory.

"Chicken," she muttered, then climbed onto the narrow bed.

A few minutes later, Curt crawled in beside her. She turned over and faced the curved wall. She needed to stop thinking about him. Now.

His broad shoulders filled the space and heated her back. The silence stretched. She listened to the water lapping against the hull, enjoyed the gentle rocking motion, and hungered to make the boat rock more. "I can't sleep," she said.

"It's only after eight here, and three in the afternoon in Korea, but it's past two in the morning for me. I'm tired."

She fidgeted and wriggled, trying to get comfortable, trying to settle her heated body, but nothing worked. Finally, Curt sighed heavily and slid an arm around her waist. He pulled her snug against him, spooning her back against his front.

"This is for comfort only."

She'd been alone and scared for so long, the feel of his hard thighs behind hers and his strong arm across her belly was comforting. For the first time in months, she dropped her guard and eased into a deep sleep.

CURT WAS PULLED from sleep by Mara, who thrashed on the bed and whimpered in misery. The sound cut right through him.

He stroked her cheek. "Mara. Wake up. It's only a nightmare."

He rubbed her back and shoulders until the thrashing stopped. After a long silence, she rolled over to face him and whispered, "Curt?"

His fingers returned to her face and confirmed her cheeks were damp with tears. He pulled her snug against him. "It was just a dream."

Her body quaked as she sobbed. He'd wondered if he would witness her inevitable breakdown, and here it was.

He stroked her hair and held her against his chest. "Sweetheart, it's over now. You're safe." But was she? All he knew for certain was he was pathetic in the wake of a woman's tears.

Crying on the stand was different. He'd hardened to that spectacle years ago. But genuine sobs rendered him helpless. He dreaded the moment she figured out he'd do just about anything to stop her from crying, possibly even make love to her.

Desperate for a distraction, he checked the time. "It's after midnight. It's Tuesday now."

She let out a half laugh, followed by a hiccupping sob. "Thank God."

"Do you want to tell me about your dream?" *Please say no.* His resistance was weak enough.

Her trembles and panting breaths eased. After a lengthy silence, she said, "I dreamt about my arrest."

He could handle this. Couldn't he? "Tell me."

"I stepped out of the woods and realized how close I was to the DMZ. I panicked."

"You ran?"

He felt her nod. "I turned and bolted back to the woods. But I'd been spotted and the soldiers chased me. I tripped over a root and stumbled, and a soldier caught my hair and yanked me backward. He threw me down." She shuddered. "There were three of them. They shouted in Korean. One tied my hands behind my back." Her whispery voice deepened. "They dragged me across rocky ground. Every few seconds, they stopped to shout and kick me in the head, stomach, and back. I have a scab on my scalp still."

A tide of anger rose at the thought of her being attacked by three armed soldiers, but he remained helpless, useless in his rage. The men who'd arrested and beaten her had probably been lauded as heroes. He wanted nothing more than five minutes alone with them. His fingers threaded through her hair, offering the compassion he was unable to express aloud.

Even as he tried to comfort her, he wondered what she wasn't telling him. It was possible she'd been raped. His pulse raced, and his skin heated. He would gladly rip the soldiers' heads off.

"Once they realized who I was, they didn't hurt me anymore."

He felt a prickle of relief, yet he couldn't help but wonder how badly she'd been hurt before they learned her identity. He tightened his arms around her.

She lifted her head and faced him. He could just discern her wide, beautiful eyes in the darkness. "I'm sorry you got dragged into this," she said.

He pressed feather-light kisses along the cut on her forehead. "I'm where I need to be." He surprised himself, because he meant every word.

"And the trial?"

He shrugged. "I'll miss a day. That's all."

"You can go back, you know. Without me."

"I'm not going to let you out of my sight until we reach DC."

"But it might be easier to travel without me."

"I was sent to North Korea to retrieve you and nearly got you killed by leaving you on the Marine Corps Base. You're my responsibility until I hand you over to the secretary of state."

She stiffened in his arms. "You do know I'm not a package, right?"

He couldn't help himself and slid his hands down her back and cupped her butt. "You're a damned enticing package."

She pressed against him; her cool fingers caressed the nape of his neck. Her mouth was a scant inch from his, and her slightly parted lips begged to be kissed.

The humid air inside the cabin thickened even more. He was nearly certain his heart had stopped, or maybe time did. He wanted—*needed*—to taste her, but if his self-control failed him now, then he'd never be able to stop with just a kiss.

And if he made love to her, he'd be disbarred.

Slowly he lifted his hands from her bottom and scooted away from her. "I'm sorry, Mara." He rolled over, flopping onto his back. "You have no idea how sorry—but I can't give you what you want right now." What *he* wanted right now.

He closed his eyes and tried to calm his racing pulse. In a matter of hours, Mara Garrett had shattered his smug belief in his heretofore steadfast self-control.

She sighed. "No. I'm sorry. I shouldn't have..." Her voice was soft, tentative, and he prayed he hadn't hurt her feelings. She was the last person he wanted to hurt.

"It's not your fault you had a nightmare. Not your fault that the only person available to comfort you is a ruthless bastard like me." He clung to that characterization. To get out of this situation with his career intact, he needed to *be* The Shark.

"You aren't—"

"Yes, Mara. I am." To put more distance between them, he could taunt her with his prosecution of her uncle, but even he wasn't that cold.

"I overheard earlier—it sounded like you got us a flight?"

"The plane should be on its way now. We'll be underway again by midafternoon local time." He reached out and squeezed her hand. "Try to get some sleep, okay?"

She squeezed his fingers in response, then, thankfully, rolled over. Several minutes later, her breathing evened out into the steady cadence of sleep.

AURORA CALLED TWO hours later. Mara slept soundly while Curt updated his co-counsel on the situation. As they spoke, the jury pool gathered in the courthouse. Aurora and another assistant US attorney would begin jury selection in an hour. All Curt could do was offer advice and encouragement while his controlling nature writhed in frustration.

If this were a state or county trial, he could count on jury selection lasting a good, long time. He'd be back in the courtroom before *voir dire* ended, no problem. But this was a federal trial, and as such, jury selection would be much faster. Plus, he had a tacit agreement with the defense not to draw out the process. There was no way they'd find twelve jurors who hadn't heard of the case, and a long, drawn-out selection process was hard on jurors. Neither side wanted to start with a pissed-off jury. As it was, he'd be lucky to make it back in time for peremptory challenges.

Call complete, he settled next to Mara, expecting to have trouble falling back asleep now that things were in motion in DC, only to open his eyes hours later to blinding sunlight. The tiny cabin baked in the late morning sun. The air was thick and his arms were full of Mara. He must have pulled her close while he slept—something he was certain he'd never done with another woman before.

Entangled as they were, sweat drenched them both. In a different situation, it would be a hot, erotic moment, but in this reality, it was utter torture. Barely clad, her petite frame, hard muscles, and spectacular breasts pressed against him, making him yearn to taste the sweat on her neck, lick her nipples into tight, hard buds, then slide deep inside her, easing the carnal ache for both of them.

How had he managed to resist her last night? He deserved a fucking medal.

She stirred in his arms, and her hip brushed his erection. Sweat rolled down his neck. He'd been told hell was hot, but he'd had no idea.

Gently, he wriggled and slid backward until he was up against the wall and Mara was no longer in his arms. Her eyes fluttered open, and he found himself staring into the most beautiful blue eyes he'd ever seen.

When had he started thinking of her in superlative terms?

*When she'd marched out to face a firing squad with strength and grace. When she learned the jet had exploded and instead of falling apart called me on my condescending attitude. When she survived a sniper attack and then was disarmingly adorable and outrageously sexy in her light-headed state.*

Damn, he had it bad for this woman. But he could handle it. He was control personified.

She rubbed her eyes and smiled, then scooted into a sitting position against the curved wall. Sweat trickled down the open V of her top, and he watched, transfixed, until the bead disappeared into her amazing cleavage.

Her nipples hardened. He finally remembered to look at her face and felt like a sheepish seventeen-year-old as her lips curved in a knowing smile. "You're a beautiful woman, Mara, and I am merely a man." She wasn't just a woman. She was a damn *siren*. He slid off the bunk, found his pants, and pulled them over his raging erection. Unfortunately, his hard-on was no less obvious, and she let out a soft, guttural noise. Oh Christ. The sound alone could make him come.

He closed his eyes, seeking strength. When he opened them, Mara met his gaze with desire as plain on her face as his was in his trousers.

He reminded himself that she only wanted him because he offered distraction from her ongoing nightmare. If she weren't so traumatized, he'd never be the recipient of that sultry, sexy look.

But even knowing that didn't stop his body from reacting.

"Mara—" *I want you. I want to toss you backward and taste every part of you. I want to make you come apart in my mouth, and then I want to slide deep inside and forget everything but your tight body.*

Jesus. He was in trouble. One thing was certain, they had hours until the jet arrived and couldn't spend them on this boat, or he'd end up satisfying their desires while destroying his career.

He stepped backward until he was against the hatchway. Three feet separated them, and he was so hard it felt as if he could span half the distance. "We may be allies now, but when this is over, we won't be friends."

Hurt flashed in her eyes. Just as he'd intended. "Is everything you say calculated?"

"No." He paused, then seriously considered her question. "Maybe."

"You're always playing chess, always looking five moves ahead."

"So?"

"You should stop being so controlling. Try living in the moment."

"The last time I made an impulsive decision, I landed in North Korea."

She cocked her head to the side. "Do you regret it?"

"Putting everything I've worked for at risk so I could save the life of my defendant's niece?" His humor fled, and he hoped Mara would hear the truth of his words. "No. Never."

Relief softened her gaze, and she smiled. "I think I'm having a positive effect on you, Counselor."

"Hardly. I've completely lost control of the situation."

"Don't you get tired of being in control all the time?"

"No."

She tossed him a challenging look. "Before we part ways in DC, I want to change that."

She might just be the woman to do it.

# Chapter Fourteen

BEN SHERROD LED his client, former Vice President Andrew Stevens, out of the packed courtroom and down the hall to a private alcove where press and jury weren't allowed. The proceedings had gone slowly as the extra-large jury pool learned the rules of the game. They'd just begun *voir dire* and already one potential juror had called a publishing house to ask for a book deal.

"You can see why Aurora Ames is Dominick's top assistant US attorney," Ben said, referring to the AUSA who'd just gotten one of the more promising members of the jury pool ejected. The man had practically glowed every time he looked at the former VP. His answers on the jury questionnaire were a defense attorney's dream, and AUSA Ames had gotten the guy ejected before strikes for cause had even begun.

Shit. His first setback and Dominick wasn't even here.

Stevens pulled out his phone and turned it on. After a moment, he cursed. "Still no calls."

"Focus on jury selection, Andrew, not your damn niece. Did you see the look on number seventeen's face when—"

"I need to talk to her."

Ben stifled a heavy sigh. "You can't. You'd have to call Dominick."

"It's bullshit that he can be alone with her when he plans to put her on the stand."

"He's alone with her because he saved her life, Andrew."

Andrew's forehead wrinkled as he pursed his lips. "Dammed North Koreans should have asked *me* to get her."

*Yes, that would have solved all your troubles with one tidy trip.*

"But they asked for Dominick," Andrew continued. "I heard it was because of the *TIME* article. How the fuck did *TIME* learn Dominick identified her as a potential witness during discovery?" Andrew flushed red.

Ben stood straighter, suspecting where Andrew was going with this diatribe. "Subpoenas are public record."

"If your office leaked it, I'll sue your ass six ways from Sunday."

Ben fought the urge to roll his eyes. "We need to talk about the jury—"

"That dammed article made Dominick look like a saint and me like a crooked politician."

Ben refrained from pointing out the accuracy of the article. Clients rarely liked that. Andrew wasn't a stupid man, but he'd been spiraling as the trial neared. Ben had seen it before. The threat of real prison time caused a panic that lowered a defendant's IQ by at least three points per day. Andrew would be a blithering idiot by the time the jury was seated if he didn't get his shit together.

"We can use the situation to our advantage," Ben said.

"How?"

"I'll impeach her as a witness. He saved her life—she'll say anything to please him."

Andrew's jaw clenched, and he looked like he wanted to punch somebody. "I don't want my niece testifying. Period."

"You should have thought of that before you introduced your niece to a Sudanese warlord and conducted an arms deal right under her nose," Ben said, revealing for the first time exactly what he'd figured out over the last months.

The former vice president's eyes bulged. "You're fired."

Ben shook his head, feeling an indulgent pity for his client. "Judge Hawthorne will never allow that. And even if she did, you'd have one hour to hire a lawyer to face *Curt Dominick* without preparation. He's the finest prosecutor I've ever squared off against, and I'm one of the few who has beaten him. You'll get five—no, make that ten—years." Ben took two steps toward the exit.

"Can you have her barred from giving testimony?" Sweat beaded on Andrew's upper lip.

Ben smiled. "No. But I can destroy her if she does."

THEY SPENT THE morning inside a Honolulu Internet café not far from the airport. They couldn't log into personal e-mail accounts without the potential to alert Raptor of their whereabouts, but, much to Mara's delight, they could anonymously search the web for news. With hours to kill and nothing to do, browsing the

Internet was a satisfying way to get caught up on what had happened in the world over the last three months, and something she usually did after a deployment anyway.

Life felt almost normal.

Except her companion was the US attorney who—according to Wikipedia—was the odds-on favorite to be named the next attorney general of the United States. And, because she was feeling naughty, from the moment she'd walked in the door, she'd begun behaving as though he were her boyfriend and he'd had to play along or make a scene.

She glanced up from the screen. "You're thirty-eight and you've never been married? What's wrong with you?"

He sent her a playful glare. "I'm married to my work."

"Oh, I get it." She turned back to the monitor. "Good thing I know how to update Wikipedia. Do you prefer the term 'Gay' or 'Homosexual'?"

He laughed. "Gay, please." Then he pointedly looked at his watch. "In another minute, you need to move on."

She grinned. "Just enough time." They'd agreed not to look at any news story about either of them, her uncle, or Raptor for too long, for fear of raising red flags. It was crazy to think Raptor could monitor all Internet browsing in all of the Internet cafés on the island, and yet the desperation that led a man to blow up a jet on a Marine Corps Base couldn't be underestimated. So in addition to catching up on the media's take on her situation, she also learned more about tabloid celebrities than she'd ever wanted to know. She pulled up the *People* article from a year ago, when after a high-profile prosecution that involved Iraqi artifacts, an Indian Casino, and an engineering firm owned by a US senator, Curt had caught the public's attention and made the magazine's sexiest men issue. But Curt closed the page before she could read the article.

"I was looking for pictures of Brad Pitt," she said.

A waitress refilled her coffee cup. "Honey, you don't need pictures of Brad Pitt when you've a hot *haole* hunk sitting by your side."

Curt smiled at the woman. "She doesn't appreciate me."

The woman perused Curt from head to toe. Clothed in Mara's landlord's T-shirt and shorts, with a day's growth of beard and a baseball cap, he looked nothing like the polished US attorney. Today he was Matthew McConaughey hot. "Sugar, I'll appreciate you." She glanced sideways at Mara. "You pretty, honey, but you ain't no Angelina Jolie. A man like him might stray if you don't take care of him. And I'm just the sort of woman to take in strays."

Curt's gaze fixed on Mara with surprising intensity. "Mar—nie is ten times more beautiful than Angelina Jolie."

Her belly fluttered. He sounded like he meant every word.

The waitress chuckled. "Oh, you are a charmer. Marnie, honey, you get bored with him, you let me know. 'K?"

Mara saw a perfect opportunity, and fixed her "boyfriend" with a challenging stare. "I'd be happier if he were a better kisser."

Curt's eyes narrowed, promising revenge.

The waitress's jaw dropped. "A mouth like that and you're complaining? Sweetie, you must not be doing it right, because his mouth was made for kissing."

"Oh, I'm doing it right. He's the one who needs help."

The woman set the half-full coffeepot on the table between them and crossed her arms. "Well, c'mon. Let's see. Kiss her. Auntie Shirley will tell you what you're doing wrong."

Mara had always loved elderly hapa-women who called themselves by their first name, and vowed to make this one an honorary auntie for life. She sent him a victorious look, and her heart went wild at the heated, promising look the prosecutor couldn't hide.

Oh yeah. He was definitely going to extract revenge. She could hardly wait.

Curt leaned forward and grabbed her chair, swiveling it so her knees met his straight on. Then, nudging her knees apart so he could get closer, he leaned toward her, his face set in a menacing scowl.

"Oh honey. There's your problem. You look like you'd just as soon bite her head off. Save biting for when you are alone."

Mara burst out laughing at the sideline coaching. "I tell him that all the time."

Curt's shoulders shook with laughter as he closed the distance. Her heart pounded as his lips hovered over hers; then finally his mouth caressed her in a fleeting, sensual brush of soft lips and breath. Shivers raced down her spine.

She parted her lips, but his mouth trailed along her cheek to her ear, where he whispered, "This is nothing compared to what a real kiss would be like." Then he lifted his head and faced Shirley.

"Good enough?"

Auntie Shirley sucked in a deep breath and patted her robust bosom. "Yes. I don't think the problem is you." She fixed Mara with a stare. "You don't like that kiss, you're *lolo*." Then she grabbed the coffeepot and marched away.

Curt leaned back in his chair, a satisfied smirk on his face.

Mara was anything *but* satisfied. She'd had a tiny taste and wanted more. How did he do that? Her libido had gone into overdrive. She wanted to jump him right here in the middle of a Honolulu café, based on nothing more than a tongueless, fleeting, wisp of a kiss.

She stood. "Be right back." She hurried to the ladies' room, where she could gather her wits. This was *not* the way to make him lose control. As far as she could tell, the only one about to lose anything was her.

In the restroom, she splashed cold water on her face and relived every second of the chaste but somehow still debilitating kiss. Then she squared her shoulders, pulled open the door, and stepped into the tiny corridor. And there was Curt.

His smolder was on full blast as he corralled her into the alcove behind the pay phone. He planted a hand against the wall above her head, blocking her in. "You want a real kiss now? Without a scorecard from Auntie Shirley?"

Her voice disappeared for a moment but eventually came out as a low rasp. "Yes, please."

And then his mouth was on hers, no longer soft or sweet, a hard pressure that had the power to melt all the bones in her body. His lips parted and—

The cell phone in his pocket vibrated against her hip.

He lifted his head.

"You answer that, and I will knee you in the groin."

He leaned his forehead against hers. "It's probably Lee, telling us our plane is landing."

"I don't care. I will still hurt you."

He closed his eyes, then sucked in a deep breath. "Break's over. Back to reality." And he answered the call.

TWENTY-FIVE MINUTES later, Curt pulled up to the guard gate at a secondary access road to Honolulu International Airport. Dread pulsed through his veins when he saw the guard's uniform. The man was a Raptor-employed security guard.

Crap. He'd gotten complacent and failed to plan for this scenario. The guard made one call after another. Each delay ratcheted Curt's tension up another notch.

Holy hell. They were so damn close to getting off this rock.

At last the guard handed him back his ID and raised the barrier. Curt drove straight to the small terminal that handled charter flights and private jets. "The jet better be fueled up. We need to take off the moment we reach the plane." Lee had assured him two well-rested pilots were ready to take over, but the refueling could take time. This jet lacked the range of the previous one, meaning they'd need to refuel before they crossed the Rockies—a complication they would figure out en route.

Relief surged when he saw a fuel truck driving away from the jet with the name TALON & DRAKE emblazoned on the side. He bypassed the parking area and headed directly for the jet. A flagger waved his wands, frantically signaling for Curt to stop. He did, but not until he was only ten yards away from the waiting jet. Reaching into the backseat to grab their bags, he said, "Crouch low and zigzag, and above all, be fast." Then, on impulse, he kissed her—a hard, fast meeting of mouths that was the least he wanted to take but the most he could give.

The flagger jogged across the pavement, reaching the vehicle just as Curt climbed out of the car. "Sir, you can't park there!"

Curt tossed him the key. "Then move it. We've got to go."

Mara ran toward the jet, and Curt breathed a sigh of relief when she was safely up the short flight of stairs. He darted forward. A moment later, he was inside and hit the button to raise the steps and seal the door.

A glance into the cockpit showed two pilots, a middle-aged man and a younger woman.

"Let's roll," Curt said. The shooter from the previous day might not be able to get a shot at Mara, but yesterday had proven a fifty-caliber round could disable the jet. He wouldn't feel safe until Honolulu was far below them.

The woman responded, "We need clearance for takeoff."

Curt gave her the code for priority takeoff. Mara stowed the bags and dropped into a seat. The pilots called in to the tower. A jet already in position landed; then all commercial traffic at Honolulu International halted. Curt closed the door to the cockpit, took the seat next to Mara, and fastened his seat belt. Less than five minutes after clearing the guard gate, they were speeding down the runway.

He held his breath. The nose lifted. At last they were airborne. If all went well, they'd be in DC in less than twelve hours. He studied his companion, the beautiful, amazing pixie he'd picked up in North Korea, and wondered how he'd ever be able to trust someone else with her safety.

The answer came with gut-wrenching clarity: he wouldn't.

# Chapter Fifteen

Mara sat in silence for the first few minutes after they were airborne. It was nutty to think Raptor might try to shoot them down, wasn't it?

But then, Raptor did have the best toys.

Now that they'd left Oahu and weren't too exhausted to talk or fearful of being overheard, it was time for her to admit to herself—and to Curt—that she agreed with his assumption that Raptor, not just Evan, was after them.

Jesus, there was a hell of a lot they needed to discuss, starting with Agent Palea's statement that Jeannie was a suspect in Roddy's murder. But first, she needed to breathe. Just…breathe.

Oahu was far below them when she finally looked around and said the first thing that came to mind. "The art was nicer on the other jet."

Curt laughed. "The other jet was owned by a billionaire. This jet is owned by JT Talon, who, while filthy rich, is not a billionaire."

"Do you think he's embarrassed by his lower-class private jet? I mean, there's not even a separate bedroom."

"I'm sure it's a source of great shame."

"I'm surprised the jet is from Talon & Drake, after you handled the prosecution of the smuggling case last year."

"I've been friends with Lee Scott for twenty years. He arranged for the jet. And as far as the prosecution, the evidence was overwhelming. It was an easy plea agreement. The press made a big deal, because they didn't want their big story to die."

"Erica Kesling is a hero among archaeologists," Mara said, referring to the woman who'd been at the center of the Talon & Drake artifact-smuggling scandal. "She's engaged to your friend Lee, right?"

Curt nodded. "When we get to DC, I'll introduce you. Up until you came along, she was the most famous—or infamous—archaeologist in the US. I'm sure she's more than happy to pass the title on to you."

Mara frowned at the reminder of her loss of privacy. She'd been changed by her experiences in North Korea—who wouldn't be—but she hadn't really considered yet how much her detainment would alter the way others viewed and treated her. Maybe Erica could offer advice on how to handle the media's relentless scrutiny.

Curt unbuckled his seat belt and went to the bar, reminding her of the first minutes of their flight after they'd escaped North Korea.

"Do I get a real drink this time?" she asked.

"I think we've both earned one." He opened the fridge, grinned, and pulled out a can of mass-produced American beer.

Mara shuddered. "I haven't survived a firing squad, a bombing, a car accident, and an attempted shooting to have my first taste of beer in three months be that crap. Is there anything *good* in there?" She stood and crossed the aisle to his side.

Curt laughed. "Lee stocked this for me. He won't touch the stuff. He included several microbrews too."

"Good man." She picked out a favorite.

Curt popped off the cap, then clinked his can against her bottle and said, "To getting the hell off Oahu."

A mix of emotions flooded her. "And farther away from North Korea," she added, then took a long swallow.

The tension in her shoulders left in a rush. Feeling dizzy, she leaned against the counter. The swaying of the jet must have gotten to her. Or was it her first taste of alcohol in months? Or the reminder that her life—whenever she got back to it—would never be the same? Whatever the cause, her knees and spine had turned to jelly.

Curt studied her, his hazel eyes full of concern. "You okay?"

She sighed. "I don't know *what* I am."

He cupped her cheek. "You're amazing. That's what you are."

Her breath caught, and she leaned toward him. He shook his head as though breaking a trance and stepped backward. "You are also dangerous." He turned and opened one cabinet after another until he pulled out a suitcase and said, "Thank you, Lee." To Mara, he said, "He sent me clothes. I'm going to change." He disappeared into the lavatory, leaving Mara to sip her beer and wonder who he would be when he came out.

She'd liked the casual, playful Curt, who'd flirted and teased and almost—damn, he'd been so close—given her the kiss of a lifetime in a Honolulu café. Now that they were alone, he'd likely put up barriers.

Damn controlling bastard. Alone was when the game could get interesting.

Several minutes later, he returned, clean-shaven and once again the high-profile prosecutor in a tailored suit. He was handsome and sexy either way, but she missed the rugged, casual Curt. "Aren't you a little overdressed for flying?"

"The clothes are my armor." He straightened his tie. "We need to talk."

His tone said it all. The Shark was back. She flopped on the sofa in disappointment. "I know."

"You've been holding out on me, Mara."

The metallic taste of fear invaded her mouth. How did he know? What did he know? All she wanted was to talk to Jeannie. After that, she'd know what to do. "What do you mean?"

"It's probable that Evan Beck shot Roddy, ran us off the road, and shot at us as we tried to board the jet at Hickam."

She nodded. Her throat was too dry to talk.

"He had access to the bases and a high-powered sniper rifle, he knows your car on sight, and he knew Roddy well enough to catch him by surprise, even as they met at your house in the middle of the night to do God knows what."

She glanced down at her hands, unable to meet his gaze as he listed the reasons he believed her ex-lover had tried to kill her—and him.

"What I want to know is, why haven't you told me everything?"

Nausea threatened. She regretted every bite of food she'd had at the café. "Everything?"

"About your engagement. And why you broke it off. I think, after all that's happened, I deserve to know."

MARA LOOKED SHOCKED. And more than a little green. Good. She'd been too out of it yesterday to confront with the question, then last night he'd seen her exhaustion had reached debilitating levels, so he'd put off the conversation until morning. But alone with her on the boat—that had been far too dangerous to his ambitions, and the café had been far too public.

"How did you know?" she asked.

"I know everything about you."

She shuddered. "Does everyone know? I mean, was it on the news?"

"No." At her relieved expression he asked, "Why does it matter? You dumped him."

She wrapped her arms around her middle. He ruthlessly shoved aside the part of him that had begun to care about her. She was a witness and a victim, not a friend.

"How did you know we were engaged?" she asked again.

"Your JPAC commander sent a dossier, which I read on the flight to North Korea."

"How the hell did he know? Evan and I were engaged for all of three days. We hadn't even announced it to family before I dumped him. Hell, the only person I'd told was Jeannie."

"You get uptight every time your relationship with Evan comes up. What gives?"

Her eyes narrowed. "Maybe the fact that he might be trying to kill us?"

"You were uncomfortable before that. Tell me."

She huffed out a sigh and looked down. "Evan is a mercenary in every sense of the word. He was paid. To seduce me. Date me. Even marry me."

Her face slowly reddened, as did his own. Hers, he was certain, in embarrassment, his in anger. He'd known Evan Beck and his father were both pricks from the moment he started investigating them, but to humiliate Mara in this way stirred violent impulses he'd been repressing for over twenty years.

"Who paid him?"

"His dad."

"How do you know?"

She bit her bottom lip. "There were a gazillion clues, I just missed most of them at the time. Overheard conversations. Evan's erratic treatment of me. He could be really charming, then, blammo—total ass. I'd walk, then he'd crawl back, turning up the charm. You see, if I dumped him, the gravy train would dry up."

She studied her hand, spreading her ringless fingers. "Raptor—the company, not Evan's dad—bought the god-awful ugly engagement ring."

"How do you know that?"

"The insurance company needed the receipt. When I saw the paperwork with Raptor's name on it, I knew. I'd wondered, because after we started dating, he bought a new car, an overpriced watch, and other items he shouldn't have been able to afford."

"His father is a very wealthy man."

"But according to Evan, his dad wasn't sharing. If Evan wanted a piece of the family business, he had to earn it. I was a shortcut into his dad's good graces. Hell, my uncle was already working for the guy. I think having me as a daughter-in-law would somehow make Robert Beck feel like he owned Uncle Andrew."

Given what he knew of the CEO, Curt had to agree. The man would buy a former president if he could, but they were out of his price range.

"Did you find proof Evan was paid?"

"Nothing that will help *you*, Mr. US Attorney, but enough to convince me Evan was making a tidy sum by screwing me."

Curt flinched but continued. This was his job. "What did your uncle say?"

"He said he didn't know anything about it, but Robert Beck had the right to give his son money if he wanted to."

"But Raptor money *isn't* just Beck's money—not anymore. Your uncle owns twenty percent of Raptor."

She glanced at him, surprise showing on her delicate features. "He's got a lot of stock, but twenty percent? He can't own that much."

Curt cocked his head to the side. "Mara, don't you know *why* I began investigating your uncle?"

"Of course. Uncle Andrew said it's because he received stock options when he took the job at Raptor, and you thought the options were bribes—but it was a legitimate business arrangement."

"They weren't options, and they weren't part of any standard employee package. Your uncle was *vested* with twenty percent of the company. Raptor is privately held. Can you tell me one good reason for Robert Beck to just give away one-fifth of his company? He bought Andrew Stevens's political power and influence, just as he used his son to buy you."

Anger flared in her deep blue eyes. "Evan didn't *buy* me. I wasn't interested in his father's money. When I found out what was going on, I dumped Evan's ass, took the gaudy pink diamond to a pawnshop, and donated the money to a Cambodian orphanage."

He kept his face blank even as his foolish infatuation deepened. They had to stay on topic. "It must have been fun being deployed with him after that."

"I switched teams. Jeannie and I weren't supposed to go to North Korea, but the forensic archaeologists who were slated to go both got really sick just before the deployment."

*That* got his attention back to the subject at hand. "You weren't supposed to be there?"

"JPAC was mindful of my family tree. They didn't want to send me on the North Korea deployment. But when the time came, no one else was available. It was hell getting clearance to enter DPRK. We didn't want to risk delaying. So I went."

"What happened to the other archaeologists, the ones who got sick?"

"They were hospitalized but recovering when I left. The doctors said they'd contracted something on their previous mission in Indonesia."

He'd be a fool if he didn't suspect Raptor had engineered Mara's and Jeannie's inclusions in the North Korean deployment. "What did your uncle say when you told him you were going to North Korea?"

"I didn't. He had too much on his mind with the trial. I didn't want to worry him."

Curt mulled this over. Mara's earlier pronouncement came back to him. *"Egypt was lonely, and Evan was hot."* He'd known already, but Mara's words confirmed her relationship with Evan had begun in Egypt.

Egypt. The JPAC deployment Andrew Stevens had visited for a photo op, and while there, Curt was certain, met with and sold arms to a Janjaweed militia leader wanted by the International Criminal Court for war crimes committed in the Darfur region of Sudan.

The former vice president had used his visit to the JPAC deployment to discreetly meet with the Janjaweed killer, but Curt couldn't prove the arms deal. Stevens had destroyed the evidence, forcing Curt to settle for the lesser charges of obstruction of justice and influence peddling.

The timing of Mara's involvement with Evan was…interesting. Especially since Robert Beck had also been in Egypt, traveling with the former vice president, ostensibly to visit his son. But of course, Robert Beck had been the one to supply the arms. Stevens was merely the broker.

Curt had suspected Evan killed Roddy because Mara's return to the United States would reveal Roddy had led her off-site and could implicate Raptor in dirty dealings in North Korea. But this could be about Egypt and the arms deal. "How did Evan take the breakup?" he asked.

"He made a show of being alternately outraged at my accusations and devastated I'd dumped him."

"And you believe he could have killed Roddy and shot at you?"

"The idea makes my skin crawl, but right now, I'll believe anything."

Except that her uncle was behind the attempts on her life.

"Could Evan have rigged the jet to blow on Oahu?"

"Easily. He's an ordnance expert." She rubbed her arms as if she were cold. "He has a military ID, which gives him access to the base. Through Raptor, he has flight line access. The hardest part would be getting close to the jet."

"Not so hard, because no one was guarding it. There are conflicting accounts. It appears the jet was refueled, and then a second fuel truck may have driven up after the first one left. Raptor is one of several contractors who provide base services including refueling. A small explosive device on a timer next to a wing tank is all it would take. If that's how it happened, then the fuel truck would have provided cover while he set the device."

She shivered at his cursory description of how her ex-fiancé might have rigged a bomb to kill her. He itched to pull her into his arms and hold her, give her comfort and a shoulder to lean on, but feared where that would lead them. Instead, he focused on her words and remembered another detail he'd wanted to follow up on. "Speaking of Evan's role as ordnance disposal technician, I want to know more about the bomb you found the last morning in North Korea."

"What about it?"

"There's no record of it. There's no mention of a bomb or Evan clearing the site in the official JPAC story. In the official version, you had a lover's quarrel with your ex-fiancé—Jeannie said he wanted the ring back—and you were so angry, you stormed off. Alone."

# CHAPTER SIXTEEN

IT TOOK A moment for Curt's words to sink in. Mara had expected him to talk about the bomb. She'd expected ambiguity, certainly. But this...this was utter betrayal.

She bolted to her feet. "No fucking way." She crossed to the bar and pressed her fists against the counter, taking one deep breath after another in an attempt to stop herself from doing something foolish. Like punching something. Or crying.

She fought to keep her voice measured. "We didn't have a lover's quarrel. I'd gotten rid of the ring nine months before, for Chrissake. We fought because I didn't like how he planned to dispose of the bomb."

"Why?"

*Careful, Mara.* "Clearing the site wasn't standard op." That was true.

"According to JPAC, he didn't clear the site. But, according to JPAC, there was no bomb."

Mara closed her eyes and remembered: Evan's decision, their argument, his asserting his power and ordering her to leave. Jeannie, standing behind Evan with wide eyes—like a kid watching parents fight for the first time. Mara had stormed off with Roddy on her heels.

They'd gotten into the Nissan Patrol, just the two of them. The others were supposed to follow. Had they? Had the four members of the team who'd been working on the other side of the ridge even known about the bomb and the orders to leave, or had Evan only issued the directive to Roddy, Jeannie, and Mara?

JPAC and the State Department had been led to believe she'd stormed off in North Korea after a fight with her ex-fiancé about an engagement ring. No wonder Curt had thought she was a twit when he first questioned her. "Why didn't you tell me about this when I first mentioned the bomb...good Lord, was that only yesterday?"

Curt's smile was as weary as she felt. "Yesterday for us. Two days ago in North Korea. Or something like that. I'm losing track.

I intended to talk to Roddy before telling you. But then Roddy ended up dead." He ran his fingers through his hair. "Who saw the bomb besides you and Evan?"

*Answer casually. Don't reveal you've thought about this for hours on end.* "No one." She looked up at the ceiling to slow her response. "Roddy and Jeannie witnessed the argument, so they knew *about* the bomb." She really needed to find Jeannie—which reminded her once again she wanted to know why Agent Palea had identified Jeannie as a suspect.

"Where was the rest of the team? Weren't there eight of you in North Korea?"

"Eight in the field, plus a liaison in P'yŏngyang. A Nissan mechanic and a medic were stationed at the base camp. Of the field team, the last morning the other four were on the opposite side of the ridge. They didn't witness my argument with Evan or, to the best of my knowledge, see the bomb."

"So Jeannie Fuller was the only JPAC employee who witnessed the argument?"

"Yes." Jeannie, her friend and protégé, had lied and let their supervisors believe Mara had behaved negligently. As if she'd storm off alone in North Korea. That was insane.

As insane as what had really happened.

Curt stood and crossed the space in three quick steps, sympathy evident in his turbulent eyes and downturned mouth, but he stopped short of reaching out to actually comfort her. "Mara, during my flight to North Korea, JPAC e-mailed me PDFs of your field journal. The last page included an account of you storming off, the crew's search for you, and their eventual expulsion from the country. According to the log, they were kicked out because of you—because you'd been arrested. The entry was signed by Jeannie Fuller."

His words crested her breaking point. Unstoppable tears rolled down, one after another as the full meaning took hold and ripped open her heart.

Jeannie really had betrayed her. Her damning statement would have ensured the entire fiasco was blamed on Mara. A simple sentence reporting Evan's command to clear the site was the difference between following orders and appalling negligence.

"Why would Jeannie do that?"

"Jeannie Fuller has a brother with a gambling problem."

Shock temporarily halted the flood of messy emotion. "Eric?"

"You know him?"

She nodded and sniffed. Curt grabbed tissues from the counter and pressed a stack into her hand. She mopped her cheeks and took a settling breath. "Eric visited Jeannie on Oahu nearly a year ago. I didn't know he had a gambling problem."

"He owed bad people big money, meaning Jeannie could be bought."

"You think Raptor paid her to lie."

"Yes."

"We need to find her."

"The FBI is working on it."

She touched Curt's arm as an idea took hold. "She probably went to Eric. She doesn't have any other family." She squeezed his bicep. "He's stationed at Davis-Monthan Air Force Base, in Arizona. We could refuel there."

He stiffened. "Another military base is dangerous. I'll call Palea, see what he knows, before we decide to do anything that drastic."

It took over two hours for Palea to talk to the FBI agent who'd interviewed Eric Fuller and get back to Curt. Seated in a plush recliner, Curt leaned back with an exhausted sigh. "Airman Fuller says he doesn't know where his sister is, but the agent who spoke to him believes he lied."

The forced air made her throat dry. Or maybe it was the awareness she could do something. She could stop running and hiding and take action. "Curt, he'll tell me."

He narrowed his eyes and fixed her with a penetrating stare. "What makes you think that?"

She shifted uncomfortably, remembering the last time she saw Eric Fuller.

He shook his head. "Don't tell me you were engaged to Fuller too?"

"Of course not! He's Jeannie's little brother and too young." She frowned. She hated this story, but it had to be told. "When he was visiting—it wasn't long after I dumped Evan—we went out for drinks one night. Evan showed up at the bar and tried to pick a fight with Eric." She allowed a grim smile. "It was appalling, juvenile, and ridiculous. Eric ignored him." Here she paused and caught her breath. "So Evan turned on me."

She heard Curt shift in his seat but didn't see his reaction because she dropped her gaze to her fingers, intertwined in a tight, painful tangle, remembering the pain that had exploded across her scalp when Evan yanked her off the barstool by her hair. She cleared her dry throat. "Evan is a highly trained operative, but Eric is ten years younger, in better shape, and doesn't have a bum knee. He kicked Evan's ass."

Curt dropped to a knee before her, forcing her to look at him. "I'm starting to like the guy."

She nodded. "After going through that…I think he'll talk to me. And I'm Jeannie's friend. He'll know I'm trying to find her to protect her."

"Are you? She lied, you know. About you." The cold pronouncement hurt. "And, Mara, you should know, Palea said preliminary examination of her home computer turned up transactions she made with foreign banks. She was well paid."

How much was selling out a friend worth? But then, how much was a brother's life worth?

The idea hurt too much to accept as fact. "There's money in my bank account too. But I didn't take a bribe."

Curt said nothing, and she wondered if he wasn't convinced of her innocence, and that idea hurt almost as much as Jeannie's betrayal. "Look, with you by my side, we can convince Eric you're willing to cut a deal with her on the bribery charge."

"I'm not in a position to make deals—"

"He won't know that. He'll tell us where she is. C'mon, Curt. We have to refuel anyway."

Footsteps sounded, and she looked up to see Curt open the cockpit door and step inside. She waited, tension coiling through her, wondering what arrangements he was making. Minutes later, he returned and dropped back into the plush recliner.

"We'll be at Davis-Monthan in three hours."

She gasped as her heart hammered. "Really?"

"We'll talk to Eric Fuller. But that's all. No matter what he tells us, we won't go after Jeannie, you understand? That's the FBI's job."

"I know." She reached across the narrow aisle and grabbed his hand. "Thank you."

"We wouldn't take the risk, except Raptor doesn't have offices in Arizona. Their closest field office is in Texas. We'll be in and out before they even know we're there."

She smiled. "I guess I should stop complaining about you being too much of a chess player and start being thankful for the strategy."

She expected him to pull away from her touch, but his fingers tightened. "When we're on the ground, you're sticking with me like glue. No talking with Eric Fuller in private—not even if he demands it."

She nodded.

"My job is to keep you safe. I'm not going to fuck it up this time." His jaw was tight, and his gaze met hers in an unapologetically hot look that somehow slipped past his rigid control. The heat in his eyes stunned her, but then, she'd been on such an emotional roller coaster, she needed to remember he'd been strapped in for the same ride.

She girded herself for another plummet and slowly stood, still holding his hand. Her belly fluttered in free fall as she lowered herself onto his lap. She grabbed the knot of his tie and began to loosen it.

His hand stopped her. "No, Mara."

"Just the tie. Please?"

Heat shimmered in his gaze, and finally he gave a quick nod. "Just the tie."

In moments, she had the noose off him, and settled against his chest. His arms closed around her. For the first time since she'd met him, she felt she understood him. He chose his armor and weapons carefully, and his shield could drop only so far when they were alone. When he was in prosecutorial mode, his actions were always calculated. She'd bet he even knew what she was going to say next.

She pressed her head against his chest and listened to his heartbeat. "What's your favorite chess piece?"

"I like the pawn, because no one sees it as a threat."

"Tell me everything will be okay."

"I can't do that."

"Tell me I'll get my life back someday."

"I can't do that either," he said.

"Then tell me you like holding me as much as I like being held by you."

His arms tightened, and his chin rubbed against the top of her head. "I like holding you. Far more than I should."

She smiled against his chest. "I want to sleep."

"Then sleep."

"I want you to hold me while I'm sleeping, like you did last night. It was the best sleep I've had in months."

His fingertips traced the cut on her forehead. "Then sleep."

She lifted her head and stared into his eyes. Her heart beat so loudly she was certain the pilots could hear. "Will you kiss me?"

"No." Even as he spoke, she felt evidence of his arousal. "Yes, I'm hard, but I won't kiss you, and I won't make love to you."

She relaxed against him. "Yet," she murmured and closed her eyes.

Curt pressed the recliner button and tilted them both backward. She fell asleep and dreamed hot, sexy, life-affirming dreams that had nothing to do with bombs, imprisonment, explosions, or shootings.

# Chapter Seventeen

The intercom buzzed, waking Curt from a light sleep. "We're thirty minutes out from Davis-Monthan," the pilot said. "We'll be on the ground just after midnight local time."

Mara stirred on his lap, and Curt allowed himself to enjoy the feeling of holding her a moment longer, telling himself he hadn't crossed any ethical boundaries, but knowing he'd come dangerously close to the line.

Her eyes popped open, and she smiled lazily. The hero worship in her gaze triggered a heady, dangerous feeling, and he fought the urge to kiss her. Since when did he have—let alone need to fight—urges?

Since a five-foot-two archaeologist with long blond hair, blue eyes, and a beautiful pixie face had taken over his life.

She stood and stretched. "How long did I sleep?"

He glanced at his watch. "Two and a half hours."

"That's all? Felt like eight. I feel wonderful."

And she looked tempting as hell. Blood returned to his legs, accompanied by the sensation of sharp pins and needles piercing his feet, but the pain was a small price for the pleasure of holding her. She really might be the one to break his control. It disturbed him to realize how much the idea appealed.

He stood and grabbed his cell phone to call the secretary of state. The man answered right away, but his voice showed he'd woken from a deep sleep. "Curt Dominick, I was beginning to think you were dead."

The man obviously hadn't lost sleep over the idea. "Sorry, sir, but calling you was out of the question while we were on Oahu. Even now, our conversation is probably being monitored."

"Please tell me this means you got off the island safely with the girl."

Curt glanced at Mara and refrained from saying *the girl* was thirty years old and every bit a woman. That sort of statement would alarm the secretary of state as much as it did Palea. "Yes, sir. We'll be in DC by morning."

"Excellent. We'll hold the press conference at Joint Base Andrews."

"A press conference puts a target on Ms. Garrett." *And I have a trial to get to.*

"You're starting to sound paranoid, Dominick."

He grimaced. He'd known this was coming. "With good reason." His gaze still on Mara, he said the words he knew she'd hate. "No press conference. She'll be taken into protective custody as soon as the plane lands." In a few hours, Mara would be out of his life. Except for when she testified, he'd never see her again.

MARA'S BODY WAS in a frenzy from the different time zones she'd been in over the last few days and didn't know if it felt like morning or night. All she knew was she was wide awake, wired, and mad as hell.

Curt intended for her to continue being a prisoner. *For my own good, my ass. He wants to make sure I don't take off without testifying.*

The jet rolled to a stop, and within minutes, the pilots had the door open and the stairway unfolded. There was no fanfare this time, just a colonel accompanied by a master sergeant waiting next to a vehicle at the end of the runway.

The senior officer introduced himself as Colonel Norris and shook hands with Curt, only greeting Mara as an afterthought. "My orders are to give you whatever you need to get you on your way." Something subtle in his tone, or maybe it was the ever-so-small curling of his lip, informed Mara he found this assignment distasteful.

"As I told you on the phone, Colonel, we're here for two things: to meet Senior Airman Eric Fuller and refuel the jet."

The colonel gestured to the master sergeant. "First Sergeant Boggs has command authority over Airman Fuller's squadron. He'll take us to his dormitory."

"Is Fuller there?"

"As far as we know. He has not been warned of your visit." The man adjusted his stance to include Mara without directly addressing her. "Ms. Garrett can wait here." He waved toward the nearby hangar.

"Ms. Garrett stays with me," Curt said.

The colonel indicated four MPs stationed around the jet. "She'll be safe. We don't intend to make the same mistake Marine

Corps Base Hawai'i made."

"No."

She was gratified by Curt's firm tone but annoyed at being left out of the conversation. "I need to speak with Airman Fuller." She crossed her arms and gave Colonel Norris a look that warned against underestimating her because she was small or a woman, a look she'd perfected for dealing with military men during her years with JPAC.

After a moment of silent standoff, the colonel said, "Fine," and led them to the vehicle. Boggs took the driver's seat while Curt and Mara climbed in the rear.

From the front, the colonel asked, "Why do you want to speak with Airman Fuller?"

Curt flashed a tight-lipped smile and said nothing. Mara followed his lead.

Colonel Norris reddened. Men like Norris were not accustomed to being ignored or denied. "I have MPs standing by at the dormitory," the colonel said. "If this is a legal matter, on base it falls under military jurisdiction."

"We're just going to ask a few questions," Curt said, unruffled. She had the feeling he was biting back the urge to cite legal precedents that proved the colonel wrong.

"It's a personal matter," Mara added. "I'm sorry it was necessary to disturb you in the middle of the night." She knew her role was to be obsequious when Curt shouldn't be, maintaining the balance of power in a way that pleased both egos.

They parked in a fire lane and followed the colonel and sergeant inside a tall dormitory building. Moments later, they were in the elevator, and Mara felt a sudden, sharp chill as the doors slid closed.

*This is about to go horribly wrong.* The elevator doors opened, and she flinched, on edge. A look from Curt conveyed his awareness of her trepidation.

Stepping out of the elevator, she noted MPs stationed at either end of the hallway. The colonel hadn't exaggerated his desire to maintain military authority.

Dim bulbs in wall sconces illuminated small patches between every second door, giving the effect of a telescoping hall. "Which room is Airman Fuller's?"

Boggs led the way. "Twenty-three."

Their footsteps padded softly on the thin carpet. Curt walked beside the colonel while Mara trailed behind. At the door, Boggs paused. "I have the authority to enter his quarters, but I'd rather knock."

"Is there a back way out?"

"The rooms don't have fire escapes."

"Then knock."

The man's thick fist met the door. The sound reverberated up and down the silent hall, but no one answered. After waiting a polite interval, Curt said, "Open the door."

The sergeant's jaw tightened, but he pulled out his key and complied. The door swung on silent hinges. Mara strained to see into the darkened room between the men's shoulders.

A sharp metallic smell enveloped her. Her gasp coincided with similar sounds from the men, and the sergeant reached inside and slapped the light switch.

The fluorescent light flickered, then washed the room in stark brightness, revealing blood on the bed, on the walls, across the floor.

Time spiraled, or maybe she did, because the next thing she knew, she was sitting on the floor with her arms clasping her knees. Curt approached, concern stamped across his features. She shook her head, unable to accept comfort, unable to do anything except maybe vomit down the garbage chute.

He knelt in front of her. "Jeannie's not there." His voice was low, husky, and filled with regret.

Relief flared, but it was short-lived as the implication became clear. "Eric?"

He nodded, and her heart split open in grief.

# Chapter Eighteen

Curt's smug assurance Raptor didn't have a presence in Arizona shattered the moment the door had swung open, and, if his hunch was right, he was now at least three moves behind a mercenary on a killing streak. He squeezed Mara's hands and said, "I need you to hold together just a little bit longer. At least until we get away from here."

He rose, pulling Mara to her feet. Behind him, Colonel Norris said, "You've got questions to answer, Dominick."

"We'll both answer questions. By phone. Right now I've got to get Ms. Garrett out of here. That blood is fresh." So fresh the streaks were still spreading down the walls. "And she's a target." He should have guessed Evan would go after Jeannie. And while they'd been holed up on a tiny boat, waiting for their jet to arrive from DC, Evan Beck had probably already been en route to the mainland on a Raptor jet. Beck had access to credentials both real and fake that would get him on Davis-Monthan without a hitch.

Mara swiped away a tear. "Curt," she said, a new urgency to her voice. "I need to tell you something." The pitch on the last word reached an alarming octave.

Those eyes that had captivated him from the start held a new emotion. Guilt. Shame. Utter horror. Oh hell. Oh crap. *Oh holy fuck.* In one moment, Curt knew with sudden, horrible certainty the rotten truth—his sweet little victim, the woman he'd saved in North Korea, the one he'd missed the first day of the trial for, and the one who'd been steadily seducing him since P'yŏngyang, had been holding out on him.

"What the hell is going on, Dominick?" Colonel Norris asked.

"Not now, Colonel," Curt said without taking his gaze off Mara.

"If you're not going to answer questions, then you're going to get the hell off my base."

"Agreed," he said, and grabbed Mara's arm and pushed her down the hall. Two dozen steps away, he backed her into the wall. He was rougher than he should be, but dammit, he was pissed. "A man is dead. I think it's past time for you to tell me what the fuck is going on."

Her eyes widened. So innocent. So beautiful. Such a liar. "I'll tell you. As soon as we're alone. Back on the jet."

"You won't put it off one more fucking second. You've had plenty of chances. On the boat, in the car, on the plane. In a box, with a fox. *Now*, Mara."

She swallowed and gripped the lapel of his jacket. "I just left one thing out. You'll understand when I explain."

"I've risked *everything* for you."

Tears slid down her cheeks. But these were the type he was immune to. "Please, Curt. I didn't know who to trust. And I didn't think—" She swiped at a tear. "I had no idea—"

He cut her off by waving an arm toward Airman Fuller's room. "Could you have prevented that?"

She shook her head frantically. "No. I don't know what's going on. I had no idea Eric would be involved. Believe me. He was a friend."

"What *do* you know?"

She pleaded for understanding with tear-filled eyes. "That last morning…the bomb we found…it was a US-made Korean-war-era smallpox bomb."

# Chapter Nineteen

Curt's hands dropped, and he stepped backward, releasing Mara from the cinder-block wall. "Sm—"

She lunged forward and covered his mouth. "Not here. We'll talk about this on the jet. I'll tell you everything."

His eyes narrowed. "You'd better." His hazel eyes were colder than she'd ever imagined they could be, which was saying something for The Shark. Heading toward the elevator, she wanted to tuck her hand in his, but all the walls between them were back, with no sign of the man who'd held her while she'd slept on the plane.

"I'm sorry, Curt."

"Save it for the jury."

She supposed she had that coming, but still, it hurt. "Cut me some slack here. I have my reasons."

He stopped and fixed her with a cold glare. "I've heard that a thousand times, from a thousand different defendants. You're no different from criminals who say they wouldn't have shot their dealer if their father hadn't beat them when they crapped their pants in first grade."

She almost choked on the fury that surged up her esophagus. Refusing to tell him about a top-secret biological weapon hardly compared. "Screw you," she rasped. "Go back to DC by yourself."

His jaw tightened while his eyes flashed fire. "I'm done playing games."

"And I was *never* playing games. I was under no obligation to tell you anything. You were the envoy, nothing more. Fly back to DC alone. I'm *not* your prisoner."

"I'm a helluva lot more than the envoy. I've given up precious days to save your sorry ass. Every attempt on your life also endangered mine, and you still kept that little tidbit to yourself. And you did it to protect your goddamned lying, cheating uncle."

"I didn't—" But she had. She'd worried from the moment she realized Curt was the envoy that if she told him about the bomb, he'd find a way to use it against Uncle Andrew.

"And, Mara, you have to return to DC with me. You've been subpoenaed."

"The subpoena blew up on Oahu."

His eyes narrowed again. "You were served."

"I never had a chance to read it. For all I know, it was a recipe for huli huli chicken."

He grabbed her arm and dragged her toward the elevator. "You're coming back with me. I will get a US Marshal, so help me God."

She pulled away from him, but those damn muscles that had impressed her yesterday now prevented her from breaking his iron grip. "I am done being a prisoner!"

The lights went out, enveloping them in utter darkness. Mara let out a squeal of surprise, then berated herself for being a damn baby.

Curt's arms came around her, protectively, as he cursed the darkness. Shouts sounded down the hall.

She gripped his shoulders. "The killer is still here," she whispered.

She felt his nod. "I don't believe in coincidences." He pulled her a few steps down the hall. "The stairs are next to the elevator."

"He could be hiding in the stairwell." He. Eric Fuller's murderer. Her ex-fiancé. *Evan.*

Curt stopped. "Shit. We can't move until the power comes back on." He pressed her against the wall and covered her with his body. Even pissed off, he protected her.

Her heart cracked wide open. Did he have to be so damn…amazing? Of course he did. He was a hero through and through. And she deserved every ounce of his hostility. She pressed her forehead against his chest and said, "I'm sorry," again.

"We'll talk about it later." But his voice was softer now, less angry.

"I trust you, Curt."

"It's about damn time."

The lights flickered, then turned on. She sighed in relief. "Elevator or stairs?"

"If the power goes off again and we're in the elevator, we're screwed."

"Stairs, then."

He gripped her hand, and they headed toward the green exit

sign. The door slammed open, hitting the wall with enough force to bounce. Two MPs charged through the opening. Seeing Curt and Mara, they stopped short. "Mr. Dominick, our orders are to escort you and Ms. Garrett off the base."

"To the jet?" Mara asked.

"No. To protect military personnel and property, Colonel Norris has ordered your jet to take off. And he wants you off the base. Now."

LESS THAN TEN minutes later, they were cut loose on the streets of Tucson in a sedan provided by the base. The moment they were alone, Mara cursed Norris's command for the jet to take off and leave them.

"It doesn't matter," Curt said. "We weren't going back to the jet anyway."

She sputtered. "But—"

"The jet would have been too dangerous. The power outage proved Fuller's killer was still there. Evan—if it's Evan—could have been trying to buy time to sabotage the jet."

"So you don't think Colonel Norris was trying to help Raptor by tossing us?"

"I didn't say that. I just said we weren't going back to the jet. At least this way we have a vehicle. We can't stay in it, though. Any number of people could know we have this car—and all government vehicles are fixed with tracking devices."

"What are we going to do?"

"I can call the Arizona US Attorney for help, but it's one in the morning. Do you know Tucson?"

"No. I've never been here."

Neither had he. Ahead, he saw a blue sign with an airplane symbol and thought maybe, just maybe, luck was on his side for a change.

"We're going to the airport?" she asked.

"We're getting rid of this car."

"But we can't rent—not without a credit card transaction, and I'm pretty sure rental cars have tracking devices. Child's play for Raptor."

He shook his head. "We'll take a taxi."

"All the way to DC?"

"No. To a strip club."

"Wow. That was *so* not what I expected you to say."

He smiled grimly. "Me neither, but from there we can find a motel that won't care about credit cards or IDs, and I can make arrangements." He glanced at his passenger. "Tonight we'll pretend we're a couple looking to take a walk on the wild side."

A dangerous heat suffused him. They'd be alone in a room built for sex, for hours. Neon and fireworks marked this hazardous path, yet this was the only possible move.

For some unfathomable reason, even though she'd withheld vital information from him, he wanted her. His vaunted control was about to be tested like never before.

An hour later, Curt shoved three twenties into the hand of a taxi driver as they idled in front of a Miracle Mile strip club. The man wore a knowing smirk, and Curt could only hope he didn't recognize either of them.

On the sidewalk, Curt pulled Mara tightly to his side as they headed down the street, seeking a seedy motel.

"Lose the tie," she said. "You look too proper for this part of town."

"That's the point. We're tourists on the wild side."

"But we don't want to be noticed."

She had a point. He gripped the knot. He should keep it on. He'd need all his armor where they were headed. He had to face a cold, hard fact: outside of military or government channels, arranging for another jet would be impossible.

That should be foremost in his mind, yet he was sweating the coming sleeping arrangements more than the knowledge he was likely to miss not only jury selection but also opening arguments and the first witnesses.

Evan Beck wasn't fooling around. He'd killed two men and nearly blown Mara's head off at Hickam. The thought of how close she'd come to dying was a sucker punch to the gut every time it crossed his mind. Which was constantly. Even when he should be thinking about the case he'd been building for the last year—the one that would cinch his place on the attorney general short list, which he'd only been working toward since he was sixteen.

But he was in Arizona—thousands of miles away from the courtroom—with the niece of the man he was prosecuting, and instead of coming up with ways to use her against her uncle in the trial, he was plagued with thoughts of other ways he wanted to use her.

If he could survive the night with his control intact, then they'd hit the road in the morning and drive without stopping—allowing for no more temptation.

And if his control failed? He'd have to decide between dropping her testimony or stepping down from the prosecution. His case or his career. If he slept with her, he couldn't have both. And the fallout could mean he'd have neither.

She'd been holding out on him.

That knowledge was a better shield than a silk tie—which he'd removed as he walked. Damn. He was already undressing and they hadn't even reached the motel.

*A smallpox bomb, a dead operative, and a dead airman. Focus, dammit.*

Mara shivered beside him, and he realized she didn't have a coat. The temperature must have dropped below fifty degrees. He slipped off his jacket and draped it over her shoulders.

"Ever the hero." She smiled and inhaled his scent from the cloth. The glimmer of pleasure on her face sent heat right to his cock.

They passed two motels, seeking to distance themselves from where the taxi had dropped them, in case the driver was questioned. At last they found one that looked perfectly disreputable. When he would have paused to rehearse their roles, she flashed a wicked look, squared her shoulders in the oversized coat, and marched toward the door. "Time for US Attorney Dominick to meet his wild side."

He was in deep shit.

MARA PLASTERED HERSELF to Curt's side as he slid cash through the slot in the bulletproof window. She blew in his ear and nibbled on his jaw. The display wasn't necessary—the guy behind the thick pane didn't look like he kept up with the news—but dammit, Curt clung to control like a man dangling by fingertips over an abyss. And with each press of her breasts against his arm, another finger slipped from the ledge.

After everything that had happened—*don't think about Jeannie, and definitely don't think about her brother Eric*—she needed tenderness, affirmation. And if she couldn't get that, she'd take the oblivion of mindless sex. Either way, she wanted him. Now.

The clerk dropped a metal key in the trough—no plastic key

cards here—along with a ribbon of condoms. Mara let out a throaty laugh and said, "For a first-time john, you sure do know the place to go."

Curt cut her a sideways glance that said he was both amused and annoyed at the role in which she'd cast him. He collected key and condoms and, fingers entwined with hers, tugged her out the door and to the stairs that led to their second floor room. On the landing, he pulled her against him. His mouth found her neck, and he said, "I thought we were a couple. Why did you make me a john?"

Because she knew it would fluster the upright attorney. She couldn't imagine the man doing anything wicked, let alone illegal. "A real couple would go to a classier place than this dump."

"We could be having an affair."

She gripped his shirt. "A man wearing clothes as expensive as yours would take his mistress to a hotel. A place that gives out condoms on check-in is for whores and johns."

His eyes narrowed in the sexiest, hottest way. The amused glare went straight to her center. "You're blowing smoke. You've never been to a place like this before."

She nibbled on his jaw and worked her way toward his ear. "This is my first time on the wild side—but I like it."

He stiffened against her, and she felt the heavy beat of his heart as another fingertip clinging to control slipped. Still gripping his shirt, she tugged him down the covered walkway. "You're wasting time. I have another appointment in an hour."

She leaned against the door and stroked his chest as he fumbled with the key. Would he fall? Or would he regain his grasp once they were alone?

The door swung open, and she tumbled inside. Gripping his bicep for balance, she pulled him in after her. He kicked the door shut behind him and caught her in his arms. A rush of victory suffused her when his mouth covered hers.

His tongue thrust between her lips, and she took him in, already drowning in the sensation of his potent kiss. She'd fantasized about this, but the reality of his surrender was a bigger rush than she'd imagined. He filled her senses with his touch, the musky smell of his skin, and the taste of his mouth as he devoured her.

"Oh God," he muttered against her lips. "I can't take this anymore."

She slid her tongue along his, drinking him in. "I need you. Now." She fumbled with the buttons on his shirt, finally freeing the top two.

He released her and pulled the shirt over his head. Ah, those glorious pecs. She ran her hands over his muscles, only breaking contact when he removed her top. His lips traced the edge of her bra, and his hands cradled her breasts.

He nibbled his way upward, nuzzling her neck as his hands dropped to pin her hips to the wall. Once again his mouth covered hers in a searing hot and thoroughly mind-blowing kiss.

When Curt Dominick let his carnal side out, the man was hot enough to melt stone.

His left hand slid upward again, capturing her breast. "You have a spectacular body," he murmured against her lips. "Keeping my hands off you. Yesterday. On the beach…" Kisses punctuated each word. "Was hell."

She kissed him, sliding her tongue along his, taking him deep into her mouth. She wanted nothing more than to do the same thing with the impressive erection currently pressing against her center and pinning her to the motel wall. She wanted to taste all of him, to look into his eyes as he surrendered his control utterly and completely, and gave in to the pleasure she could give him and came in her mouth.

Her hands trailed down his chest and found his fly. She popped the top button, then touched the zipper. His hands closed over hers, stopping her.

He closed his eyes and pressed his forehead to hers. His breathing was ragged. "We can't do this—"

*No.* A fingertip had gained purchase. "Don't you dare back out on me now, Curt."

"I want you. I've never wanted anyone as much as I want you right now."

"No problem, because you can *have* me."

"We can't. *I* can't."

"Please, Curt. I *need* this."

His mouth lit on her cheek, her brow, her neck. "So do I, sweetheart. But if I have sex with you, then put you on the stand, I'll be disbarred."

"Then don't put me on the stand."

The lips against her throat paused for a heartbeat; then he reared back. "Fuck. You're doing this on purpose, aren't you?"

His eyes narrowed. "What's your goal here, Ms. Garrett? Are you doing this to help your goddamned uncle?"

Her wildly thumping heart split open. How could he think she'd be so mercenary?

Cold, hard eyes pierced her with a glare. "Are you trying to get out of testifying?"

She swung out to slap him, but he caught her wrist before impact. He grabbed her other arm and pinned her to the wall with both hands up. "Or do you want me disbarred?"

# Chapter Twenty

JESUS. HE WAS too stupid to live. How could he have kissed her? How could he have forgotten everything that mattered to him?

Her eyes burned with anger as she glared at him, trapped between his body and the wall, her hands pinned beside her face with her fingers curled into eye-gouging claws. Her magnificent breasts heaved as she struggled against him. She might be strong and fit, but he was twice her weight with twice the muscle.

"You are such an ass. For a Harvard-trained lawyer, you really are stupid."

"I agree."

She stopped struggling, but he didn't relax his grip. Her knee came up, but he blocked her with his own. He thrust his knees between her legs, preventing her from trying again.

She wriggled against the intrusion, her crotch nestled on his thigh, and let out a small, guttural sigh. His body responded to her arousal just as quickly. What the fuck? They were both spitting mad and hot for each other at the same time. "I hate to break it to you, darling, but I'm not into rough sex."

Again she glared at him. "Neither am I. But I'm into *you*, dumbass."

"I don't believe you."

"No kidding."

Small and fine-boned, she'd been held prisoner in a dark cell for two months and had at times been blindfolded and handcuffed—and he was manhandling her in the worst way, making him question every virtue he thought he had. "If I let you go, are you going to scratch me or kick me in the balls?"

"I won't scratch you."

He smiled. Damn, only she could make him smile in this situation. He pressed his thigh against her center and she gasped. "Dammit, Curt. It's obvious I'm turned on. Allow me some dignity and let me go." She was a proud woman. That had been apparent from the moment they met, and now he was bringing her low in a despicable manner. The starch left her spine. "Please."

He dropped her hands, lowered her feet to the floor, and stepped back, wary of quick movements on her part.

She stayed against the wall and stared at him, the fight in her gone. A tear rolled down her cheek, but it lacked the quality of courtroom hysterics and cut straight to his heart.

"Why did it have to be you?" She shook her head in disbelief. "Clinton, Richardson, even Jesse Jackson—I'd have been grateful, but I wouldn't have fallen for them. No, I get *you* as my rescuer. Young, handsome, powerful, and utterly heroic. You are a potent combination, and in my fractured state I didn't stand a chance. Not even the fact that you're trying my uncle could get in the way of my foolish fascination.

"No, Curt. I don't want to make love with you because it will gain me a damn thing. In fact, I'm pretty sure the only thing you can offer me is pain. But I want you because I'm stupid and vulnerable and weak and lonely, and a thousand other things, all unflattering and embarrassing." She pushed off the wall and headed to the bathroom. "I'm going to take a shower. When I come out, we're going to pretend I didn't make a big fool of myself—"

"You didn't—"

She cut him off with a swift arm motion. "And you didn't make an even bigger ass of yourself. We'll pretend this didn't happen."

She was right. He was a complete ass. As far as he knew, the last guy she'd been with was Evan, a man who'd been paid to date her, had assaulted her after their breakup, and now was probably trying to kill them both. He itched to pull her back into his arms, to make it up to her with his mouth and hands. To erase all the harsh memories by making love to her. But he couldn't. That path led to disbarment and destruction.

"We'll pretend we didn't get out of control, and that you didn't insult the hell out of me."

She was right. They had to pretend nothing happened. "Mara—"

"And I *will* tell you about the smallpox bomb."

Fuck. What was wrong with him? How could he have kissed her, started to undress her, when she still hadn't explained the smallpox bomb?

SHE TOOK A long hot shower, washing Curt's touch from her skin. A half hour later, she emerged from the bathroom, at last composed enough to face him. Curt sat on the bed with the prepaid phone to his ear. He took one look at her, said a quick good-bye, and dropped the phone.

Her heart squeezed, as it always did at the sight of him. Disheveled again with half a day's growth of beard, he was so appealing, so magnificent, she probably could have come while they kissed if he'd applied only the slightest bit more friction.

She had forgotten her number one rule: never trust a man with ambition.

For Evan, she'd been a ladder, a way back into his father's good graces after a botched military career, with the levels of their courtship providing the rungs. But Evan was merely the last and most successful in a line of men who'd wanted to use her to gain access to her uncle. Then there was her uncle, who'd used her job with JPAC, visiting her for photo ops that softened his image and encouraged the military vote. He'd used her, and she'd spent years looking the other way.

She should have guessed Curt was just another man with ambition who wanted to use her. "What if I refuse to testify?"

His face revealed no emotion. "Then you'll go to jail."

"You wouldn't do that to me. Not after what I've been through."

"I don't bluff, Mara. There's no need when I hold all the cards."

"You really are ruthless. All you care about is your case."

He didn't flinch. "It's about time you figured that out. Now, tell me about the smallpox bomb."

MARA PACED THE dingy room, and it took all of Curt's effort to keep his brain on her words and off the shape of her ass or the bounce of her breasts beneath the thin T-shirt. Over the years, he'd taken pride in the fact he wasn't ruled by his dick like so many he knew. Even many of the greats he admired—politicians with brilliant minds—had fallen into that trap. But not him, no, he'd been smug in his belief he'd never be so stupid.

Then he met Mara. She'd entered his life and rocked his world. Forbidden fruit until after the trial. But when the trial was over, if her loyalty to her uncle remained, they'd never speak again.

So he drank her in now. The sexy sway of her hips, the flutter of her blond hair as she pulled it back from her face in a repeated, unconscious action. Those luminous deep ocean blue eyes that conveyed exactly what she was feeling at any given moment. All the pieces of her came together to create a work of art, a masterpiece that was Mara Garrett.

She paused in her pacing. He noticed because her breasts stopped bouncing, and he was sorry for the interruption. "Earth to Curt? Hel-*lo*?"

He shook his head. "Sorry. Lack of sleep is getting to me, I guess." *Liar.*

She smiled. "Liar."

Hell. He had to add mind reader to her other attributes.

"For the record, you're the one who stopped us from having sex."

He grimaced. "I thought we were going to pretend that didn't happen."

"It would be easier if you didn't look at me like I'm dinner."

"I am not." But of course, he was. She had utterly decimated his legendary control in—what, three, or was it only two?—days. He stood from the bed and pulled off the bedspread. It was cheap and scratchy and would probably melt in a warm dryer, but it was their only hope to get through this conversation in a timely manner so they could sleep for a few hours before hitting the road. He draped the blanket around her shoulders and gathered it in his fist at her throat. "Tomorrow we're going to buy you a burka."

Her eyes flashed with heat.

He retreated to the bed. "You were telling me about JPAC's Research and Investigation Team—RIT, I believe you called them."

She smiled. "You *were* listening."

"My brain is capable of multitasking."

"Magna cum laude at Harvard?"

"Summa. Now tell me about RIT." He leaned against the headboard to watch her pace, the bouncing of her breasts now thankfully cloaked.

"I was curious about that particular North Korean plane wreck from the start, because of the accounts RIT gathered. Two fighter pilots witnessed the 1952 crash. Neither one knew what happened. It was a crisp, clear summer day. Not a cloud in the sky or an enemy for miles. No one fired on them from the ground, but all of a sudden, Captain Baldwin's plane started to go down. They radioed him, but he didn't respond. There was no distress call, nothing. He dropped at full speed, but in the last seconds appeared to slow, making the other pilots think he was fully conscious—at least at the end."

"What do you think happened?"

"There are accounts of pilots deliberately crashing their planes. Not many, but it did happen. But Baldwin was highly respected, heavily decorated. He was one of the air force's first Aces—the air force was new, having just branched off from the army in 1947."

"An Ace doesn't crash on purpose."

"Never."

"Was your job to find his remains or solve the mystery of his death?"

"Find his remains."

"What happened that last morning in North Korea, after you found his remains?"

"I found Baldwin's dog tag and some bones, and Jeannie started to remove them. I studied the lay of the land, and, figuring remains may have washed downslope, grabbed a rake and shovel and followed the drainage. A few scrapes later I found a section of fuselage. Inside, coated in dirt, I found two bombs. One fractured, one battered but intact."

"How did you know it was a bomb?"

She shrugged. "I dig in combat plane wrecks. I've found bombs before."

"But these were different."

"Very. We train for unexploded ordnance at JPAC. I've seen pictures of prototype weapons—real and imagined—so if we come across something odd—be it American, Russian, Japanese, Korean, or whatever—we'll recognize it. What I found reminded me of an E120 biological bomblet, but an earlier version. Cruder but definitely American."

Curt sat up straight. "It was obviously a biological weapon?"

"No, but it was different. Really different. The usual protocols couldn't apply, so when Evan ordered the site cleared, I was upset. We argued. He insisted on detonating it. I thought that was a terrible idea."

"But as ordnance disposal expert, he got his way." The wooden headboard squeaked as he shifted position. Just hearing her say Evan's name made him itch to strangle the operative.

"Yes."

"So why are you certain it was a smallpox bomb?"

Mara opened the concealing blanket and lifted the hem of her shirt, exposing her midriff. "Because, when I was in North Korea, I got sick." For the first time, Curt noticed tiny pockmarks marring her otherwise perfect skin.

# Chapter Twenty-One

Evan maintained a constant speed, following the red pickup truck from a distance. He was hot on Jeannie's trail and about to clean up the last loose end. She'd fled the base in her brother's red pickup when the FBI came sniffing around. The greedy bitch didn't even know her little brother was dead. Her frantic and repeated calls to her brother's cell had all gone unanswered. You'd think she'd get the hint. With one hand Evan shut off the phone. The calls had become annoying.

He'd been locked onto Jeannie's phone for the last hour, and he'd easily caught up with her as she circled the city, trying to get ahold of her brother.

It was a shame Mara and the US attorney had been so damn careful with his phone. They'd made things damn near impossible for Evan, forcing him to go after Jeannie instead of twiddling his thumbs on Oahu waiting for a lead.

Evan's own phone rang, from the ringtone he knew it was his father—a call he couldn't avoid. "I'm on it, Dad," he said by way of greeting.

His father cursed loud and long. "Jesus. You had the chance to get the girl on the base. What the fuck happened?"

Evan wasn't actually sure which girl his father meant, but it didn't matter. He was right on both counts. "I'd have gone after the plane, but the colonel ordered the pilots to take off, and Mara and Dominick were whisked away before I could get a lock on them, so I'm after Jeannie."

"Don't fuck up, Evan. We've got *maybe* one more shot at this. As it is, the FBI is focusing on you, and you know Raptor can't be implicated."

"Dominick must have made the decision to drive. He'll be late to the trial."

"It would be better if he *never* makes it to the trial, but it's vital Mara never gets there. Don't screw up. Not again."

"I'd like to remind you that *Roddy* is the one who screwed up in the first place."

"He was under your command."

And it was *Evan's* fault Mara had escaped Roddy? Hell, if the linguist had just gotten Mara to the Joint Security Area as planned, they'd have had their international incident without Raptor looking guilty. Roddy's claim he'd overheard threats to Mara's safety would have been the perfect cover. And while it might have taken weeks to negotiate Roddy's and Mara's releases from the country, Raptor, Roddy, and even Mara would have come out of the ordeal squeaky clean.

JPAC would have been ejected as planned and Evan would have been able to smuggle out the bomb without the need to bribe Jeannie to keep quiet about Roddy leaving with Mara and returning alone. If all had gone as planned, there was a small—admittedly, very small—chance he could have won Mara back someday.

But Mara escaped, and Roddy panicked. He'd returned to the site instead of finding her in the woods. Against all odds, Mara had survived. Now she could point out every lie.

Roddy had tried to protect himself by mailing a bomb fragment to Mara's address—his own residence inside the Oahu Raptor compound was decidedly out of the question—to use as leverage against his employers. Fortunately, Evan had found the souvenir when he'd caught up with Roddy at Mara's.

Roddy's fuckup had become Evan's problem because he was the only logical scapegoat. His history with Mara gave him cause to stalk her for personal reasons. He'd bet the FBI was following that logic already, and his dear old dad would be the first to sell him out.

The truck signaled for the next exit. Was Jeannie stopping for gas? Turning back? It didn't matter what her plan was. If she pulled off the road, it was time for him to make his move.

"Dad, I've got Jeannie in my sights. Give me ten minutes, then I'm on Mara and the US attorney. What do you know about where they are?"

"The car they'd been given was found at the airport. I've got a team interviewing shuttle, bus, and cab drivers now. One thing we know for certain, they didn't fly out of Tucson."

"Call me when you locate them. I've got a loose end to tie up." He tossed the phone onto the passenger seat and exited the interstate, an idea forming for how he could use Jeannie to track his ex-fiancée.

MARA COULDN'T HAVE said what Curt thought she'd said. He planted himself before her and ran a finger over the scars on her hip. "You had smallpox? But you're fine." Her evidence was a dozen fine pockmarks on her body.

"I was vaccinated. All military personnel deployed to Korea are vaccinated." She twisted and showed him a flowerlike pockmark on her creamy shoulder. "So my case was mild, but I knew what it was."

"But how? The bomb was intact."

"One of them was. The other cracked apart when I uncovered it. We'd been warned smallpox can survive for years in an undisturbed environment. Those bombs were buried inside the fuselage of an F-86 Sabre and weren't touched for six decades."

"How did you explain your illness to your captors?"

"The spots were mostly under my clothes. Thanks to the vaccine, I didn't develop a fever. I felt like crap, but that was all." She wrapped the blanket tightly around herself and resumed pacing. "When I got sick, I was grateful I was in an isolated cell. I was very careful not to touch anyone or anything that might spread the virus."

"What about meals? I'm guessing they didn't let you wash your own dishes."

"I was given weak, disposable chopsticks and my kimchi was always served in a disposable bowl—I assume because metal and ceramic could have been used as a weapon—so I didn't have to worry some poor dishwasher would get sick. And never once in my months of captivity did they change my bedding, thank goodness."

She paused in her pacing and met his gaze. "Aside from fearing I'd contaminate an unvaccinated population, I was also terrified I'd be executed on the spot if my illness were discovered. But my interrogators were very formal and didn't touch or come close to me. They didn't even question me every day. I knew I was in the clear once the pox scabs fell off—which happened quickly—again probably thanks to the vaccine."

Jesus Christ. She'd been a prisoner in North Korea and had to hide *smallpox* from her captors? Curt was, quite simply, dumbfounded. And in awe.

"It all makes sense, Curt. The pilot didn't have a mechanical failure. He knew what he carried on that plane. He was headed to P'yŏngyang and chose to crash the plane into a hillside rather than drop weaponized smallpox on a populated area. The average North Korean probably didn't have access to the vaccine in 1952. So many would have died." She stopped pacing and faced him. "He was a hero, in the truest sense of the word. He chose death to protect thousands of people he would never know."

MARA ACHED WITH exhaustion and crawled into the bed while Curt turned off the light. He spoke softly in the darkened room. "Mara, tell me one thing. Even knowing all this, how can you still defend your uncle?"

She'd known this question was coming. "My uncle didn't have anything to do with Roddy driving me away from the site or my contracting smallpox."

"Don't be naïve. It's obvious what happened. Evan and Roddy were there to retrieve the bomb."

She twisted to face him. "You think that's what this is about? Why Evan might be hunting me?"

"You don't?"

She flopped onto her back as a knot formed in her belly. "But they couldn't smuggle a biological weapon out of North Korea. The protocols there were unreal. It's impossible." A thousand anxieties had plagued her detainment in North Korea, but this fear had never occurred to her. Hell, if she'd thought anyone could steal the smallpox bomb, she'd have demanded to talk to the president and secretary of state the moment they were out of North Korean airspace.

"That's why they needed you. Your arrest caused an international incident and JPAC was ejected without following the normal protocols. How much do you want to bet that concealed within the remains returned to the US with the team was one smallpox bomb? A bomb that is now in the hands of Raptor. I'm willing to bet half a million dollars."

"I didn't receive a payoff."

"But someone sure made it look like you did."

"It doesn't make sense. Maybe Evan and Roddy did steal the bomb, but they are just two people. They aren't Raptor. Over the years I've worked with several Raptor operatives. I know them. I can't think of a single reason they'd want a smallpox bomb."

"They're mercenaries. Everything they do is for money. Including trading arms with war criminals." Curt's voice held frustration mixed with exhaustion. "You must know my investigation into your uncle's shady financial dealings led to a suspected arms deal."

"I know you claim he sold arms to a warlord in Darfur. But that's impossible."

"He did it, Mara."

"But you never found any proof."

"No, because he destroyed it. I can't get him for the arms deal, but I can nail him for destroying documents that had been subpoenaed."

She turned away and fluffed her pillow. Was it naïve to still have faith in her uncle? She thought she'd left naïveté behind in North Korea.

Curt's voice broke the tense silence. "Why didn't you tell me about the bomb before?"

She settled her head onto the old, flat pillow, and stared at the ceiling. Mirrored, like any good hourly motel should be. It was too dark to see her unhappy reflection. All that was visible was the light from the alarm clock and the street lamp glow that bled around the curtains.

"As far as I knew, the bombs had been destroyed in place by Evan on a remote North Korean hillside. I didn't know they were in play and was afraid you'd want to somehow use the information that I'd uncovered a biological weapon against Uncle Andrew—which you do—and there is no evidence he had *anything* to do with it. Furthermore, your investigation could expose the fact that the US really did test smallpox bombs on North Korea. Do you realize what the North Korean government would do with that information?"

"It wouldn't be pretty."

"Aside from heightened tensions, they'd order troops to comb the hillsides for more weapons. They'd desecrate every American crash site. Appalling enough they've got nukes, what if they ended up with smallpox as well?"

"Some believe they already have smallpox."

She twisted to face him, barely making out his profile in the dark. "I planned to tell about the bomb. When I got to DC, I was going to tell the secretaries of Homeland Security and State."

"It would have been nice if I'd been on your short list. It's my job to prosecute high crimes, and I know how to keep secrets." His words expressed hurt, while his arms enfolded her.

She pressed her nose against his chest and breathed deeply. "When we met, the one thing I knew about you is that you are prosecuting one of the people I trust most in the world."

"Trust. Present tense." His arms fell away.

She closed her eyes, missing his warmth. He'd made his terms clear. But she'd known her uncle a hell of a lot longer than Curt Dominick. "Yes."

# Chapter Twenty-Two

FINGERS OF LIGHT reached around the edges of the blinds, letting Curt know dawn had arrived in Tucson.

*Tucson.* Day two of jury selection and he was in Tucson, quite literally in bed with the defendant's niece. In sleep, her smooth skin and delicate features didn't hold the weariness and anxiety he'd grown accustomed to seeing on her face. Her soft lips relaxed, and all he wanted to do was gather her against him and explore her mouth with his own.

Hell, he wanted to explore *all* of her with his mouth. He'd never felt such relentless desire. But then, in the past, when he developed emotions that bordered on uncontrollable, he'd moved on. Life was safer that way. He'd have done the same with Mara, except he was stuck with her.

He needed her to testify. She could show a pattern of corruption. He couldn't forget that. And deep down he knew what happened on that North Korean hillside was connected to Raptor, but there was no way to draw the line all the way to Stevens.

Yet.

Another man had died. Mara needed to tell an investigator what she knew about Jeannie and Eric Fuller without mentioning the smallpox bomb. The existence of weaponized smallpox was a top-secret security threat that could cause nationwide panic. For that reason, his suspicions could be divulged only to the head of Homeland Security, the State Department, or the Department of Justice. All three would be notified as soon as Curt could safely do so.

Raptor had strong ties to the military and fingers in the FBI. Aside from Palea and a handful of others, he didn't know who he could trust. Curt wished he could call Bixby, the president's chief of staff, but that number was one of many in his cell phone that had been compromised.

The bed creaked as he sat up to see the digital clock. Last night, he'd called the Arizona US attorney, a woman he knew only by reputation. She'd promised him a car and cash, to be delivered to the Denny's restaurant down the street in an hour. If they hurried, they'd be able to have a decent breakfast before hitting the road.

After quick—and separate—showers for them both, they were seated in a back booth. The waitress had just delivered their food when a man approached their table. "I have your vehicle, Mr. Dominick," he said, sotto voce.

Mara growled with the fierceness of a mama bear protecting her cub. "I'm starving, and this is the first meal since North Korea that wasn't prepared in a microwave or takeout. I'm eating here."

The young attorney had been in the process of offering Mara his hand, but as she was intent on maintaining a death grip on her overloaded plate, he shifted to Curt. "Assistant US Attorney Anthony Palazzolo."

Curt shook his hand and slid over in the booth. "Have a seat."

The man sat and eyed Mara nervously as she made quick work of an omelet and hash browns. "I have some questions for you, Ms. Garrett," he said softly. "About your relationship with Eric Fuller."

"Before we start, Mr. Palazzolo," Curt said, "we need assurance that no one will know your office provided us with assistance. It's imperative."

"I've been instructed to turn over my notes to FBI Agent—" He pulled out a notebook and glance at the page. "Kaha'i Palea, in Honolulu. He, in turn, will pass the information to the local FBI without revealing who conducted the interview."

Curt smiled. "After we reach DC, you can talk to the local agents directly. But since you've brought us a car, no one can know you've helped us until she's inside a safe house in DC."

"Aren't you being a little extreme, sir? It's my understanding that the chief suspect is her ex-boyfriend, who by all accounts was obsessed with her." The man again checked his notebook. "The victim, Eric Fuller, was in a very public fight with the suspect ten months ago. And, according to witness statements, the two men fought over Ms. Garrett. Right now this looks like simple domestic violence."

MARA DROPPED HER fork as the food she'd been savoring turned bitter in her mouth. Curt leaned toward Palazzolo and spoke in a low but menacing tone. "You can believe whatever you want, Mr.

Palazzolo, but your boss assured me she'd conceal the fact her office aided us until after we are safely in DC."

Curt Dominick in protective mode was a sight to behold.

Palazzolo leaned away and looked as though he would slide to the floor given the opportunity. "Absolutely, sir." He cleared his throat and sat upright again. "But it's my job to question her."

Curt's nod was as clipped as his name. "Proceed."

Mara told the assistant US attorney about her broken engagement and the humiliation of realizing Evan had been paid to date her. As she spoke she pushed her food around on her plate, no longer hungry. A sip of cold coffee indicated the interview had taken far too long. "We should hit the road," she said.

Curt nodded. He dropped cash on the table, and Palazzolo led the way out of the restaurant and to a white SUV parked in the corner of the lot. "The SUV is property of the Tucson office." He reached into his breast pocket and pulled out an envelope. "The keys and ten thousand dollars, cash."

Mara startled at the large sum but supposed at this point they needed to be prepared for anything.

"I'll make sure the money and vehicle are returned to your office immediately upon our arrival in DC," Curt said, tucking the envelope into his own breast pocket.

"One last item," Palazzolo said. He pulled a handgun from his pocket. He slid the weapon open in a practiced movement, showing the chamber was empty, then handed over the gun, grip first, before producing a bullet magazine. "I understand you are trained to use a Glock."

Curt nodded and took the clip, tucking it in his pants pocket, while the gun had gone into his jacket.

Palazzolo turned to her. "My boss wanted me to pass on a message to you, Ms. Garrett. Her father fought in World War II. He came home, but many didn't. Her father often wished the MIAs could be found and properly buried, and she wanted me to thank you for the work you do."

After his earlier assessment and dismissive attitude toward the danger she was in, his change in demeanor surprised her. She smiled and tilted her head to see his face, but the morning sun hit her in the eyes. "Thank you, Mr. Palazzolo."

The man ducked his head. "Be safe," he said and left them.

Strangely energized, she plucked the keys from Curt's hand.

"I'm driving first shift." She circled the vehicle to the driver's door. They had a car, money, a weapon, and nothing but open road between here and DC. This was the closest thing to freedom she'd felt in months.

Curt remained on the pavement, staring at her with the strangest look on his face. "Stop dawdling and get in," she said. "Maybe we can make it to Oklahoma City by midnight."

He shook his head as though to clear it and circled the vehicle.

HE WAS LOSING his mind. He had to be.

What was happening to him? One moment he was collecting cash and a gun from an assistant US attorney—a bizarre occurrence all by itself—and the next he'd been ensnared as the morning sun glinted off Mara's blond hair, her blue eyes warmed with pleasure, and that elusive, charming dimple peeked over the horizon of her smile.

He'd spent the entire interview with Palazzolo adding up the facts and trying to decide if the theory Evan pursued her out of jealousy had merit. Only to have her once again take his hardened, suspicious heart and shatter it to dust with a radiant smile.

It wasn't just the smile, it was the deep-seated pride she took in the work she did. He'd met so many frauds in his line of work, men and women who ran charitable foundations not for the cause but for the accolades. Mara was the real deal. Her work meant something to her.

As a man devoted to his profession, he respected that.

How was it possible? How could he be falling for her?

Helpless, hopeless, he wrenched open the door and slid into the passenger seat. Mara put the vehicle in reverse. In his mind, he stopped her by cupping her face between his hands and kissing her. It would be a swift, hot kiss. He'd slide his tongue between her lips, drink in her shocked gasp and warm response. But he couldn't. It was only a possibility in an alternate universe. One in which she wasn't a witness and he wasn't The Shark.

In this reality, she backed out of the space with smooth efficiency, and in minutes they were on the interstate. Curt glanced at his watch, then pulled out the prepaid cell phone and called Aurora, who should be midway through lunch recess. After she answered, he asked, "Did you get the warrant to trace the money in Garrett's account?"

Mara stiffened beside him, but she'd known about this warrant. "Yes. The money was easy to trace—no laundering even attempted."

"Where did the money originate?"

"Dear old Uncle Andrew."

Curt closed his eyes and sucked in a deep breath. *She'd been shocked. She hadn't known about the money.* He repeated these phrases over and over again, hating how much he wanted to believe them. He'd never wanted to believe in anyone before. In his world, everyone was a potential suspect and individuals were ruled out based on evidence. He'd never cared which way the evidence cut, so long as it led to someone he could prosecute.

But today, right now, he didn't want to believe the woman he was risking everything to protect—even his role as lead prosecutor in her uncle's trial—had taken a payoff from his defendant.

He had to look at all the facts, no matter how distasteful. What did she have besides a few dots on her belly to back up her smallpox-bomb story?

"There's more," Aurora said. "Some of the money left her account before we could put a freeze on it."

"How much?"

"Fifty thousand went to Jeannie Fuller's account."

Cold gripped him in the gut. "She's been with me and hasn't had access to her account at all." Had she? He'd showered on the boat and again in the motel. She could have completed a transfer using the cell phone.

"You know how easy it is to set transfers up ahead of time."

"Three months ahead of time?" he asked.

"What's going on?" Mara asked. Her knuckles tightened on the steering wheel again.

He shook his head and shifted in his seat. Into the phone, he said, "Forward the information to the Arizona FBI, all of it."

"Already done." Aurora paused. "Curt, as your co-counsel, I need to know something before we put Garrett on the stand. Are you involved with her?"

He closed his eyes. He'd known she'd ask this. "No." A kiss wasn't a relationship.

"Don't split hairs with me. We don't need a Clinton-like denial to bite us in the ass."

He ground a palm into his forehead, hating everything about this conversation. He'd like to keep something private, hold precious one morsel of the elation he'd experienced when his control had vaporized, replaced with the need to taste her, touch her, and brand himself with her energy. "When she takes the stand, you'll question her, not me."

Aurora sighed. "Be careful. She could be trying to help her uncle by getting you disbarred. Half a million bucks for your disbarment is a small price to pay for a wealthy man facing prison."

He'd only be disbarred if he slept with her. Extenuating circumstances made the kiss explicable, even excusable. But still, he felt like a nineteen-year-old boy with his hands in the pants of a seventeen-year-old piece of jailbait. On the surface, harmless and consensual, but legally, a big fucking mistake.

## CHAPTER TWENTY-THREE

A HUNDRED MILES outside Tucson, they stopped at a discount department store for snacks, clothing, a car cell phone charger, and more minutes for the phone. In and out of the store in record time, Mara had purchased comfy yoga pants and T-shirts for the drive—the sum total of her belongings since the jet had taken off with her duffle bag inside.

She'd fared better than Curt, though; his laptop and case files would reach DC long before he would. He spent hours on the phone, consulting with his co-counsel when she was on break from jury selection, and the rest of the time, it sounded like he spoke to another assistant US attorney who was managing the office in his absence.

If the one-sided conversation she heard was any indication, the man had a stunning workload. How on earth had he found the time to build a case against her uncle?

Driving felt futile, each mile only a tiny step closer to their eventual goal. Curt needed to get to the trial, and she… What was she heading towards?

She was supposed to testify and have a conversation with a few of the president's top security people. But then what? Would she be set adrift, or would she be protected?

Why was Evan hunting her? Was it possible that he was—as he'd always claimed—devastated by her accusations and rejection and had gone off the deep end? Was there any merit to the jilted-lover scenario?

She'd always known his feelings had been real. She'd never have fallen for him if there hadn't been genuine emotion—a true relationship—between them. But she'd been disgusted by the catalyst for that relationship—the urging of his father to seduce her—and appalled by the payoffs he'd gladly taken for succeeding.

He'd assaulted her when she'd dumped him. That alone argued for domestic violence. But Assistant US Attorney Palazzolo hadn't known about the smallpox bomb, and his accusations fell flat when that was taken into consideration.

Curt was silent in the passenger seat, a rare moment when he wasn't managing someone two thousand miles away, so she asked the question that bugged her most. "What on earth would Raptor *do* with a smallpox bomb?"

"A: reverse engineer it and make more. B: use it to stir up fear. C: sell copies to the highest bidder. Or D: all of the above."

Cold fear invaded her belly. Since it hadn't occurred to her that the bomb could have left North Korea, the harm Raptor could do with it hadn't penetrated. "What do you mean, stir up fear?"

"Americans will spend a lot of money on the military when they're afraid. Between Raptor's military training grounds and the national and international private security side of the business, they'd make a killing off a good old blame-it-on-terrorists patriotism-inducing scare."

"How long do you think it would take to reverse engineer a smallpox bomb? They've had two months already."

"I don't know." The side of his fist hit his knee. "And I have no clue who to trust. People could be infected already. How many days after exposure before you showed the first symptoms?"

"Eleven days." She paused. "Isn't there someone we can call?"

"Just saying the word smallpox on a cell phone can get the conversation flagged. Homeland Security has bots that scan the airwaves. If Raptor has hooked into their system, they could use that to get a lock on our location."

"What about the friend you called to get us the Talon & Drake jet, Lee Scott? Isn't he a technology security guy? Can he encrypt our calls?"

Curt's body went rigid. "Lee?" He paused, then said, "Mara, that's brilliant. I've been hoping for a lead on which Raptor facility is the most likely to have the technology to replicate the bomb. Lee can research that for us."

She smiled, knowing in her gut they were on the right track, but all the while wondering what this meant for her uncle. Uncle Andrew wasn't greedy. Human lives weren't worth less than government contracts to him. No. This had to be the brainchild of Evan and his vulture of a father.

IT TOOK LEE a few hours to set up the encryption on the prepaid cell phone. The only problem was the security was only effective for calls between equally secured numbers. Meaning calls to Lee were safe, but a call to the president's chief of staff, who utilized different security, was out.

Curt told Lee about Raptor and the smallpox bomb.

"Have you listened to the news today?" Lee asked, his voice full of alarm.

"No."

"A congresswoman from Virginia proposed a new bill that would change the definition of the types of operations that can be conducted by private security companies. They would have the ability to act with military force but without government oversight. It may even redefine them as domestic first responders."

"Does it stand a chance in hell?" Curt asked.

"There is support. Private military and security is a lot cheaper and everyone is looking for ways to cut the federal budget. But it's by no means an easy sell. Unless of course, we have an act of terrorism on American soil to scare the hell out of everyone."

Curt swore. "Lee, I want to know every piece of land that son of a bitch Robert Beck owns—not just the parcels owned by Raptor. But only search *public* databases." He didn't need any illegal hacking to mar this investigation. Given the nature of mercenary work and the top-secret contracts Raptor already held, it was going to be damn hard to convince a judge to give him a search warrant.

"I'll also search under Evan Beck. Do you want a search on Andrew Stevens as well?"

Curt glanced sideways at the woman driving the car. Her faith in her uncle remained strong, which pissed him off no end. She was a smart woman, and she was being pigheaded. "No need. I have that information already. Call me if you find anything."

BY TWO IN the morning Central Time, they'd put Oklahoma City far behind them. With at least eighteen hours of driving time remaining, there was no way they'd reach the trial before jury selection and opening arguments were completed the following day.

They'd taken turns napping while the other drove, although Mara had only pretended to sleep. It was hard to let her guard down after months in captivity. But even so, she felt strangely wired, wide-awake and yet hypnotized by the monotonous flashes of reflective lane-marker bumps. The road went on forever into the darkness, yet it felt as if the inside of the SUV was all that really existed. They were the only two people in the world.

"Talk to me, Mara. I'm tired."

She twisted in her seat and faced him. "What do you want to talk about?"

"JPAC. Deployments. Your uncle's surprise visits to Vietnam, the Philippines, and Egypt."

"Subtle, Dominick."

"I'm Dominick now?"

"It's better than calling you The Shark."

He cut her a glance with an indignant smile. "You call me The Shark one more time and I will spank you."

"Kinky. I'm not so much into spanking, but I suppose you could convince me."

Curt shifted in the driver's seat, and she hoped she'd caused a painful tightening of his slacks at the crotch. His voice came out husky. "We can negotiate that when the trial is over."

He wanted to fool around with her after the trial? It was hard to believe they could get involved, but for the first time since this crazy journey started, she could imagine…something. "Negotiate, or plea bargain?" she asked.

He grinned. "Depends on what you have in mind."

"Why don't we just go tit for tat?"

"As long as you provide the ti—"

She held up a hand to stop him. He was obviously feeling plucky at this hour. "Funny, but I'm talking about now. Tell me why Palea asked questions about my mail, and I'll tell you about my uncle and JPAC."

"Palea found an envelope. Someone mailed something to you from South Korea the day after you were arrested."

"What do you think it was?"

"It's tit time. Tell me about your uncle's visit to Vietnam."

"He was still vice president then and had about six months left in office."

"Tell me something I don't know."

"He spent more time with Evan than he did with me. Tat. Why would anyone mail something to my address from South Korea?"

"I think Roddy screwed up and hoped to save himself. Maybe he sent the original pages from your field notebook, before Jeannie changed it. Proof things weren't kosher."

She frowned. "Do you think Roddy was supposed to kill me

that day?"

Curt squeezed her knee. "I don't know. If you'd disappeared, how would the North Korean government have reacted? Would they have let JPAC leave or detained everyone? I think Roddy needed to get you to the Joint Security Area and raise a fuss about your safety. JPAC would probably have been ejected—which would have allowed Evan to smuggle out the bomb."

The green glow of the dashboard lights revealed the tightness of Curt's mouth. "Unfortunately, we still can't prove Raptor is behind anything. My actions, my evidence, are bound by law. Theirs are not."

"They blew up a jet."

"If we can't prove Evan was following orders, Raptor will get away with it."

The acid in her stomach churned. "They're going to blame it all on Evan—and on me, for dating him."

"Your turn. Tell me about the time your uncle visited you in Egypt."

"Why?" Exasperation and frustration made her voice harsh. "He was no longer vice president when he came to Egypt! What does it matter?"

"Because the arms deal with the Sudanese warlord—a Janjaweed militia leader and a wanted war criminal—took place in Egypt. Mara, it happened right under your nose."

The air inside the car turned thick, nearly solid, too concrete to inhale, let alone pass through constricted lungs. The knot that had been sitting in her belly for weeks suddenly melted into a pool of boiling acid and pulsed up her esophagus. He spoke with such conviction, such assurance. And she knew him well enough by now to know there had to be some kernel of truth, or he wouldn't be so certain. And yet, she *knew* her uncle wasn't the corrupt man Curt believed him to be. "No. Fucking. Way."

"He did, Mara."

"Vice presidents smile prettily with elementary school children and attack the opposition party with pit-bull tenacity. They don't make arms deals."

"He wasn't VP when he conducted the deal."

"Is that why you want me to testify? I promise you, Curt, I don't know a damn thing. I've never met anyone from Darfur or even Sudan. Hell, I don't even know what Janja-whatever means."

"Janjaweed. Darfur isn't an ethnic or religious conflict—it's nomadic tribes versus sedentary. Janjaweed is a blanket term to describe the nomadic Arab gunmen who see no problem with killing entire villages so they can take their water and grazing land."

"I know what war criminals do. Before I worked for JPAC, I worked in Bosnia for the International Commission for Missing Persons. I excavated mass graves—sites where entire villages had been lined up and shot in the name of ethnic cleansing. I recovered the remains of children and babies, some still locked in their mother's arms. My uncle would *never* cut a deal with someone who would do that."

"He did, Mara."

"Well, if that's why you want me to testify, you've wasted a trip to North Korea. I can't help you."

He shot her a frustrated look. "Don't be insulting. I didn't go to North Korea because I want you to testify."

She had to admit, that was unfair of her. He'd been nothing but heroic.

"And if I thought you could testify about the arms deal, I'd have your uncle on charges a lot worse than obstruction of justice and influence peddling."

"Then why am I testifying?"

"You're a character witness."

Incredulous, she snickered. "I'm a *character* witness? You mean I get to tell everyone that after my father, Uncle Andrew is the best, most wonderful man I've ever known? Well, hell, Curt, why didn't you tell me that in the first place? I'm in."

"No, Mara. You're not going to tell everyone what a paragon he is. You're going to tell the jury what he did for you."

"What the hell are you talking about?"

"I'm talking about how Andrew Stevens used his power and influence to get you into Stanford and even snagged you a full scholarship you didn't deserve."

# Chapter Twenty-Four

Evan's frustration boiled over. "I've got a plan, Dad. Either way, she'll come to us."

"I'm sick of waiting. I think you've got a soft spot for the girl."

Evan gritted his teeth. "Mara's a job, Dad. I swear. I forgot to adjust the scope because the damn thing is too fucking complicated and I didn't have much time. When I took the shot, her head was in the crosshairs." So maybe he did feel a bite of pain when he pulled the trigger. That was his own business. He hadn't been *trying* to fail. Lord knows he knew the consequences, and given the choice between his life and Mara's, he'd choose himself every time.

"If Mara has a chance to breathe one fucking word about smallpox to the wrong person, we're fucked. The plan was an anonymous attack at the Macy's parade. But if there is any chance Mara knows what she saw in North Korea, al Qaeda won't be blamed, we will."

"She couldn't possibly know," he repeated for the hundredth time. "She saw a bomb but didn't know what it was." Even as he said the words, he rubbed the scars on his thigh. His father didn't know it was a vaccine-resistant strain, didn't know Evan had been sick, because Evan had quarantined himself during the contagious period and contained the damage.

Mara couldn't know about the biological weapon, because if she'd gotten sick, there was no way North Korea would have let her go. But even so, she could pinpoint Roddy as the man who'd led her off-site. So Roddy had been taken care of. And Jeannie, with her second thoughts on selling out, she was a liability too. Then her brother had admitted to knowing about the bomb. Jeannie really should have kept her mouth shut.

"At this point, they'll blame me as her crazy ex anyway. I'll take her out, then start over, with a new name."

"If you succeed, you'll get a new name," Robert Beck said. "If you fail, you're on your own."

ALARMED BY THE greenish tinge to Mara's features, Curt parked on the deep shoulder a safe distance from the quiet interstate. As soon as the car stopped, she flung open the door and tumbled out into the chilly, star-filled Oklahoma night.

He braced, almost expecting her to run. But they were a hundred miles from nowhere. Tension dissipated when, a few feet from the SUV, she stopped and hunched over with her hands on her knees.

He jumped out and circled the vehicle. "Are you going to be okay?" he asked. From the look of her, it was a stupid question.

She shot him a glare over her shoulder. "You're wrong. Uncle Andrew didn't—"

He took a step closer. "From your reaction, I'm guessing you didn't know—but you must have suspected."

"The admissions department took pity on me! My dad had just died—"

"He'd died two years before, and you fell apart. Your grades tanked. All that is understandable. But no. Stanford doesn't grant admission or full scholarships based on sympathy."

"There was an interview—I flew out and explained my grades and why I'd bombed the SAT exam."

"I'm sure you were very convincing. But the interview was a formality—and a fraud. Your admission was decided when your uncle secured government funding for a university study and pushed through a higher education bill with two-million in earmarks for Stanford. Your four years as an undergrad and two years in the master's program cost taxpayers over two million dollars. But it didn't cost you a dime."

"Before my dad died, I was a great student. And my last six months of high school, I got my shit together. I *earned* my spot at Stanford."

He'd never felt like such a shit revealing corruption in his life. This truth hurt her in ways he hadn't anticipated, but it was too late to turn back now. "No, Mara. I'm sure you would have earned it, if your dad hadn't died, but the truth is, your efforts were too little, too late. Based on Stanford's admissions criteria at the time, there is no way you should have been accepted, let alone received a free ride." He paused. "It's called influence peddling, and your uncle was very, very good at it."

"Are you saying I'm in trouble? Am I facing charges?"

"No. Even if I wanted to—and I don't—I couldn't charge you. Or your uncle, for that matter. The crime ended when you finished grad school and stopped receiving the scholarship, which was over five years ago, so the statute of limitations has passed."

She slid down the side of the SUV and rested her head against the lower door panel. "If he's not being charged with this, what do you want from me?"

"You can show a pattern of corruption."

"I didn't know. And I don't believe it."

Why did he feel a stab of guilt at the pain in her voice? This was his job. It was what he did best. "You don't have to believe it. You only have to answer questions truthfully."

"Can I plead the fifth?"

"No." He slid down beside her. Gravel bit into his butt, and he shivered in the chill air. "You've been subpoenaed, and thanks to the statute of limitations, I can't use anything you say against you. Fifth amendment doesn't apply."

She swiped at her cheek. "I was a wreck when my dad died." She turned to him. "He was killed in a commuter plane crash. I woke up one day, and he was just…gone."

Curt put his arm around her, but she leaned away from him, rejecting the feeble comfort he offered. Her reaction stung. He dropped his arm and scooted sideways, a sharp rock added injury to the insult.

"I was depressed—in a dark, terrible place. When I finally got my shit together, it was because Uncle Andrew sat me down and gave me something to work toward. He said it wasn't too late for me to get into a good school." She swiped at another tear. "He believed in me. He believed I had it in me to pull out of the darkness, to take control of my life. He saved me."

"*You* saved you. He just gave you a reason. Who suggested Stanford, you, or him?"

"California sounded so glamorous. And so wonderfully far away from the mess I'd made of my life in Michigan."

"That's not what I asked."

Her voice dropped. "Honestly, I'm not sure, but I think it was Uncle Andrew. My grades were awful. But I busted my ass—worked with tutors in math and science. The extra work couldn't change my grades, but it ensured I was ready for the college-level coursework. I was told by the admissions board they'd reviewed work I'd done and had decided to make an exception for me."

Curt sighed and swept aside the pebble that was digging into his tailbone. "You worked hard at Stanford. You earned your degrees, and no one can take that from you. But you didn't get there on your own merit. Your uncle made it happen. And what he did was illegal."

She took a deep breath but said nothing.

Curt knew her family couldn't afford Stanford. Stevens hadn't been a wealthy politician. He couldn't have made a legal donation to secure her acceptance and he sure as hell couldn't afford the steep tuition. Andrew Stevens didn't come into money until later, after he left politics and joined Raptor.

He plucked the offending pebble from the ground and tossed it into the darkness beyond the roadside shoulder. "Deep down, you must have known."

She picked up a pebble and weighed it in her hand before following his lead and hurling it into the darkness. "I was eighteen, self-absorbed, and recovering from a debilitating depression. No. I didn't know." She chucked another rock. "You're supposed to be my white knight, but instead you're telling me one of the things I've done that I'm proudest of is tainted."

"Like your uncle, I'm not what you've made me out to be." He dragged his fingers through his hair. "Christ, is there a man in your life you *haven't* idealized?"

She crossed her arms. "Evan comes to mind."

"Before you found out what a scumbag he is, I bet you thought he hung the moon."

She flinched and looked down.

Curt stood. "Look, I know you lost your dad when you were young, and that led to some…issues…but you can't continue idolizing every man you meet. Most men are pricks. Present company included."

She glanced up at him. Her eyes glistened in the moonlight. "I only idolize the ones who fly halfway around the world to save me from a firing squad."

He took her hand and pulled her to her feet. "I don't deserve it." He pulled her into his arms and sighed, hating what he had to tell her next. "You should know, the money in your account came from your uncle."

Her beautiful eyes widened in shock. "Uncle Andrew deposited a half-million dollars in my bank account? Why would he do that?"

"I was hoping you could tell me."

"I haven't seen or spoken with him in months."

"Aurora thinks he paid you to get me disbarred."

Her gaze hardened, and she stiffened in his arms. "Screw you," she said, trying to wriggle from his grasp. "I was horrified when I learned my boyfriend had been paid to seduce me. I would never—"

"I didn't say I agreed with her. But you should know, your account is frozen pending investigation. If nothing comes up, then there may not be any legal reason you can't keep the money."

"I wouldn't keep it. I highly doubt Uncle Andrew has that much money to spare. His legal bills must be astronomical."

He'd been wavering between sympathy and frustration, but the concern in her voice for her scumbag uncle pushed him over the tipping point. "I don't get it. I don't understand how you can cling to belief in your uncle in spite of all the evidence against him." He backed her up against the SUV until they were nose to nose. "He's chief of operations of Raptor, and Raptor operatives are trying to *kill* you. They killed Roddy, shot at you, and killed Eric Fuller. I've just explained to you how he used his power and influence to buy your way into Stanford. I've pointed out the payoff he got from Raptor and how he sold weapons to a war criminal. He's been using you and JPAC for years for dirty deals. And yet you're concerned Andrew Stevens can't afford to plant money in your account—money that makes you look like an accomplice?"

She clamped her jaw shut and glared at him. "You haven't proven a damn thing. You've made a lot of broad accusations, but where is the body of evidence? Where is the smoking gun? If you could prove the arms deal, he'd have been indicted for it."

"You found a smallpox bomb and then Roddy kidnapped you in North Korea. Do you really think that was a coincidence?" His voice rose as his anger reached new levels.

"And how the hell does that have anything to do with my uncle? That's Raptor, through and through."

"Your uncle works for Raptor! He owns one-fifth of the company!"

"So? That's not a controlling interest. Sounds to me like Robert Beck is your real problem. Did you decide to go after my uncle because he was more famous than Beck? Are you so ambitious you don't care if the defendant is guilty so long as he's a big name?"

Her words sent ice down his spine. That she, of all people, could believe such a thing cut him to the core.

"No, Mara. I went after your uncle and not Robert Beck because I can prove—beyond a shadow of a doubt—your uncle destroyed files that had been subpoenaed. I've got him on the cover-up, and he was stupid for not rolling on Robert Beck. Because Beck has been my primary target all along."

MARA WRAPPED HER arms around her middle and shivered. "Can we hit the road again?"

Curt nodded, then reached to straighten a tie he wasn't wearing. "I'm going to miss tomorrow anyway. Let's find a motel. Get some decent sleep."

"But we need to get back. The smallpox bomb—"

"Lee's finding out what he can, and getting five or six hours of sleep won't make much difference but will make for safer driving tomorrow."

Her bones, or maybe it was her soul, ached as she climbed into the passenger seat. The interior heat hit her chilled skin and enveloped her in a cocooning warmth.

She was in a daze, reeling from all that Curt had told her. Had her uncle really used legislative bribes to get Stanford to admit her?

Why hadn't she ever wondered about the miraculous scholarship? She'd just accepted it as her due. Her due. She was a self-pitying, self-absorbed teen who thought no one had ever had to deal with a trauma as bad as hers.

She'd been embarrassed, even ashamed, over the years as she healed, grew, and came to her senses. But none of that felt nearly like the shame she felt now.

Had she taken a scholarship from a more needy student? Stolen a spot in her class from someone who'd worked harder and deserved it more?

Or was Curt wrong? Maybe her essay and interview really had been brilliant, had proven her drive and brains and garnered her not only acceptance and a scholarship but also a plum job in the library, where she could study during her shift and was rarely bothered by students.

*Oh shit.* Her Stanford-educated brain had to admit that when put that way, the math didn't add up.

They reached an exit, and Curt left the interstate without comment. She pulled her knees to her chest as he passed two big-name motel chains to the center of the rural community. "I doubt they have by-the-hour motels here. We need a mom-and-pop place," he said.

A few minutes later, he found a tiny, eight-room motel perched at the edge of the main road. The neon vacancy sign glowed like a beacon and looked like it dated to the 1950s—which had to be when the motel was built.

Together they approached the night window. He hit the buzzer. Was it less than twenty-four hours ago they'd done the same thing in Tucson? But then she'd been all over him. She'd wanted him, wanted to be his lover, even if only for an hour in a sleazy motel.

Now sex was the furthest thing from her mind.

Lights came on in the room beyond the window, and a boy—he couldn't be more than twelve—appeared. He yawned and slid a piece of paper through a hole in the windowpane. "We've only got one room left." His eyes drifted from Curt to Mara. "A single. That okay?" The question was cursory—the boy went through the motions of his job with the sleepy movements of an often-repeated task.

"Fine," Curt said. "Cash okay?"

The boy nodded. "Just fill out the card and give your license plate. Fifty for the night."

Curt slid a fifty-dollar bill through the window, and the boy passed him the key on a brown, diamond-shaped plastic keychain, the kind she remembered from her childhood, with the number eight printed on it. "Eight is on the end. Checkout is at noon."

"Thanks," Curt said and took Mara's hand, sliding his fingers between hers.

What was his game? When was Curt the prosecutor and when was he a man?

She didn't really need to ask that question. With the exception of a few minutes in Tucson, he was *always* a prosecutor.

The brass number eight was attached to the door with a loose center screw. The number lay on its side, defeated, or maybe the room represented infinity. She hoped to see endless possibilities beyond the solid wood portal, but when the door swung inside on creaky hinges, all she found was a motel room.

Old but clean, with a table, two chairs, a nightstand, and a bed. The full-size mattress suddenly looked even smaller than the V-berth bunk they'd shared…how many days ago? Days and crossed time zones made no sense anymore. Now she tracked the passing of time in miles.

And revelations.

She dropped the plastic bag filled with clothes purchased somewhere in Texas on the table and flopped onto the bed.

"Sorry there's only the one bed," Curt said as he unbuttoned his shirt. "But I'm not sleeping on the floor."

Mara was exhausted and emotionally wrung out, but the last thing she expected to feel was a hint of anticipation as he peeled off his shirt. Her toes curled as each button revealed another patch of firm muscle. It was criminal how sexy this man was and shameful how titillated she was under the circumstances.

He caught her gaze. His eyes darkened, nostrils flared, and his hands slowed.

The air thickened. She took a deep breath, forcing oxygen into her lungs. "I'm so tired, I don't care," she lied, then darted into the tiny bathroom and splashed cold water on her face.

Her heart beat rapidly as she fought urges she could not, would not, give in to. After minutes of deep breathing, she found her composure and left the safety of the bathroom.

Curt was stretched out on the bed, all lights but the dim nightstand bulb extinguished. He rose and passed her, toothbrush in hand. She slid under the covers on the far side of the bed, presenting her back to the now empty room. A few minutes later, he joined her. The nightstand light went out with a click, and he slid under the covers, the old bed drooping under his greater weight.

She slid toward him. Really, it was gravity's fault.

She didn't turn, didn't acknowledge the man beside her. From his breathing, she could tell he was battling the same preposterous desires.

Minutes passed. The ticking of the old clock did nothing to ease the tension. Instead the sound reminded her of the passing of time, and suddenly she felt like she was hurtling toward DC.

She'd been telling herself she'd be safe in DC, but now she questioned that assumption. The fear Robert Beck would inflict smallpox on an unsuspecting community merely for financial gain made her pain at Curt's assertion she hadn't really earned her spot at Stanford seem selfish and petty.

These thoughts twisted in her mind, and her anxiety intensified. It didn't help that the blankets were thin and the night cold.

She turned to face the man who had saved her life and torn her world apart. The neon motel sign glowed behind the closed curtain, allowing enough light to discern his open eyes. "Go to sleep, Mara."

"I'm cold."

He let out a sigh and pulled her against him. She twisted so her back spooned against his front. Warmth seeped from his body to hers. His breath caressed her neck as his arms held her in a tight grip, and heat spread from her scalp to her feet. Curt's arms represented safety. Something she'd been short on for far too long.

# Chapter Twenty-Five

MARA WOKE WITH a jolt. Sunlight streamed through the thin curtain. A glance at the clock revealed she'd slept for six hours. The bed next to her was empty, but the sound of the shower told her Curt hadn't abandoned her in this remote Oklahoma town.

The direction of her thoughts startled her. She had no reason to believe he would abandon her like her team had, but what would happen after she testified? Would she face the legal equivalent of wham, bam, thank you, ma'am? Her government would no longer need her, but what about Curt? Had he meant his flirtatious joke yesterday?

How would she feel about him if he succeeded in sending Uncle Andrew to prison?

The shower stopped. A quick glance around the room showed he'd taken all his belongings—including their cash, cell phone, and car keys, into the bathroom with him.

He didn't trust her.

But had she ever given him reason to?

A minute later, the door opened and he appeared, wearing a towel around his hips and shaving cream on his face. Her heart gave a lurch at the casual intimacy. At some point on this ridiculous journey, the attraction had transformed from simple lust to something deeper.

No. She was just following her usual pattern—as he'd so deftly pointed out last night—and was idolizing him. There was nothing more to it than that. She cleared her throat. "I remembered something. About Egypt."

He took a startled step forward, and the towel around his hips slipped an inch. "What?"

Did he have to have such amazing abs? She lifted her gaze, focused on the white cream on his jaw, and tried not to think about how good it would feel to have his hard body against hers. "Because he was no longer VP when my uncle came to Egypt, there wasn't a press corps. No photographers. No fanfare."

Curt nodded. "I knew that."

"The photos, the ones that ended up on the AP wire, were taken with my camera."

"I knew that too."

"That evening, after the official photo op, we had dinner in the local village. It was a community affair—the village elders, a gift exchange. The usual. I don't speak the language and, having been through a number of those, was bored. But I had my camera with me. So I took pictures. Lots of them."

His hazel eyes widened. He took a step toward her, then stopped and shook his head. "Who attended the dinner?"

"Uncle Andrew, his Secret Service detail, Robert Beck, Evan, Roddy, Jeannie, the rest of the JPAC team, a few dozen villagers."

"He still had Secret Service protection?"

"Former vice presidents may maintain protection for six months." She frowned, feeling certain he was asking questions he knew the answers to. Again.

"How many agents were there?"

"Is this a real question, or a test?"

"Real," he said.

She tried to remember. One agent, handsome, dedicated, and competent, had always caught her eye. Had he been there? No. None of the regulars had been present. "I'm not sure, but I think there were only two."

"And you have pictures of all of this?"

"Yes."

"Of your uncle at a dinner with locals. In Egypt."

"Yes. Dozens of them." She could tell the idea excited him.

"Where are they?"

"The photos are on my computer."

The flash of glee in his eyes disappeared so quickly she could almost believe she'd imagined it. He pivoted into the bathroom.

"I don't think you'll find anything, but I thought you should know."

He applied the razor to his cheeks. "It's worth a try. I'll call Palea."

Done shaving, he leaned over the faucet and splashed water on his cheeks. The motion made the towel slip again, which he caught, just in time. Holding the towel up with one hand, he grabbed a washcloth and wiped his face dry.

Her belly churned even as she watched Curt with avid interest. If her uncle hadn't done anything wrong, then she hadn't just betrayed him to impress Curt. If her uncle was truly innocent, then he had nothing to fear from random snapshots.

Maybe now, when Curt was pleased with her, was the time to tell him about tossing his name out as a potential envoy when her interrogator kept insisting no one short of a sitting cabinet member—preferably the secretary of state—would do.

They'd wanted someone with power, with clout, and with the ear of the president. Not someone formerly powerful. Not an ambassador or a humanitarian. They'd wanted a representative of the president.

The demands were impossible, and she'd countered with Curt's name as merely another avenue to pursue. The *TIME* issue must have come out within days of her offhand suggestion, elevating Curt's visibility and upping his appeal.

But she'd known, even then, even when she never thought they'd choose him, that his selection would mess with her uncle's prosecution.

No. Now wasn't the time. That revelation could happen when they parted ways. Or never.

She took a deep breath. "What comes next? Breakfast, then drive to DC?"

"Palea wants you to text Jeannie. He thinks she might answer you."

She jumped to her feet. "You're just telling me this now?"

"I talked to him right before I got in the shower. You were sound asleep. We'll figure out what you should say on the road."

Anxiety twisted her belly. She was worried and heartsick for Jeannie. Leaning against the open bathroom door, she met his gaze in the mirror. "Do you think she knows about Eric?"

"I don't know. But Palea thinks she's alive."

Water droplets speckled the smooth skin of Curt's muscular back. Slowly, she raised a hand. With gazes locked in the mirror, he said nothing as she traced a pattern on his skin, connecting the dots. His mouth tightened, but he didn't stop her. Emboldened, she stepped closer. With her hand flat against the warm skin of his shoulder, she leaned against him and pressed her cheek against his spine, then closed her eyes and breathed in the clean scent of soap, shampoo, and skin.

She felt the rise of his back and heard the accompanying deep, guttural breath. Slowly, he twisted, and she leaned back, expecting him to step away. But his arms surrounded her, halting her retreat.

She snuggled against his chest.

His mouth pressed against her hair. "You'll be protected in DC. We've got safe houses there and FBI agents I know and trust."

"I'll be a prisoner. Again."

He tilted her face up and cupped her cheeks in his palms. She thought he was going to kiss her, but at the last moment, his lips landed on the healing cut on her forehead.

The words she wanted to say clogged in her throat. Making love with him would get him disbarred, and his work was his life. She needed to stop wanting the impossible.

With regret, she stepped back and pulled the door closed as she left the bathroom. "Hurry up," she said through the panel. "Just once I want to eat a decent breakfast without being in a rush."

CURT TOOK THE first driving shift of the day and chuckled when Mara vehemently expressed her disappointment in his choice of breakfast—a fast-food restaurant with a drive-through window.

"All I've eaten since I met you is junk! I feel fat and bloated and want to go for a run."

"You could stand to gain a few pounds," he said, noting that she did look like she'd gained weight since Monday in North Korea. Her cheeks held a healthier glow, and the fatty food they'd subsisted on had more bulk than the fare she'd been given in North Korea.

"Yeah, but I don't need greasy-food pounds. When we get to DC, I'm going to eat nothing but fresh salad for days…" She let out a soft sigh. "I had hardly any produce in North Korea. The sad part is, I probably ate better than the average citizen."

"I'll take you to my favorite Italian—" He stopped, realizing he'd been about to make a promise he could not fulfill. When they got to DC, this would end. She would be placed in a safe house until it was time for her to testify, and he would convict her uncle.

She brushed crumbs off her lap and tucked away the empty food bags, ignoring his aborted offer. From the center console she plucked the brand new prepaid cell phone they'd picked up before they'd purchased breakfast. "Okay. Time to text Jeannie. I need to say something so she knows it's me." She paused, staring at the phone. "How about 'Jeannie, you changed my field notes in NK.

Please call me. I can help you.'"

"Sounds good. Send it."

"Is the FBI hoping to trace Jeannie through her response to me?"

"They tried to get a lock on her number yesterday. Her phone is off. Right now the goal is information, to confirm she's alive and to convince her to head to the nearest FBI office."

Mara quickly typed out the message and hit Send. He wished he could check the text, but he needed to watch the road. Besides, he trusted her. Didn't he?

After everything she'd been through, the jury was going to love her. Hell, they might even forgive her uncle for the Stanford influence peddling, because it had helped her when she was young and shattered.

Even Curt was considering forgiving the son of a bitch for that one.

He glanced at his watch. They probably *already* loved her. If the selection process had gone smoothly, the jury had been selected and opening arguments would commence after the lunch recess, and he still had a thousand miles left on this nine-thousand, five-hundred-mile journey from hell.

In the seat next to him, Mara gripped the phone as if her life depended on it.

"Turn off the phone and pull out the battery. We'll check at random intervals for a response."

She sighed heavily. "I'm terrified something has happened to her."

"Save your sympathy for someone who deserves it. She took a bribe and sold you out."

"Her brother is dead."

"And it's her fault he was even involved."

"Everything is black-and-white with you, isn't it?"

"When it comes to prosecuting, guilt is guilt."

"But you plea bargain."

"Not all crimes are created equal. A shoplifter doesn't deserve the same penalty as an abusive husband. And a shoplifter who can help me convict the wife abuser can cut a deal."

"But you don't handle those kinds of cases."

"I can't. I oversee three hundred and fifty assistant US attorneys. I rarely try cases at all anymore."

She shot him a speculative look. "You said the courtroom was your happy place, and yet you've made no secret of the fact you want to be the next attorney general. Why do you want a job that removes you from the courtroom?"

He clamped his jaw shut and focused on the road.

"Oh no you don't, Dominick. You know all my secrets. Time to spill yours."

"I'm not the one under investigation here."

"So it's tit for tat."

"That game ended last night." He tightened his grip on the steering wheel. "It's complicated."

"You don't let anyone inside, do you?"

He cut a glance sideways. "Other women have aired that complaint, but you're the first one I haven't slept with first."

"You're probably a crappy boyfriend."

"The worst. I'm neglectful and obsessed with my work."

She laughed. "Don't put that in your eHarmony profile."

"I'm not looking, Mara. I like my life fine the way it is."

"God. You probably get great play from that line—the ultimate challenge. You're the George Clooney of the legal profession."

He laughed. "I don't suffer for lack of attention, but it's not a line. I'm always upfront."

"I shudder to think of how many women have fallen at your feet."

He gave in to dangerous curiosity and asked, "Are you one of them?"

"Not anymore. I've sworn off superhero lawyers. They don't put out. A woman has needs."

He laughed again. She ought to come with a warning label. He'd nearly jumped in the sack with her in a sleazy motel in Phoenix, and honestly could have made the same mistake in Oklahoma.

Before he'd boarded the jet in DC to retrieve her, he'd arrogantly believed he understood her. But he'd been utterly and completely wrong. Whether she was marching out to face a firing squad, diving into the ocean to wash rivers of blood from her skin, or revealing she'd been ill with smallpox, she rose to every challenge in a way he'd never imagined the Mara Garrett he'd read about could.

Every moment they were together made him more determined to figure her out, to reconcile the woman she was with the woman he'd believed her to be. But that was a hazardous road, filled with perils he'd sworn off years ago.

"If you won't tell me why you want to be attorney general, I'm going to guess."

"Let it go, Mara."

"No way. You've given me something to puzzle over besides Jeannie. Let's see… You are the great-grandson of a former US attorney general who died in disgrace and ruin after he was caught in a sex scandal with a ferret, and your lifelong goal is to restore the family name."

He snorted. "Um, no."

"How many miles do we have left? A thousand? I wonder how many guesses I could come up with over the course of a thousand miles? I bet one would come close. How about this, you had a dog when you were twelve—"

Oh Lord, she really was going to keep guessing, needling him until he divulged his past.

"—and his name was General, and he—"

He broke. "I was arrested when I was sixteen."

She gasped, and her jaw snapped closed.

He noted the upcoming mile marker and wondered how far they'd drive in blissful silence.

She lifted her feet from the floor and twisted sideways in the seat. "No. Way. *You?* Oh my. Nope. I don't think I would have guessed that."

He frowned. Not even a tenth of a mile.

"So. What happened?"

He shouldn't have said anything. She'd have tired of guessing after an hour or two.

"C'mon. Spill. You don't get to drop a bombshell like that, then clam up."

She was either the world's greatest interrogator, or she'd done more damage to his patience than he'd guessed. He'd like to tell himself it was the former but knew it was the latter.

"I was in a fight. At school." He glanced sideways at her, taking in her bare feet propped on the seat, followed the line of her delicate ankles to the full breasts pressed against her knees, and upward to those mischievous blue eyes. A perfect package he wanted to possess but couldn't, and a reminder of the pain of being sixteen and in love. "Over a girl."

She raised a pale blond eyebrow.

"The guy pulled a knife on me." He returned his focus to the road ahead. "I, um, won. He went to the hospital—"

"Not from the knife—"

"No. I disarmed him. It was a fair fight." Tightness gripped his shoulders, as it always did when remembering the rage and violence he'd unleashed. "We were students at a private prep school. When he pulled the knife, he announced he could kill me without repercussions because I was a scholarship nobody while *his* dad was a senator."

"So he had the knife, but you were arrested."

"Bingo." He reached to straighten his nonexistent tie. The silk accessory was always a reminder of his success, but today it was absent in favor of comfort, so he wiggled his toes inside his shoes. Expensive, well-made shoes. Lawyerly shoes. A symbol of how far he'd come since he was the brainy fourteen-year-old on scholarship, with nothing but thrift-store footwear to shod his rapidly growing feet.

There was so much more to the story, and for some crazy reason, he *wanted* her to know. To understand him. Because no one had in the longest time.

It had been years since anyone had even asked.

"When I was fourteen, I was picked on a lot at that school. I was the poor kid who'd skipped two grades. I outscored everyone on the exams and blew the curve. My classmates were rewarded with things like trips to Europe for getting As, and I kept screwing that up for them. I'd been taking karate for several years and thought I could handle myself, so one day an argument came to blows. I was younger and weaker and had my ass handed to me. So I started lifting, bulked up, and trained in other martial arts. By my senior year—when I was sixteen—I didn't know what I was capable of."

"And you got in a fight again." The vibrant energy that accompanied his initial revelation had left her as the conversation became serious. "And beat the crap out of him because he'd pulled a knife on you."

But it hadn't been the knife; it had been his opponent's words. Curt's girlfriend had found a new guy, without the courtesy of breaking up first. The boy's taunts had triggered heartache, which unleashed primal violence.

"My first time in a courtroom, I was a defendant. The case against me was dropped after my ex-girlfriend recanted and admitted the other guy brought the knife to school to threaten me. Her father—a prominent attorney—and the senator sent the happy couple to the Virgin Islands for a week to recover from the emotional trauma."

"He didn't get into trouble for bringing a weapon to school?"

"He said he was invincible because his dad was a senator. And he was right."

"And you've worked your whole life to change that."

"Yes. And as attorney general, I'll ensure no one believes they are above the law." The moment the case was dismissed, he'd felt a rush of clarity. He shelved his application to MIT for a degree in chemical engineering and applied to Harvard, all while fearing his violent action had made acceptance impossible.

When his acceptance letter arrived, he'd vowed he wouldn't screw up again. He wouldn't squander the opportunity he'd been given.

Violence existed inside him, and heartache had released it, so he swore off love and relationships in favor of career and never regretted his decision. Now, twenty-two years later, he was on the cusp of achieving his ultimate goal, and for the first time since he was sixteen, he felt something for a woman he couldn't push away.

He shook his head at the irony and pressed the accelerator to the floor. The sooner they got to DC, the sooner he could be himself again.

Miles passed under the tires, while minutes inched by. He wasn't entirely certain the space-time continuum had remained constant during the endless drive, but would wait to do the math when he got home.

Mara checked the phone at random intervals as planned, and three hours after sending the initial text, she received a reply: TRYING TO CALL. LEAVE PHONE ON.

"That could have been sent by anyone," Curt said.

"Should I ignore it?"

"No. Tell her to call at three Eastern Time." He signaled for the next exit.

"Why are you pulling over?"

"We're going to switch drivers so I can talk to Jeannie—if it's Jeannie."

"She won't talk to you."

"She should. No one knows how to cut a deal with a conspirator better than me."

"Maybe she's not a conspirator."

"She took a payoff. She might be a victim, but she's also a conspirator."

"It looks like I took a payoff too, but I didn't."

Curt was silent.

Her face flushed. "Damn it! You know I—"

"Jeannie altered your field notebook and lied about why you left the site," he said, cutting off her outrage. "Records in her computer show her brother's gambling debts were paid by an offshore account that contained a hundred grand. She's a conspirator."

"Let me talk to her first; then you can float deals. Okay?" She tapped out a text message while Curt pulled to the side of the frontage road. She shut off the phone until the appointed time.

Mara jolted when the phone rang at three o'clock sharp. She held the phone between them, and caller ID showed a number. "That's Jeannie," she confirmed.

"Answer on speaker phone."

She took a deep breath and hit the button. "Jeannie, do you know what happened to your brother?"

"Yes, Mara. She does," a man said.

Mara gasped.

Curt snatched the phone and hit Disconnect. He snapped plastic in his rush to pry off the back and pluck out the battery. "Was that Evan?"

Her face was sickly pale. "Yes."

# Chapter Twenty-Six

Curt threw the SUV in drive and floored the accelerator. "We don't know what kind of toys Raptor has for hacking phones. That shouldn't have been a long enough connection to lock in on our signal, but we can't take the chance. Use the other phone to call Palea. Tell him Evan found Jeannie."

She blanched even paler. "Do you think she's still alive?"

What could he say? There were no words to soften this blow. He reached across the console and squeezed her hand. "It doesn't look good for her."

"I'm going to be sick."

"Can you hold it together until we put some distance between us and where we answered the call?"

She nodded, her lips tightly sealed. She gripped his fingers to the point of pain.

His gut churned. "We should change our route. Go north or south, then resume east." Opening arguments were probably wrapping up now. Tomorrow the first witness would take the stand, and again he wouldn't be there.

"No, Curt. You can't miss any more of the trial." The death grip on his fingers intensified.

"I'll miss all of it if Evan finds us."

"What if we find him?" she asked in a low, quiet voice. "And we were ready for him."

Raindrops splattered the windshield, the first drops of what promised to be a nasty storm. Curt flipped the wipers on and tightened his one-handed grip on the wheel. "Ready for him?"

"He's after me. What if we let him find me? We could be waiting for him…"

He took his eyes off the developing squall to glare at her. "*Waiting for him?* You want to be bait?" Fear tore through him with the ferocity of a lightning bolt. "No. No fucking way, Mara."

"Why not? I'll be bait when I testify. Raptor could have a whole squadron of operatives outside the courthouse, waiting for me."

The road darkened as they entered the heart of the storm, forcing him to release her hand and take the wheel in a two-handed grip. "You'll be surrounded by FBI agents." Even as he said the words, he wondered how he could go on if he failed her.

DARKNESS HAD LONG since fallen when Lee called. Curt was driving, so Mara answered the phone. "Raptor has facilities in Hawai'i, Texas, Alaska, Virginia, and Montana," he said. "Don't tell Curt this, but I did a little *research* into company flight logs." Mara took that to mean he'd hacked into Raptor's system—a feat that drew her admiration. Curt hadn't been kidding about Lee's technical skills. "Four days after Roddy and Evan returned from North Korea, they took a Raptor jet and flew to Virginia with a stopover at the Texas compound."

"They could have delivered the bomb to Texas or Virginia," Mara said.

"That's my thinking. Virginia is the most likely choice. That's where their technological hub is, and where they'd most likely have the ability to reverse engineer the bomb."

"Where in Virginia is it?"

"Not far south of DC. Their home office is in the city, but that's primarily the business wing—"

"Yes, I know about the DC office. It's where my uncle works."

"Right. Sorry."

After she hung up, Mara relayed the flight information, but not how Lee had obtained it.

"He hacked Raptor, didn't he?"

She shrugged, refusing to be the snitch.

"Interesting, but useless. I can't tell a judge about those flights in my request for a search warrant."

AT ONE A.M. Eastern time, they crossed the state line from Tennessee to Virginia. In seven hours, they'd reach DC. Mara was at the wheel for the momentous crossing.

"Pull over at the next exit," Curt instructed. "We need gas and I need to stretch my legs."

The gas station was a huge truck stop with attached diner. Big rigs flanked both sides of the lot, engines idling as their drivers filled up on coffee and food.

She shivered as she reached for the pump. The pullover they'd purchased in Amarillo couldn't compete with the cold late-October Virginia night. Curt removed his jacket and draped it over her shoulders. "We should've bought you a warmer coat at Target."

She slipped her arms through the sleeves and looked damn cute in the oversized coat. "Thanks," she said, pulling it tighter around her midsection. "Damn, it's cold here." Her teeth chattered.

"Go inside and get some coffee," he said. "I'll pump the gas."

She cocked her head to the side. "You sure?"

This was a break in their protocol. He hadn't left her side in days. He nodded toward the bright windows of the well-lit diner. "I'm watching."

She stepped forward and brushed her lips over his, a soft kiss that made him want more. He caught her arm, pulled her against him, and kissed her deeply. Igniting fires he shouldn't, taking pleasure he couldn't have.

This was foolish. Wrong. He released her mouth. Her eyes were hot, smoky with arousal, and her breath came out in uneven pants.

"When this is over, Mara, I'm going to take you somewhere quiet and safe, and make love to you for days." He shouldn't have voiced the fantasy he'd harbored for thousands of miles, but she'd decimated his control.

"When this is over, we probably won't be on speaking terms."

He pressed a finger to her lips. "Who said anything about talking?"

She chuckled. Her forehead rested against his chest for a moment; then she took a deep breath and said, "I'll get coffee."

With that, she dashed to the diner. He turned back to the tank, inserted the nozzle, then remembered he needed to give the clerk in the glass booth cash to get the pump started. He reached for the money envelope, but it was in his coat pocket. Circling around the vehicle to catch up to her, he came face-to-face with Evan Beck and his Glock 23.

# Chapter Twenty-Seven

Mara stood just inside the diner, staring out the window, frozen in fear. One moment she'd been in a dreamy haze, and the next she glanced through the window and saw Evan. With a gun. Aimed at Curt.

She patted the coat pockets and found the gun they'd been given in Arizona. The bullets, sadly, were still in Curt's pants pocket.

Could she pull off a bluff with a mercenary who knew her well?

She had to. Curt's life depended on it. She eased open the door, wincing at the bell that jangled. But Evan was too focused on Curt to turn around, and Curt was too smart to give away her approach.

A semitruck pulled into the lot with an earsplitting screech of hydraulic brakes. Mara used the cover of noise to dart forward, charging Evan.

He spun at the last second, but his face showed no surprise at seeing her. He shifted, pointing the gun at her. He hesitated for one frozen instant, and Mara launched herself at him feetfirst.

A shot rang out, flying high as she slammed into the injured knee that had forced Evan's medical discharge from the marines.

He howled in agony and dropped to the ground, his gun still clenched in his hand. His body collapsed on hers, a two-hundred pound heap that crushed her into the litter-strewn ground. She lashed out, kneeing, biting, and punching everything she could reach, ignoring a sharp pain in her thigh as they grappled on the jagged pavement.

He tried to get his arm around, to free the gun from the tangle of their bodies. She landed a blow to his groin, and he grunted.

Pinned beneath him, she heard him mutter something and stopped fighting. "What?"

"Jean—" Evan's words cut off as Curt kicked Evan in the side. He tumbled to the right, off her.

Had Evan's initial hesitation been real, or had she imagined it?

Curt lifted Evan by the throat. His grip on the two-hundred-pound mercenary appeared effortless in his rage, making Evan look like he had no more substance than a rag doll.

"Wait, he said something about Jeannie!" Mara yelled, scrambling to her feet.

Curt's wild, angry eyes turned to her in the same moment he released Evan's throat. Evan crumpled when the leg with the shattered knee touched pavement.

She scrambled for Evan's gun and realized he landed on it when he fell. She lunged for it, too late. He was already bringing the gun around.

Curt grabbed her, shoved her behind him, and kicked Evan's gun hand in the same moment. The gun swung inward and upward as it fired. Evan's lower jaw exploded.

Her ex-fiancé's glazed eyes met hers. He aimed the weapon at the remainder of his face and pulled the trigger.

# Chapter Twenty-Eight

THE BRIGHT PARKING lot was even brighter under the onslaught of ambulances, police cars, and eventually, news vans. Curt watched the scene from the inside of an FBI sedan, answering questions from a local agent. Mara was being interviewed separately in a nearby vehicle.

"You must be relieved Ms. Garrett is out of danger. Now you can return to DC and the trial without having to worry," the agent said.

"She's still in danger," Curt said. "Evan Beck was operating on orders from Raptor."

"I never took you for a conspiracy theorist, Mr. Dominick."

Curt bristled at the derision in the man's tone. "I'm not."

"You sure sound like one. Raptor is after her?" The younger man laughed. "Word from the SAC investigating the murder at Davis-Monthan Air Force Base is Evan Beck was working alone. The evidence shows he was obsessed with Garrett. She dumped him, and he took it hard. He was jealous of Airman Fuller—had been since he caught them out on a date last year. When she got all sorts of attention for being detained in North Korea, he snapped. This isn't an international incident; it's domestic violence, pure and simple."

*Shit.* At some point in the last forty-eight hours, the tide had shifted in Raptor's favor. The mercenary organization had deep pockets and important friends. He'd known from Palea the pressure had been on to put the kibosh on the investigation, and now it appeared someone high in the hierarchy had caved.

He glanced toward the vehicle where Mara was undergoing a similar interview and felt sick. She was a sitting target, and these baby agents had been ordered to decorate her in neon.

The prepaid cell phone vibrated against his hip. "I need to take this call."

"We're not done—"

"I'm the US attorney for the District of Columbia. I don't answer to you." He exited the vehicle and answered Palea's call.

"Curt, you need to get Mara out of there."

Dread crawled up his spine. "I was just thinking the same thing, but I want to know how *you* came to that conclusion."

"The powers that be are putting pressure on me to attribute the crimes to Mara's stalker ex and close the case. I'm having trouble fighting them, because Evan *did* commit all the crimes on Oahu."

Curt swore. "Either someone took a payoff, or they're returning a favor." *This* was why he wanted to be attorney general.

"My thoughts exactly," Palea said.

His gaze remained fixed on Mara. He could tell she argued with the agent questioning her from her flailing arms and the set of her chin. "If Evan acted alone, then there's no reason to continue protecting her."

"Bingo. She'll be on Raptor's home turf without a safe house or security detail."

The vehicle holding Mara pulled forward. "Gotta go." Curt jammed the phone into his pocket and ran in front of the car. The driver slammed on the brakes. The bumper stopped an inch shy of Curt's knees.

The agent poked his head out of the window. "Out of the way, Mr. Dominick. I'm taking Ms. Garrett to DC. Your job is done."

Anger surged through him. After everything he'd been through with her, this dipshit agent thought he could just drive off with Mara? *Hell no.*

He wanted to pummel the man. The violence he'd avoided for so long beckoned. With iron will, he held anger at bay and spoke through stiff lips. "She needs to go to the hospital. Now. She needs stitches for that cut on her thigh."

"Amazing you can diagnose her from the front bumper, Mr. Dominick. I heard you were a good lawyer but didn't realize you were a doctor too."

Was it possible Raptor's campaign to ruin him had succeeded where so many others had failed over the years? They'd managed to bring him low in the eyes of the FBI. He'd lost the status and respect he'd earned through years of work as a federal prosecutor.

Tomorrow he'd worry about what this meant for his career, but right now he had a bigger concern. He met Mara's gaze through the windshield. "Get out of the car, Mara."

She wrenched open the door. The agent at the wheel caught her arm. The man's voice was muffled through the glass, but his menacing tone was clear. "You're making a big mistake, Ms. Garrett."

Mara nodded toward Curt. "I look forward to when he becomes attorney general, so I can watch him fire your ass." She jerked her arm out of his grasp. "I *told* you I need to see a doctor." She climbed out of the car and slammed the door. She straightened her shirt, which was coated in blood, some Evan's, some her own. She had road rash on her arm, bruises on her face, and true to his word, a cut on her thigh, probably caused by a shard of glass as she rolled on the pavement with Evan. All her wounds lent credence to the claim she needed to see a doctor.

Curt remained planted in front of the vehicle until she reached his side. "Thanks," she murmured.

He gripped her arms, his heart hammering at the knowledge she'd almost been taken from him. "You okay?"

"My thigh stings like a bitch, and these idiots seem to think Evan's hunting us was nothing more than a lover's spat. I'm pissed, in pain, and exhausted, but okay."

He leaned forward and whispered in her ear, "Do you have the money envelope?"

She nodded, the motion of her head bumping his chin. Her soft hair tickled his nose as he breathed in her scent. He wanted to hold her against him and bury his face in her neck, but the FBI agent watching through the windshield would cause problems if he did.

Anxiety twisted his gut. He couldn't believe it had come to this and was terrified of what would happen to her. But he didn't have a choice. He slipped the prepaid cell phone and bullet magazine into her pocket and whispered, "When you get to the hospital, run. I can't protect you anymore."

# Chapter Twenty-Nine

"Unless Ms. Garrett is under arrest, you don't have the right to ride in the ambulance." The paramedic stood in the open ambulance doorway with her hands planted on her hips, blocking Mara's view of the FBI agent standing outside the vehicle trying to finagle his way in.

Inside, Mara leaned back on the gurney, relieved the paramedic hadn't budged.

The agent tried a new tactic. "Ms. Garrett claims she needs protection. I'm offering that."

The medic glanced over her shoulder at Mara. The woman was young, early twenties, but she carried herself with an air of confidence Mara found comforting.

Evan was dead, Raptor was still after her, and she was on her own.

"Do you want protection, Ms. Garrett?" the woman asked.

She gripped the gurney, trying to still shaking fingers. "Not from him."

"There's your answer," the medic said.

"What hospital are you—"

The door slammed closed on the question, and the medic smiled at her. "He was kind of a dick. I don't blame you."

"He wants to take me to DC. I don't want to go to DC."

"That's kidnapping." To the driver she said, "Let's go." The woman sat on a bench seat beside her as the ambulance started to move. "What hospital do you want to go to?"

"Depends. Is the agent following us?"

The woman stood and gazed out the rear window. "He's talking with the US attorney. Damn, he's even better looking in person."

Mara smiled as the knot in her belly loosened a bit. "I take it he's been on the news a lot."

"You both have. The press is only capable of covering one story at a time, and the fact that you disappeared after your jet blew up on Oahu means this week's story is you." With a grin, she said to the driver, "Do you think we should tell Brian Williams or Wolf Blitzer our story of taking the notorious Mara Garrett to the hospital?"

"I've always had a thing for Elizabeth Vargas," the man at the wheel answered.

The woman winked at Mara. "Don't worry. We're kidding. So which hospital?"

The knot returned with new intensity. She didn't know the paramedic or driver, and what she was about to say would make her sound paranoid, but she had no choice if she wanted to live. "The man who died at the truck stop wasn't the only person hunting me. He worked for Raptor—do you know who they are?"

The woman nodded.

"Raptor operatives are probably monitoring your radio. They'll be waiting for me at whatever hospital you broadcast as our destination. I don't care where you take me, so long as you don't tell the world."

"Why didn't you want the fed to ride with us if you really need protection?"

"With Evan dead, he believes I'm out of danger. He wants to drag me back to DC—exactly where Raptor expects me to go—without providing protection."

The medic cocked her head. "Does the FBI have the right to drag you to DC?"

Mara took hope from the fact she hadn't declared her a nutjob—yet. "There was a subpoena for me to testify, but Curt Dominick won't have it enforced."

"He told you that?"

At this moment, Curt stood in the center of a ring of sharks. She couldn't pour blood in the water by repeating his final instructions to a stranger. "He knows how much danger I'm in."

The woman was silent for a long moment. Finally, she said to the driver, "I don't believe in taking chances. Radio we're going to Anthem."

After the driver finished that task, he said, "Where *are* we going, Kaitlin?"

Kaitlin pierced Mara with a stare. "You're legit? This shit is real, mercenaries stalking you?"

"I know it sounds nuts. But there's no way Evan Beck could have stalked me for almost five thousand miles without technical support from Raptor. He caught up with us at the truck stop after brief cell phone contact nine hours before. The problem is, he's not *that* good."

"What are you going to do?"

"Run. Hide."

"How will you run?"

"I don't know. I need a vehicle."

"Any chance you know how to ride a motorcycle?" the driver asked.

Kaitlin looked over Mara's shoulder into the cab of the vehicle. "You thinking what I'm thinking, Gary?"

"Yes," the man said.

A flicker of hope ignited in Mara's acid-filled belly. "Yes, I know how to ride a motorcycle."

"Call Tyson," Gary said.

"Who is Tyson?" Mara asked.

"My boyfriend. He's a motorcycle mechanic. He's got a project bike he's been trying to sell. If you take it, you'll be doing me a favor. I want it out of the garage." She pulled out her phone.

"It's nearly three in the morning. You can't call him now."

Kaitlin shrugged. "It's either wake him or wait until my shift is done at eight. But if we get an emergency I have to respond to, then it could be much later."

The sooner she left the area, the safer she'd be, so she didn't protest further as Kaitlin called her boyfriend. The fact that these strangers were willing to help her had her fighting back tears.

After Kaitlin hung up she said, "Tyson says it's yours for fifteen hundred. But if you don't have money, you can owe him. It's not like we don't know who you are." She rolled her eyes. "And he'll just spend the money on a new project bike anyway."

"I've got cash."

Kaitlin made a face. "You sure? 'Cause really, you can owe him."

"Sorry. But I'll feel better if I pay him now." Who knew how long she'd be in hiding? It could be months before she could pay him back.

"Fine. We'll take you to my house. Tyson's waiting for you. Then we'll return to our headquarters and put word out on the radio you jumped out at a stoplight. If no calls come in, we can give you about a thirty-minute head start."

"Thank you." Mara gripped the woman's hand. "Will you get in trouble?"

"I'm an EMT for a private ambulance service. I get paid ten dollars an hour. I don't give a shit if I get in trouble, and neither does Gary. Do you, Gary?"

"Semper fi," Gary said.

"You're a marine?" Mara knew better than to ask if he was a former marine, even though the man had obviously left the service.

"In service for over twenty years," the man said. "I've been following your story. We all have. I'll do whatever I can to help you."

"And Tyson was in the army," Kaitlin added. "He served in Afghanistan."

This explained why they were willing to help her, and she was humbled by their unquestioning support. She'd been isolated for so long, she'd forgotten what her work meant to military personnel. She'd spent so much time blaming herself for what happened in North Korea, she'd assumed her entire country blamed her too. And Curt, the only person she'd spent any time with since her captivity, he'd been suspicious of her at first, confirming her assumption.

She didn't blame him for that. It was an impossible situation, and he was just being…Curt.

Now she remembered the line of marines who had saluted her in Kaneohe, and a sob rose in her chest. "Thank you."

"Do you know who blew up the Marine Corps runway in Hawai'i?" Gary asked.

"I think it was the dead guy at the truck stop."

"Good. Raptor is run by a shit-hot civilian prick who should be fragged."

Her sob became a laugh. She and Curt had avoided the military, because of Raptor, but now she realized they'd also been avoiding the very people who were her best allies. "Hell yes," she answered.

"You see anyone in the rearview?" Kaitlin asked Gary.

"No one looks like they're following."

"Twist around a bit. We need to be certain before we go to my place."

They drove around for twenty minutes, then finally approached Kaitlin's street. During the drive, the woman cleaned and bandaged the cut on Mara's thigh.

They stopped a block from Kaitlin's, and Mara jumped out the back followed by the young EMT.

A man stepped from behind a high fence, and Kaitlin greeted him with an exuberant kiss. Then she introduced Mara to her boyfriend. "Give her a helmet too, Ty." To Mara, she said, "Promise you'll wear it, or the deal is off."

Mara smiled. The young woman was an EMT through and through. "It'll be a good disguise."

Satisfied, Kaitlin jumped back into the ambulance, and she and Gary departed.

Wind stirred tree branches, which creaked and whistled in the inky darkness, sending adrenaline surging through her. Mara followed Tyson down the block to a small house in the middle of the quiet street. She winced at the idea of revving a motorcycle in the middle of the night and was relieved to see the bike was an old BMW, not a loud Harley.

Tyson gave her a quick rundown on the condition of the bike. He yawned several times, and she had a feeling he'd give her a detailed description of all the work he'd done, if he weren't eager to go back to bed. She paid him and less than ten minutes after arriving was on the bike, heading north.

Sporting bandages on one side and smallpox scars on the other, she was completely on her own for the first time since she emerged from the woods to find herself on the edge of the DMZ. Another minefield was now before her, and with Evan dead, she had no idea what her enemy looked like. But for the first time since this nightmare started, she knew what she needed to do. Evan had given her direction with his last words: *"Jeannie is alive."*

# Chapter Thirty

Curt spent hours with the FBI, first delaying them from following Mara to the hospital, then on a false hunt for Mara, all to buy time for her escape.

The two EMTs who'd taken her to the hospital were interviewed, and Curt believed with a prosecutor's instinct they'd done more than watch Mara climb out of the ambulance at a stoplight, but he gave no hint of this suspicion to the frustrated FBI agents.

Dawn lit the sky as one of the agents begrudgingly gave Curt a lift to a nearby airfield. There he caught a commuter flight and a short while later was forced to wade through a throng of reporters at National Airport. The only other option had been to fly through Joint Base Andrews, but he wouldn't go through another military base until he was certain Raptor no longer tailed him.

He forded the gauntlet of vultures, his only weapon the words, "No comment," which he wielded over and over on his way to a waiting limousine.

Bixby, the president's chief of staff who'd set him on this crazy journey five—*or was it six?*—days before, waited inside the vehicle. "The president can't meet with you."

Frustration stirred with the confirmation the president was distancing himself from Curt, but he was too exhausted to care. "You mean won't."

"That too."

"Fine. Then I'll head home and shower before going to the courthouse."

"That'll have to wait. We're going to the State Department. The secretary is waiting for a debriefing."

"Good. I need to talk to him."

Bixby sighed and said, "This will blow over, Curt."

He nodded and closed his eyes as he leaned against the plush seat. He'd known Bixby only a few years but liked the man. "It looks to me like the Justice Department needs to clean house."

"You're still in the running for the job." The man paused.

"The president wants to appoint you, but you've got to show you can survive the confirmation process. You've got to win this case. A win will restore your credibility."

"Restore? I didn't think it was *that* bad."

"It's worse. A witness at the truck stop says he saw you kiss Garrett before she went inside. The morning talk shows are going nuts."

He ran his fingers through his hair. He couldn't lie. He couldn't tell the truth. He shrugged. "She's not testifying. The morning talk shows can go to hell."

"Win the case, Curt."

"I intend to." Curt paused and stared at Bixby. At this point, the more people who knew, the safer Mara would be. He hit the button to close the divider so the driver couldn't eavesdrop. "There's something you need to tell the president."

THE SECRETARY OF state met with Curt in a conference room. Curt quickly told the man about Mara's encounter with the smallpox bombs. The man listened quietly, then said, "I'll ask the president to convene an informal cabinet meeting and will need you to present evidence at the meeting. Can you prove Ms. Garrett found the bombs?"

"Not at present, sir, but I'm seeking search warrants for all of Raptor's facilities."

"Keep me posted on your progress. And Dominick, it's very important the press doesn't get wind of this. Tension between the US and North Korea is bad enough as it is. Allegations of biological weapons testing on the Korean peninsula in the fifties could lead to war today. And with North Korea, we're talking nuclear war. Any statements regarding US testing and use of biological weapons would threaten national security and leave you open to prosecution under 18 USC Section 798: Disclosure of Classified Information."

Curt was used to citing chapter and verse of the US Code. He was unaccustomed, however, to having the code cited to him. "I never grant interviews and have been very careful with this information for that very reason."

"Also, with regard to Ms. Garrett, if she reveals to anyone she believes she found a smallpox bomb—"

"She doesn't believe it; she knows it. But rest assured she

won't tell anyone."

"Good." The man stood and walked Curt to the door. "Thank you for your service in retrieving Ms. Garrett."

Curt turned to the door, one item checked off on his long to-do list. He needed to get home and shower before heading to court, and he was anxious to call the prepaid cell phone and check on Mara. He needed to know she was okay.

"Dominick," the man said with a note of uneasiness. "One more thing. I'm hearing whispers… There is concern you've fixated on Raptor to the point of obsession, and these smallpox allegations will only exacerbate that."

There it was. Said aloud. Frankly, hearing the words was a relief. It was better than being quietly discredited until he woke up one morning without a career, without support, without a future. "Evan Beck wasn't acting alone."

"Can you prove that?"

"No. But someone flew Evan to the mainland. Someone provided him with weapons and the technology to track us." He swallowed his anger. The man had merely repeated allegations most people would only whisper behind his back.

But Curt hadn't gotten where he was by backing down at the first sign of trouble, and silence now would only aid Raptor. Bad enough he'd given Raptor a victory when he cut Mara loose. He wouldn't fail on his own turf. "Mr. Secretary, I expect a full investigation into Raptor's actions. If it isn't done, I will use the full power of my office to push for congressional hearings on the matter."

The secretary grimaced. "Keep a lid on the smallpox allegation, and rest assured Raptor will be investigated by Homeland Security."

"I expect a full report." He turned and left, knowing in his gut sending Mara away had been the only safe choice.

She was everyone's pawn, but no one, not even Curt, had been willing to protect her flank.

He paused on his way out of the building, suddenly chilled by the realization that in telling Mara to run he'd distanced himself from her. He bore bruises and aches from the struggle with Evan, but pain of a different sort lanced through him. After all his blustering about his own importance, Mara probably wondered why he hadn't pushed for protective custody. She probably believed he'd chosen his career over her life.

And deep down, he feared that was exactly what he'd done.

HE ARRIVED AT the courthouse just minutes before the trial was supposed to adjourn for the weekend break. A feeling of peace settled over him as he entered his domain. The courtroom was packed, and hundreds of heads turned when he entered.

Judge Hawthorne, a tiny woman—as small as Mara—always managed to look imposing from the raised bench. She glanced at him over the top of her rimless glasses and smiled, showing the stained front tooth that had appeared in more than one op-ed caricature.

A buzz erupted in the room as Curt made his way down the center aisle, and Hawthorne's gavel met sound block with impassive effort. She hated resorting to the gavel to restore order and only did it with vigor when her ire was raised. "Nice of you to join us, Mr. Dominick."

He nodded and crossed to the prosecution table, dropping into the empty seat next to Aurora. "Sorry for the delay, Your Honor."

The darkened tooth made another appearance. "Glad you're okay."

Ben Sherrod, Stevens's attorney, called attention back to him with a dramatic sigh. "Your Honor, I believe you were about to rule on the objection—"

"I haven't forgotten, Counselor. Overruled." She glanced at her watch. "At this time, we will break for weekend recess." Judge Hawthorne's gaze landed on Aurora, not Curt. "Ms. Ames, you may finish questioning your witness when court resumes on Monday morning at nine a.m." To the witness, she said, "You are excused until then." The gavel fell, and the courtroom erupted into low-voiced conversations.

The twelve jurors and two alternates filed out, casting curious glances in his direction. Aurora had briefed him nightly, and he identified several from her descriptions. He had a lot of catching up to do, but it could be worse.

For the first time since he'd entered the room, Curt's gaze landed on Mara's uncle, who sat at the defendant's table. The man put effort into avoiding eye contact.

Those dangerous, unacceptable emotions surfaced. She deserved so much more than she'd received from everyone. Including Curt.

Andrew Stevens stood and exited the courtroom at his attorney's side. No pause, no hesitation, no questioning look about the well-being of his niece. Mara's mother was a different story. Seated in the first row behind the defendant's table, she met Curt's gaze, her own full of worry.

He responded with a slight nod, the barest communication, but he knew the woman caught his meaning because she flashed a wide, relieved smile, so much like Mara's it hurt.

Aurora jabbed him in the shoulder, drawing his attention away from Mara's mother, and pegged him with a penetrating look. "About time you got your ass here, Dominick."

"We need to talk. At the office or over dinner, your choice."

"Both. Takeout. We'll eat at the office. We've got a lot of work to do."

Sam Harder, the AUSA who'd filled in during Curt's absence, said sotto voce to Curt, "Be careful. You're up on the dartboard in her office."

"Again?" He glanced at Aurora, who refused to look at him as she gathered her binders. Curt stacked several legal pads. "What's her aim been like?"

"Dead center."

"Thanks for the warning."

An hour later, carrying a bag overloaded with Chinese food in one arm, Curt unlocked the door to the lobby of the US Attorney's Office located in the Judiciary Center Building on Judiciary Square, just a few blocks from the Federal Courthouse. His own picture graced the wall above the receptionist's desk, keeping company with the president, the attorney general, and, because Curt was also the local district attorney, the mayor of DC.

Aurora and Sam followed him inside, each carrying a box of files. "We're set up in the main conference room," Aurora said with a nod toward the hall.

In the room, she dropped the box on the table, kicked off her shoes, and brushed them aside with an angry swish of her feet before plopping into the most coveted and comfortable conference room chair. "Spill, Dominick. Where is Garrett?" Her words were sharp little daggers, conveying more anger than she'd expressed during their numerous phone conversations.

"I have no idea." Which was true. She hadn't answered the phone when he'd called earlier.

Sam, who had similarly flopped into a chair, sat up straight.

"What?"

"I assume you know Evan Beck ambushed us last night."

"I received your message on my office phone *this morning*," Aurora said. "You should have woken me up at home." Her glare was at full potency. "I'm acting as lead prosecutor on *your* case, and you left me out of the loop."

Ah, at last, the source of her anger. He hadn't called her at home because he would have had to reveal that Mara had fled, and he hadn't been prepared to discuss the trial implications. But she'd probably guessed that—hence, the resentment. "Sorry, AA, but I was busy dealing with cops, medics, and the fact that a psycho with a gun got the jump on me. Next time I'll try to consider *your* feelings."

"You know how much I hate sarcasm."

"Sam, did the sense of humor we ordered for Aurora arrive while I was gone?"

"It wasn't powerful enough to overcome her innate inability to detect nuance. We sent it back."

Aurora's glare held the hint of a smile. It was probably all he'd get from her in this mood, but it was enough to loosen the chunk of ice on her back. "While I was dealing with the cops, Mara went to the hospital. She had a severe cut on her leg. She talked her way out of the ambulance en route to the hospital. I don't know where she is."

"Did she run because she refuses to testify? We can get a federal marshal—"

"No marshals. She ran from Raptor. She was resigned to testifying, but the FBI wouldn't promise to protect her."

"How did she manage it?" Aurora asked.

Curt stiffened. Aurora was going to flip. "She had nine thousand in cash on her."

Aurora's fist hit the table. "Of all the stupid… You gave her the money?"

"The money was in my coat, which I had given to her because she was cold." True, but he'd have given her the money even if she hadn't been wearing the coat.

Aurora glared at him. "We need to find her. I want her on the stand on Wednesday."

"No. She's not testifying."

He braced for another thump on the table, and Aurora didn't disappoint. "Shit, Curt. I knew that's what you were leading up to.

Did you fuck her?"

He held his anger in check. Lashing back would only turn a difficult situation into a disaster. "No, Aurora, I didn't sleep with her. Testifying would be a death sentence for her."

"Don't you think you're being a bit melodramatic?"

"No." *Dammit*, he hadn't believed Aurora could be influenced by whispered allegations. He glared across the conference table. "You have no idea what I've been through in the last five days." He stared her down until she flinched.

Finally, with a tight jaw, she said, "What are we going to do?"

"We'll prove our case without laying the foundation of previous influence peddling. We couldn't charge him with that anyway." He straightened his tie. "A week ago, we thought we wouldn't have Mara to testify because she was a prisoner in North Korea. We go back to the game plan we'd set up then." He turned to Sam. "Is the press still clamoring to know if she'll testify?"

"More than ever with the trail of stiffs you encountered."

"Two is not a 'trail.'" But, assuming Jeannie's fate, in all, four people had died.

"According to my tenth-grade geometry teacher, it *is* a line."

Curt rolled his eyes. "Monday, I want you to release a statement saying the prosecution has no intention of calling Mara Garrett to testify."

"Do I give a reason?"

"No."

"Will the Arizona US Attorney's Office go after her for the nine grand?" Sam asked.

"How did you know that's where we got the money?"

"We received an invoice."

Unease trickled down his spine, but he was safe in DC and had made arrangements at the truck stop to return the SUV to Arizona. "Don't pay it. I've already transferred the money."

Aurora's eyes narrowed. "With US Attorney's Office funds?"

"No. My own. Raptor is after Mara. She needs the money to stay in hiding. I'd give her more if I could."

"Doesn't the State Department want to talk to her?"

"I've told them everything. Mara is a free woman—if hiding counts as being free."

"She can't hide forever," Sam said.

"We need to nail Stevens so he'll roll on Raptor. Only then will Mara be safe."

# Chapter Thirty-One

Mara headed north, riding all night and into the following day, stopping, finally, to rest for a few hours when exhaustion and cold made the drive dangerous. She found a hospital in a busy city and tucked herself in a corner waiting room where she slept for a few hours before hopping back on the bike and heading toward the town where she grew up and the one person she believed could help her. It was late afternoon on Friday when she rolled into a parking lot in front of a stately Michigan State University building. She climbed off the motorcycle and stretched. She shivered, not from the frigid air but because it was time once again to remove the helmet.

The stone façade of the research building looked imposing, but she knew this campus and this building. The man she hoped to see today had been a childhood friend. She stiffened her spine and slid the helmet off, then pulled on a knit winter cap she'd purchased at a truck stop and tugged the earflaps forward.

After locking the helmet in the saddlebag, she made her way to the front door, tucking her head down as she passed students on the stairs.

She wound her way through the building, which echoed hollowly late on Friday afternoon. At last she found Michael's office, and disappointment shot through her when she read the sign next to the door. He didn't have office hours until Monday. She'd known it was a long shot, but desperation had led her to Michael first.

Now she'd have to hide out in the area for three days before she could see him. Three days would pass in which Raptor could finish replicating the smallpox bomb. Three days would pass before she could begin the hunt for Jeannie. In the grand scheme of things, three days wasn't much, but given the enormity of what had passed in the previous five days, it felt like a lifetime.

CURT WORKED LATE on Friday night. Aurora quickly thawed and focused her sharp legal mind on the case, and Sam did his best to ease tension while demonstrating his own skill with the intricacies of federal case law. Curt had been hesitant to bring the man on at the last minute, but Aurora had been correct in selecting the hungry assistant US attorney. They filled Curt in on the missed *voir dire*, as well as the first day of testimony. By the time he drove home through the empty city streets, he felt confident the trial was on the right track and they'd have a conviction against Stevens.

Now all he had to do was protect Mara and stop Raptor from committing a terrorist act on American soil.

No problem. If he were fucking Superman.

Which, despite Mara's foolish faith in him, he definitely was not.

As soon as he reached his Georgetown condo, he grabbed his phone. Lee had promised him his landline was secure and traps had been set that would alert him if the system were breached. With that assurance, he dialed Mara. As he waited for the call to connect, he eyed his stark bachelor furnishings. He'd never spent enough time here to bother making it feel like home, but now he wondered what Mara would say when—*if*—she saw the place.

Her home—which she was away from at least half of each year—had been full of knickknacks and treasures, items she'd collected in her travels. Color and warmth had infused the place with a homey feeling, even during a murder investigation.

She'd made her home a special place to return to. He, on the other hand, put in ridiculously long hours at the office, and made his home into a cold, unfeeling place that drove people—especially himself—away.

Oh Christ. He was obsessing over Mara Garrett and her as-yet-nonexistent thoughts on his home décor. He'd officially lost it.

His call rolled to voice mail, which he'd never bothered to set up. Dammit.

He set down the phone. Physically turned his back on it and marched into his bedroom. It had been a week since he'd gotten a decent night's sleep, but he doubted being home would change that. How could he sleep when Mara was out there, unprotected?

In his bedroom, he had his tie off and was unbuttoning his shirt when the phone rang. He lunged for it. *Jesus*, he was supposed to be control personified. A ruthless shark. But he couldn't resist and proved to be all too human when he read the display. Mara.

His heart crashed wildly in his chest and tangled with other internal organs. He hit the Answer button so hard he jammed his finger.

"Curt?" she said.

The smooth alto of her voice took the starch out of him, and he dropped to the bed, clutching the phone to his ear. He might be pathetic, but he was happy. Maybe there was a benefit to this whole emotion thing. "Thank God. Dammit, Mara, don't ever make me wait that long to hear from you again."

She laughed. "It's only been, what...twenty hours?"

"Twenty-three," he corrected. "Where are you? Are you safe?" He wanted to see her, touch her. Hold her.

"I'm in Michigan."

His heart picked up speed. "You didn't return to East Lansing, did you? Crap, Mara, your hometown is the first place they'll look."

"No. I'm at a vacation cottage on a small lake. It's a few hours away, close to Lake Michigan. No one is around because it's off-season."

The pounding in his chest eased. Slightly. "Promise me you'll be careful."

"I promise."

"You need to call me every day. If I don't know you're safe, I think I'll go insane." *Jesus.* He'd just said those words to his defendant's niece. And the scary part was he didn't give a shit.

She huffed out a sigh, and he could picture the rise of her chest at the familiar sound. "Good, because I'm a little freaked out, and I need a friend."

A friend. Truth was, he wanted much more than friendship from Mara, and now that she wasn't going to testify, he could pursue her without consequences. "Court is in session weekdays from nine to four. I have a new cell, which Lee has promised is secure, so outside of court, even if I'm in a strategy session with Aurora, I'll take your call.

"Aurora will love that."

"I work twenty hour days; it's none of her damn business who I talk to when I take fifteen minutes for myself."

"God, you turn me on when you talk like that."

He chuckled. "And you turn me on when you breathe." He paused and turned serious again. "I paid back the nine thousand dollars. No one will search for you because of the money."

"I'll pay you back. I just can't access my own money right now…"

"I know, love. Don't worry about it." *Love.* The word had slipped out—naturally. As if it were a word he used all the time.

"What the hell are we going to do about the bomb? And how long will I have to remain in hiding?"

"I'm working on both situations. We'll find the bomb, nail the bastards, and then you'll be safe."

"It's going to take months, won't it?"

He hated the distress in her voice but couldn't lie. "I hope not."

"I can't hide forever. I'll run out of money."

"Sit tight for now. We'll figure something out. I promise."

ROBERT BECK POURED himself a stiff drink, drank it in one swallow, and slammed the glass down. Something broke—either the glass or the tabletop, he wasn't sure which. And he was fairly sure the blood that soaked the glass surface was his, but he couldn't feel the cut, so it didn't matter.

His son was dead. Gone. Killed by the bitch who'd ruined everything. He'd heard the allegations and thanked God he had allies who could derail the investigation. But he couldn't think about that now. Right now all he had was rage.

Mara Garrett had caused his son's death as surely as if she'd pulled the trigger. He'd been told Evan had turned the gun on himself, but he didn't believe it. Evan was a fighter, not a quitter. If Garrett didn't shoot him, then it was Curt Dominick. Regardless, he wanted them both dead. With Dominick publicly gunning for him, he'd have to be careful and bide his time. But Garrett? Well, he had a plan for her.

She would pay for Evan's death. She would suffer. And then she'd die.

# Chapter Thirty-Two

MONDAY AFTERNOON, MARA returned to the university building, hoping Michael Reilly would be there. She wore heavy, almost garish makeup and a wig of long, thick, chestnut curls. She'd done the best she could to disguise herself.

Inside the building, a blast of heat enveloped her, causing her chilled skin to burn, providing the perfect excuse to cover her face. Pressing cold fingers to blazing cheeks, she headed down the main hall.

A door banged open in front of her, and she startled; then a sea of students spilled into the hallway. No one paid any attention to her. Her breathing eased as she wound her way through the crowd. Her short stature made it easy to avoid eye contact. She could do this.

She reached his office and hesitated outside the door. In coming to see him, she was endangering him. It was a horrible, awful feeling to know she was risking another person's life without their knowledge or consent. But the alternative was to let Raptor get away with stealing a smallpox bomb.

Her days as a Star Trek geek offered guidance but little solace. *The needs of the many outweigh the needs of the few.*

She pushed open the door without knocking and felt a rush of relief when her old friend uttered an absentminded "Office hours aren't until three o'clock," before he looked up to see her. His gaze was puzzled for a moment, but then turned startled as recognition settled over his features. As she'd feared, the wig and makeup delayed identification for only about ten seconds. But then, Michael knew her better than most.

She closed and locked the door as he said, "The wig really isn't you, doll."

She smiled at Michael's familiar endearment. "It was the only decent one they had at the thrift store."

"I'd ask why the getup, but I've been watching the news."

She flopped into the chair in front of his desk. "I'm so sorry to do this to you, Michael, but I need your help."

"Name it."

"I need you to do something for me. But it's a secret. And it involves national security. And it's dangerous."

"Mowing-the-lawn-barefoot dangerous? Or skydiving dangerous?"

"Hunted-by-mercenaries dangerous. It-could-get-you-killed dangerous."

He flashed a wry grimace. "I'm so…*flattered* you thought of me."

A half laugh, half sob escaped. "I'm sorry, Michael. There's no one else who can help me. No one I can trust."

He leaned forward. "What's going on?"

"I need you to run a blood test to prove I was ill with a virus, but it's complicated, because I was also vaccinated."

"That's going to be tough. What virus are we talking about here?"

She took a deep breath and said the word that endangered them both. "Smallpox."

Thirty minutes later, Michael escorted her outside—through the back door. After hearing her improbable tale, he'd taken a blood sample.

Curt had been saying all along they had no body of evidence to prove Raptor had been hunting her. Mara's blood contained some of the proof they needed to remove the tarnish from Curt's heretofore sterling reputation.

Michael understood she'd call him for the results. They stood next to the motorcycle, and she shivered, already chilled by the cold autumn wind. Her old friend hugged her. "You be careful," he said.

"You too. If anything odd or suspicious happens—anything at all—contact Curt Dominick right away, okay? I'm so sorry to do this to you."

He chucked her under the chin. "Are you kidding? I'm an epidemiologist. This is seriously exciting stuff for me."

She lowered her voice. "Raptor doesn't play games. I don't want you to get hurt. If they find out what you are doing… What *are* you doing, anyway?"

"I need to get the lab techs to run cytokine assays on your blood, looking for evidence of recent infection. I can turn it around in twenty-four hours. Raptor will never know."

"Good."

She climbed on the bike and tugged on the helmet. In minutes she was back on the freeway. She'd lied to Curt about her location. She'd never gone near Lake Michigan or the lakeside cottage community. She'd spent the last three days in a dingy Lansing motel. Today she'd head south, then east, for a rendezvous with Jeannie. If Evan had been telling the truth and Jeannie was still alive, Mara had a plan to find her. Jeannie had some serious explaining to do.

THAT EVENING SHE stopped at a library in Toledo and logged into her Twitter account for the first time in months. She sent a simple direct message to Jeannie: "You've really hit the jackpot. We need to talk." She was in and out of the library in less than five minutes. Now all she needed to do was get to the rendezvous location and wait.

She had no doubt Raptor would see the message and trace her login to Toledo. She needed to put miles between herself and the library before she stopped for the night.

Four hours later, she settled in a Pittsburgh motel room and called Curt. Cold, tired, and knowing he'd flip if he knew what she was doing, she inserted buoyancy into her voice and described the flight of birds across the Lake Michigan sand dunes. Remembering the forecast for western Michigan, she added, "I think it's going to snow soon."

"Do you like snow?"

"Living in Hawai'i, I missed skiing and ice skating, all the things I did as a kid."

"I like snow for about three days. After that, I'm done for the season."

She flopped back on the motel bed, closed her eyes, and focused on his voice. "Do you ski?"

"I love skiing. I just hate dealing with snow when I'm not skiing."

"We should go togeth—" She stopped herself. She'd entered the unspoken forbidden zone—talk of a future that included them spending time together.

"I'd like that," he responded, crushing the boundary with ease.

She rubbed her temples and felt the shimmery ache of wanting the impossible. "Are you any good? Because I'm a black-diamond girl."

"Mara, haven't you figured out yet I'm good at everything I do?" The flirtation in his tone sent a rush of heat to her center.

She let out a long, slow breath. "You're killing me here, Dominick."

"Me too." He sighed. "I wish we'd met in a different way. If things had gone as I'd originally planned, we'd have met when you were deposed."

But what could have been wasn't any better than what was. "I'd have been hostile toward you."

"Yeah, well, I'd have been awed by your strength, intelligence, humor, and your seriously stupendous body."

Mara glanced down, surveying her attributes. "You like my body?"

"Fishing, Mara?"

"A girl likes to know she's attractive."

"Throw me a bone first. What would you have thought of me if we'd met over a deposition?"

"One glimpse of your cocky grin and I'd probably have melted at your feet," she said.

"If we'd met over depositions, after the trial I'd have asked you out on a date."

She sighed. "But I'd be in Hawai'i, or Cambodia, or God knows where." *But definitely not in a dive in Pittsburgh.*

"This is my fantasy, and in my fantasy, you're still in DC."

She laughed. "Okay, in that alternate universe, I'm in DC, but I'd probably say no."

"I'd ask again."

"Persistence. I like that." Mara wished they were talking on an old-fashioned, corded landline, like the one on the nightstand next to her. Her fingers itched to thread between the loops of the cord, as she'd done when she was in high school and talked to a boy.

"I'd win you over with Redskins tickets."

She sat up sharply. "You can get Redskins tickets?" She loved football, and her two favorite teams were the Detroit Lions and the Washington Redskins.

"Mara, I'll do whatever it takes to get tickets if it means securing a date with you."

"Okay, so we go to a game. Are we talking playoffs?"

"Not so fast. Our first date wouldn't be the game. The game is the second date. I'll only take you to the game if you go out to dinner with me first."

"Clever. That way I can't use you to get to the game, then ignore you the whole time."

"Exactly."

She dropped back onto the lumpy mattress. "I bet you're actually a decent lawyer."

He laughed. "That's what they tell me."

"So where do you take me for dinner?"

"My place?"

"No way. Too obvious you're just trying to get in my pants."

"But that *is* what I'm trying to do."

She'd been chilled from the ride on the motorcycle, but his voice had a strong warming effect. "I bet you can't cook."

"I was hoping you'd cook for me."

She laughed. "On our first date? No way." God, she was enjoying this game.

"Okay, so I take you someplace nice, but not quiet or formal. A loud, crowded restaurant with great food."

"People will recognize us there."

"They'll recognize *me*. In this fantasy, you weren't arrested in North Korea and are still anonymous."

"What do people say when they recognize you?"

"Women say hi, then slip me their card in a way that makes it clear what they want."

"So I'll see what a hot commodity you are."

"Yes."

"Will you act apologetic about it—these women pursuing you, when it's obvious we're on a date?"

"I think it would be smarter of me to put an arm around you."

A thrill shot through her, and this wasn't even *real*. "So you'd be sending the women a signal *and* have an excuse to touch me."

"I *am* known for my intelligence."

She laughed. "You win. It would work. I'd probably crawl all over you to stake my territory."

"Naturally." His low voice held an irresistible confidence.

"Where does your plan go from there?"

"A moonlit walk through the monuments?"

"In late November? It'd be freezing."

"You'd need my arm around you."

She smiled, since he couldn't see it, but assumed a stern voice. "Let's get one thing straight, Dominick. You may think I'm easy based on past behavior, but in this scenario we barely know each other. I'm not sleeping with you on the first date." *As if.* She'd totally jump him given the opportunity.

"Fine. We'll take a cab to your place, and I escort you to your door."

"But when I'm in DC, I usually stay at my uncle's."

"So you're staying at a hotel, or you've rented a place. Wait. This is my fantasy. In my fantasy, you've moved to DC."

"Why would I do that?"

"Well, there was this hot prosecutor you met, and he *lives* in DC."

"No. This is *our* fantasy, and in our fantasy there is no way I'd quit my job and move here before our first date. I'm staying at a hotel." She glanced around the motel room, taking in the twenty-year-old industrial carpeting, the cracked green plastic patio chair and table, and the lingering scent of cigarettes, even though it was supposed to be a nonsmoking room. "A really nice one," she added. "Very expensive. Paid for by your office because you dragged me there to testify."

"My office can't pay your bill after the trial is over—"

She huffed a sigh. "Fine. I stayed after the trial ended on my own dime, because there was a hot prosecutor who called me the day the trial ended…"

"After sentencing, you mean. Damn, we really should wait until after the appeal—"

"Do you even know what the word *fantasy* means?"

He laughed. "Oh, Mara, we really are screwed, aren't we?"

Eyes closed again, she said, "Leave reality out of it. I'm enjoying this. Okay, we get out of the cab at my hotel…"

"My arm is around your shoulders, and I'm wondering if you're going to let me explore your stunning cleavage. We walk toward the entrance, but I pull you to the side."

"Where are your hands?"

"I pull you against me so we're chest to chest. My arms are loosely around your waist, my hands flat on your back."

"Nice."

"I tell you I had a great time, and that I'm picking you up at ten for the game the next day."

"Do you kiss me?"

"No."

This time her gasp was indignant. "Why not?"

"Because you kiss me first."

"Oh. You know, you're right. I probably would."

"What do you think as you kiss me for the first time, Mara?"

That moment would forever be vivid in her mind. "Your mouth on mine makes me feel alive again."

His breathing turned ragged. "And I feel like I'm kissing lightning. Every touch burns."

She paused. "Seriously? You expect me to believe *that's* what you thought?"

"Well, that sounded better than admitting the way you sucked on my tongue made me wonder what else you could do with your mouth."

She chuckled. "Point taken. Okay. I'm lightning. And by the way, since you mentioned it—I can do a lot."

He groaned. "Damn, woman. You are cruel."

"Thank you. And on that note, I thank you for a lovely evening and escape into the hotel."

"Fine. Then I dive into the Potomac River and, finally cooled off, take a cab home."

She laughed again. "Goodnight, Curt."

"Goodnight, Mara."

CURT SET THE phone on the bedside table and fingered the football tickets he'd secured with her in mind, hoping with all his heart Mara could come out of hiding in time to use them.

# Chapter Thirty-Three

The US Attorney's Office was busy at eight o'clock on a Thursday night. Curt didn't have the luxury of keeping courtroom hours and usually put in six to eight hours in the office after court adjourned at four. His private line rang, and for a moment his heart picked up speed in the hope it was Mara, then slowed knowing she wouldn't call his work number.

The caller was Palea. "I'm having one badassed *lolo* day."

"What's wrong?" Curt asked.

"Do you want the good news or the bad news first?"

"Bad."

Palea snickered. "Should have guessed. I got the report from evidence. Garrett's hard drive was wiped clean. Professionally."

"They finally delivered on the subpoena?" Curt asked. He'd been waiting for the FBI to give Palea access to Mara's computer since last Friday.

"That was the good news."

Curt grunted. "That's the crappiest good news I've ever heard. They stopped stalling on the subpoena only to tell us we can't get anything from the hard disk?" *Dammit.* He'd really been hoping Mara's photos from Egypt would be the key, and the fact that her hard disk had been cleaned while she was in North Korea only confirmed his suspicions.

Palea cleared his throat. "Curt, if you know how to get in touch with her, find out if she backed up online or to a hard disk. The wipe was thorough. I want to know what Evan was so anxious to get rid of."

"I keep a fireproof box in the crawl space. Before a deployment, I back up everything and the hard disk goes into the box," Mara said to Curt when he finally got to speak with her later that night.

Her answer surprised him. "Why don't you just store the computer in the fireproof box?"

"Theft is rampant on Oahu, and my house is vacant for

months at a time. I'd rather lose the computer than force a meth-head to search for the valuable stuff. It's in the back corner of the crawl space, obscured by a bunch of worthless crap."

"You're very careful."

"My next-door neighbor's house was broken into a year ago. I don't have much of value, but there is some heirloom jewelry and my father's watch."

"Did Evan know about the firebox?"

"He would have called me paranoid—he always grabbed at any excuse to bring me down—so I didn't tell him."

If the man's head hadn't been blown off, Curt would gladly have decked him. "Hiding a backup hard disk is brilliant, not paranoid."

"Thank you. I think so too." Her low voice was filled with warmth that carried over the distance between them and settled in his chest. She continued. "It came in handy too. Twice I came back from deployment to a crashed hard disk."

The mellow feeling left in a flash, and Curt sat bolt upright. "Twice? Before or after Egypt?"

She sucked in a sharp breath. "It was an operating system failure…" Her words trailed off.

"Before or after Egypt?" he asked again.

"Shit." He could imagine her sitting there, eyes closed in resignation as another violation by Raptor became clear. "After."

"Both times you restored the data with your backup disk?"

"Yes."

"Evan must have wondered where the hell your backup was. Let's pray he didn't find your hiding place this time." He glanced at the clock. He wanted to stay on the phone with her and enjoy this, his favorite part of his day. But the case took precedence over imaginary dates with a beautiful woman. "I need to call Palea. It's early enough in Hawai'i. Maybe he can get the hard disk tonight. Can I call you later?"

"You sound tired."

He *was* tired but thought he'd been hiding it well. "I'm fine."

"Liar."

He yawned. "Tomorrow night?"

"Date three. I wouldn't miss it."

"It's date four, and I'll pick you up at ten. Dress is formal. Very formal."

# Chapter Thirty-Four

"THE PROSECUTION RESTS, Your Honor."

"Thank you, Mr. Dominick. Mr. Sherrod, is the defense ready to present their first witness?"

"Yes, Your Honor."

"Excellent. We will take the lunch recess. At one thirty, we will continue with the defense's first witness. The jury may be excused." The gavel fell, and the jury silently filed out of the room.

Juror seven looked pleased—possibly relieved at reaching a trial milestone. Two weeks into the proceedings and the prosecution had presented their case. The jury had been sequestered since opening arguments, and it was beginning to weigh on them.

Curt hated sequestering juries. But this trial had gotten so much press, it was inevitable. The jury, of course, hated *him* for it. He was the one who'd filed charges, he was the one who made them give up Halloween with their children, to try a man who'd been a beloved national figure.

This afternoon, the defense would have their turn. Right now it looked like Stevens would take the stand on Monday, and the trial would go to the jury Tuesday or Wednesday. The end was in sight, and then he could focus on Robert Beck and Raptor.

Curt's alarm went off at four every morning, and most nights he was lucky if he made it back into bed before midnight. Each day he managed over three hundred and fifty lawyers, ran a media circus of a trial, and spent the spare moments in between haggling with the FBI over search warrants and the Raptor investigation.

It was no wonder his nightly phone dates with Mara were the highlight of his day. The surprising part was that he'd successfully convinced himself to stop questioning his sanity and just enjoy…her.

And tonight, he had a special date planned.

Far too many hours later, he was settled on his couch with a glass of champagne in his hand and a beautiful woman on the phone. "Okay, then. On what date *do* you intend sleep with me?"

he asked. He was starting to feel strangely desperate.

"I'm not sure." Mara's smooth voice never failed to turn him on.

"You mean I could get lucky at any time?"

"Pretty much."

"I still say the football game was a date."

"Lee and Erica were there. I never agreed to a double date."

"But we didn't go *with* them. Lee has season tickets, and he hooked me up with the guy who holds the tickets for the seats next to his."

"And how does a US attorney justify buying scalped tickets?"

"They weren't scalped. I bought the tickets at face value."

"And the ticket holder's daughter's artwork for an exorbitant sum. That's scalping."

"I happen to think the five-year-old has talent," he said dryly.

Mara laughed.

Curt grinned. Her laughter, her voice, everything about these conversations made him feel vibrant. Alive. A warm buzz that had nothing to do with the champagne and everything to do with her. "Fine. Our second date was the Smithsonian American Indian Museum."

"You really got off cheap on that one. A free museum."

"Hey, I spent a fortune on a little girl's artwork so we could go on a nondate to a football game."

"I thought it was an investment."

He chuckled. "It was. In you."

"Ohhh. Good one. Okay, I'll let you cop a feel."

"Before or after dinner?"

"Depends. Where are you taking me?"

"We're going to the White House for a State Dinner."

She let out a low whistle. "Pulling out the big guns. Okay, I'm *slightly* impressed by the venue for date four, but you should know, this isn't my first State Dinner."

"France. Four years ago, when your uncle was in office. I've seen pictures, and you were stunning in that dress."

"The low-cut blue one?" He could hear the smile in her tone. "Thank you."

"No. Thank *you*."

"So what State Dinner is this?"

"I think we need something exotic. Maybe Asian?"

"I've spent enough time in Asian countries recently, thank

you."

He cringed. "Oh. Yeah. My bad."

"How about South Africa? I've never been there."

"Okay. South Africa. State Dinner. You're wearing blue. Or barely wearing blue."

"And you look hot in a tux," she said. "So, who are we seated next to?"

"You don't want to sit at the president's table?"

"We're too controversial. We're at a table by the kitchen, sitting with the Taiwanese ambassador or a Tibetan holy man. The guy they had to invite but shoved in the corner to keep from pissing off China."

He chuckled. "I'm not impressing you with my connections at all, am I?"

"No. But it's so sweet of you to try."

"Sweet. Just what I was aiming for."

"How's this for sweet? The blue dress is backless. I have to wear an adhesive bra or the whole world will see my goods. Guess what I rub on my nipples to make it stick?"

She'd struck him speechless.

"Honey," she said.

He sucked in a sharp breath. "No way."

"It wouldn't really work. But this is fantasy. In this fantasy, my bra adheres to my breasts with honey."

"Works for me." He closed his eyes, lost in the erotic image of a honey-coated Mara. "Let's skip the dinner part of this date and get to afterward…"

"You were charming and witty and had everyone at our table enthralled with your legal exploits."

"Then we leave in a limousine."

She chuckled. "Fastest State Dinner ever. Okay, with the privacy shield up, I pour you a drink and tell you I'd like to go back to your place."

*Hot damn, it's about time.* With the phone in one hand, he reached for the open bottle of champagne on the coffee table and refilled his glass. He'd begun preparing for his nightly "dates" with Mara more meticulously than he ever had for actual dates.

Tonight he had a chilled bottle of high-end champagne to go with this high-end fantasy. Next to the bottle sat the embossed invitation to the Indonesian State Dinner, due to take place in a few weeks. Given his tenuous reputation, he'd been surprised to make the cut. Tonight he allowed himself to fantasize she would be his date, wearing a sexy blue silk gown, high heels, and a thin coating of honey.

"How long is the drive to your place?" she asked.

"Ten minutes."

"I sip the champagne, then kiss you."

"I pull you onto my lap and deepen the kiss," he added.

The sound she made was the sexiest guttural purr Curt had ever heard. "The limousine stops in front of your building, but neither of us notices."

"Eventually, the chauffer politely informs us we need to get out."

"You've lost the bow tie."

"They're overrated."

"And a few buttons on your shirt might have popped off. We're disheveled and stumble out of the limo like two kids on prom night."

"And I'm so hard, I *feel* eighteen again."

Her voice dropped to a husky whisper. "Are you hard right now, Curt?"

"Beautiful, I get hard every time I hear your voice."

Her sultry laugh only made the ache worse. "Good. Because I'm so turned on I'm shaking."

"I can help you with that."

"I wish."

"What are you looking at right now, Mara?"

She paused, then said, "The fireplace. Flames licking the logs."

Curt leaned to the side and flicked the switch that turned on his gas fireplace. In seconds, flames danced before him. "How does the heat feel?"

"Not as good as your hands would."

"Words are all we have. So let's use them." He paused and took another sip of champagne. "We stumble through the lobby of my building and into the elevator."

"Can we do it in the elevator? I'm really, really aroused."

He chuckled. "I am *the* US attorney for the District of Columbia. I can't have sex with you in an elevator."

"Okay, USA Dominick. I merely kiss you silly in the elevator. How many flights?"

"Eight."

"Not a long ride, then."

"We enter my condo. You hate it, by the way."

She burst out laughing. "You've thought about this."

"Honey, I've thought about *all* of this, every minute of every day."

"Why would I hate your home?"

"It's a place to sleep, shower, and shave. I rarely even eat here."

"We'll talk about your decorating skills later. Right now I'm more interested in your anatomy."

"Inside, I scoop you up and kick the door closed. I carry you into the living room and set you down in front of the fireplace." Curt's gaze fixed on the stretch of carpet in front of the hearth. He could almost picture Mara there.

"Only one button, at the small of my back, holds my gown on, and I undo it. It falls to the floor and pools at my feet."

"So you're wearing an adhesive bra, a thong, and four-inch heels?"

"I never mentioned a thong or four-inch heels."

He chuckled. "I filled in a few details."

"Fine. I just pulled off your shirt so I could get to those pecs."

Curt loosened his collar but otherwise remained clothed. Tonight was for Mara and only for Mara. "What are you wearing right now?"

"It's not sexy. I don't have much."

"Mara, you could make a garbage bag sexy. Regardless, take it off."

She let out a hesitant sigh. "Have you ever done this before? Phone sex?"

He closed his eyes and conjured her smell, the texture of her skin. "No. I've never wanted or had a reason to. I want to make love to you, Mara, and the phone is all we have."

MARA RELAXED, KNOWING this was a first for him too. Their phone dates had been sexy, fun, a forbidden pleasure with a forbidden man. But part of the exhilaration was the utter shock of knowing something about *her* drew out Curt's warm, sensual side. He'd been so funny, so charming, so damn sexy on their pretend dates, they felt real.

But if he'd done all this before, then the sexy, sweet victory of breaching the barriers erected by The Shark and captivating the man would be gone, taking her libido with it. She settled on the cheap Atlantic City motel room bed, wishing she could be honest with him about her location, but knowing he'd freak and the mood would be lost if she were.

She stared at the old radiator in the corner. It wasn't a wood fireplace with dancing flames, but at least it was warm.

"I reach out and cup a breast," he said. "My thumb brushes across your nipple."

"Hey, wait. Am I still wearing the bra?"

"It's imaginary. Imagine it's gone."

She laughed and pinched her nipple and rolled it between her fingers, picturing Curt's hand in place of hers. "My breasts are tight. Ready for your mouth."

He let out a soft groan, and she wondered if he, like she, was thinking of their brief, forbidden touches in a different seedy motel room. "I suck on one and cradle the other in my hand. I alternate between the two and watch how the nipple contracts with the attention. You really have beautiful breasts, Mara."

"Thank you. I need you to kiss me some more. I could kiss you for hours."

"Same here. So we kiss. For hours. We don't stop as we lie down on the rug, in front of the fire. Your tongue and mine meld together. You taste like champagne."

She smiled. "You're still dressed, but I cradle you between my thighs as we make out. You are so hard, your cock presses against me, and I want you so bad I start fumbling with your fly." She slid her hand between her thighs and rubbed, imagining Curt between her legs. Remembering how he'd smelled, how he'd cradled her when he'd held her in bed.

"I stop you. I want to go slower. I take both of your hands and pull them up, over your head. I kiss you deeply while pressing deeper between your thighs, grinding against you."

"I want more."

"And you get more. I leave your mouth and trail kisses down your body. Again I taste those perfect, honey-coated breasts. Then my mouth slides lower, across your flat abdomen. My tongue traces a line from your belly button downward, until I get to the top of your thong."

Mara followed his words with a hand trailing down until it hovered at her panty line. "Then what?" she asked in a choked voice.

"The thong must go. I pull it off, and you're naked before me. I spread your thighs and smell the sweet scent of your arousal. With a finger, I separate your folds, and touch your clitoris. I roll it between my thumb and forefinger, just like I did your nipple."

Mara jolted, electrified by his words. "I rock up against you and demand more."

"I give it to you. With my tongue. I suck on your clit, then explore your opening. You're swollen, ready for me, and taste like heaven."

Mara found a pleasing rhythm with her fingers, surprised at how uninhibited she was. She felt as if she really were laid bare before him, really had given him free access to her most intimate places. "I want you inside me, Curt."

"I want that too, love." He sighed, then continued. "But I'm going to make you come with my mouth first. Are you close, Mara?"

"I was close when you answered the phone."

He chuckled. "I slide my fingers inside you, then rub a slick finger over your clit. I keep up the friction with my tongue and thumb, while two fingers thrust inside."

Her breathing became a ragged pant as the sound of his voice and the pressure of her fingers brought her closer to the edge.

"Your thighs tighten. I can feel your whole body coil when you clench down on my fingers."

"Oh. Curt—"

"That's it, sweetheart. Come for me. Feel my mouth on your clit, my fingers inside you."

Her eyes were closed. His voice reached across the miles to caress her soul. She could feel his hands, his mouth, his heartbeat. He was here with her, and it was his touch that pushed her quaking body over the edge. A powerful orgasm rocked her. She let out a guttural cry.

"God, that's sexy," Curt said. "I wish I could see your face and follow up by sliding inside you. I want to make you mine."

*I am yours.*

A moment passed before the quaking stopped and she could speak. "When can we do this for real?"

"I don't know, sweetheart. The trial will be done soon. We'll figure something out once it's over."

After he sent her uncle to prison. Christ, what was she doing falling in love with this man?

# Chapter Thirty-Five

The call came from Palea at midnight. "Curt, I'm e-mailing you a photo from Mara's hard disk right now. I think you'll find it interesting."

Curt ran his fingers through his hair and shook his head. Weeks of being short on sleep had caught up with him. Add to that his incredible date with Mara and the erotic dreams that followed, and he'd uncharacteristically failed at hiding his groggy state.

"This better be good. Tonight was the first night I've gone to sleep before midnight in days." He slipped from the bed and padded into his office.

"Depends, is nailing Beck and Stevens on the arms deal *good*?"

Adrenaline shot through him, eclipsing fatigue. "You've got the arms deal?"

"In HD clarity."

He dropped into the office chair and woke his computer. It took a few minutes for the e-mail to download. "High-res digital camera?"

"You can count the pores on the Janjaweed militia leader's ugly face."

Curt opened the preview image. "Holy fuck." There he was. A mass murderer sitting two feet away from Andrew Stevens. "Shit, Palea. The prosecution rested today."

"Get it in on cross."

"I can't. Not without Mara to authenticate it."

"You definitely need her. The others are all dead, missing, or in on it. Robert Beck is next to Andrew Stevens. Roddy Brogan is with Jeannie Fuller behind the VP, and I think that's Evan Beck's shoulder on the right. But Curt, zoom in on the Secret Service agents in the background."

Curt did as instructed. "Palea, you fucking genius. Those aren't Secret Service agents. Those are Robert Beck's top operatives."

"Merry Christmas, *brah*."

This was his birthday and Christmas rolled into one. Mara had taken a picture of Raptor's CEO, Raptor's chief of operations, two operatives contracted out to JPAC, and two operatives pretending to be Secret Service agents, all meeting with a Janjaweed militia leader who was posing as an Egyptian villager. The meeting took place in a remote Egyptian village in the midst of a JPAC recovery operation, but Curt strongly doubted any of those people were there to mourn the American soldiers who died in Egypt during World War II.

"WE'LL NEED GARRETT to authenticate it," Aurora said, sitting in front of her computer while Sam hovered over her shoulder and Curt leaned against a file cabinet. It was three in the morning on Saturday, and even though the trial wouldn't resume until Monday, this couldn't wait until dawn. She cursed, then said, "Why didn't Palea get this photo to us yesterday, before we rested?"

"The FBI did everything they could to deny access to Mara's computer—which they'd confiscated from a crime scene. I had to get a subpoena, just to find out the disk had been wiped." He crossed his arms. "Then, when I learned where the backup hard drive was"—Aurora's eyes flickered, telling him she'd guessed how he'd managed *that*—"he had to go through hoops to retrieve it so it would have a clean chain-of-evidence."

Aurora growled. "Goddamn politics."

Curt leaned forward and reached for the mouse. With a click, he opened another picture. "This is the photo of the warlord that Palea used for comparison."

Sam pointed to the pictured man's left cheek. "Same scar. Same goofy grin. He knew Garrett was taking his picture and didn't care."

"I think Evan Beck saw what she was doing," Curt said, "and tried to block the shot. They started dating in Egypt. I'm guessing he was trying to get access to her camera and computer." Anger simmered over the idea a scumbag like Beck had ever touched her, let alone did it to serve Raptor. "He crashed her hard disk twice but didn't know where she kept the backup."

"If we get this accepted into evidence, we can motion to have the charges conformed to the evidence," Aurora said. "The arms deal would be a slam dunk after that."

Curt shook his head. "We can't do that without Mara to authenticate."

"We can bring her in as a rebuttal witness. Odds are Stevens will take the stand, so get him to deny the photo is authentic and she's in."

"We don't need the photo for this trial," Curt said. "We can save it for Beck. We've got Stevens on obstruction and influence peddling. He won't get off."

"Dammit, Dominick! Have you gone soft? We both know the obstruction charge could result in a presidential pardon. If we can prove the arms deal, he'll get ten years—and it will be damn hard for any president to issue a pardon."

Shit. Aurora was right. His gut clenched, and a piece of his heart ripped open.

He'd always thought the worst part of falling in love was the inevitable pain of breakup, but now he understood the truth. The worst part was knowing he would devastate her by doing the one thing he had to do. "I can get her here before this goes to the jury."

# CHAPTER THIRTY-SIX

IT WAS TIME to move to a new motel. Mara never spent more than two nights in the same place and left the Atlantic City dive without regret, knowing the next stop on her tour of the seedy casino fringe would be neither better nor worse. At least in Atlantic City she had plenty of options. She was merely another person wishing to remain anonymous in a place known for attracting the dregs of society. Atlantic City lacked even the questionable class of Las Vegas.

The motel she checked into at three in the afternoon on Saturday was as shabby and worn as the last. Her third-floor room boasted bars on the window and a surprisingly solid door with a massive dead bolt.

This was as safe as she would get, if she didn't mind feeling imprisoned. Again.

She didn't bother to unpack her paltry backpack of supplies gathered from thrift stores in Michigan, Ohio, and Pennsylvania. She never left a thing behind when she went anywhere. She could, and would, flee at any time.

She'd been in Atlantic City since Tuesday night and planned to give Jeannie a few more days before she would drive two hundred miles away and try Twitter again.

Two and a half years ago, before Evan, before indictments, before Raptor had so thoroughly infiltrated JPAC, Mara had flown to DC to visit her uncle at the same time Jeannie had flown to New York to visit her hometown. At the end of their respective visits, they'd met up in Atlantic City for a girl's weekend. Mara had never been into gambling. Casinos were Jeannie's thing—and now, Mara realized, her brother Eric's as well—but Mara had enjoyed the in-house spa while Jeannie parked herself in front of a slot machine and tapped the electronic buttons to her heart's content.

On the second night of their long weekend, Mara found Jeannie in the back corner, feeding a quarter slot machine. Ready to leave for dinner, Jeannie hit the button one last time. Symbols lined up, and she won the jackpot. Nothing life-changing, but the four-hundred-dollar payout bought dinner that night and was the highlight of an enjoyable weekend.

Mara knew Jeannie would understand her cryptic Twitter direct message. If Jeannie read it and wanted to see her, she'd know to find Mara in the same corner of the casino where she hit the jackpot. Mara went to the casino every day and waited, sometimes for five minutes, and sometimes for hours.

Jeannie would show up. She had to. Her brother was dead, she was on the run, and she probably had as many questions as she had answers. If nothing else, Mara would drag her ass to DC so she could tell the Departments of State and Homeland Security what had happened in North Korea and Curt could get his search warrants for Raptor facilities.

But to do that, she needed to find Jeannie, without making it easy for Raptor to find her. She'd head back to the casino in an hour, but for now, all she wanted to do was flop on the bed and watch the news.

She flipped through the cable news channels, looking for stories about Curt so she could see his face even though the thought of calling him made her blush. She'd had phone sex with the man, but she was the only one who'd gotten off.

She was being such a *girl*, with her day-after doubts, but still couldn't help but worry—what if when she saw him again, the wonderful man who'd taken her on several dates and courted her with such ardor on the phone turned back into the ruthless prosecutor?

His picture flashed on the screen, followed by a photo of her uncle. The reporter said her uncle's defense was falling apart and laid odds Uncle Andrew would opt to take the stand on Monday because he was certain to lose otherwise.

There were exactly two men alive who mattered to her: an uncle she adored and a hero she was falling in love with. But one's success meant the other's destruction. There could be no happy ending for both.

The phone rang, and in spite of her mixed feelings, she lunged for it. Her days were filled with tawdry casinos and dingy motels. Curt and their imaginary relationship was her sole escape from the depressing landscape.

"Hi, Gorgeous. I'm sorry I didn't call sooner. Today has been nuts."

His warm tone sent quivers straight to her crotch. "It's okay. I didn't expect to hear from you until tonight."

"I've been thinking about you." His voice deepened and became suggestive. "All day."

Her heart went into overdrive. "I've been thinking about you too."

"Good. Mara, the trial will wrap soon. Another few days and it's done. Raptor might step up efforts to find you after the trial, expecting you to make a move. I want you to come to DC."

The suggestion startled her. "You mean now?"

"Yes. They won't expect it. They won't be looking for you here."

"But why DC? I could go anywhere." *And I need to find Jeannie.*

"Because I'm here." He paused. "And it's time for you to come forward. I need you to tell the secretary of state about the smallpox."

She pursed her lips and debated her options. Finally, she said, "I went to see an epidemiologist. I've got blood-test results. You can prove I had smallpox without me being there."

Tension and more than a little anger entered his voice. "You did *what*?"

"I saw an epidemiologist. He's someone I know, from Michigan. He was safe. He ran a blood test and found antibodies—or something like that—that proves I had smallpox."

"And you didn't tell me?"

She frowned. "Because I knew you'd be upset."

"With good reason. Jesus, Mara. What sort of risks are you taking? You're supposed to be sitting tight in the lakeside cottage and staying safe."

She bristled at his tone. "But you just asked me to go to DC. How is that *playing it safe*?"

"At least here I can protect you!" His voice rose with every word. "And any blood test you had wouldn't be valid in a court of law without a clean chain-of-evidence."

"So what? You can use it to get a search warrant. How about thanking me instead of yelling at me?"

"I'm not—" His words broke off.

"Yes. You are," she said softly.

He huffed out a heavy sigh. "I'm sorry. You're right. But, Mara, I'm scared to death for you. I hate it that you're hundreds of miles away and I can't watch over you. I want you here. With me."

She closed her eyes. She wanted more than anything to go to DC, to see him, to feel like she could have some semblance of a life. "I'm afraid. The risk would be so high in DC. I'd be trapped indoors."

His voice turned Barry White–deep. "You'll be trapped with *me*."

"Sounds like a booty call to me."

"Bonus."

She laughed, but tension still coiled through her. "I'm not sure, Curt."

"Give it a day. Think about it."

"Do we still have a date tonight?"

"Of course. I've been looking forward to it all day."

Afraid he'd reject her if she didn't give him what he wanted, a torrent of emotion flooded her at hearing the warmth in his voice. She'd been with manipulative Evan just long enough to rattle her confidence when it came to relationships. She closed her eyes and gripped the phone in a tight fist. She didn't speak until she was certain she could keep her heart out of her voice. "What do you have planned?"

"I was thinking we'd go to your hotel room. Or my place. We'll get takeout and eat in."

"And fool around?"

"It's like you read my mind." She could hear the smile in his tone.

She sighed and spoke the truth that had been nagging at her all day. "It's not like this is real, Curt."

"Mara, this is more real than any relationship I've ever had. The dates are pretend, but the connection? It's genuine." He paused. "You've turned my world upside down. Just talking to you on the phone wakes something inside me that's never been there before. I'm ass-over-teakettle, sweetheart."

Guilt swamped her. How would he react when he realized she'd been lying to him? That she hadn't told him—or anyone—Evan's last words. She'd withheld information from the FBI to protect Jeannie. "Dammit, Curt. Every time I manage to convince myself I'm only falling for you because you're my incredible-savior-superhero, you go and say something like that and give me hope this is real. And you know what I hate? Hope. It's a fucking four-letter word." *And I can't afford to hope when no matter what I do, someone I care about will suffer.*

His soft chuckle carried across the line.

"It's not funny. Hope has brought me nothing but pain and disappointment."

"Oh, sweetheart, I'm not laughing at you. I'm relieved. Your moment of silence after I told you how I feel scared the hell out of me."

*He feels insecure too?* She cradled the phone, pressing it with painful intensity against her ear. "What are we going to do?"

"Come to DC, we'll figure it out from here."

She couldn't. Not yet. "I don't know, Curt. I need to think."

"Don't think about it too long."

"I'll have a decision for you tomorrow."

"Okay." He sighed, and a long silence ensued. Finally, he said, "Mara, I'm falling in love with you."

LEE SCOTT SHOWED up at Curt's Georgetown condo at eight on Sunday morning. Curt answered the door armored in his version of casual Sunday attire—a business suit minus the jacket and tie. He raised a curious eyebrow at Lee's uncharacteristically early arrival, then stepped back to allow him to enter. "Did you get in a fight with Erica or something?"

Lee shook his head. "Get your coat. If you have coffee made, fill two travel mugs. We've got to leave. Now. My car is gassed up and ready to go."

"I've got coffee. Come in and tell me what the hell is going on."

In the kitchen, Lee wasn't surprised to see a Sunday morning political news program on the television. He turned the set off. He needed Curt's undivided attention.

Curt poured coffee. "Where are we going?"

"We need to be in Atlantic City before noon." Lee's gaze cut to the clock, and adrenaline shot through him. Four hours. Without traffic, they might be early.

"Why?"

There was no way to soften this news. "Mara is not in Michigan. She's in Atlantic City, trying to find Jeannie Fuller. An hour ago, via Twitter, Jeannie sent a direct message to Mara saying she'd meet her at noon today."

AN HOUR LATER, with DC thirty miles behind them, Curt still found it difficult to breathe. Of all the crazy, foolish, idiotic, dangerous things to do. Mara was about to rendezvous with Jeannie, a woman who had sold her out once already and later left her own brother to die at the hands of Evan Beck.

What was she *thinking*?

More curses ran through his mind. How many times was he going to drop everything to save Mara from a firing squad? Because sure as hell meeting with Jeannie was even more dangerous than the damn North Koreans.

Thank God he'd asked Lee to put his hacking skills to work on finding her after their conversation yesterday. He didn't want to know how Lee had done it or what laws he'd broken. All he wanted was Mara safe.

So he could throttle her.

Curt drove far too fast and prayed he wouldn't have to explain himself to police, while Lee had his computer open on his lap in the passenger seat, tracking Mara's movements when her phone checked in with cellular antennas.

"You promise Raptor can't do the same thing?" Curt asked.

"Aside from the fact that they don't have her number, I've also secured her signal. I can get around it, because I'm the one who encrypted it. But Raptor can't hack a phone that doesn't show up during their scans, and her signal is invisible to everyone but me."

Curt frowned and kept his eyes on the road ahead. "Don't tell me any more."

"Don't worry. It's mostly legal."

Yeah, it was the "mostly" part that worried him. He turned up the radio and said, "I can't hear you."

Lee tapped away at his keyboard. A minute later, he said, "Her phone has checked in with the same antenna for the last hour, and it's not near any casinos. We don't have to worry unless Mara heads to a casino before noon."

"*If* you're right about the meeting place being a casino." *Oh Jesus.* What if Lee was wrong? *Don't think about it. Just drive.* "Where is she now?"

"From the map, it looks like she's outside the casino district."

"That fits for the kind of motel she'd choose. She'll find a place that doesn't bat an eye at cash and won't check ID." The thought of Mara exposing herself in Atlantic City, when Raptor's base of operations was only four hours away, sent his blood pressure through the roof. *And for Jeannie, of all people.* "Any action on Mara's Twitter account?"

"Since you asked fifteen minutes ago? No. She hasn't logged in to Twitter in a week. She doesn't know Jeannie plans to meet her today."

"If it's Jeannie who responded."

"Yes. If."

"Has Jeannie gone onto Twitter again?"

"Also no." Lee closed the laptop. "Curt, when are you going to be honest with me?"

He stiffened. "What do you mean?"

"Mara is more than just a witness. You care about her."

"I do. But until the trial is over, there's nothing I can do about it."

"Are you going to tell her you want her to testify?"

Curt tightened his grip on the steering wheel and fixed his gaze on the road ahead. He hated what he had to do but couldn't see any way around it. She would be a rebuttal witness. He didn't have a subpoena anymore, and couldn't get one until Stevens said something she could rebut. So if he told her, and she fled… He didn't even want to consider that possibility.

Lee must have guessed what his silence meant, because he said, "Do you have any idea what this will do to her? You're going to fuck over any chance of a relationship with her for your trial."

"Her uncle is a traitor to his own country. He has to pay."

"You and Mara will end up paying too."

"You think I like this? This isn't my first choice. Not by a long shot. But I can't only pursue justice when it's convenient for my love life, and if I don't get Mara on the stand, Stevens and Beck will go on with their dirty deals. People will die. Hell, I'm fairly certain Beck's got big plans for his new smallpox toy. Stopping him is bigger than me or my desire for a relationship with Mara. And, if after seeing the evidence against her uncle, Mara still worships the man, well then"—a wave of regret rolled through him—"she's not the woman for me."

Lee's laugh held no humor. "Man, you are so fucked. Either way."

"Yeah. Tell me something I don't know."

AT ELEVEN FORTY-FIVE, Mara walked by the slots as if she were heading to the restaurant on the other side, scanning faces and alert for anyone noticing her. But the off-season patrons all held the blank stares of habitual gamblers. The flashing lights of the loud machines had a lock on their attention, blocking everything else.

She entered the restaurant and scanned the crowd. Her heart leapt at the sight of a woman at the buffet who was the right height and build. She crossed the room to the food line, only to be disappointed when the woman twisted and Mara caught a glimpse of her profile. Not Jeannie.

Curt had told her Jeannie withdrew twenty-five thousand dollars from her bank account before fleeing Oahu two weeks ago. With that kind of money, she could hide for a while—far longer than Mara, whose reserves were rapidly dwindling. With the right connections, Jeannie could buy an ID and credit card. She could build a new identity. She could travel with ease and purchase plane tickets on commercial airlines. She could distance herself from her brother's grisly murder.

Jeannie's face hadn't been on the news as Mara's had. She was safely anonymous. But she must have questions about her brother. She must realize Mara was her only hope if she were ever to come out of hiding.

*Dammit.* Jeannie should have shown up by now. This was Mara's seventh day in Atlantic City. The casino staff was starting to notice her. Maybe it was time to give up.

She could go to DC and enlist Curt's help. His friend Lee could monitor her Twitter account and let her know if Jeannie responded.

But Curt would flip. He'd be livid and, worse, hurt that she hadn't confided in him. She did a mental headshake as she stepped back out onto the main casino floor. One more day. She could give Jeannie one more day.

She crossed the card room floor. Next she'd swing by the pool and arcade, then the spa. Anything to kill time and give Jeannie a chance to show up, without leaving Mara a sitting duck in the back of the casino. The damn building didn't have enough exits for her liking.

Her cell phone rang, and she startled.

Curt. It had to be Curt. She plucked the phone from her pocket and answered.

"Do you see the man in the Aloha shirt?" Curt asked.

Adrenaline shot through her system. She spun and saw a tall—very tall—man, young, boyish looking, leaning on a slot machine, and staring directly at her. The man waved, beckoning her toward him. In her ear, Curt said, "That's Lee. He's safe. Follow him."

"I can't. I'm—"

"I know exactly what you're doing, Mara, and if you think I'm going to let you risk your life for that rotten, betraying bitch, think again. *Follow Lee!*" The last words were a roar.

In spite of Lee's imposing height, he looked safe, nonthreatening, probably due to the familiar, colorful shirt. Her feet obediently followed Curt's shouted instructions.

Within striking distance, Lee's arm snaked out and gripped her shoulder. He was fast. Shockingly so. And with a reach that shouldn't have surprised her given his height. Jesus. He was probably a foot and a half taller than her.

"Nice to meet you, Mara," he said and dragged her toward the front door.

He stopped and swore, and Mara saw what halted him in the same moment. Jeannie Fuller. Entering the casino.

Mara lurched forward, toward her friend, but the grip on her arm stopped her. Lee yanked the phone from her grasp and said, "Trouble, Curt. Meet us at the back entrance." With Mara in tow, he spun and bolted for the rear of the casino floor.

"Wait! I want to talk to her."

"Not a chance in hell," Lee said, dragging her along.

Mara dug in her heels and struggled against him. She twisted her arm, and amazingly, broke free. She shot forward, then skidded to a stop. Two men had entered the casino behind Jeannie. Both had the bearing of Raptor operatives.

Jeannie had betrayed her again.

# CHAPTER THIRTY-SEVEN

CURT SAW JEANNIE and the two goons enter the casino right before Lee shouted into the phone. He'd pulled onto the wide, twisty road that circled the casino before Lee even started speaking. They had planned for this. Lee would get her to the rear exit.

Raptor couldn't afford to open fire in a crowded casino. Mara had done that much right in choosing the meeting place. Now Lee and Curt had to do their part to save her.

Later he'd ask her the important questions, like why she hadn't confided in him. But right now, all that mattered was getting her out of there. Thank God, Mara was a runner. If anything, she'd be faster than Lee sprinting across the casino floor.

Curt reached the back entrance—a full mile and a half around the building from the front—at the same time the door burst open, and Mara shot through with Lee at her heels. Lee pointed to his gray sedan, and Mara veered in his direction. She yanked open the rear door and tumbled in, Lee right behind her. Curt hit the gas, and they were peeling away from the curb as Lee caught the door and pulled it shut.

He didn't look back to see if they were followed. It didn't matter. They had to assume Raptor would hack the hotel security camera to get the license plate. Within the hour, they'd know Lee was helping them.

But at least for now, Mara was safe.

"I THINK," LEE said, climbing between the seats to the front of the vehicle, "I can hack the camera and erase the footage before Raptor sees it."

Mara sat bolt upright, still catching her breath, still trying to figure out what had just happened. "You can do that?"

"I don't want to hear about it," Curt said from the driver's seat.

Mara focused on Lee, because if she looked at Curt, met his angry gaze in the rearview mirror, she just might fall apart.

"How?"

Lee plucked a laptop from the floor, flipped it open, and answered in a stage whisper, as if Curt couldn't hear him, "He doesn't know it, but on the drive down I hacked the security cameras of all the major resort casinos. I didn't know which one we'd find you in."

"That can't be easy," Mara whispered back, impressed.

"It's not." He grinned and winked at her.

Curt kept his gaze on the road. Mara had to admit this was a terrible position for him to be in, knowing his friend was breaking the law to protect her. She touched Curt's shoulder. He stiffened.

She dropped her hand and slumped back against the rear seat, feeling rejected, hurt. "I'm sorry, Curt. I—"

"Don't," Curt said, his voice clipped, full of righteous anger. "Don't even try to justify it to me."

She didn't know at this point if she could justify her decisions to herself. Jeannie had sold her out to Raptor. Again.

What would make her bring members of the same organization that had killed her brother to a rendezvous with Mara?

The thought of what it would take to bring Jeannie so low twisted her gut. She had probably been through a hell Mara didn't want to imagine. "We need to go back. Jeannie needs help."

"There's been an APB out on Jeannie for two weeks now," Curt said. "I called the local FBI office on the drive up and told them to have a team ready. As soon as we knew which casino, I updated them. If Jeannie is smart, she'll make a scene and won't leave the casino with the Raptor operatives, giving the FBI the opportunity to take her into protective custody."

Relief filtered through the heartache. They hadn't abandoned Jeannie to monsters. She pulled her knees up and hugged them to her chest. "Where are we going?" she asked.

"I've arranged for a safe house in DC," Curt answered, his words even colder than before.

This was hardly the reunion she'd imagined with the man who'd been so hot and enticing on the phone. "I thought the FBI wasn't going to protect me."

"I just needed time to make it happen."

"How safe can it be? Isn't the FBI caving to pressure to blame everything on Evan?"

"There are a handful of agents I've known for years and trust."

"And I've known Jeannie for years—"

"I said don't, Mara. You may have known her for years, but nothing she's done lately has proven her trustworthy. You're as blind about her as you are about your uncle, but this time, you almost got yourself killed." His voice rose. "What if I hadn't asked Lee to find you? What if we hadn't gotten there in time?"

"Why did you?" she asked, lashing out like the cornered, wounded animal she was. "Why the hell did you find me? It was *my* business I was in Atlantic City. Not yours."

"Curt," Lee said, "pull over. Let me drive."

"No. Driving the car is the only thing that's keeping me sane right now."

"I beg to differ," Lee said. "There is nothing sane about the way you're driving."

Mara looked at the speedometer and blanched. They were going ninety. Curt hadn't driven that fast in trafficless, middle-of-the-night Oklahoma. He eased off the gas, and the car slowed.

"Pull over," Mara said. "I'll jump out at the next rest stop. I'm not your problem anymore, Dominick."

"The hell you will. You're going to DC and the safe house. Period."

"Get this straight, US Attorney Dominick, I am *not* your prisoner." He was as bad as the Korean People's Army, and she was sick of it.

Curt's knuckles whitened on the steering wheel. "Ms. Garrett, I kindly ask that you take the protection I have gone to great lengths to acquire for you." The words were spoken through gritted teeth. "I would be ever so grateful, seeing as how I'm doing my best to *save your goddammed foolish ass!*"

So much for courtship and telephone dates. They had come full circle and were right back where they started. "Fine," she said through stiff lips. She'd go to the safe house. It would buy her time to think.

She swiped at the stupid, foolish tear that trailed down her cheek before Curt or Lee could see it. What happened to the man who'd wined and dined her with imaginary dates? Where was the man who thought he was falling in love with her?

"MR. SHERROD, IS your next witness ready?" Judge Hawthorne asked.

"Yes, Your Honor. At this time, the defendant, Vice President

Andrew Stevens would like to testify."

Noise in the gallery peaked. Judge Hawthorne gave her trademark look over her glasses to the spectators but didn't resort to the gavel. Even so, the noise stopped. The crowd had been trained.

"We are nearing the lunch recess and as Mr. Stevens's testimony should take significant time, we will break. Court will resume at one thirty. The jury is excused."

Aurora whispered to Curt, "Nice. The reporters will have just enough time to file a noon report."

Curt wondered if Mara was watching the news. In a matter of minutes, Stevens's intention to testify would hit the airwaves. What would she think of that?

Anger had crackled between them yesterday when he left her at the safe house. In the end, Lee had stepped outside, leaving Curt alone with her.

She'd been tense, hurt, and defensive. And he had to admit he was behaving like a complete ass. The sight of Mara fleeing that casino, knowing Raptor operatives were in pursuit, had rattled him much more than he'd anticipated.

He'd crossed the living room of the safe house and took her small, stiff body into his arms. *"I'm upset because I was terrified. I care about you, Mara. You're worth a thousand Jeannies."*

*"I was trying to find her for you."*

*"For me?"*

*"I was going to convince her to come to DC and tell the FBI or Homeland or the State Department about Raptor. If she told the truth, you'd get your search warrants in a heartbeat."*

*"Jeannie's word isn't worth spit. She took a payoff from Raptor. She has no credibility. Your word is the only one that will convince a judge to issue a warrant."*

She'd crumpled then, pressed against him, and he'd held her while she quietly sobbed, as he should have done right after they'd escaped North Korea.

Now, a day later, his only hope to salvage a relationship with her when this was over was pinned on shattering her allegiance to her uncle. She was going to hate him when she realized he'd asked Lee to find her so he could drag her here to testify. But maybe, if she knew the atrocity her uncle had committed in selling arms to a war criminal, she'd understand.

Mara had seen the devastation of war crimes firsthand. She'd excavated mass graves in Bosnia. Her uncle had used her work with JPAC as a cover for illicit meetings with the worst sort of war criminal, and he'd followed that by using JPAC for recovery and theft of biological weapons. By all rights, Mara should despise her uncle, but Curt knew his own actions would cut just as deep.

# CHAPTER THIRTY-EIGHT

LATE TUESDAY MORNING, Curt finally got his chance to question Andrew Stevens. He led with harmless questions designed to put the man at ease. A half hour into questioning, he finally got to the heart of the matter. "Mr. Stevens, have you ever been to Egypt?"

Stevens stiffened in the witness box. The bastard didn't want that line of questioning. Too bad.

"Objection, question on cross-examination goes beyond scope of direct," Stevens's attorney, Ben Sherrod, said.

"Your Honor, Vice President Stevens spoke of his travel to foreign countries as part of his work for Raptor," Curt said.

"Overruled. You may answer the question, Mr. Stevens."

"Yes. I've been to Egypt once. But it wasn't for Raptor, or as vice president. I was visiting my niece."

"Objection, witness's answer goes beyond the scope of the question," Sherrod said with barely restrained annoyance.

"Mr. Sherrod, he's *your* witness. Overruled."

Curt smiled as Ben Sherrod gritted his teeth. Sherrod hadn't stood a chance of winning that objection, but he'd managed to remind his defendant to keep his answers simple.

"You weren't there on a Raptor assignment?" Curt asked.

"No."

"Then why was Raptor's CEO, Robert Beck, also present?"

"Objection," Sherrod said. "Assuming facts not in evidence."

"I'll rephrase, Your Honor. Mr. Stevens, did Raptor's CEO, Robert Beck, join you in Egypt when you visited your niece?"

"Yes. He came along so he could visit his son, Evan Beck, a Raptor operative who worked on a contract basis with JPAC."

"Did anyone else travel with you to Egypt?" Curt asked.

"Two Secret Service agents."

"You were no longer vice president, but you still had Secret Service protection?"

Stevens twisted in the witness box and faced the jury on his left. He flashed his friendly, politician smile. "It is allowed for six months for former vice presidents."

Juror three, a middle-aged school teacher, smiled back for the fifth time since Stevens took the stand.

"When did you stop receiving Secret Service protection?"

"I don't remember the exact date."

"Is it safe to assume it was six months after January 20th?"

"Reasonable. It might have been a little earlier."

"And two Secret Service agents traveled with you to Egypt?"

The man let out an annoyed sigh, and Curt could just bet the former vice president had the jurors in the palm of his hand. That was about to change. "Yes."

"Did a photographer travel with you to Egypt?"

Stevens finally turned back to Curt. "No. This was a private visit."

Curt met his gaze. "Photographs of the trip appeared on the AP wire. Who took those photos?" Defendants usually looked away, but not Stevens.

"My niece. Mara has an excellent digital camera and a good eye."

"Let the record show that the person the defendant refers to is his niece, Mara Garrett," Curt said.

Stevens cleared his throat. "Yes. Sorry."

Mara was a heroine to most of the people who'd followed her story in the press. Every time Stevens referred to her in a warm, avuncular way, the jury's attention level peaked. Sherrod had certainly told him to mention Mara as often as possible under cross.

Aurora handed Curt the first photo they planned to introduce. A familiar jolt ran through him at seeing Mara's face in the picture. "Permission to approach the witness?"

"Proceed," Judge Hawthorne said.

Curt left the podium and handed Stevens the photo. "Was this photo taken on that trip?"

Stevens shrugged. "I assume. The background looks right. I visited Mara a few times on different deployments. They blur together a bit."

"Your Honor, I offer this photo as exhibit sixty-six and ask that it be accepted into evidence."

"Your Honor, a moment while I review the photo?" Sherrod asked.

"Certainly."

Sherrod flipped through the proposed exhibit binder and

found the photo. After a moment of study, he said, "No objections."

"Let the record show exhibit sixty-six has been accepted into evidence."

"May I publish this to the jury?"

"You may."

Curt approached Juror One and handed him the photo. The man studied it, then passed it to the next juror; they'd gotten used to passing exhibits over the last few weeks.

He returned to the podium and received another photo from Aurora. Equally innocuous, taken later in the day and also one that had been picked up by the Associated Press. Curt went through the same process and the photo was admitted as exhibit sixty-seven without argument.

"Your Honor, at this time I would like to show the defendant a third photo, taken the same day, which only recently came into prosecution's possession."

Sherrod shot to his feet. "Objection, prosecution did not supply defense with the photograph during discovery."

"Your Honor," Curt said with his most conciliatory smile, "chain-of-evidence will show we only discovered this photograph the day before yesterday, and therefore were unable to provide it during discovery."

"Sidebar. Now." Judge Hawthorne didn't look pleased. Curt calculated the odds of showing the photo to Stevens at fifty-fifty.

"What's the deal with this photograph, Dominick?"

He handed the judge a copy. "It was recovered from Mara Garrett's backup hard disk. I want Stevens to look at the picture and tell me if he remembers when it was taken."

Ben Sherrod looked at the picture. His eyebrow rose. "Obvious forgery," Sherrod said.

"The chain-of-evidence is clean," Curt added.

"Mr. Dominick, you can't ask for a photo to be admitted without authentication." Judge Hawthorne's tone was mildly annoyed.

"Stevens can authenticate it. As you can see, he was there."

Hawthorne paused. Finally, she said, "I'll allow you to show the defendant the photo."

Curt's heart thudded and adrenaline pulsed. When he'd told Mara the courtroom was his happy place, *this* was what he'd meant. The rush of assured victory. "Thank you, Your Honor."

Sherrod returned to his seat, his movements stiff. He was worried. Very worried.

As he should be.

Curt delivered the photo to Stevens and lingered by the witness box. "Do you recognize this photo, Mr. Stevens?"

He caught the slight widening of the man's eyes before he got his reaction under control. Having seen what he wanted, Curt retreated to the podium.

Stevens looked to the jury, not Curt, as he gave his answer. "No."

"Was it taken by your niece?"

To Sherrod's credit, he kept his mouth closed.

"It's not possible. The photo is a complete forgery," Stevens said.

"Your Honor, at this time I ask that the photo, marked proposed exhibit sixty-eight, be introduced into—"

Again, Sherrod shot to his feet. "Objection! Lack of proper foundation."

Judge Hawthorne glared at the defense attorney. "Sit down, Mr. Sherrod. Your objection is sustained. Introduction of the photo into evidence is denied." Gavel met sound block, underscoring her ruling.

Curt smiled, having gotten exactly what he wanted. "No further questions, Your Honor."

"Mr. Sherrod, do you wish to redirect?"

"No, Your Honor."

"The witness is excused."

Stevens returned to his seat at the defendant's table.

"Mr. Sherrod, do you have another witness?"

"No, Your Honor. At this point, the defense rests."

Noise rose in the gallery, even among the jurors as they sat straighter, stretched, and looked relieved their odyssey was almost over.

After another glare from the judge, the room settled. "Mr. Dominick, does the prosecution wish to present rebuttal argument?"

"Yes, Your Honor."

Disappointed sighs rose from the jury.

"Is your first witness ready?"

Curt looked at his watch. "I can have the witness brought to the courthouse in twenty minutes."

The judge frowned. She was as anxious as the jurors to end this. "As we are nearing midday, we will recess for lunch. Have your witness here by one thirty, Counselor." Judge Hawthorne dropped the gavel.

THE FBI AGENT in the vestibule startled her by opening the front door and peeking into the living room. "Ms. Garrett, you have a visitor."

A visitor? Who the hell knew she was here? "I was told I couldn't have visitors. Curt said—"

"This visitor was sent by Mr. Dominick." The door opened wider, and a man she'd never seen before passed through.

Mara instinctively stiffened and took a step backward.

"Ms. Garrett? I'm a federal marshal. I'm here to escort you to the courthouse. You've been called to testify."

Her brain shut down. This could not be happening.

But it was. She was taken from the safe house, led to an SUV parked out front. Two FBI agents waited inside the vehicle, protection for the drive across town.

They wound through the familiar streets of DC, taking her ever closer to a man who'd tried to sweet-talk her into coming to DC, but when that failed, he'd set his hacker friend to finding her.

They circled the federal courthouse and entered the parking garage.

*"You're worth a thousand Jeannies."*

*"Jeannie's word isn't worth spit… Your word is the only one that will convince a judge to issue a warrant."*

But he hadn't wanted her here for a warrant to find the smallpox bomb. No, they really *had* come full circle. He'd raced to save her only because he wanted her to testify.

*"I'm falling in love with you."*

She'd heard those words in her mind a thousand times since he'd uttered them. She'd believed he had stayed away from the safe house the first night to give them both time to cool off. And last night, when he didn't appear, she'd convinced herself it was because her uncle had taken the stand, and he'd understood how hard that was for her.

The vehicle stopped by the garage elevator. Curt stood by the curb. Her heart lurched at the sight of him, as it had from the first moment she saw him.

An agent opened the SUV door. She climbed out and approached the man she'd thought she was falling in love with. Curt's expression sent chills up her spine. He looked like he did in the photos with the North Korean dictator. An empty suit. Expressionless.

After all they'd gone through together, she was once again face-to-face with The Shark.

# CHAPTER THIRTY-NINE

THE LOOK ON her face nearly killed him, but it was the blow to his cheek that made his head spin. Not a dainty slap from his pixie. No. She'd decked him with a closed fist.

The marshal caught her wrist as she pulled back for a second blow, and dragged her away from him. The two FBI agents flanked her.

"Mr. Dominick, do you intend to press charges?" one of the agents asked.

"No. I deserved it." Cupping his sore face, he turned and headed to the elevator.

"Goddam you, Curt! You son of a bitch!" Her rant continued, getting more and more creative as she went. She'd clearly spent a lot of time in the field with marines.

Inside the elevator, he said, "You can call me every name you want, but at one thirty you're going to testify."

"I will not."

"You have no choice, Mara. I didn't want to do this, but it became necessary."

Inside, the marshal led them to a private room. "Will you be safe with her?" he asked, nodding toward Mara and smiling a little too much.

"Probably not. But I can take it. I want the two agents to guard this room. Right now the fact that no one knows she's here is the best protection for her."

The door closed behind him, and they were alone. She spun around and swung at him again. This time he caught her wrist. It wouldn't do for him to face the jury with a black eye. He held her wrist above her head and felt the prick of a thousand daggers from her gaze.

"You're falling in love with me, huh?"

"Yes. I am. Every word was true."

"Jesus, Curt. I trusted you." Her voice dropped to a whisper. "How could you do this to me?"

She crumpled before him, and all he could do was pull her

against him and pray she'd let him hold her.

She didn't.

The moment his arms closed around her, she let out a guttural shriek that hurt worse than any blow and shoved him away. "Leave me the hell alone."

He stepped back. Fire blazed in her eyes. Explaining was impossible at this point. Later, he'd have his chance—if watching her testify didn't kill him first. "A bailiff will escort you to the courtroom when it's time."

"MR. DOMINICK, ARE you ready to call your first rebuttal witness?"

"Yes, Your Honor. The prosecution calls Mara Garrett to the stand."

At least one jury member gasped, while the gallery exploded with conversation. Judge Hawthorne was forced to resort to the gavel to restore order. "Mr. Dominick, please tell the court exactly what Ms. Garrett is expected to rebut."

"She will authenticate proposed exhibit sixty-eight and in so doing will impeach the testimony of the defendant."

"Objection, Your Honor!" Sherrod said. "Prosecution is trying to use rebuttal to try the case by introducing evidence not part of case in chief."

Judge Hawthorne glared at Curt. She wasn't pleased with his surprise witness, but he knew the foundation for calling Mara was sound. "Sidebar, gentlemen."

They met again beside the bench. Sherrod spoke first. "Your Honor, in light of recent events, the witness's testimony may be biased in favor of the prosecution. She may wish to please the man who rescued her from a firing squad."

"Mr. Dominick," Judge Hawthorne said, "if I let you put her on the stand, Ms. Ames will examine the witness and questions will be limited to the photograph and contents thereof."

"Yes, Your Honor."

"Then I will allow the witness to be called."

"Thank you, Your Honor."

"Mr. Dominick. I advise caution here. If I see anything that indicates you hold undue influence over the witness, I will have you barred from the courtroom during questioning."

MARA WAITED IN the witness room, alone. The room was cold. Freezing. It might be the coldest room she'd ever been in in her entire life. Then there were the painful knots in her stomach. The dull ache of fear and betrayal was back, but this time it came from a different source.

Why the hell had she ever allowed herself to start hoping again?

Now she waited in a frigid witness room, watching the second hand slowly rotate around the clock face. This felt just like her cell before the firing squad. At least the North Koreans had had the grace to give her a blindfold. Curt would make her look her uncle in the eye as she gave testimony against him.

And how in the hell had he managed to call her to testify? Hadn't the prosecution rested days ago? None of this made sense.

A few minutes after Curt left her, Aurora Ames, a tall, polished blonde, showed up with clothing, makeup, and hair products. She'd told Mara she could use or ignore the makeup and brushes, but the clothing change wasn't optional because the judge didn't allow jeans in her courtroom.

When Mara threatened to wear the jeans anyway, she was informed the judge would find her in contempt. It wouldn't get her out of testifying, but it would seriously screw up her day.

So Mara had changed. She ran her fingers over the quality garment and wondered who had picked it out for her—Curt or the sharp-eyed assistant US attorney.

Bored and anxious, she'd ended up playing with the makeup and fiddling with her hair. She studied her reflection in the mirror. The stupid, girlish part of her wondered what Curt would think when he saw her.

She ruthlessly crushed that thought under the classic, low-slung, navy-blue heels provided by the District of Columbia's US Attorney's Office.

A bailiff opened the door. "It's time."

# Chapter Forty

SHE ENTERED THE packed but silent courtroom alone. Her heels clicked on the hard floor, making her feel self-conscious and exposed. She paused before the witness box, raised her right hand as instructed, and took the oath that bound her to the truth. After taking her seat in the raised box to the judge's left, she scanned the courtroom.

The jury sat to her left, only a few feet away, and each of the fourteen members stared at her with avid interest. The face of the middle-aged man on the end was easy to read: *Things have finally gotten interesting.* The elderly woman in the middle of the front row smiled encouragingly. None of the other jurors would meet her gaze.

"Thank you for joining us, Ms. Garrett," Aurora Ames said, drawing her attention to the podium placed between the prosecution and defense tables.

Mara realized her navy suit was similar to Aurora's and felt a bitter twinge. She'd been dressed to match the blue team. "I wasn't aware I had a choice."

She made the mistake of glancing toward the prosecution table, directly in front of her. There he sat, serious and silent. The man who'd tried to lure her here with words of love, and when that failed, came after her with deceit and righteousness. She took a grounding breath and allowed her gaze to stray to the defendant's side and met the sad eyes of her uncle.

She'd prepared to face his condemnation, but he didn't look angry. He looked…pained. Behind him sat his wife, Aunt Clara, and next to her was Mara's mother.

She hadn't seen her mom since last Christmas, and her longing to leap out of the box and throw herself into her mother's arms was overwhelming. Tears ran down her mother's face, and Mara's breath hitched.

"Ms. Garrett, will you please answer the question?" the judge said, interrupting her thoughts.

Mara faced the woman seated above her. "I'm sorry, Your

Honor. I didn't hear it. I haven't seen my family in months. I'm a little overwhelmed."

"You may have a moment to collect yourself," the judge said.

"Thank you." She took a deep breath, then nodded toward the AUSA waiting at the podium.

"Your Honor, if it pleases the court, I'd like it entered into the record that Ms. Garrett is testifying unwillingly," Aurora Ames said.

The man seated next to her uncle said, "Objection, Your Honor."

"On what grounds?" the judge asked.

"Argument improper."

"Sustained."

"I'll rephrase, Your Honor," Aurora said. "Ms. Garrett, are you willingly testifying in the matter of the United States of America v. Andrew Stevens, defendant?"

The volley of statements bounced around the courtroom quickly. Lost, she sat mute in the box, wondering if she was supposed to answer or not.

"You must answer the question, Ms. Garrett," the judge said.

She cleared her throat and allowed her gaze to land on Curt. He looked…fierce. Intent. On her. She maintained eye contact as she answered. "Well, it's not a firing squad, but no, I don't want to be here."

He didn't flinch, but a member of the jury laughed, then slapped her hand over her mouth. Mara felt a small amount of satisfaction at getting a reaction out of *someone*.

Aurora Ames smiled. "Well then, let's get this over with." The woman looked toward Curt, seated next to the podium at the prosecution table, and took the piece of paper he offered her. To the judge, Aurora said, "Permission to approach the witness, Your Honor?"

"Granted."

Aurora stopped in front of the witness box and handed Mara the paper.

Mara glanced at the oversized photograph, then looked sharply at Curt when she realized what she held. She felt dizzy with the shift in mental gears. This had nothing to do with Stanford University and undeserved scholarships. This was Egypt. This was the arms deal that supposedly happened under her nose.

Curt simply nodded, his expression showing no shift in

emotion. No encouragement, no sympathy. No sorrow. No regret.

"Ms. Garrett, do you recognize this picture?" Aurora asked, drawing her gaze away from Curt and back to the woman who stood before her.

She cleared her throat. "Yes."

"Who took the photo?"

"I did."

"When did you take it?"

"Nearly a year and a half ago. When I was in Egypt with JPAC and Uncle Andrew visited."

Aurora rattled off a date and asked Mara if it was correct.

"That sounds right."

"Does this appear to be an exact replica of the photo you took?"

"Yes."

"Why did you take the photo?" Aurora asked.

"Objection, relevance," Uncle Andrew's lawyer said. Mara studied the man, who had the same polish as Curt. He wasn't pleased to see her in the witness seat. Well, that made two of them.

"Your Honor," Aurora said, "the prosecution is seeking authentication of the photograph. The photographer's thoughts at the time the photo was taken will help establish its authenticity."

"Overruled. You may answer the question, Ms. Garrett."

"I was bored, so I started taking pictures."

"But why did you photograph *this* man?" Aurora persisted.

She studied the image, then met Aurora's gaze. "I was fascinated by the Egyptian man's eyes and the jagged scar. He looked battle-worn. He kept himself apart from the other villagers. I was trying to capture that." Her gaze shifted from Aurora to Curt. "Then he smiled and seemed delighted I was photographing him, so I snapped a few more."

"Did you speak with him?"

"Not that I remember."

Curt shifted subtly in his seat, and she realized she'd been staring at him. Even sitting quietly at the prosecution table, he looked like he owned the room. This was his world. His arena. It was like the sun had somehow found a way into this packed, windowless chamber and shone only on him.

"Do you remember the people standing in the background when you took the shot?" Aurora asked.

Mara returned her attention to the assistant US attorney. "Yes."

"Can you name the other people in the photo?"

"Objection," her uncle's attorney said as he jumped to his feet. "In describing the photo, witness is, in a sense, displaying evidence prior to its introduction."

Aurora pivoted toward the bench. "It goes toward authenticating, Your Honor. Are all the people present in the photograph people she remembers being there?"

"Overruled."

Aurora turned back to Mara.

"I can't name the Secret Service agents, but the other people are Roddy Brogan, Jeannie Fuller, Robert Beck, and my uncle, Andrew Stevens. Centered is the Egyptian man. On the right you can see Evan Beck's shoulder."

Shuffling in the gallery and jury box told her the two dead men's names were noticed by the onlookers, but Mara remained focused on the photograph, on the small part of Evan's anatomy visible on the edge as she continued. "I remember Evan started to walk in front just as the shutter clicked, which irritated me. He knew about the delay on the digital camera and should have waited."

"Was Mr. Beck deliberately trying to obscure the shot?"

"Objection," Sherrod said, "conjecture."

"Withdrawn." Aurora glanced at Curt, then slapped Mara with her next question. "I understand Evan Beck was your fiancé?"

She tossed Curt a glare, then answered. "Ex-fiancé. We were engaged for three days."

"And Roddy Brogan, were you friends with him?" Aurora's tone was casual. Friendly. And it rankled.

As if the humiliation of admitting under oath she'd been engaged to the monster who'd killed several people and hunted her across the country wasn't enough, now she was being asked to describe her friendship with the man who set her up for a firing squad. She was as sick of the bared-teeth politeness of the US courtroom as she was of the blatant hostility she'd endured in the North Korean one.

"Yes. We were. Right up until he kidnapped me in North Korea, left me near the DMZ, then returned to Hawai'i with the rest of the team."

Gasps came from the jury and the gallery, and Mara realized

this was the first time the public heard her account of the ordeal.

"Objection!" Sherrod said, projecting his voice over the growing noise. "Question was answered, but then the witness gave testimony on a subject far beyond the scope of the question posed."

The spectators' chatter ballooned to a roar.

Mara gave her inquisitor a tight, satisfied smile, and to her surprise, saw glee in the other woman's eyes.

The judge called for silence and banged her gavel, showing agitation when the pounding had no immediate effect. A dozen thumps later and the room began to quiet.

"Ms. Garrett," the judge said, her irritation now directed at Mara. "You are to limit your answer to the question posed. The objection is sustained and the witness's remarks are to be stricken from the record."

"Your Honor, at this time the prosecution asks for exhibit sixty-eight to be entered into evidence."

"Objection!" Sherrod jumped to his feet.

Judge Hawthorne sent him a sharp glare and told him to sit with an angry flick of her wrist. "Overruled. Exhibit sixty-eight is entered into evidence."

"Your Honor, may I publish this photo to the jury?"

"Proceed."

"Thank you."

The procedure took several minutes, giving Mara the opportunity to meet her uncle's gaze. He looked stricken, possibly even a little green.

She finally gave in and shifted her gaze to Curt, who'd remained silent throughout the courtroom uproar. A mix of emotions played across his handsome features as he stared at her with an unwavering intensity. Remorse, pain, satisfaction, and something that looked a lot like caring, but she wouldn't open the door to that possibility. That would leave her vulnerable to the vicious bitch hope.

"Your Honor," Aurora Ames said, again drawing the attention of everyone in the room. "At this time I'd like to show Ms. Garrett prosecution exhibit twenty-seven, already accepted into evidence."

"Proceed."

Aurora's shoes echoed in the now silent chamber as she approached Mara with another paper in her hand. She flashed a crisp smile that wasn't entirely devoid of warmth and offered the photo. Mara's gaze dropped to the picture, and surprise rippled through her when she recognized the central figure.

"Ms. Garrett, is this a picture of the same man you photographed in Egypt?"

She nodded.

"You need to answer verbally, Ms. Garrett," the judge said. "For the record."

"Sorry. Yes. That's the battle-weary Egyptian. He has the same scar, the same eyes, and the same smile."

"Let the record show Ms. Garrett has identified war criminal and the leader of Darfur's Janjaweed militia as the same man she photographed with Andrew Stevens and Robert Beck."

Time froze after Aurora's statement. Darfur. Janjaweed. Maybe time hadn't frozen; maybe her heart had just stopped beating. Her uncle really was a…a monster.

In an instant, her heart resumed, only now it raced at the same speed as the uproar in the courtroom. Sherrod jumped to his feet, shouting objections so fast Mara couldn't catch them all. The judge used the gavel to quiet the courtroom and reprimanded everyone.

Mara met Curt's gaze, and he nodded. Not an I-told-you-so sort of nod, just a confirmation that said, *this is why I had to hurt you.*

Uncle Andrew really had traded arms with a war criminal. And, just as Curt had claimed, he'd done it right under her nose.

Her stomach flipped. He'd brought a baby-killing warlord to a JPAC deployment. The man had been fed and cared for by the local villagers in a dinner Mara had arranged.

She felt dirty. Sick. And used. By a man she'd trusted her whole life.

"Your Honor, I have no more questions for this witness," Aurora said.

"Does the defense wish to cross-examine?" the judge asked.

"No, Your Honor." No indeed. Sherrod looked like he couldn't get her off the stand fast enough.

"Ms. Garrett, you may be excused."

Mara stood and walked out of the now silent courtroom with her head held high. She had no idea what she was walking toward, but she knew exactly what she was walking away from.

# Chapter Forty-One

MARA LEFT THE courtroom with the same dignity and grace she'd shown in North Korea, but without the blindfold—both mental and literal—that had hampered her then. She knew without a doubt what sort of man her uncle was, and from the pain Curt had glimpsed in her eyes, she resented the messenger as much as she despised the message.

He'd lost her.

*For now.* He wasn't a man to give up, not when he wanted something as much as he wanted her. She'd awoken his heart, making it impossible for him to go back to being the cold, emotionless shark motivated only by ambition.

Outside the courtroom, the two FBI agents would be taking her back to the safe house. She would remain in protective custody for the foreseeable future. Fewer than ten people knew the location of the house, Curt and Lee included. Tonight he would go to her and begin his campaign to win her back.

But first, he had work to do. The next witness was a facial-recognition expert who would rebut Stevens's statement that Secret Service agents had traveled to Egypt with him. If all went well, closing arguments would be presented tomorrow, and Curt could refine his plan for wooing Mara while the jury deliberated.

He stood and addressed the judge. "Your Honor, at this point the prosecution calls—"

"Your Honor." Curt turned to see Stevens standing next to his seated lawyer. Ben Sherrod didn't look pleased. "I request a private meeting with the prosecution."

The gallery broke out in low murmurs, akin to the buzzing of bees.

Judge Hawthorne glared at the gallery over the top of her glasses while addressing Stevens. "You're out of order, Mr. Stevens."

"I know, Your Honor. But before we proceed, I'd like to speak with Mr. Dominick. Alone."

"What is your purpose?"

"To negotiate a plea bargain."

Ben Sherrod was on his feet, objecting to his own client's words.

The buzzing became a strong wind. In seconds, it was a gale.

Hawthorne pounded her gavel with more vigor than Curt had ever seen. "The defendant's words are to be stricken from the record. The jury is excused and will wait in the jury room."

The furor died down as the jury filed out, casting glances at Stevens on their way.

Judge Hawthorne glared at the former vice president. "Mr. Stevens, were you hoping for a mistrial with that stunt?"

"No, Your Honor. I want to plead guilty."

"You had that opportunity before the trial."

"Yes, Your Honor."

Judge Hawthorne turned her attention to Curt. "Mr. Dominick, are you willing to entertain a plea bargain?"

"After the next witness, I intend to ask the charges be amended to conform to the evidence presented. I will not settle on the lesser charges of obstruction and influence peddling."

"I'll plead to everything—even the arms deal," Stevens said. "I just want to *talk* to you."

The noise from the gallery couldn't be contained. "Chambers! Now!" The judge stood and marched to the door behind the bench. Stevens followed with his angry lawyer by his side. Aurora and Curt were the last ones through the door.

They crowded into the judge's chambers; Hawthorne took a seat behind her desk while the rest stood. "What the hell do you think you're doing, Mr. Stevens? You *know* better than to make statements like that in front of spectators."

"Your Honor, I don't care what happens to me. I never have. But I came to the conclusion I'm protecting the wrong people, and I need to do something about it. If that means confessing and going to prison, so be it."

Sherrod clapped his hand on his client's shoulder. "Shut up, Andrew."

Stevens shook off his attorney's hand. "You're fired, Ben."

"You intend to negotiate a plea bargain without your lawyer?" Judge Hawthorne asked.

"Yes. Mr. Dominick and I are going to talk. Alone."

"Is that acceptable to you, Mr. Dominick?"

"I will not make concessions, but I'd like to hear what he has to say."

"Court will adjourn for the day, but I won't release the jury until we have a signed agreement. Settle this tonight, gentlemen. We have a jury sequestered, and I don't want them held for another day without cause."

THE DRIVE BACK to the safe house—located on a state-named street north of Embassy Row and her uncle's former residence at the Naval Observatory—was long thanks to vehicle changes to ensure they weren't followed. At last they drove down the steep driveway and into the basement garage. It was a nice house, if one liked being a prisoner.

Mara did not.

Inside, she paced the living room and shouted in the direction of the closed front door, "Protective custody, my ass. That bastard just wants to keep me here in case he needs me to testify again."

But the agent on the other side of the door had stopped responding to her complaints.

She stopped and stared at the gas fireplace, remembering the phone sex with Curt and his attempt to use the fireplace as a visual link between them. To think she'd felt guilty for lying.

When it came to deceit, she had nothing on him.

Had the "dates" merely been bait?

Curt *was* a good chess player. Laying the trap for over a week, saying the right things to make her laugh, make her care; it had probably come easily to him. All so he could call her to DC with the snap of his fingers. And it would have worked. He'd just gotten impatient.

Well, he and Lee *had* saved her from Raptor again. She had to give them credit for that.

What the hell was she going to do?

Raptor still hunted her. A smallpox bomb could go off at any time. Testifying hadn't decreased her danger, and she wouldn't be able to come out of hiding until Raptor was charged. She couldn't do it alone. She needed the FBI. Dammit all to hell. She needed Curt.

In DC, Curt *was* the law. Raptor's home office was in DC, and prosecution of the CEO would go through the US Attorney's Office.

How else to bring them down? She'd once thought she could

turn to her uncle, but that road was decidedly closed.

There was only one avenue that didn't include Curt: the State Department. She had information on a smallpox bomb, and it was time to use it. She marched to the front of the house and pounded on the heavy door.

The door opened, and the agent looked amused. "What can I do for you, Ms. Garrett?"

"I need the secretary of state's phone number."

ROBERT BECK ANSWERED the phone on the first ring; he'd been expecting this call.

The caller didn't bother with pleasantries. "Are you watching the news?"

"Yes. Stevens rolled."

"If he knows what's good for the girl, he'll take all the blame."

It didn't matter what was good for the girl. There was nothing Stevens could do to save Mara Garrett now. "The words of a desperate man are hardly proof," Robert said.

"Your people fucked up. Your son most of all. We've managed to put the lid on the smallpox rumors, but if Garrett manages to produce proof, we're screwed."

"Without a blood test, they can't prove a thing. Our intel into the Centers for Disease Control hasn't shown any tests for smallpox. To convince a judge, Dominick would have to go through the CDC."

"Our only hope to move forward with the plan is to make Mara Garrett and her blood disappear from the face of the earth."

Robert needed that bill to pass, and the smallpox bomb was the ideal shortcut to getting the votes he needed in congress. "The incinerator at the Virginia lab. We just need to get her there."

"You need to take care of Dominick as well. He'll never believe your son acted alone. And if he becomes attorney general, he'll have enough power to destroy Raptor."

"We need to find the fucking safe house where he's stashed her."

# Chapter Forty-Two

CURT FACED THE former vice president across the conference table armed with pen and notepad. The man had refused to allow the conversation to be recorded.

"I didn't know Raptor was after Mara," he said.

"I find that hard to believe, sir. You aren't a stupid man."

Stevens raked his gray hair with his fingers and sighed. "Wanna bet?" He then sat up straight and focused his clear blue eyes on Curt. "I thought it was Evan, obsessing. I never really liked the little shit."

"I beg your pardon, sir, but if you didn't like him, why didn't it upset you that your business partner paid him to date your niece?"

"He didn't. He paid him to destroy the pictures she took in Egypt. Evan started to date her to get close to her, but he seemed to really care about her." The man's wrinkles seemed to have deepened in the last hour.

"If he was paid to destroy the photos, you really should demand a refund."

"Mara must have switched the memory card, and he destroyed the wrong one. Scared the hell out of me when the Egyptian photos appeared on the AP wire."

Curt smiled, figuring that must have caused a panic for him and Robert Beck. "Hadn't you told Mara to release the photos to the AP?"

"Of course. I didn't want her to think there was anything odd about the trip, and all my other trips had included a publicity photo shoot. But I didn't think there would *be* any photos to release. Evan said he'd erased them." The man flashed an ironic smile. "Think of the trouble she'd have saved you if she'd released the photo with the warlord."

"No such luck."

"JPAC returned to Hawai'i just days after the arms deal was completed. At that point, we realized she'd probably downloaded the photos to her computer. It was necessary for Evan to stay close to her."

Curt's hand clenched into a fist. "You paid an amoral sociopath mercenary to date your niece. You're truly uncle-of-the-year material."

"I didn't know that's what Evan was. He cared for her. *I* didn't like him, but she was happy."

He'd give anything to be able to punch this man. Evan had emotionally denigrated Mara to the point she'd lost sight of her own value, and after she ended the relationship, the man assaulted her. "Your definition of happy is seriously fucked."

"I didn't know." He dropped his head into his hands. "I thought he loved her. When she broke up with him, he went nuts, so when I heard the jet had exploded, I thought he'd truly lost it."

"You're full of justification for ignorantly endangering Mara, but how do you excuse bringing a Janjaweed militia leader to a JPAC deployment?"

Stevens lifted his head from his hands and sat up straight. "I was trading arms for hostages."

Curt set down his pen and stared at the man, incredulous at his audacity. "You're claiming you pulled an Iran-Contra?"

"Yes."

Curt didn't begin to believe him but was curious about the story the man had obviously worked hard to fabricate. "Fine. I'll bite. How did it start?"

The former vice president sighed. "I first got to know Raptor and Robert Beck during my downsizing government initiative—continuing the work Al Gore started when he was vice president. Beck's organization interested me because they didn't have to go through sixteen layers of bureaucracy to buy a ream of paper. They were more efficient, cheaper, and got results. Robert Beck began talks with me toward the end of my term about joining the organization as chief of operations. I liked the idea.

"Just before my term ended, those six reporters were taken hostage in Darfur. I worked with the State Department, trying to negotiate their release, and it became clear it wouldn't happen through diplomatic channels. I also happened to be sick to death of diplomatic channels."

The man glanced down at his hands, which curled into fists. "The president couldn't do anything. The military couldn't get close to the Janjaweed. The CIA was having their own problems. We benefited from their intel, but Raptor operates on different rules and could do more. I approached Robert Beck, and he and I worked out an arrangement.

"It took us months to pull it off—yes, after my Secret Service detail was gone. Two of Raptor's top operatives posed as my detail so Mara and her JPAC team wouldn't get suspicious."

"Why go to all that trouble?" Curt asked.

"We wanted as many Raptor operatives to provide security as possible. The Janjaweed bastard wasn't the most trustworthy."

"Yet you gave him advanced weaponry."

"It was the only way to save the hostages. Mara's work provided the perfect cover. I had a reason to be there; the militia leader would go unnoticed by the JPAC team. While we were there, handing over arms, the hostages were being released in Sudan. And US government officials were, for the most part, unaware their lives were bought with guns. Not even the president knew."

"Protecting him from scandal or yourself from prison?"

"Myself. We hoped if we operated outside government channels, no one would find out."

"But I started investigating the influence peddling and picked up the trail."

"We managed to destroy the paper trail, but it was too late. Then you had me on obstruction." He paused and stared at Curt. "I'm not ashamed of what I did. If the hostages had been killed, the US would have become embroiled in another Middle East/North Africa conflict, and frankly, our military is stretched thin as it is."

"So noble. But you still armed a known war criminal."

Stevens shrugged. "In politics you have to make deals with the devil if you want results."

Curt leaned forward and glared at the man whose covert deals had caused the woman he loved to face a firing squad. "Tell me about North Korea. I want to know about the smallpox bombs."

THE PROSECUTOR'S WORDS gave Andrew a jolt. "How do you know about the bomb?"

"Bombs. Plural. I know about them because your niece got sick while in a North Korean jail cell."

That knocked the wind out of him. "Mara had smallpox?"

"Fortunately, she'd been vaccinated and only had a mild case."

Blood left his face and gathered with acid in his stomach. "The

North Koreans didn't… They could have assumed she'd been sent to infect them. They would have killed her…"

"I believe that was their plan, but they didn't know about her illness. She was able to keep it hidden."

"She must have been terrified."

The Shark nodded. "She wouldn't have been there, wouldn't have been terrified, if Raptor operatives hadn't used her."

Guilt swamped him. He'd failed Mara yet again. "I didn't know about that until she said it on the stand. I'd only heard the official version—she'd fought with Evan and stormed off. Mara is…temperamental… It made sense."

The younger man's face reddened and his eyes narrowed. "Do you know your niece at all, sir?"

"Of course I do! She's like a daughter to me."

"I am so fucking sick of that line. From both of you. Obviously, neither one of you has taken a solid look at the other since she was in braces. Mara is not 'temperamental,' and you are not a goddamned saint."

Andrew was taken aback. "She thinks I'm a saint?"

"Don't take it to heart. She tends toward delusion at times and thought *I* was a superhero."

Andrew smiled. For a moment—just one small instant—the stress that was his constant companion faded. "Is there something between you two?" He had to admit the prosecutor would be worlds better for Mara than the mercenary.

"Not anymore. Bringing her in to testify killed any heroic thoughts she had about me."

"I'd offer to talk to her on your behalf, but I have a feeling she won't listen to me after today." He paused. "But I'm glad you put her on the stand, because I was about to go down silently to protect an ideal that doesn't exist."

"Explain."

"You were right about everything. The arms deal, and the cover-up to hide it. Iran-Contra taught us even though the intention is good, the American people are not fond of arming enemies."

"But you did it anyway." Dominick remained impassive. The only flicker of emotion he'd shown was when Mara was mentioned.

"I did. Then your office began to investigate some of my previous political dealings. One thing led to another, and the next thing I knew we were shredding files and doing our best to make the arms deal disappear. It became clear my only hope was the cover-up would be enough to beat the charges." Andrew looked at the man who'd put him through the wringer over the past year. "It wasn't. My own lawyer thought I was guilty."

"Because you are."

"True."

"Get to the smallpox, Mr. Stevens."

"My initial plan for the Raptor/JPAC joint venture came about because JPAC had access to places where even the CIA can't operate. I knew about the smallpox bomb—I made a point of learning whatever I could when I had access to state secrets in my capacity as vice president. My plan was for Raptor to locate the smallpox bomb and destroy it."

"It's a good story. Your niece might even buy it."

"We'd already successfully destroyed two other bombs."

Dominick tilted his head in interest. "Smallpox?"

"No. A Cold War–era anthrax bomb in China and a chemical weapon in Vietnam."

"Can you prove this? That you located and destroyed them?"

"Of course not. We weren't nearly so sloppy after the arms deal."

Dominick sat back again. "I'm not fond of fairy tales, Mr. Stevens."

Andrew sat forward. "I don't give a shit if you think I'm guilty. I've already accepted I'm going to prison. What I need is for you to believe Beck is guilty. I realize now he developed his own ideas about our mission. He knows how to conduct covert arms deals, and now he's got a smallpox bomb in his possession."

"What made you come to that conclusion?"

"Mara wasn't even supposed to go to North Korea. As my niece, she had a higher profile than the others. But the other archaeologists got sick—easily engineered—and Mara went."

"Why would Beck want Mara on the team?"

He'd been pondering that ever since the idea first germinated. "To create an international incident so they could get the bomb out of the country instead of destroying it on-site, and to keep me on edge as the trial drew near. My guess is Robert didn't like my noble goals—"

"Apparently delusion runs in the family."

Andrew smiled at that one. "I think Robert got greedy. He

must have decided he didn't want to find and destroy anymore. He's had nearly three months to replicate the smallpox bomb."

"Did anyone outside of Raptor know what you were doing?"

"One person. I told him in the strictest of confidence, my backup against getting caught. Someone who holds sway with the president, should I need a pardon."

"You sold arms to a war criminal and you're hoping for a pardon? Do you know how those arms were used?"

Andrew shook his head.

"Your Janjaweed buddy led the massacre of a remote village. He wanted their water supply and killed every man, woman, and child to get it."

The words cut. But he'd known it wouldn't be pretty. "I freed six American reporters who were taken hostage. Had they been killed, we would have conducted airstrikes on the region. Those same civilians could have died, as would American soldiers."

The prosecutor leaned forward. "Who did you tell? Was it an administration official?"

Andrew clasped his hands and leaned on his wrists. He wasn't praying. It was too late for that. Nothing could save him now, not even the talented prosecutor who might be in love with his niece. But the man could save Mara, and she needed a hero now, more than ever. "I told the secretary of state before the arms deal, and have continued regular updates ever since."

# Chapter Forty-Three

Curt informed Judge Hawthorne a plea agreement would be delivered for her approval in the morning, convinced her to sign wiretap warrants for those the former vice president had implicated, and then spent an hour arranging Andrew Stevens's relocation to a safe house. He had a long-ass night ahead of him, drafting the agreement and getting the surveillance in place.

In Andrew Stevens's plea, no mention would be made of biological or chemical weapons, or trading arms for hostages. Stevens had agreed to cop to the arms deal without excuses or justifications.

Try getting a presidential pardon for *that*.

Yet, Curt did believe his fairy tale. A zealot for his cause, the man saw himself as honorable. But if Stevens hadn't pushed for the smallpox bomb recovery, the bomb would still be in North Korea, safely buried on the same hillside where it had rested undisturbed for over sixty years. Yes, there was a danger it could have fallen into a dictator's hands, but falling into Robert Beck's hands was just as bad.

Once arrangements had been made for Stevens, Curt grabbed his coat. He had a ton of work to do, but dammit, he needed to see Mara. He needed to begin his campaign to convince her of his own fairy tale, his own honorable intentions. But deep down, he feared Mara would see him as another misguided zealot.

He took a taxi to Union Station and from there took one Metro train after another, randomly changing lines and direction. Finally, he exited the Metro at Cleveland Park and caught another taxi, which dropped him a few blocks from the safe house. It was after nine by the time he trudged down the cold city block. The residential streets were quiet, making it easy to spot someone following him. The cloak-and-dagger routine would, in most circumstances, make him feel ridiculous, but Raptor *was* out there, *was* looking for Mara, especially now that the news had carried the story of Stevens's courtroom confession.

Each wasted minute hurt. He didn't have much time to see her, and the moments dwindled before he'd even arrived.

The house was small, a single-story two-bedroom with a steeply sloped driveway that led to a basement garage. A nondescript house nestled between similar houses, the only difference was the porch had been enclosed to create a vestibule, which provided a workstation for the FBI agent assigned guard duty.

Curt paused in front of the security camera, hit the buzzer, and was quickly admitted. "What's her mood?" he asked after shaking hands with the guard.

"She's crabby. There's been some ranting."

Curt grimaced. "She say anything about me?"

"Nothing I could repeat." The hulking agent ran a hand over his bare scalp. "My mother taught me better than to use language like that."

"I'm going in."

The guard smiled. "You got body armor on?"

"Will you lend me yours?"

He laughed. "No way. Really, most of all, you need a cup."

Curt winced. "I'm going in unprotected. No matter how much I scream, don't come in."

The guard gave him a knowing look and said, "Good luck."

Curt took a deep breath and prepared to do battle.

THE MOMENT MARA heard the door, she knew who it would be. Who else would show up at this hour? She looked about the living room and grabbed the first loose objects to come to hand. But the remote control wouldn't hurt him enough and the lamp would hurt too much.

He approached with the unwavering determination of a Terminator as she tried to decide which weapon to hurl at him. She was still weighing her options when he was upon her. He touched her wrists, wrapping his fingers and gently twisting in a way that forced her to drop both items without hurting her, then continued forward, still holding her wrists, until her back was against the wall.

Once again he pinned her wrists above her head and pressed his body to hers. But this time he wasn't restraining or interrogating her. His body was taut with tension and his hazel eyes bright with emotion. Without saying a word, he invaded her mouth in a hot, searing kiss that put the gas fireplace to shame.

She melted and molded against him. The carnal kiss conveyed passion his earlier kisses had hinted at, but this was Curt, unleashed.

Being a weak fool, she reveled in the heat. His mouth devoured, blazing a hot trail across her cheek, to her ear, down her sensitive neck. He released her hands so he could cup her breasts, and she didn't hesitate to thread her fingers through his hair, to grip his wide shoulders and trace the muscles that never failed to fascinate.

At last, fantasy, desire, passion, and need could be satisfied. His mouth returned to hers, and she sucked on his tongue, unable to get enough of kissing him. This was real. Not shared fantasy, not incomplete, aching memory.

The frenzy of his initial possession slowed into something more leisurely, more thorough, but more intense. He explored her mouth as his hands investigated her body. She purred with satisfaction. She'd longed for this since they'd shared a narrow bunk in Hawai'i.

He broke the kiss and leaned his forehead to hers, his breathing ragged. "Let's get one thing straight. When I told you I'm falling in love with you, I meant it. I've never said those words to anyone before, and I wanted to say them to you while I had the chance."

She caught her breath and waited for her emotional compass to right itself. How did she feel about this declaration?

Giddy, certainly.

Satisfaction was there too.

As was elation.

And don't forget lust.

But then there was hurt. And resentment.

And fury.

She pushed at his shoulders, and he fell back, freeing her. "Goddamn you, Curt Dominick. Do you really think you can just march in here, kiss me silly, and I'll just melt at your self-righteous feet? Of all the egotistical, supercilious…"

"I may be self-righteous and egotistical, but I am *not* supercilious!"

She cast him a satisfied glare. She'd hit a nerve. Good. "You tried to lure me here with lies. You didn't tell me the real reason you came after me—instead you yelled at me for taking risks when you were the one who would expose me. Raptor knows I'm in DC now. Thanks to *you*! You can't just kiss me and expect me to forget."

"I planned to enter on my knees and beg you to understand. But then I saw you and needed to kiss you more."

She crossed her arms. "I need the knees and the begging."

FOR OVER TWENTY years the idea of being brought to his knees by love had filled Curt with dread, but now he couldn't drop fast enough. He took her hands in his. "You win."

He felt cocky, victorious. Her response to his kiss told him this case was his. The jury was favorable.

She snatched her hands from his. "You risked my life by bringing me here. All to save your goddamned career."

Cockiness fled, and fear rushed into the void. This was so much darker, deeper than the fear he'd carried of emotional attachment. This was fear of living the rest of his life without a heart.

He dropped farther, to his heels. "I've given up so much for my career, and will probably give up more in the years to come, but give up you? Never. If I had to make a choice between career and you, I'd quit tonight." He studied his hands, unwilling to meet her gaze. "What I did to get you here to testify, I didn't do for me or for my career. I did it for justice."

When she remained silent, he dared to look up. "Justice was served today."

Her eyes were shuttered, giving no hint of her reaction.

The remote silence from his warm, vivacious pixie hit him like a sucker punch. He'd counted on too much, taken the hero worship to heart, and assumed her forgiveness was a foregone conclusion.

For a smart man, he really was stupid. And an ass.

"I'm not a superhero, Mara. I never have been, but neither am I the kind of man to risk your life just to save my career." He felt the burn of tears but held them in check. "From the moment you stepped into that courtyard blindfolded and handcuffed, you have made me question all of my smug—and yes, *supercilious*—assumptions about you. But, if you believe I was acting to save my ass, then I failed to show you who *I* am."

"At least you've cured me of idealizing you."

He smiled without joy. "Progress."

"Did it even occur to you to *ask* me?"

"What if you'd said no? What if you'd bolted? I had a narrow window of time to get you on the stand, but more important, if you'd fled, I couldn't protect you. Yes, I risked your safety in bringing you here, but I worked damn hard to make sure you'd be protected. I even ensured no one knew you would testify until moments before you were on the stand. Raptor didn't have time to respond."

"But did you consider I might have said yes?" The pain in her eyes smothered the last embers of his hope.

"I couldn't take that chance." He rose to his feet. "I hate the machinations that were required, but I did what I had to do." He crossed the living room, putting space between them, knowing he was back on his feet but emotionally still on metaphorical knees, and there was nothing left to do but tell her. "You're the last person in the world I want to hurt, the last person I want to endanger." He turned back to face her. "I'm in love with you, Mara. Hopelessly, helplessly in love with you."

She took a step toward him, then stopped and stared at him. All he could do was stare back and let her see the truth in his eyes. After a lifetime of hiding behind a cold façade, it wasn't easy to let the shield go.

Speechless, she stood in the middle of the room. Finally, she lifted a hand in the air and studied it wonderingly. "I'm so afraid to believe you, I'm trembling." He saw her shaking fingers and the shivers that traveled up her arm.

He crossed to her in three quick strides and held out his own hand. "And I'm so scared you *won't* believe me, I've been shaking since I was on my knees." He took her hand in his and stilled both their tremors.

She let out a half sob, half laugh. "This is nuts. I started falling for you the first moment I saw you, and I've been second-guessing myself every moment since." She studied their entwined hands. "I can't fall in love with *you*. I can pretend to date you, but a real relationship is crazy. You're a legendary crusader for justice, and my uncle is an arms dealer. You'll be the next attorney general, and I helped create an international incident."

His heart pounded as hope sprang anew. "Sounds like a perfect match to me." He pulled her against him, slowly, giving her a choice, then cradled her face in his hands. "I'm sorry, Mara. It killed me to know how much my actions would hurt you."

She gripped his tie, pulling him down as she rose on her toes. When their lips were millimeters apart, she said, "Promise you won't ever manipulate me like that again."

He raised his voice to be heard over his loud, racing heart. "I promise."

Her lips touched his. A soft, fleeting kiss, and it took all his willpower not to crush her in a demanding embrace. The only way to win was to surrender and grant her complete control.

Still gripping his tie, she said, "I have something I need to tell you."

Fear surged at her trepidation. "Hopefully it's that you love me?"

She shook her head, and his heart dropped. He rallied a second later. Dammit. He'd convince her to love him. She was a jury of one, and he would sway her. "Give me time, then. That's all I ask."

She laughed. "No. It's not that. I mean, I do love you, but it's not that."

Relief flooded him. "Wow. And people say men are bad at romance. Could you say that again, but without the other stuff?"

"It's my fault you were the envoy."

Her words took him aback. "Your fault?"

"I suggested your name to my interrogator. They wanted—"

He planted his mouth on hers before she could finish. He lifted his head long enough to say, "I don't give a damn," then resumed kissing her. Fear, tension, anxiety all left him at once, and now, all he felt was the urgent need to make her his. He dropped small kisses along her jaw, traced her ear with his tongue, and murmured his intention against her skin.

She lifted his head and gazed into his eyes. "If you'd asked me to testify, I don't know how I would have answered. But I'm glad you forced me. I know if I hadn't testified, I'd have regretted it."

This was her gift, absolving him. He sucked in a deep breath, continually amazed by her. "About your uncle, I need to tell you—"

"No. Not now. He doesn't get to share this moment. This is for us." She smiled wickedly. "You are finally going to put out." She worked the knot on his tie.

He grinned and began unbuttoning her blouse. "Yes, ma'am." When he had her shirt open, he lowered his mouth to her breast, laving the hard nipple through the thin satin of her bra. She let out a soft moan and ran her fingers through his hair. "You're mine," he said, feeling positively Neanderthal and enjoying every primal-possessive moment. He slid a hand over her butt and down her thigh, then moved upward to press against her center. "And I'm going to have you."

She tugged his shirt from his slacks. "Promise me the guard won't interrupt us."

He glanced toward the door. "I'm pretty sure he knows what we're doing."

She laughed and pushed his jacket and shirt down his shoulders.

He let go of her long enough to remove both items, then nodded toward the fireplace. "I want to make love to you in front of the fire, like we did on our fourth date."

"Third. The football game wasn't a date."

He chuckled, tossed her over his shoulder, and deposited her in front of the hearth. He reached for the clasp on her slacks. "You're wearing too much."

"So are you." She tugged on his belt.

Their arms tangled at cross-purposes. He stepped back and removed his pants, while she doffed her blouse and slacks. She reached for her bra, but he stopped her hands and traced the cups with deliberate slowness.

She purred with impatience and unhooked the back, then slipped the straps from her shoulders. He caught the cups before they slid off and instead revealed her magnificent curves in slow millimeters. Nipples exposed at last, he covered one with his mouth while rolling the other between his fingers.

"You really do have spectacular breasts." Her skin was hot in his hands. He tasted her other breast, and she panted his name.

Every sensation was heightened, intense. He'd never known what he was missing, engaging in sex without love. This was new. And incredibly hot. She moaned and closed her eyes. The pleasure on her face pushed his arousal to a new level as satisfaction shot through him.

This beautiful woman was his. All his.

He pulled her against him and captured her mouth in another searing kiss. Her hands found his erection, and he groaned as she put his staying power to the test.

"Condoms," she said. "Please tell me you have condoms."

"I do." He released her to rummage in his jacket pocket and returned with a box.

"You're prepared."

He hooked a finger inside the top of her panties and pulled her closer. "I wasn't afraid to hope." He dropped to his knees, pulling down her underwear as he went. She obliged by stepping out of the skimpy satin.

He knelt before her, bringing his face level with her breasts. He kissed a trail south while his hands slid between her thighs and stroked between her legs. With a gentle nudge, he indicated she should widen her stance. She groaned and obeyed, spreading her legs for his touch.

He breathed in her scent and slid a finger inside her. Holy crap, she was *so* ready for him. He gazed upward. With closed eyes, she whimpered. It was the most erotic thing he'd ever seen.

His mouth found her center. She gripped his shoulders and rocked on her heels. He separated her folds with his tongue and groaned at her slick heat. "I've been aching to taste you forever," he said against her center. "And now I'm going to feel you come against my mouth, just like we talked about."

She was sweet and hot against his tongue, and with each stroke she let out a sexy whimper. He felt her knees tremble and knew she perched on the precipice of orgasm. The fire warmed his bare back and sweat beaded on his neck while her breath came out in sharp pants. She pulled back from his mouth, attempting to stop him from making her come. "Make love to me, Curt. Now."

He shook his head and laved her center while sliding fingers inside her slick heat. "Come for me, sweetheart."

"No."

He cupped her bottom and pulled her to his mouth. He licked her clitoris, then sucked on it and lightly grazed it with his teeth. He felt the exact moment she tumbled off the precipice, and only iron will kept him from following.

He maintained pressure with his tongue, and her orgasm continued until her knees gave out. He caught her and lowered her to the carpet. The scratchy rug wouldn't do for the first time he made love to her. "Be right back," he said and escaped into the bedroom. A moment later, he returned with blankets and pillows and spread them out before the fireplace.

She stretched out with a sated smile. He lay down beside her and gathered her against him. Golden firelight caressed her smooth skin as her mouth relaxed in a sensuous smile. He kissed her, a slow, thorough kiss, claiming her for his own.

She reached for the condoms and opened a foil packet, then slid the latex over his erection, and he gasped at the feel of her hand as she explored him, cupped his testicles, and slid her hand up his hard shaft.

How had he managed to resist her on their journey? All he wanted was to bring her pleasure, make her laugh, and take away her sorrow. Love her body and mind.

She opened her thighs and gripped his hips, pulling him to her. Unable to resist a moment longer, he pressed against her opening. His lips found hers, and he delved into her mouth with slow, sensual need.

"Please," she begged.

"Now," he agreed and filled her in one swift motion.

She was so hot and slick and, *sweet Jesus*, tight, he could come right now. Lightning-like jolts of pleasure shot through him. He held still, reveling in the thrill of being inside her, with her. He kissed her, deep and slow.

Her hands cradled his face. "I love you, Curt."

And with those words, his heart soared. Unable to remain still a moment longer, he thrust with slow, deep strokes. Those lightning jolts intensified with each thrust. She moaned and gasped, and he felt like the superhero she wanted him to be. In moments, she was frantic and trembling, but despite her urging, Curt maintained the slow, erotic pace. In absolute control. He slowed further when she begged him to go faster. "No, love. Don't rush."

His mouth found her nipple, and she clenched tightly around his cock. He let out an uncontrolled groan and quickened the pace.

She smiled and clenched tighter, rocking her pelvis into his. Another notch of control slipped, and he moaned against her chest, "Mara, you're killing me."

"Come for me, Curt."

"Not yet."

She gripped his butt and ground her hips against his, and it was his turn to tumble off the precipice. He thrust into her hot, urgent, and, thankfully, bringing her over the same edge. He came in a single burst of lightning that erupted from his core.

He collapsed, bathed in sweat and panting.

She ran her fingers through his hair. "You're mine. Finally." She let out a contented sigh. "The moment you put yourself between me and the firing squad, I fell, hard."

He slid out of her and adjusted his position, rising up on his arms as he did so. Bending his elbows, he lowered himself, push-up style, and kissed her, an openmouthed kiss that promised hours more of pleasure. He dropped down on one elbow to her side. "I was taken with you the moment I saw your dignity and strength." He traced circles on her belly. "I haven't let myself get close to someone since I was sixteen because I was afraid of not being in control. I sent a kid to the hospital—"

"He pulled a knife on you."

"I know. But when I think about Evan—and what he did to you—I want to dig up his body and kill him again. I'm a prosecutor; I'm supposed to believe the system will mete out justice. But no judge or jury could bestow what Robert Beck and the others deserve. I spend my nights searching for the evidence necessary to convict him, when all I really want is to go to his house and tear him apart with my bare hands."

"If you do, promise me you'll let me kick him in the balls a few times."

Since he'd never allow her within a mile of Robert Beck, he said, "Sure." The mantel clock chimed, and he sat up and cursed. "Hell. I was supposed to meet Aurora twenty minutes ago to draft the plea bargain. I didn't want to do this—make love to you and run—but we can't release the jury without a signed agreement, and they're sequestered. It would be shitty to keep them longer just because I'd rather spend the night making love to you."

He left her side to dispose of the condom. When he returned, she handed him his clothes. "When can you come back?" she asked.

The firelight on her skin tested his commitment to the very nice jurors who'd given up weeks of their lives for civic duty. But he had a duty to them. "You'll be moved tomorrow. It's not a good idea to keep you in the same place for long. Your uncle rolled on Raptor. His word alone isn't good enough for indictments, but you can back up several of his claims. Beck will be twice as anxious to get to you." While he spoke, he pulled on clothing.

She wrapped the blanket around her naked body and moved to the couch. "Why did he do it? My uncle has his faults, but greed isn't one of them."

"It's a long story—and I'll tell you the whole saga later—but the truth is, we were both right about him, and we were both wrong."

"What do you mean?"

He'd looked forward to this moment ever since he'd determined Stevens had told him the truth. He could restore a small amount of honor to her view of her uncle. "He traded the arms for hostages, and—he claims, and I believe him—the plan to get the smallpox bomb was originally to destroy it in place. Robert Beck, with the help of Evan and Roddy, betrayed him."

"He gave weapons to a war criminal." Her lips tightened. "In Bosnia I saw firsthand what war criminals do. Killing children is just as heinous in Darfur. He's going to prison?"

"He'll get five to ten years."

She pulled the blanket tighter and looked down. "A lot of people died thanks to those weapons, didn't they?"

The best estimate was a hundred and twenty, but after trying to shatter her relationship with her uncle for weeks, he found he couldn't deliver that blow. He stopped dressing and knelt before her. "Stevens arranged the deal, but it was Beck who took blood-soaked money from a Janjaweed militia leader. You'll remain in protective custody until after Beck is convicted."

"How long will that be?"

He had to tell her the truth, no matter how much she'd dislike it. "At least a year."

"A year?" She looked crestfallen. "Will you be able to visit me?"

"I won't work the case. We're involved, and you're a key witness. I expect a special prosecutor to be appointed. So yes, I will be able to visit you. Often. And not in an official capacity."

Her eyes widened. "I thought special prosecutors only investigated government officials? Raptor is private. Are you saying a politician is involved?"

He'd hoped to avoid telling her the rest until after her meeting with the secretary of state. He probably already suspected he was under investigation, but if Mara accidently tipped him off, it would be that much harder to gather evidence. But she had a right to know the truth. "Yes—"

A knock on the door interrupted him. "Mr. Dominick, Ms. Garrett," the guard said, "the secretary of state is here to see you."

# Chapter Forty-Four

Curt faced Mara with wide, shocked eyes. "How did he find you?"

"I called him," Mara said. Her heart began to pound, and she didn't know why. "He finally called me back about ten minutes before you got here. I gave him this address so he could come over tomorrow and interview me. Why would he be here now?" But she didn't need to ask that question; understanding came crashing down before the words left her mouth.

Adrenaline flooded her system. Through the door she heard the secretary demand entrance, but the guard refused him.

Curt scooped up her clothes and dropped them on her lap. "Play along," he whispered. "Act normal. Raptor won't strike while he's here, but when he leaves, I'm getting you out of here."

She pulled on her underwear as Curt grabbed his shirt and slipped it over his head. He crossed the room to the door. "Give us a minute," he yelled.

"Mr. Dominick," the secretary said through the door, "I don't have time—"

"She's naked," Curt said, cutting him off.

Mara laughed in spite of the churning in her belly. She still didn't understand how the secretary could be involved. Jesus, she'd really screwed up.

"We need more evidence against him for an indictment," Curt whispered. "If he believes I'm here just to get in your pants, he might feel complacent and make mistakes."

She fastened the slacks and adjusted the blouse. Curt stood in front of her and gripped her shoulders. "You ready?" he asked.

She nodded.

He kissed her, a firm, openmouthed kiss that restored her confidence. He leaned his forehead against hers and whispered, "I love you," then shouted toward the door, "Come in."

His mouth was on hers when the door slammed into the wall.

"Of all the stupid, unprofessional—" the secretary blustered. "Jesus, Dominick. You've not only destroyed your shot at attorney general, you'll be lucky if you aren't disbarred."

In a remarkable display of indifference to the man's predictions, Curt's lips remained on hers throughout the tirade.

He lifted his head and smiled at her, his hazel eyes bright with emotion; then he flipped an internal switch and faced the secretary in full shark mode. "The trial is over, Mr. Secretary. I'm free to pursue a relationship with Ms. Garrett."

The elder man paused, and Mara studied him. He'd aged since she met him last—at least three years ago, when he'd still been in the senate. His stately gray hair had fewer streaks of brown now, and the world map of wrinkles around his eyes had deepened.

"So the news was accurate? Stevens pled guilty?" he asked, scanning Curt.

Curt threaded his fingers through hers and squeezed. "Yes."

"Did he implicate Raptor?"

Curt raised an eyebrow. "I'm not at liberty to divulge anything until the indictments come down."

The man stepped farther into the room. "If he did, Stevens's word won't be good enough. He'll say anything to get a reduction in sentence."

Mara bristled. She knew the penalty for arms trafficking with foreign agents was five to ten years, and according to Curt, that was what he would receive. Her uncle had received no concession for naming names.

"Mr. Secretary," Curt asked. "Why are you here?"

"I wanted to check on Ms. Garrett before I have her moved."

Curt stiffened. "Why do you think you're moving her?"

The man approached the sofa, saw the pile of blankets and pillows before the hearth, and shook his head in disappointment, then sat on the edge of the seat, as though fearing sex cooties.

Mara snickered.

"She asked for my help. I'm helping her. She said she didn't want to be under your control." The man flicked a cold glare at Curt. "I could assume her opinion has changed, but before I believe that, I'm going to insist on speaking with her alone."

Curt's grip on her fingers tightened. "No."

She squeezed back. "It's okay. He's right. I did say I didn't want to be under your control. I was"—she grinned sheepishly—"upset."

With a guard outside the door, it had to be safe to speak alone with a man who desperately wanted to avoid being implicated. "Why don't you wait outside?" she said to Curt.

Curt's stare was short but meaningful; then he leaned down and kissed her. "You've got one minute." He stepped into the vestibule, leaving her alone with the man who was fourth in line for the presidency and who was probably up to his eyeballs in dirty deals with Robert Beck.

THE GUARD GREETED Curt with a smirk. "Impressive, Mr. Dominick."

Curt grimaced. "She's not a conquest. I'm nuts about her."

The bald, hulking agent grinned. "Hell, we all figured that from the insane security you set up for her."

"Which is compromised now. We need to leave."

The man's brow furrowed. "You don't think the secretary—"

Curt gave a short nod. "We need to leave. Now. You have a car?"

The man nodded. "In the garage."

"Get it. We'll meet you out front."

The man snatched keys from his desk and darted out the door. Curt plucked out his cell and hit the button to dial Lee. He had no choice but to bring Mara to Lee's place while he arranged for a new safe house. As he waited for Lee to answer, he pivoted and returned to the living room.

"We're not done talking, Mr. Dominick," the secretary said with a glare.

Lee answered as Curt said, "I don't care. I'm feeling uneasy. Mara, we're leaving." Into the phone he said, "Got that?"

Lee answered, "What's going on?"

Mara nodded and bent down to retrieve her shoes. An engine revved behind him, and he glanced over his shoulder to see if the agent had extracted the car from the garage that quickly. Bright, blinding lights cut through the vestibule window and shone through the open door.

Curt jammed the phone into his pocket and lunged for Mara. He gripped her arm and shoved her ahead of him. The engine roared as they dove for the bedroom door on the far side of the room.

Behind them, the vestibule crashed inward, and a backward

glimpse revealed a truck. Beaming headlights canted upward as the vehicle came to a stop half in the vestibule, half on the front steps. Then the room exploded in a flash of orange.

# Chapter Forty-Five

Blinded by smoke and deafened by the explosion, Curt covered Mara as best he could as debris rained upon him. He placed his mouth next to Mara's ear and shouted, "You okay?" but could barely hear his own words above the ringing in his ears.

He felt her nod, and again shouted. "The bedroom! We can get out that way." He rose to his knees, uncovering her.

He nudged her forward, but she shook her head. Her muted yell barely penetrated. "The secretary! Where is he?"

Curt didn't give a damn about the man, but it was clear Mara wouldn't budge until they'd located the undeserving bastard. He'd been a few feet to the right of Curt before the blast, so he groped in that direction and quickly found him. A heavy object had landed on top of the man, who was conscious and struggling. Curt guided Mara to grab one of the secretary's wrists and together they tugged him out from under the debris and into the closest bedroom.

The doorframe was skewed, making it impossible to close and block the roiling black smoke from entering the room, but still, visibility was better and the smoke wasn't yet thick.

A quick perusal showed Mara was scraped and likely bruised, but otherwise unharmed. The secretary was a different story. A large shard of wood protruded from the man's back. Curt had no idea how deep it penetrated, but unless they got out of here fast, the man wasn't likely to survive.

Curt bent down beside him. With his mouth next to the secretary's ear, he shouted, "You stupid fuck. They betrayed you."

The secretary wheezed and grabbed Curt's shirt, pulling him down to speak into his ear. Curt could just make out his words. "Raptor. They weren't…supposed…while I'm…here…"

"Mercenaries aren't big on loyalty," Curt said.

"Robert Beck…he gave the orders…every time."

"I need you to live so you can say that under oath."

"I won't."

He wouldn't live, or wouldn't testify? Curt didn't have time to argue either way. The house vibrated, and he felt a shift. Had the ceiling over the living room collapsed?

A noxious wave of smoke poured into the room. They had to get out of here before the whole structure went down. He leaned into Mara and shouted, "The window!"

She shook her head. "It's barred."

"Shit."

"This way!" She tugged his arm and led the way to an attached bathroom. The air was clearer in the small room, and he could see the window she pointed to. "It's so small, it wasn't barred!"

The window, located high on the wall in the toilet alcove, was tiny. Only a pixie like her could fit through. He climbed on the seat and wrenched up the pane. Fresh sweet air wafted in, and he sucked in a deep breath, then pulled Mara up beside him. "I'll lift you."

He boosted her so she could slide through feetfirst. In seconds, she was outside, gripping the edge before she realized his predicament. "Curt. How will you—"

His hearing had improved slightly, and he hoped hers had too. "I love you!" he shouted. The noxious smoke was filling the bathroom. "Go!"

"No, Curt!" She gripped the edge and boosted herself back into the window. "I won't leave you."

A coughing spasm overtook him. Unable to speak, he shoved her back through the window. She fought him. He lifted her fingers from the sill and let go.

He couldn't see, couldn't breathe. He stepped to the top of the tank and poked his head out the window. He took a deep breath of the cool night air. He rubbed his eyes to try to clear his vision of the black, burning smoke and saw Mara was gone.

SHE HAD TO get Curt out of the house. She groped around the shattered structure, wiping her eyes, which burned and ached. Her hearing was returning in slow degrees. She rounded to the front yard and caught her breath.

The front of the house was gone. The vestibule and two front rooms—the kitchen above the garage and the adjacent living room had collapsed inward. The remaining structure was shaped like the inward curve of a cresting wave, and from the looks of it, the wave was about to break.

She thought she could hear sirens in the distance, but it could just be the ringing in her ears. Regardless, Curt needed help *now*.

Headlights appeared up the road. Mara ran into the street and waved frantically for the driver to stop.

Brakes squealed, and the sedan halted inches from her.

"A man is dying in there. I need your car. Now!"

The teenage boy looked confused. "Is this a carjacking? What happened to that house?"

Flames shot out of the crumbling house behind her. There was no way Curt could escape through the front. "Get out of the fucking driver's seat and give me your car!"

Shockingly, he did.

Mara slid behind the wheel and threw the car in gear. She hit the curb and tore up the neighbor's lawn, racing toward the side and rear of the burning house. She aimed for the barred master bedroom window.

She didn't feel the impact. She didn't feel a damn thing as the sedan slammed into the wall.

# Chapter Forty-Six

CURT USED THE lid of the toilet tank to smash the window, trying to make the opening wide enough to accommodate his shoulders. Black smoke filled the bathroom, and he gasped for air through the window. The walls around him shook ominously.

The house was going to collapse. Soon.

A crash sounded in the next room, loud enough to penetrate his muted hearing. The house rumbled as the walls quaked. Soon had become now. But while the house rocked on its foundation and bits of ceiling rained down, the roof remained above him. If that hadn't been the sound of the bedroom collapsing, what was it?

With a sharp shove, he opened the bathroom door and got a lungful of black smoke, but two lights cut a swath through the darkness. Headlights?

He crawled through the smoke and paused beside the secretary, still lying belly down on the floor. He checked for a pulse and found none. He skirted around the man, saying a silent prayer for the FBI agent, hoping the man had fared better in the concrete basement than they had inside the house.

He followed the light beams to the wall. Sure enough, a vehicle protruded into the room. He traced the outline of the car, seeking a break in the wall he could slide through, but the opening was no wider than the vehicle that had made it.

His lungs ached for air as he searched for the door handle. At last he gripped it, and muscles burned as he wrenched the battered door open. Inside, his groping hands found warm skin and a woman he recognized by touch. "Mara!"

Nothing. "Mara! Answer me!"

Still no answer. He could see nothing and knew he had to get out of the smoke now, or suffocate. As would she.

The only way out was through the vehicle.

He slipped inside, careful as he climbed over Mara's unconscious form, terrified she'd been badly injured by the impact. He felt cloth draped on her lap and hoped to hell that was the deployed airbag. He searched for a seat belt crossing her chest and found none. She'd driven into a wall—to save him—without thought for her own safety.

He climbed to the back of the vehicle and, bracing his shoulder against the front passenger seat, he kicked out the rear window. Debris rained into the gap, but there was an opening, with blessed fresh air.

He gripped Mara's shoulders and tugged her over the seat, across the back, and through the broken window. He emerged into a starry, smoky night, and gathered Mara in his arms.

Following the ruts in the grass, he sucked in deep, rasping breaths of air and headed toward the street, to a group of onlookers. A man broke free from the group and tried to take Mara from him, but Curt gripped her tighter and refused.

He could barely walk, but he'd never let her go.

A safe distance from the house, he dropped to his knees and gently laid her down on the grass. Behind him, the house rumbled. Curt turned in time to see the remaining section collapse.

Sirens wailed as an ambulance and fire truck screeched to a halt in front of him. The firefighters leapt from the vehicle, and Curt called out to one of them, "There's probably a man trapped in the basement garage. Another is in the master bedroom—but he's dead."

The man nodded and began shouting orders to the other firefighters.

Another man crouched in the grass in front of Curt. "You need a medic."

"I'm fine, but she needs help." He wiped grit from his burning eyes, and saw the man wore a medic uniform. "She drove a car through the wall to get me out and wasn't wearing a seat belt."

The man checked her pulse and shined a flashlight in her eyes. "She's so small, the airbag probably knocked her out."

"She's inhaled a lot of smoke," Curt added, choking out the last words.

"As did you," said another man from behind him. He slapped a plastic cup over Curt's mouth and nose, and cool oxygen eased the pain in his constricted chest.

"Let's get you in the ambulance," the second medic said.

"I won't leave her." He couldn't trust anyone with her life. That lesson had been shoved down his throat often enough.

"We can transport two."

In moments, Mara was on the gurney, and Curt followed her into the back of the ambulance. The door slammed shut, and they wound their way between fire trucks en route to the hospital.

Curt crouched beside the gurney where Mara lay, and held her hand. Glancing toward the front, he could see through the gap between the driver's and passenger's seats and out the windshield. Rain had begun to fall, and the lights of the city blurred under the wiper blades.

The medic perched on the opposite side of Mara called out her stats to the driver, who used the radio to relay the information to the waiting hospital.

To Curt, the man said, "Her numbers are solid. It was probably just the airbag. She'll have a nasty headache when she wakes up, but she'll be fine."

His gut clenched, he wanted desperately to believe she was okay. Mara was right; hope was a four-letter word.

"Relax, dude. She's gonna be fine."

Curt gazed through the front window again. The city blurred as they shot through town with sirens blaring, but something wasn't right. Weren't the hospitals in the other direction?

Mara's eyes fluttered open. She coughed and wiped her eyes. After a glance at the medic, she found Curt's gaze and smiled, then did a double take and sat bolt upright. "George? What the hell are you doing here?"

"My boss wants to talk to you."

Without hesitation, Mara backhanded the man across the jaw. To Curt, she said, "He's a Raptor medic who works with JPAC."

Curt launched himself at the man, but the ambulance swerved, throwing him off balance. He hit George with only a glancing blow. The man recovered quickly as the ambulance rocked sideways again, sending Curt into the opposite wall.

George plucked Mara from the gurney. His thick fingers closed around her throat. "Back off, Dominick. Whether she lives or not is up to you."

CURT'S GAZE MET Mara's and silently conveyed a thousand different promises, starting with revenge, ending with love, but most of all asking for trust.

He had a plan. Her job was to play along and not screw it up.

"Dominick, I'll let her breathe if you put your hands in the air and sit on the gurney."

Curt did as instructed, and the hands at her throat loosened.

They rolled through the rainy streets of DC, finally coming to a bridge, crossing the Potomac and entering Virginia. George stood with his back to the side panel, Mara stood in front of him, his hands slack on her throat.

"Where are you taking us?" she asked.

"Shut up," George answered and tightened his grip.

"You hurt her, and you're a dead man," Curt's voice was cold and his body rigid. He was a cobra looking for an excuse to strike, eyes clear with deadly intent.

George got the message, and his fingers loosened. She tried to push away from him, but he maintained a grip, even as he was careful not to hurt her.

"No talking," George said in a feeble attempt to assert his dominance. Mara had no doubt Curt could safely extract her from George, but they still had the driver to worry about, which had to be why Curt didn't make a move.

At this point, she was certain where they were headed: Raptor's Northern Virginia compound, the Raptor facility where they built their fancy toys. The lab, where the smallpox bomb was probably located.

Ironic that Curt had been trying to get a warrant for the place for weeks. If only the FBI knew they were being taken there now.

Did the FBI even know they were missing yet? How long had she been unconscious?

Her head throbbed, and she was so tired she wanted to collapse, but she refused to lean against George. Her knees began to shake. "Please. I need to sit."

George dropped into the seat beside the gurney and pulled Mara onto his lap. Revulsion swirled in her belly, and she leaned forward, attempting to sit on the very edge of his knees. His arm locked around her belly, and he pulled her firmly onto his lap, her back to his chest. The arm around her waist slid upward, and he groped her breast.

The stupid man chuckled at the rage in Curt's gaze.

Mara knew Curt was about to strike and jabbed her elbow into George's sternum, using the momentum to dive forward, out of Curt's way.

She scrambled to the back of the ambulance, then turned to see Curt lift George by the shirt and slam his head into the panel.

He released him and struck George in the face with several flat-handed blows.

George's blocks were ineffective and his punches never made it past Curt's lightning-quick reflexes. The ambulance lurched to a stop. Mara's belly dropped when the driver slipped an arm through the wide gap between the front seats and aimed a gun at Curt's head. "Stop!"

Maybe Curt didn't hear him, Mara wasn't sure, but he kept pounding on George. She threw herself forward onto the gurney, determined to prevent Curt from being shot.

The gun swung in her direction. Curt dropped George.

"Glad I finally got your attention, Mr. Dominick," the driver said.

Mara met the driver's gaze. The man smiled. Cold dread spread down her spine. Robert Beck stood in the pass-through to the cab, and his gun was aimed at her forehead.

# Chapter Forty-Seven

"George, get in the fucking driver's seat," Robert Beck said.

Curt's heart went into overdrive at seeing the gun on Mara. His mind raced, trying to come up with a reason for the man to keep her alive, but came up blank.

George grunted, shoved Curt back, then swung at his jaw. Curt used the momentum of the blow to pitch backward, landing him squarely between Beck's gun and Mara.

He straightened on the gurney, tucking Mara behind him.

Beck dropped into the paramedic's vacated chair while George settled in the driver's seat. Through the front windshield, Curt saw a road sign and realized they were less than five miles from the compound. *Shit.* Why Beck hadn't just killed them as soon as they were inside the ambulance, he didn't know, but he had no doubt once they were inside the gates, they'd only have minutes left to live.

His cell phone remained in his pocket; he could feel it against his hip. He had no idea if it had been damaged in the blast or even remained connected to Lee. If it was still on, he knew Lee would be locked on to the signal and phoning the GPS coordinates to the FBI. With luck, that stop by the side of the road was enough for agents to catch up.

"I'm shocked to see you risking yourself this way, Beck. This is the sort of dirty job you leave to your operatives."

"After what you did to Evan, I want to personally watch you both die."

"Evan had smallpox," Mara said from behind him. "Did you know that?"

Beck flushed red. "You lie."

"He did. They ran a cytokine assay on his blood after he died, and found evidence he'd been sick."

She was blowing smoke. No such tests had been done on Evan's blood, but he had to admit, her words rattled Beck.

"I had smallpox, and they did the same test on me. We can prove Evan and I were sick with the same strain. You can't start a smallpox epidemic. No one will believe it was al Qaeda or the North Koreans, or whoever you planned to blame it on. They'll know it was Raptor."

"Nice try, but I know the CDC hasn't done any tests for smallpox."

"I didn't go to the CDC. I went to an epidemiologist at a university. He knows everything, and when I disappear, he's going public."

Beck laughed. "Ms. Garrett, you've disappeared so many times already, everyone will believe you've merely gone into hiding again. This time with your lover, who has thrown away his career for you."

"No one will believe that about Curt."

"Are you kidding? He's been acting paranoid since meeting you. I've been hearing for weeks how you've damaged him. And then there's what you did to poor Evan. They'll believe it."

Sirens sounded behind them. Curt said a silent prayer that Lee had sent the cavalry, but regardless, it was now or never. He had to take down Beck before they entered the compound. The moment Beck's gaze flicked to the rear window, Curt struck. He smashed Beck's gun wrist to the side, then pinned him against the bulkhead by the throat. With his free hand, he repeatedly slammed Beck's wrist into the corner edge of the pass-through until his wrist snapped and the gun dropped.

Beck was a businessman, not a mercenary, and the blows he tried to land with his good hand were ineffective.

The ambulance veered suddenly, then rocked from side to side. George couldn't stop because of the pursing police cars, so he used the motion of the speeding vehicle to prevent Curt from seizing control. Curt was tossed to the left, forcing him to let go of Beck.

To catch his balance, he grabbed at the bulkhead behind the driver's seat. Catching a handhold, he pulled himself into the opening between the cab and rear of the ambulance.

George hit the accelerator, knocking him off-balance. Grappling for purchase, his free hand slipped along the driver's seat base and caught on the seat-belt latch at George's right hip.

George twisted the steering wheel, again rocking the bulky vehicle side to side. Curt released the handhold and took a swing at his head, but missed as he was bounced like a ping-pong ball in the opening between the front seats.

His grip on the latch slipped, but he caught the attached belt, jerking it tight as he lurched backward. George grunted, and Curt angled forward to see the shoulder belt pressed against the man's neck.

He gripped the belt tighter and looked over his shoulder to check on Mara. She was right behind him, holding the rail of the locked-down gurney with one hand and Beck's gun in the other, trained on the CEO.

Curt turned back to George, who hadn't slowed the vehicle. With the ambulance tilting, swaying, and speeding down the interstate, Curt leveraged himself behind the driver's seat and braced his foot on the bulkhead.

He yanked on the belt, and George shuddered, but didn't—couldn't—make a sound.

George slammed on the brake pedal in what must have been an attempt to dislodge Curt. Mara slammed into his back with a grunt.

Thanks to his firm foot against the partition, neither Curt nor Mara flew between the seats and through the windshield. The ambulance came to a stop as George grappled with the seat belt, silently fighting for air.

Curt twisted the belt in his hands, tightening the pressure until the man passed out.

# Chapter Forty-Eight

TWO HOURS LATER, an FBI agent insisted Mara don a biohazard suit to enter the lab. A ridiculous precaution, since she'd already *had* smallpox. But she did as instructed, and minutes later she confirmed they had located the bomb she'd found in North Korea.

Task complete, she exited the lab and doffed the bulky suit. From there an agent led her to a waiting vehicle, and her heart swelled when she saw Curt inside. She hadn't seen him since the first minutes after the FBI had taken Robert Beck into custody at the roadside. They'd had to be questioned alone about what had happened in the safe house and in the ambulance.

She slid into the seat and right into his arms. She snuggled against his side in contented silence.

Finally, Curt said, "They found the agent in the garage. He was inside the SUV when the bomb went off. Thanks to the concrete walls and sturdy vehicle, he was trapped but unharmed."

She smiled. "I heard. I'm relieved."

"Jeannie's going to be okay."

Jeannie had been found inside the compound when the search warrants were served. She claimed she'd been a prisoner, but it would be her word against Beck's. Mara believed her and feared the woman had been put through hell.

"She's not ready to see you," he added.

"I know. We'll talk eventually." She sighed and snuggled closer. "I think every part of me aches. I feel like I smacked into a wall."

Curt threaded fingers through her hair. The tickling sensation felt heavenly. "Next time, will you please wear a seat belt?"

She closed her eyes and smiled. "Are you kidding? After what I saw you do with the seat belt to George?" She shook her head. "Seat belts are dangerous." She opened her eyes. "Thanks for saving my life again."

"I think we need a score card to figure out if we're even."

"That depends. You took out both George and Beck, but I was the one who had a gun on Beck in the end. So is that one or two?"

"I'm pretty sure it's two."

She chuckled, then turned serious again. "How did you know the secretary of state was involved?"

"Your uncle told me he kept him informed, and everything clicked into place. When I spoke to him about the smallpox bomb, he shut me down in no uncertain terms. He used all the right words and excuses, but it didn't sit right. Then there's the fact that Raptor knew where we were in Hawai'i, Arizona, and Virginia. In Hawai'i and Arizona, the military appeared to be the weak link. But Virginia… I thought Evan had tracked us through the phone, although I couldn't figure out how he did it, because the connection was so brief.

"Before I arrived in DC, my office was billed for the ten grand the Arizona US Attorney's Office gave us. It turns out the USA's assistant had also cc'd the bill to the State Department. That was all the secretary needed to determine who had provided us with a vehicle. As I mentioned before, all federal vehicles have tracking devices."

"Would that have been enough to indict him?"

"No. He *did* follow up on the smallpox with the president. He did everything right, while quietly discrediting you and me. Last night I got the judge to authorize a wiretap, but he might have walked if Robert Beck hadn't betrayed him by ordering the attack on the house while he was still inside."

Her eyes drifted closed. She hadn't been this tired since the first day they met—the longest day of her life. "Are you always this busy?" she asked. "Because every time I'm with you. it's nonstop. You promised me dates with dinners at restaurants and fun football games. But all I get are explosions, men trying to kill me, and we hardly *ever* eat."

"I've got tickets to a football game a week from Sunday."

She bolted upright. "You really got tickets?"

"Of course. I bought the tickets and a five-year-old's artwork."

"I thought you'd made that up. It was an adorable story."

"It was pure wooing gold. Wait until you see Katie's drawing. You'll be crawling all over me." Curt's grin set her heart pounding. He had a new smile, just for her, and it conveyed all the intensity of his feelings as well as a hint of their shared intimacy and a promise for more.

"Can we really go to a football game? In public? Don't I need to hide?"

"Beck has lost his mercenary army. He can't pay the bills, so his employees won't take orders from him anymore. It's one of the nicer things about mercenaries. Zealots are so much harder to stop." He lifted her fingers to his lips. "So, Mara, will you come with me to the football game?"

She grinned. "I'm pretty sure you're supposed to take me out to dinner first."

# EPILOGUE

CURT AND MARA stood on the fringes of the small graveside gathering in Arlington Cemetery. The remains of Captain Allen Baldwin, the man who'd piloted the F-86 Sabre she'd excavated that last day in North Korea, were being laid to rest at long last, and Mara didn't want to draw attention away from the man being honored by making her presence known. Weeks had passed since the explosion at the safe house, and the excessive media attention had finally died down, but the press still occasionally followed them.

Curt held her hand as the flag was carefully folded and presented to the man's widow. The widow was flanked by her children and grandchildren, several of whom were Mara's age, reminding her so much of her own family and how her grandmother had longed for a ceremony like this one.

Someday, perhaps, JPAC would return to North Korea and retrieve her grandfather's remains, but Mara wouldn't be on the crew. Nor would Jeannie. Jeannie's legal troubles were still being sorted out, but it looked like she'd get probation in exchange for her testimony against Beck.

Mara had seen her, briefly, at Jeannie's brother's funeral, which Curt and Mara had flown across the country to attend. Now, here she was, again dressed in black, attending the last of the memorials related to the North Korean deployment and Raptor's foray into biological weapon manufacture and homegrown terrorism.

Robert Beck, two scientists, and his four most loyal mercenaries were being held without bond. They had enough to convict them without her testimony, and Mara had no reason to fear any rogue operatives would target her.

Still, she'd breathe easier when the convictions were handed down.

The ceremony ended, and they waited for the crowd to disperse before she approached the freshly filled grave. From her purse she pulled a JPAC coin, a grinning skull on one side with the words "Search, Recover, Identify" on the back. She set the coin in the loose soil and whispered her thanks to the man who'd given his life to prevent the US from committing a wartime atrocity.

The cold December wind cut through her wool coat, and she shivered as they walked up the path toward Curt's car. Days like today made her miss Hawai'i, yet she looked toward the coming mainland winter with a surprising amount of hope.

They returned to Curt's condo, where she'd been staying since Beck's arrest. The press no longer camped outside his building. Life was starting to feel almost normal.

Inside his home, she kicked off her shoes and walked straight to the fireplace, where she warmed her chilled hands while Curt checked messages. A few minutes later, he approached her from behind and wrapped his arms around her waist. "Just got word, a man has stepped forward with an offer to buy all of Raptor's assets."

She frowned. "Raptor isn't dissolving?"

"He says he wants Raptor's existing government contracts in addition to the various training grounds and compounds."

"If Raptor keeps operating, am I in danger?"

"My source says no. The man is Alec Ravissant. He's an Army Ranger. Sterling reputation. He's agreed to government oversight and says he's determined to redeem the organization. The deal won't go through without a thorough vetting, and so far he looks good."

She let out a sigh of relief. The fact that Raptor was in limbo had been weighing on her.

Curt's arms tightened around her waist. His hard body warmed her back. "You're safe."

His lips found her temple and he kissed a trail down her neck. She twisted in his arms and faced him. Her mouth met his in a long, leisurely kiss. Eventually she rocked back on her heels and smiled. "I appear to be living with you," she said. Not the words she'd planned to say, but, with the last funeral over, she no longer had a reason remain in DC. No reason, that is, except Curt.

His mouth curved in her favorite smile. "You just noticed?"

She nipped at his chin. "I don't want to go back to Hawai'i."

His grip on her hips tightened. "Good, because I want you here. With me. But you should know I'll go wherever you decide."

Tiny bubbles of joy expanded in her chest. She'd expected his response but still liked hearing the words. "I've been thinking I could apply for a job at the Naval History and Heritage Command in Anacostia. It wouldn't be JPAC, but it could be meaningful." She paused, wondering how he'd react to her next statement. "When I get back on my feet financially, I'd like to find a way to fund a scholarship—to Stanford. I can't pay it back, but I can pay it forward."

His eyes lit. "I think that's a fabulous idea. I can support you; then any salary you earn can go straight to the scholarship."

Emotion flooded her. She kissed him, accepting his offer without words. He let out a guttural groan that told her he enjoyed this method of negotiation.

She broke the kiss and glanced around the room. "There is one caveat. If we're going to stay here, we need to do something about your condo." She pretended to shudder. "It's a shame Raptor blew up a perfectly nice safe house and left this place intact."

He chuckled. "Before you were here, I was never home. Now when I'm home, all I see is you."

She grinned. "Good one."

"I'm getting good at this relationship thing."

She scoffed. "Yeah, it's been days since you've tried to read me like a chessboard."

"I can't help it. That's how my mind works." He kissed her again. "There was another message on the answering machine. The White House wants a definitive answer on whether or not we're going to attend the State Dinner next week."

"They really want us there, don't they?"

"It would be good PR after what happened to the secretary of state."

She frowned. "I'm willing to go. But it won't be nearly as fun as the pretend one."

He raised his eyebrows suggestively. "We can do for real what we talked about."

"Sex afterward was a given."

He laughed. "No, I mean put in a token appearance and leave."

"We could bail before the first course?"

"Yes. I have a different appetizer in mind."

She grabbed his tie and pulled him to her for a leisurely kiss. With her mouth on his, she backed him toward the bedroom as she undressed him. He was naked from the waist up by the time she pushed him backward onto the bed. "If you bring the champagne, I'll bring the honey."

He tugged on her arm, and she toppled forward, landing on his chest. "Check," he said. In a swift motion, he flipped her so she was pinned to the mattress beneath him. Hazel eyes alight, he grinned a sexy, confident grin. "And mate."

# Author's Note

For more information on the Joint POW/MIA Accounting Command and the work they do, please visit their website at www.jpac.pacom.mil.

Thank you for reading *Body of Evidence*. I hope you enjoyed it!

If you'd like to know when my next book is available, you can sign up for my new release e-mail list at www.Rachel-Grant.net. You can also like my Facebook page at www.facebook.com/RachelGrantAuthor or follow me on Twitter at @RachelSGrant. I'm on Goodreads at www.goodreads.com/RachelGrantAuthor, where you can see what I'm reading and post reviews.

# ACKNOWLEDGEMENTS

THANK YOU TO my friend and Joint POW/MIA Accounting Command archaeologist Richard Wills, for answering all my questions about JPAC protocols and for describing your experiences working in the Democratic People's Republic of Korea. This book wouldn't have been possible without your insight.

Thank you to author and Centers for Disease Control and Prevention Infectious Disease Specialist Jennifer McQuiston and her colleagues Mary Reynolds and Andrea McCollum for answering my questions about smallpox. Their opinions do not represent the opinions of the CDC, and any factual inaccuracies in this book are my mistake, not theirs.

Thank you to author and Air Force Reserve public affairs officer AJ Brower, for answering my questions about US Air Force bases and dormitories.

Thank you to attorneys Steven Burke, Shauny Jaine, and Kenneth Kagan, for answering my legal questions and explaining the difference between case-in-chief and rebuttal, and the rules of evidence for both.

Thank you also to Courtney Milan for answering random questions about U.S. law and lawyers when I didn't know what I needed to know. Also, I can't remember who suggested it, but I must thank either Courtney or Mr. Milan for naming my mercenary organization.

Thank you to both the plaintiff's and defendant's attorneys who selected me to be juror number nine in a civil suit just weeks after I began writing this story. I was utterly grateful for the opportunity to learn about our court system from a juror's perspective. Thank you also to my fellow jurors, who left me with nothing but respect for our system and pride in how honorable and conscientious our compulsory volunteers are.

Thank you to all the authors who critiqued this book, with a special shout out to the authors who dropped everything to read for me (sometimes more than once) when I needed it most: Elisabeth Naughton, Darcy Burke, Kris Kennedy, Jill Barnett, Mary Sullivan, Carey Baldwin, Amy Atwell, Krista Hall, Jennie Lucas, Gwen Hernandez, and Elizabeth Heiter.

Heartfelt thanks to my blogmates at www.KissandThrill.com for putting up with me on this publishing journey. I'd be nowhere without your support, and your friendship means the world to me.

Thank you to the Northwest Pixie Chicks for the best annual writing retreat every year. You all inspire me.

Thank you to the RWA® judges who made this book a finalist in the Golden Heart® contest two years in a row. Those contest finals opened so many doors for me, for which I'm grateful.

Huge thanks to my agent, Elizabeth Winick Rubinstein at McIntosh & Otis, for pushing me to be a better writer and for believing in me. Your support has meant more than I can say, and without you, this book would be so much less.

As always, thank you to my family. Everything I do, every word I write, is for you.

THANK YOU TO the men and women of the Joint POW/MIA Accounting Command who work in difficult and often uncomfortable conditions to bring our lost servicemen and women home.

Lastly, thank you to all the men and women, past and present, who have served in the US armed forces.

# Books by Rachel Grant

Evidence Series:

Concrete Evidence (#1)

Body of Evidence (#2)

Withholding Evidence (#3)

Incriminating Evidence (#4)

Covert Evidence (#5)

Grave Danger

Midnight Sun

Read on for a preview of

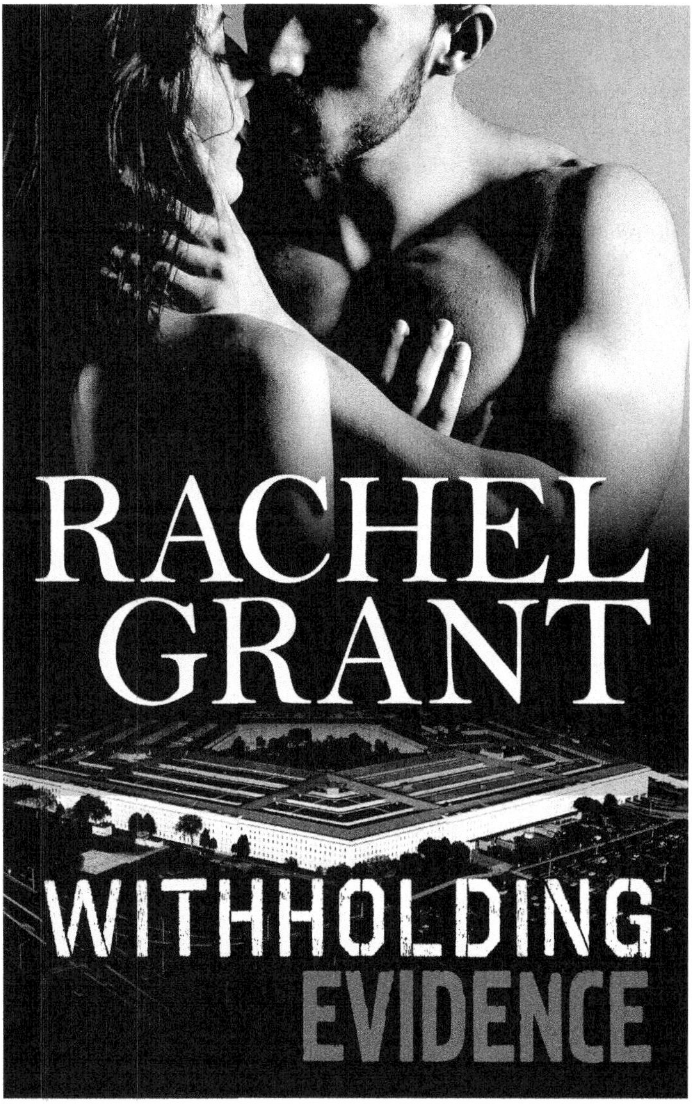

*Some secrets are worth dying for…*

Military historian Trina Sorensen has a nearly impossible task before her: get recalcitrant but tempting former Navy SEAL Keith Hatcher to reveal what happened during a top secret Somalia op five years ago. Recent history isn't usually her forte, but the navy wants an historian's perspective and has given her the high security clearance to get the job done.

Keith isn't just refusing to tell Trina about the op, he's protecting a national secret that could destroy the lives of those he cares about the most. But not wanting to talk about a covert mission doesn't mean he isn't interested in spending time with the sexy historian, and the first time they kiss it's explosive.

When the past comes pounding on Keith's door, he'll do anything to keep Trina safe… Anything, that is, except tell her the secret that could get them both killed.

# Chapter One

*Falls Church, Virginia*
*August*

TRINA SORENSEN STIFFENED her spine and rang the town house doorbell. She couldn't hear a chime, so after a moment of hesitation, she followed up with a knock. Seconds ticked by without any sound of movement on the other side. She rang the bell again, and then repeated the knock for good measure. The front door was on the ground floor, next to the garage. Glancing upward, she checked out the windows of the two upper floors. No lights on, but at nine in the morning on a hot August day in Falls Church, that didn't tell her anything. If the man she hoped to meet was home, he'd have to descend at least one flight of stairs, possibly two.

*Patience.*

She was about to ring the bell again when the door whipped open, startling her. She stepped back, then remembered she needed to project poise and straightened to meet her target's gaze.

Keith Hatcher was even more handsome in person than in his official navy photo, but she couldn't let that fluster her. It just meant he'd been blessed with good genes, a rather superficial measure of a person, really.

She took a deep breath and held out her hand. "Mr. Hatcher, Trina Sorensen, historian with Naval History and Heritage Command. I'd like to ask you a few questions about Somalia." She cringed as she said the last part. Too perky. Too eager. That was *not* how to approach a former navy SEAL when asking about a mission.

Sporting tousled dark hair that suggested he may have just gotten out of bed, and wearing low-rise jeans and nothing else, the man leaned an impressive bare bicep against the doorframe and raised a quizzical thick eyebrow. "Trina? Cute name." He smiled.

"It fits." He reached out and touched the top of her head. "But I think you should go back to the day care center you escaped from and leave me alone." He stepped back, and the door slammed shut.

She jolted back a step. He did *not* just pat her on the head and slam the door in her face.

Except that was exactly what Senior Chief Petty Officer Keith Hatcher had done.

She was aware she looked young, but dammit, she was thirty-one freaking years old—the same age as Hatcher. In fact, she was a few weeks *older* than him. She squared her shoulders and rang the bell again.

Seconds ticked by. Then minutes. She pounded with the side of her fist.

Finally the door opened. "Yes?" He leaned against the doorjamb again, this time stretching out an arm to touch the hinged side of the opening. His body language conveyed amusement mixed with annoyance.

"Senior Chief, I'm *Dr.* Trina Sorensen"—she never referred to herself with the pretentious title of doctor, but figured his crack about day care warranted it—"and I'm researching your SEAL team's work in Somalia five years ago for Naval History and Heritage Command and the Pentagon. You must answer my questions."

"Dollface, it's Sunday morning. The only thing I *must* do today is jack off."

She crossed her arms. "Fine. I can wait. It'll be what, one, maybe two minutes?"

The man tilted his head back and laughed. She saw her opportunity and ducked under his arm, entering, as she'd suspected, an enclosed staircase. The door to the left could only go to the garage. She went straight for the stairs, heading up to his home. Her heart beat rapidly at her own audacity, but she was never going to get the information she needed to do her job from the SEAL without taking risks.

"What the hell?" he sputtered, then added, "Who do you think you are, barging into my home?"

"I told you. I'm Dr. Trina Sorensen from NHHC," she answered as she reached the landing that ended in the most spotless mudroom she'd ever seen. She crossed the room and stepped into his kitchen. Equally spotless. Either he had an amazing cleaning service, or he was a total neat freak. Given his disheveled appearance, she'd expected a disheveled home.

She leaned against a counter as he paused in his own kitchen doorway. His mouth twitched, but his jaw was firm, making her think he couldn't decide if he was annoyed or amused.

"I'll wait here while you masturbate. We can start the interview when you're done."

Amusement won, and a corner of his mouth kicked up. He took a step toward her. "It'll go faster if you help me."

Her heart thumped in a slow, heavy beat. Barging into his home might've been a mistake. She frowned. *Of course it was a mistake.* "I'm good to go. Already took care of business this morning in the shower. You go ahead without me."

He barked a sharp laugh, then shook his head. "What do you want, Dr. Sorensen?"

"As I said already, I'm here to ask you questions about Somalia." She pulled her digital recorder from her satchel. "Do you mind if I record our conversation?"

His brown eyes narrowed. "Hell, yes, I mind. More importantly, we aren't having a conversation. You are leaving. Now. Before I call the police."

"Please don't be difficult. I'm just doing my job."

"SEAL ops are classified." All hint of amusement left his voice, leaving only hard edges.

She sighed in frustration. Hadn't he bothered to read any of her e-mails? "I sent you what you need to verify my security clearance in my e-mail. And my orders came directly from the Pentagon."

"I don't give a crap if the pope sent you on orders from the president. I'm not telling you shit about a place I've never been."

He expected her to accept that and walk away? She'd never have gotten anywhere as a military historian if she allowed the men in her field to brush her off. "Oh, you've been to Somalia all right. You were there on a reconnaissance mission, gathering data about a rising al Qaeda leader who was taking advantage of a power vacuum created by ongoing interclan violence."

He crossed his arms and spoke softly. "I have no clue what you're talking about."

The man had a solid poker face; no hint that she'd surprised him with the paltry facts she knew. So he was handsome and big and had the most gorgeous sculpted pecs and abs she'd ever seen, and he was sharp to boot. "I'm researching various SEAL actions in Somalia over the last two decades, starting with Operation Gothic Serpent and ending with yours."

He cocked his head. "Who is your boss?"

"Mara Garrett, interim director of the history department at Naval History and Heritage Command."

His eyes widened when she said her boss's name. At last, a break in the poker face. Did he recognize Mara's name from her trouble in North Korea, her notorious run-in with Raptor, or because he knew Mara was married to the US Attorney General? Regardless, the name Mara Garrett opened doors, and Trina had one more threshold she wanted to traverse—from the kitchen to the living room, where she could conduct a proper interview.

"The work I did when I was in the navy is classified. Not only do I not have to tell you about an op I was never on in a country I've never visited, but I could also get in serious trouble if I *did* tell you a damn thing about the places I *have* been."

She handed him her card. "But you do have to answer me. The Pentagon wants this report. Your input is necessary." This project was her big break. Future naval operations could depend on her findings, and the biggest of the brass were eager for this account. She was already having visions of moving out of the cubicle next to cantankerous Walt. She could have walls. And a door.

"But, you see there, dollface, that's the problem. I'm not in the navy anymore. I don't take orders from the Pentagon. I don't have to follow commands from anyone, least of all a five-foot-nothing librarian who invaded my kitchen without my permission."

She straightened her spine and threw back her shoulders, determined to reach her full height. "I'm five foot three. And I'm an historian." Her glasses slipped, and she nudged them back to the bridge of her nose.

He chuckled, and she flushed. She'd have been better off if she hadn't corrected him on the librarian label as she adjusted her glasses.

"Whatever, doll. Listen, you have one minute to get out of my house, or I'm going to assume you've decided to watch me jerk off after all."

She couldn't look away from the brown eyes that held hers in a tense gaze. Just her luck that he was so frigging gorgeous. Attractive men made her self-conscious. Especially ripped, half-naked ones. "I'm not playing games, Senior Chief. I'm just here to do my job."

He smiled slowly and reached for his fly.

KEITH LAUGHED AS the woman bolted down the stairs and out of his town house. He was sort of sorry to see her go, because that exchange had been fun—certainly worth getting out of bed for.

He waited until he heard the front door slam, then followed and locked the door. What kind of fool showed up at a guy's house at nine on a Sunday morning and expected him to be forthcoming about an op that was not only top secret but was also the single greatest and worst moment of his military career? As if he'd tell her—or anyone—about Somalia.

He'd been debriefed after the op. The people who needed to know what happened knew everything. It was enough for the powers that be, and it was enough for him.

He climbed the stairs and returned to his kitchen, where he made a pot of coffee. The woman—Trina—had been hot in a sexy, nerdy-librarian sort of way. There was probably a fancy name for the way she wore her hair in that twist at her nape, but to him it was a bun. And the little glasses with the red rims? Sexy as hell the way they slanted over her hazel eyes.

Did she dress the part of librarian on purpose, or was it some sort of weird requirement of her profession? It was too bad she hadn't decided to stay, because he had a hard-on after watching her march up his stairs in that straight skirt that cradled her ass.

He'd always had a thing for librarians—or historians—whatever.

If she had a PhD, she was probably a lot older than she looked. *Thank goodness.* Of course, she could be some sort of Doogie Howser genius.

Mug of coffee in hand, he headed into his office, woke his computer, and clicked on the mail icon. Had she really e-mailed him? It seemed like he'd have noticed.

New e-mail notifications came pouring in. Shit. How long had it been since he loaded e-mail? He checked the date of the first ones—from his dad, of course. These were nearly two weeks old. Oh yeah, he'd been so upset after the last round of antigovernment, antimilitary e-mails from his dear old dad, he'd turned off the mail program and took it out of start-up so it wouldn't run unless he initiated it. For some reason that had felt easier, less final, than blocking his father's e-mail address.

Thanks to the constant barrage of ranting messages, three months ago Keith had set his phone to only load e-mails from a select number of approved addresses. In the last two weeks, since he shut off mail on the computer, he'd received e-mails from the people who mattered to him on his phone, allowing him to forget he wasn't receiving everything on the computer.

He scanned the list, deleting the ones from his dad without opening any. Each time he tapped the button, he felt a twinge of guilt. It was time to block Dad once and for all. Yet he still refused to take that final step and wasn't quite sure why.

Misguided hope the man would change, he supposed.

After he'd deleted several e-mails, the name Trina Sorensen popped to the top of the list—the time stamp was last night. He scrolled down further and found four e-mails from her in the last week.

He opened her most recent message, noting the return address was indeed official navy. He scanned the contents. Huh. She'd told him that since he hadn't responded to her previous inquiries, she would be stopping by his house this morning, and if he didn't want her to show up, he should reply.

He lifted a finger to hit the Delete button and paused. Dammit. He owed her an apology.

Then he smiled, remembering that tight ass and those sexy calves. He'd liked the way she was quick with a comeback and didn't back down easily.

He wouldn't apologize via e-mail. He wanted talk to her in person so he could see her again. No way was he going to tell her about Somalia, but he could explain that in person too. Sort of.

Maybe his interest in the historian was only because he was bored. But at least she'd given him a reason to get out of bed this morning. Unemployment was for shit. He needed to *do* something.

An e-mail from his buddy Alec Ravissant reminded him of the garden party this afternoon at the home of Dr. Patrick Hill, the head of The MacLeod-Hill Exploration Institute in Annapolis, Maryland. Rav was running for the open Senate seat in Maryland, and the party was intended to introduce Rav to Hill's extensive connections in local politics and the military.

Hill's guests would be power-hungry high-society and military personnel. People who wanted to ingratiate themselves with military leaders, like the socialite made infamous in the Petraeus scandal a while back.

*Sorry, Rav. No way in hell.* Keith might be bored in his very early retirement, but he wasn't bored enough to attend a party that would require fending off the advances of married women while their husbands stood idly by, either oblivious, uncaring, or hoping their wives' infidelity would gain them admission into the centers of power.

Christ. He was starting to sound like his dad.

Just before he hit the Delete button, his eye caught the note at the bottom. Curt Dominick would be there, and Rav wanted to introduce them. Keith knew the US Attorney General had been the one to finally convince Rav to run for the Senate, so it was no surprise that Dominick would attend. He was both a power player and a good friend of Rav's. What gave Keith pause was realizing the man's wife, Mara Garrett—who happened to be sexy Trina the historian's boss—would probably attend as well.

Something Rav had said rang a bell—didn't the MacLeod-Hill Institute have some sort of oceanic-mapping joint venture with the navy? Specifically with the navy's underwater archaeology branch?

A quick Google search answered that question—yes—and revealed that the navy's underwater archaeology department was part of Naval History and Heritage Command.

Well, that changed everything. He'd lay odds everyone at NHHC with a connection to the MacLeod-Hill project had been invited to the party. This could be the perfect opportunity for Keith to apologize to the historian.

# About the Author

Four-time Golden Heart® finalist Rachel Grant worked for over a decade as a professional archaeologist and mines her experiences for storylines and settings, which are as diverse as excavating a cemetery underneath an historic art museum in San Francisco, survey and excavation of many prehistoric Native American sites in the Pacific Northwest, researching an historic concrete house in Virginia, and mapping a seventeenth century Spanish and Dutch fort on the island of Sint Maarten in the Netherlands Antilles.

She lives in the Pacific Northwest with her husband and children and can be found on the web at Rachel-Grant.net.

Printed in Great Britain
by Amazon

28876527R00169